DEAD SIMPLE

PETER JAMES

PAN BOOKS

First published 2005 by Macmillan

This edition published 2011 by Pan Books
an imprint of Pan Macmillan, a division of Macmillan Publishers Limited
Pan Macmillan, 20 New Wharf Road, London N1 9RR
Basingstoke and Oxford
Associated companies throughout the world
www.panmacmillan.com

ISBN 978-0-330-47486-3

5 7 9 8 6 4

A CIP catalogue record for this book is available from the British Library.

Typeset by SetSystems Ltd, Saffron Walden, Essex
Printed and bound by CPI Group (UK) Ltd, Croydon, CR0 4YY

Praise for the Roy Grace series

'Genuinely frightening'
Evening Standard

'This is the first in a new crime series which promises to be both fascinating and destined for the bestsellers'
Independent on Sunday

'Peter James's superior thriller . . . gripping . . . nail-biting . . . a satisfyingly complex puzzle'
The Times

'Ingenious plotting, high suspense and tight writing should guarantee instant lift-off for this new series'
Daily Mail

'A terrific tale of greed, seduction and betrayal'
Daily Telegraph

'Peter James is a very gifted writer and he kept me guessing with his relentless pacing and suspense. I would be reading what I thought was a lead to the climax, only to notice I was only halfway through the book. This book is a gem'
Crimespree

'A page-turner from start to finish, this is a book you will start and not put down until the end. Totally gripping and one of those rare crime books that are as good as they advertise themselves to be'
Book Place

'At a time when more than ever we feel beholden to be seen with pretentious novels which, in the privacy of our own homes, we find hard to pick up, what a relief to finally find a book which is well nigh literally impossible to put down'

Julie Burchill

'Mystery novels make very special Christmas presents . . . Especially when they are so well crafted, good and surprising as *Dead Simple* by Peter James'

***Brigitte*, Germany**

DEAD SIMPLE

Peter James was educated at Charterhouse then at film school. He lived in North America for a number of years, working as a screenwriter and film producer before returning to England. His novels, many of which have been *Sunday Times* Top 10 bestsellers, have been translated into thirty-four languages, with world sales of 11 million copies. Three books have been filmed. All his novels reflect his deep interest in the world of the police, with whom he does in-depth research, as well as science, medicine and the paranormal. He has produced numerous films, including *The Merchant of Venice*, starring Al Pacino, Jeremy Irons and Joseph Fiennes. He divides his time between his homes in Notting Hill in London and near Brighton in Sussex.

Visit his website at www.peterjames.com
Or follow him on Twitter @peterjamesuk
Or Facebook: http//www.facebook.com/peterjames.roygrace

Also by Peter James

DEAD LETTER DROP
ATOM BOMB ANGEL
BILLIONAIRE
POSSESSION
DREAMER
SWEET HEART
TWILIGHT
PROPHECY
ALCHEMIST
HOST
THE TRUTH
DENIAL
FAITH
PERFECT PEOPLE

Children's Novel

GETTING WIRED!

The Roy Grace Series

LOOKING GOOD DEAD
NOT DEAD ENOUGH
DEAD MAN'S FOOTSTEPS
DEAD TOMORROW
DEAD LIKE YOU
DEAD MAN'S GRIP
NOT DEAD YET

ACKNOWLEDGEMENTS

Writing is always regarded as a solitary occupation, but for me it is a team effort, and I owe a great debt to several people who have very generously given me their time and input, in so many areas. In particular I want to single out Detective Superintendent Dave Gaylor of Sussex Police, who gave me many suggestions for this novel, tirelessly read and reread the manuscript at many stages, and opened every door that I needed in different divisions of Sussex Police – I could never have written this without him. And I would like to thank the many officers of the Sussex Police Force who were so welcoming and helpful to me, in particular Detective Sergeant Keith Hallett of the Sussex Police Holmes Unit, Detective Inspector William Warner and Senior Scenes of Crime Investigator Stuart Leonard.

I would like to thank also Dr Nigel Kirkham MRCPath and his team at the Brighton and Hove Mortuary, where I long hope to remain a day visitor rather than an overnight guest, my good friend James Simpson, my film and television writing partner, Carina Coleman, who acted as my unofficial editor and gave me some brilliant insights, Mike Harris, Peter Wingate Saul, Alan Tonks, Greg Shackleton, police surgeon and coroner Dr Peter Dean. And Helen Shenston, who gave me the faith and encouragement that kept up my enthusiasm for this book during my bleakest days.

I want to thank also my wonderful new agent, Carole Blake, for her faith in me, and the fantastic team at my new publishers, Macmillan, in particular David North and Geoff Duffield and my editor Stef Bierwerth, who is a total treasure.

And both Geoffrey Bailey and Tony Mulliken for their enduring support and belief in me. And, as ever, my faithful hound Bertie and my more recent canine friend Phoebe, who both tolerated my writing – albeit with some reluctance – as tedious interludes between their walks.

Peter James
Sussex, England
scary@pavilion.co.uk
www.peterjames.com

DEAD SIMPLE

1

So far, apart from just a couple of hitches, Plan A was working out fine. Which was fortunate, since they didn't really have a Plan B.

At 8.30 on a late May evening, they'd banked on having some daylight. There had been plenty of the stuff this time yesterday, when four of them had made the same journey, taking with them an empty coffin and four shovels. But now, as the white Transit van sped along the Sussex country road, misty rain was falling from a sky the colour of a fogged negative.

'Are we nearly there yet?' said Josh in the back, mimicking a child.

'The great Um Ga says, "Wherever I go there I am,"' responded Robbo, who was driving, and was slightly less drunk than the rest of them. With three pubs notched up already in the past hour and a half, and four more on the itinerary, he was sticking to shandy. At least, that had been his intention; but he'd managed to slip down a couple of pints of pure Harvey's bitter – to clear his head for the task of driving, he'd said.

'So we are there!' said Josh.

'Always have been.'

A deer warning sign flitted from the darkness then was gone, as the headlights skimmed glossy black-top macadam stretching ahead into the forested distance. Then they passed a small white cottage.

Michael, lolling on a tartan rug on the floor in the back

of the van, head wedged between the arms of a wheel-wrench for a pillow, was feeling very pleasantly woozy. 'I sh'ink I need another a drink,' he slurred.

If he'd had his wits about him, he might have sensed, from the expressions of his friends, that something was not quite right. Never usually much of a heavy drinker, tonight he'd parked his brains in the dregs of more empty pint glasses and vodka chasers than he could remember downing, in more pubs than had been sensible to visit.

Of the six of them who had been muckers together since way back into their early teens, Michael Harrison had always been the natural leader. If, as they say, the secret of life is to choose your parents wisely, Michael had ticked plenty of the right boxes. He had inherited his mother's fair good looks and his father's charm and entrepreneurial spirit, but without any of the self-destruct genes that had eventually ruined the man.

From the age of twelve, when Tom Harrison had gassed himself in the garage of the family home, leaving behind a trail of debtors, Michael had grown up fast, helping his mother make ends meet by doing a paper round, then when he was older by taking labouring jobs in his holidays. He grew up with an appreciation of how hard it was to make money – and how easy to fritter it.

Now, at twenty-eight, he was smart, a decent human being, and a natural leader of the pack. If he had flaws, they were that he was too trusting and on occasions, too much of a prankster. And tonight that latter chicken was coming home to roost. Big time.

But at this moment he had no idea of that.

He drifted back again into a blissful stupor, thinking only happy thoughts, mostly about his fiancée, Ashley. Life was good. His mother was dating a nice guy, his kid brother had just got into university, his kid sister Carly was backpacking in Australia on a gap year, and his business was going incredibly well. But best of all, in three days time he was going to be marrying the woman he loved. And adored. His soul mate.

Ashley.

He hadn't noticed the shovel that rattled on every bump in the road, as the wheels drummed below on the sodden tarmac, and the rain pattered down above him on the roof. And he didn't clock a thing in the expressions of his two friends riding along with him in the back, who were swaying and singing tunelessly to an oldie, Rod Stewart's 'Sailing', on the crackly radio up front. A leaky fuel can filled the van with the stench of petrol.

'I love her,' Michael slurred. 'I sh'love Ashley.'

'She's a great lady,' Robbo said, turning his head from the wheel, sucking up to him as he always did. That was in his nature. Awkward with women, a bit clumsy, a florid face, lank hair, beer belly straining the weave of his T-shirt, Robbo hung to the coat tails of this bunch by always trying to make himself needed. And tonight, for a change, he actually *was* needed.

'She is.'

'Coming up,' warned Luke.

Robbo braked as they approached the turn-off and winked in the darkness of the cab at Luke seated next to him. The wipers clumped steadily, smearing the rain across the windscreen.

'I mean, like I really love her. Sh'now what I mean?'

'We know what you mean,' Pete said.

Josh, leaning back against the driver's seat, one arm around Pete, swigged some beer, then passed the bottle down to Michael. Froth rose from the neck as the van braked sharply. He belched. ''Scuse me.'

'What the hell does Ashley see in you?' Josh said.

'My dick.'

'So it's not your money? Or your looks? Or your charm?'

'That too, Josh, but mostly my dick.'

The van lurched as it made the sharp right turn, rattling over a cattle grid, almost immediately followed by a second one, and onto the dirt track. Robbo, peering through the misted glass, picking out the deep ruts, swung the wheel. A rabbit sprinted ahead of them, then shot into some undergrowth. The headlights veered right then left, fleetingly colouring the dense conifers that lined the track, before they vanished into darkness in the rear-view mirror. As Robbo changed down a gear, Michael's voice changed, his bravado suddenly tinged, very faintly, with anxiety.

'Where we going?'

'To another pub.'

'OK. Great.' Then a moment later, 'Promished Ashley I shwouldn't – wouldn't – drink too much.'

'See,' Pete said, 'you're not even married and she's laying down rules. You're still a free man. For just three more days.'

'Three and a half,' Robbo added, helpfully.

'You haven't arranged any girls?' Michael said.

'Feeling horny?' Robbo asked.

'I'm staying faithful.'

'We're making sure of that.'

'Bastards!'

The van lurched to a halt, reversed a short distance, then made another right turn. Then it stopped again, and Robbo killed the engine – and Rod Stewart with it. *'Arrivé!'* he said. 'Next watering hole! The Undertaker's Arms!'

'I'd prefer the Naked Thai Girl's Legs,' Michael said.

'She's here too.'

Someone opened the rear door of the van, Michael wasn't sure who. Invisible hands took hold of his ankles. Robbo took one of his arms, and Luke the other.

'Hey!'

'You're a heavy bastard!' Luke said.

Moments later Michael thumped down, in his favourite sports jacket and best jeans (not the wisest choice for your stag night, a dim voice in his head was telling him) onto sodden earth, in pitch darkness which was pricked only by the red tail lights of the van and the white beam of a flashlight. Hardening rain stung his eyes and matted his hair to his forehead.

'My – closhes—'

Moments later, his arms yanked almost clear of their sockets, he was hoisted in the air, then dumped down into something dry and lined with white satin that pressed in on either side of him.

'Hey!' he said again.

Four drunken, grinning shadowy faces leered down at him. A magazine was pushed into his hands. In the beam of the flashlight he caught a blurry glimpse of a naked redhead with gargantuan breasts. A bottle of whisky, a small flashlight, switched on, and a walkie-talkie were placed on his stomach.

'What's—?'

A piece of foul-tasting rubber tubing was pushing into his mouth. As Michael spat it out, he heard a scraping sound, then suddenly something blotted the faces out. And blotted all the sound out. His nostrils filled with smells of wood, new cloth and glue. For an instant he felt warm and snug. Then a flash of panic.

'Hey, guys – what—'

Robbo picked up a screwdriver, as Pete shone the flashlight down on the teak coffin.

'You're not screwing it down?' Luke said.

'Absolutely!' Pete said.

'Do you think we should?'

'He'll be fine,' Robbo said. 'He's got the breathing tube!'

'I really don't think we should screw it down!'

''Course we do – otherwise he'll be able to get out!'

'Hey—' Michael said.

But no one could hear him now. And he could hear nothing except a faint scratching sound above him.

Robbo worked on each of the four screws in turn. It was a top-of-the-range hand-tooled teak coffin with embossed brass handles, borrowed from his uncle's funeral parlour, where, after a couple of career U-turns, he was now employed as an apprentice embalmer. Good, solid brass screws. They went in easily.

Michael looked upwards, his nose almost touching the lid. In the beam of the flashlight, ivory-white satin encased him. He kicked out with his legs, but they had nowhere to travel. He tried to push his arms out. But they had nowhere to go, either.

Sobering for a few moments, he suddenly realized what he was lying in.

'Hey, hey, listen, you know – hey – I'm claustrophobic – this is not funny! Hey!' His voice came back at him, strangely muffled.

Pete opened the door, leaned into the cab, and switched on the headlights. A couple of metres in front of them was the grave they had dug yesterday, the earth piled to one side, tapes already in place. A large sheet of corrugated iron and two of the spades they had used lay close by.

The four friends walked to the edge and peered down. All of them were suddenly aware that nothing in life is ever quite as it seems when you are planning it. This hole right now looked deeper, darker, more like – well – a grave, actually.

The beam of the flashlight shimmered at the bottom.

'There's water,' Josh said.

'Just a bit of rainwater,' Robbo said.

Josh frowned. 'There's too much, that's not rainwater. We must have hit the water table.'

'Shit,' Pete said. A BMW salesman, he always looked the part, on duty or off. Spiky haircut, sharp suit, always confident. But not quite so confident now.

'It's nothing,' Robbo said. 'Just a couple of inches.'

'Did we really dig it this deep?' said Luke, a freshly qualified solicitor, recently married, not quite ready to shrug off his youth, but starting to accept life's responsibilities.

'It's a grave, isn't it?' said Robbo. 'We decided on a grave.'

Josh squinted up at the worsening rain. 'What if the water rises?

'Shit, man,' Robbo said. 'We dug it yesterday, it's taken twenty-four hours for just a couple of inches. Nothing to worry about.'

Josh nodded, thoughtfully. 'But what if we can't get him back out?'

'Course we can get him out,' Robbo said. 'We just unscrew the lid.'

'Let's just get on with it,' Luke said. 'OK?'

'He bloody deserves it,' Pete reassured his mates. 'Remember what he did on your stag night, Luke?'

Luke would never forget. Waking from an alcoholic stupor to find himself on a bunk on the overnight sleeper to Edinburgh. Arriving forty minutes late at the altar the next afternoon as a result.

Pete would never forget, either. The weekend before his wedding, he'd found himself in frilly lace underwear, a dildo strapped to his waist, manacled to the Clifton Gorge suspension bridge, before being rescued by the fire brigade. Both pranks had been Michael's idea.

'Typical of Mark,' Pete said. 'Jammy bastard. He's the one who organized this and now he isn't bloody here . . .'

'He's coming. He'll be at the next pub, he knows the itinerary.'

'Oh yes?'

'He rang, he's on his way.'

'Fogbound in Leeds. Great!' Robbo said.

'He'll be at the Royal Oak by the time we get there.'

'Jammy bastard,' Luke said. 'He's missing out on all the hard work.'

'And the *fun*!' Pete reminded him.

'This is fun?' Luke said. 'Standing in the middle of a sodding forest in the pissing rain? Fun? God, you're sad! He'd fucking better turn up to help us get Michael back out.'

They hefted the coffin up in the air, staggered forward with it to the edge of the grave and dumped it down, hard, over the tapes. Then giggled at the muffled 'Ouch!' from within it.

There was a loud thump.

Michael banged his fist against the lid. 'Hey! Enough!'

Pete, who had the walkie-talkie in his coat pocket, pulled it out and switched it on. 'Testing!' he said. 'Testing!'

Inside the coffin, Pete's voice boomed out. 'Testing! Testing!'

'Joke over!'

'Relax, Michael!' Pete said. 'Enjoy!'

'You bastards! Let me out! I need a piss!'

Pete switched the walkie-talkie off and jammed it into the pocket of his Barbour jacket. 'So how does this work, exactly?'

'We lift the tapes,' Robbo said. 'One each end.'

Pete dug the walkie-talkie out and switched it on. 'We're getting this taped, Michael!' Then he switched it off again.

The four of them laughed. Then each picked up an end of tape and took up the slack.

'One . . . two . . . three!' Robbo counted.

'Fuck, this is heavy!' Luke said, taking the strain and lifting.

Slowly, jerkily, listing like a stricken ship, the coffin sank down into the deep hole.

When it reached the bottom they could barely see it in the darkness.

Pete held the flashlight. In the beam they could make out the breathing tube sticking limply out of the drinking-straw-sized hole that had been cut in the lid.

Robbo grabbed the walkie-talkie. 'Hey, Michael, your dick's sticking out. Are you enjoying the magazine?'

'OK, joke over. Now let me out!'

'We're off to a pole-dancing club. Too bad you can't join us!' Robbo switched off the radio before Michael could reply. Then, pocketing it, he picked up a spade and began shovelling earth over the edge of the grave and roared with laughter as it rattled down on the roof of the coffin.

With a loud *whoop* Pete grabbed another shovel and joined in. For some moments both of them worked hard until only a few bald patches of coffin showed through the earth. Then these were covered. Both of them continued, the drink fuelling their work into a frenzy, until there was a good couple of feet of earth piled on top of the coffin. The breathing tube barely showed above it.

'Hey!' Luke said. 'Hey, stop that! The more you shovel on the more we're going to have to dig back out again in two hours' time.'

'It's a grave!' Robbo said. 'That's what you do with a grave, you cover the coffin!'

Luke grabbed the spade from him. 'Enough!' he said, firmly. 'I want to spend the evening drinking, not bloody digging, OK?'

Robbo nodded, never wanting to upset anyone in the group. Pete, sweating heavily, threw his spade down. 'Don't think I'll take this up as a career,' he said.

They pulled the corrugated iron sheet over the top, then stood back in silence for some moments. Rain pinged on the metal.

'OK,' Pete said. 'We're outta here.'

Luke dug his hands into his coat pocket, dubiously. 'Are we really sure about this?'

'We agreed we were going to teach him a lesson,' Robbo said.

'What if he chokes on his vomit, or something?'

'He'll be fine, he's not that drunk,' Josh said. 'Let's go.'

Josh climbed into the rear of the van, and Luke shut the doors. Then Pete, Luke and Robbo squeezed into the front, and Robbo started the engine. They drove back down the track for half a mile, then made a right turn onto the main road.

Then he switched on the walkie-talkie. 'How you doing, Michael?'

'Guys, listen, I'm really not enjoying this joke.'

'Really?' Robbo said. 'We are!'

Luke took the radio. 'This is what's known as pure vanilla revenge, Michael!'

All four of them in the van roared with laughter. Now it was Josh's turn. 'Hey, Michael, we're going to this fantastic club, they have the most beautiful women, butt naked, sliding their bodies up and down poles. You're going to be really pissed you're missing out on this!'

Michael's voice slurred back, just a tad plaintive. 'Can we stop this now, please? I'm really not enjoying this.'

Through the windscreen Robbo could see roadworks ahead, with a green light. He accelerated.

Luke shouted over Josh's shoulder, 'Hey, Michael, just relax, we'll be back in a couple of hours!'

'What do you mean, *a couple of hours*?'

The light turned red. Not enough time to stop. Robbo accelerated even harder and shot through. 'Gimme the thing,' he said, grabbing the radio and steering one-handed around a long curve. He peered down in the ambient glow of the dash and hit the *talk* button.

'Hey, Michael—'

'ROBBO!' Luke's voice, screaming.

Headlights above them, coming straight at them.

Blinding them.

Then the blare of a horn, deep, heavy duty, ferocious.

'ROBBBBBBBBBOOOOOOOO!' screamed Luke.

Robbo stamped in panic on the brake pedal and dropped the walkie-talkie. The wheel yawed in his hands as he looked, desperately, for somewhere to go. Trees to his right, a JCB to his left, headlights burning through the windscreen, searing his eyes, coming at him out of the teeming rain, like a train.

2

Michael, his head swimming, heard shouting, then a sharp *thud*, as if someone had dropped the walkie-talkie.

Then silence.

He pressed the *talk* button. 'Hello?'

Just empty static came back at him.

'Hello? Hey guys!'

Still nothing. He focused his eyes on the two-way radio. It was a stubby-looking thing, a hard, black plastic casing, with one short aerial and one longer one, the name '*Motorola*' embossed over the speaker grille. There was also an on–off switch, a volume control, a channel selector, and a tiny pinhead of a green light that was glowing brightly. Then he stared at the white satin that was inches from his eyes, fighting panic, starting to breathe faster and faster. He needed to pee, badly, going on desperately.

Where the hell was he? Where were Josh, Luke, Pete, Robbo? Standing around, giggling? Had the bastards really gone off to a club?

Then his panic subsided as the alcohol kicked back in again. His thoughts became leaden, muddled. His eyes closed and he was almost suckered into sleep.

Opening his eyes, the satin blurred into soft focus, as a roller wave of nausea suddenly swelled up inside him, threw him up in the air then dropped him down. Up again. Down again. He swallowed, closed his eye again, giddily, feeling the coffin drifting, swaying from side to side, floating. The need to pee was receding. Suddenly the nausea wasn't so bad any more. It was snug in here. Floating. Like being in a big bed!

His eyes closed and he sank like a stone into sleep.

3

Roy Grace sat in the dark, in his ageing Alfa Romeo in the line of stationary traffic, rain drumming the roof, his fingers drumming the wheel, barely listening to the Dido CD that was playing. He felt tense. Impatient. Gloomy.

He felt like shit.

Tomorrow he was due to appear in court, and he knew he was in trouble.

He took a swig of bottled Evian water, replaced the cap and jammed the bottle back in the door pocket. 'Come on, come on!' he said, fingers tapping again, harder now. He was already forty minutes late for his date. He hated being late, always felt it was a sign of rudeness, as if you were making the statement, *my time's more important than yours, so I can keep you waiting* . . .

If he had left the office just one minute sooner he wouldn't have been late: someone else would have taken the call and the ram-raid on a jewellery shop in Brighton, by two punks who were high on God-knows-what, would have been a colleague's problem, not his. That was one of the occupational hazards of police work – villains didn't have the courtesy to keep to office hours.

He should not be going out tonight, he knew. Should have stayed home, preparing himself for tomorrow. Tugging out the bottle, he drank some more water. His mouth was dry, parched. Leaden butterflies flip-flopped in his belly.

Friends had pushed him into a handful of blind dates

over the past few years, and each time he'd been a bag of nerves before he'd shown up. The nerves were even worse tonight, and, not having had a chance to shower and change, he felt uncomfortable about his appearance. All his detailed planning about what he was going to wear had gone out of the window, thanks to the two punks.

One of them had fired a sawn-off shotgun at an off-duty cop who had come too close to the jewellery shop – but luckily not quite close enough. Roy had seen, more times than he had needed, the effects of a 12-bore fired from a few feet at a human being. It could shear off a limb or punch a hole the size of a football through their chest. This cop, a detective called Bill Green who Grace knew – they had played rugger on the same team a few times – had been peppered from about thirty yards. At this distance the pellets could just about have brought down a pheasant or a rabbit, but not a fifteen-stone scrum prop in a leather jacket. Bill Green was relatively lucky – his jacket had shielded his body but he had several pellets embedded in his face, including one in his left eye.

By the time Grace had got to the scene, the punks were already in custody, after crashing and rolling their getaway Jeep. He was determined to stick them with an attempted murder charge on top of armed robbery. He hated the way more and more criminals were using guns in the UK – and forcing more and more police to have firearms to hand. In his father's day armed cops would have been unheard of. Now in some cities forces kept guns in the boots of their cars as routine. Grace wasn't naturally a vengeful person, but so far as he was concerned, anyone who fired a gun at a police officer – or at any innocent person – should be hanged.

The traffic still wasn't moving. He looked at the dash

clock, at the rain falling, at the clock again, at the burning red tail lights of the car in front – the prat had his fogs on, almost dazzling him. Then he checked his watch, hoping the car clock might be wrong. But it wasn't. Ten whole minutes had passed and they hadn't moved an inch. Nor had any traffic come past from the opposite direction.

Shards of blue light flitted across his interior mirror and wing mirror. Then he heard a siren. A patrol car screamed past. Then an ambulance. Another patrol car, flat out, followed by two fire engines.

Shit. There had been road works when he'd come this way a couple of days ago, and he'd figured that was the reason for the delay. But now he realized it must be an accident, and fire engines meant it was a bad one.

Another fire engine went past. Then another ambulance, twos-and-blues full on. Followed by a rescue truck.

He looked at the clock again: 9.15 p.m. He should have picked her up three-quarters of an hour ago, in Tunbridge Wells, which was still a good twenty minutes away without this hold-up.

Terry Miller, a newly divorced Detective Inspector in Grace's division, had been regaling him with boasts about his conquests from a couple of internet dating sites and urging Grace to sign up. Roy had resisted, then, when he started finding suggestive emails in his inbox from different women, found out to his fury that Terry Miller had signed him up to a site called U-Date without telling him.

He still had no idea what had prompted him to actually respond to one of the emails. Loneliness? Curiosity? Lust? He wasn't sure. For the past eight years he had got through life just by going steadily from day to day. Some days he tried to forget, other days he felt guilty for not remembering.

Sandy.

Now he was suddenly feeling guilty for going on this date.

She looked gorgeous – from her photo, at any rate. He liked her name, too. Claudine. French-sounding, it had something exotic. Her picture was hot! Amber hair, seriously pretty face, tight blouse showing a weapons-grade bust, sitting on the edge of a bed with a miniskirt pulled high enough to show she was wearing lace-topped hold-ups and *might* not be wearing knickers.

They'd had just one phone conversation, in which she had practically seduced him down the line. A bunch of flowers he'd bought at a petrol station lay on the passenger seat beside him. Red roses – corny, he knew, but that was the old-fashioned romantic in him. People were right, he did need to move on, somehow. He could count the dates he'd had in the past eight and three-quarter years on just one hand. He simply could not accept there might be another Miss Right out there. That there could ever be anyone who matched up to Sandy.

Maybe tonight that feeling would change?

Claudine Lamont. Nice name, nice voice.

Turn those sodding fog lamps off!

He smelled the sweet scent of the flowers. Hoped he smelled OK, too.

In the ambient glow from the Alfa's dash and the tail lights of the car in front, he stared up at the mirror, unsure what he expected to see. Sadness stared back at him.

You have to move on.

He swallowed more water. Yup.

In just over two months he would be thirty-nine. In just over two months also another anniversary loomed. On 26 July Sandy would have been gone for nine years. Vanished into thin air, on his thirtieth birthday. No note. All her belongings still in the house except for her handbag.

After seven years you could have someone declared legally dead. His mother, in her hospice bed, days before she passed away from cancer, his sister, his closest friends, his shrink, all of them told him he should do that.

No way.

John Lennon had said, 'Life is what happens to you when you're busy making other plans.' That sure as hell was true.

By thirty-six he had always assumed Sandy and he would have had a family. Three kids had always been his dream, ideally two boys and a girl, and his weekends would be spent doing stuff with them. Family holidays. Going to the beach. Out on day trips to fun places. Playing ball games. Fixing things. Helping them at nights with homework. Bathing them. All the comfortable stuff he'd done with his own parents.

Instead he was consumed with an inner turbulence that rarely left him, even when it allowed him to sleep. Was she alive or dead? He'd spent eight years and ten months trying to find out and was still no nearer to the truth than when he had started.

Outside of work, life was a void. He'd been unable – or unwilling – to attempt another relationship. Every date he'd been on was a disaster. It seemed at times that his only constant companion in his life was his goldfish, Marlon. He'd won the fish by target shooting at a fairground, nine years ago, and it had eaten all his subsequent attempts to provide it with a companion. Marlon was a surly, antisocial creature. Probably why they liked each other, Roy reflected. They were two of a kind.

Sometimes he wished he wasn't a policeman, that he

did some less demanding job where he could switch off at five o'clock, go to the pub and then home, put his feet up in front of the telly. Normal life. But he couldn't help it. There was some stubbornness or determination gene – or bunch of genes – inside him – and his father before him – that had driven him relentlessly throughout his life to pursue facts, to pursue the truth. It was those genes that had brought him up through the ranks, to his relatively early promotion to Detective Superintendent. But they hadn't brought him any peace of mind.

His face stared back at him again from the mirror. Grace grimaced at his reflection, at his hair cropped short, to little more than a light fuzz, at his nose, squashed and kinked after being broken in a scrap when he'd been a beat copper, which gave him the appearance of a retired prize fighter.

On their first date, Sandy had told him he had eyes like Paul Newman. He'd liked that a lot. It was one of a million things he had liked about her. The fact that she had loved everything about him, unconditionally.

Roy Grace knew that he was physically fairly unimpressive. At five foot, ten inches, he had been just two inches over the minimum height restriction when he'd joined the police, nineteen years back. But despite his love of booze, and an on–off battle with cigarettes, through hard work at the police gym he had developed a powerful physique, and had kept in shape, running twenty miles a week, and still playing the occasional game of rugger – usually on the wing.

Nine-twenty.

Bloody hell.

He seriously did not want a late night. Did not need one. Could not afford one. He was in court tomorrow, and needed to bank a full night's sleep. The whole thought of the cross-examination that awaited him pressed all kinds of bad buttons inside him.

A pool of light suddenly flooded down from above him, and he heard the clattering din of a helicopter. After a moment the light moved forward, and he saw the helicopter descending.

He dialled a number on his mobile. It was answered almost immediately.

'Hi, it's Detective Superintendent Grace speaking. I'm sitting in a traffic jam on the A26 south of Crowborough, there seems to be an accident somewhere ahead – can you give me any information?'

He was put through to the headquarters operations room. A male voice said, 'Hello, Detective Superintendent, there's a major accident. We have reports of fatalities and people trapped. The road's going to be blocked for a while – you'd be best turning around and using another route.'

Roy Grace thanked him and disconnected. Then he pulled his BlackBerry from his shirt pocket, looked up Claudine's number and texted her.

She texted back almost instantly, telling him not to worry, just to get there when he could.

This made him warm to her even more.

And it helped him forget about tomorrow.

4

Drives like this didn't happen very often, but when they did, boy, did Davey enjoy them! He sat strapped in the passenger seat next to his dad, as the police car escort raced on in front of them, blue lights flashing, siren *whup, whup, whupping,* on the wrong side of the road, overtaking mile after mile of stationary traffic. Boy, this was as good as any fairground ride his dad had taken him on, even the ones at Alton Towers, and they were about as good as it gets!

'Yeeeha!' he cried out, exuberantly. Davey was addicted to American cop shows on television, which was why he liked to talk with an American accent. Sometimes he was from New York. Sometimes from Missouri. Sometimes Miami. But mostly from LA.

Phil Wheeler, a hulk of a man, with a massive beer belly, dressed in his work uniform of brown dungarees, scuffed boots and black beanie hat, smiled at his son, riding along beside him. Years back his wife had cracked and left from the strain of caring for Davey. For the past seventeen years he had brought him up on his own.

The cop car was slowing now, passing a line of heavy, earth-moving plant. The tow-truck had 'WHEELER'S AUTO RECOVERY' emblazoned on both sides and amber strobes on the cab roof. Ahead through the windscreen, the battery of headlights and spotlights picked up first the mangled front end of the Transit van, still partially embedded beneath the front bumper of the cement truck, then the rest of the van, crushed like a Coke can, lying on its side in a demolished section of hedgerow.

Slivers of blue flashing light skidded across the wet tarmac and shiny grass verge. Fire tenders, police cars and one ambulance were still on the scene, and a whole bunch of people, firemen and cops, mostly in reflective jackets, stood around. One cop was sweeping glass from the road with a broom.

A police photographer's camera flashed. Two crash investigators were laying out a measuring tape. Metal and glass litter glinted everywhere. Phil Wheeler saw a wheel-wrench, a trainer, a rug, a jacket.

'Sure looks a goddamn bad mess, Dad!' Missouri tonight.

'Very bad.'

Phil Wheeler had become hardened over the years, and nothing much shocked him any more. He'd seen just about every tragedy one could possibly have in a motor car. A headless businessman, still in a suit jacket, shirt and tie, strapped into the driver's seat in the remains of his Ferrari, was among the images he remembered most vividly.

Davey, just turned twenty-six, was dressed in his uniform New York Yankees baseball cap the wrong way around, fleece jacket over lumberjack shirt, jeans, heavy-duty boots. Davey liked to dress the way he saw Americans dress, on television. The boy had a mental age of about six, and that would never change. But he had a superhuman physical strength that often came in handy on call-outs. Davey could bend sheet metal with his bare hands. Once, he had lifted the front end of a car off a trapped motorcycle by himself.

'Very bad,' he agreed. 'Reckon there are dead people here, Dad?'

'Hope not, Davey.'

'Reckon there might be?'

A traffic cop, with a peaked cap and yellow fluorescent waistcoat, came up to the driver's window. Phil wound it down and recognized the officer.

'Evening, Brian. This looks a mess.'

'There's a vehicle with lifting gear on its way for the lorry. Can you handle the van?'

'No worries. What happened?'

'Head-on, Transit and the lorry. We need the van in the AI compound.'

'Consider it sorted.'

Davey took his flashlight and climbed down from the cab. While his dad talked to the cop, he shone the beam around, down at slicks of oil and foam across the road. Then he peered inquisitively at the tall, square ambulance, its interior light shining behind drawn curtains across the rear window, wondering what might be happening in there.

It was almost two hours before they had all the pieces of the Transit loaded and chained onto the flatbed. His dad and the traffic cop, Brian, walked off a short distance. Phil lit a cigarette with his storm-proof lighter. Davey followed them, making a one-handed roll-up and lighting it with his Zippo. The ambulance and most of the other emergency vehicles had gone, and a massive crane truck was winching the front end of the cement lorry up, until its front wheels – the driver's-side one flat and buckled – were clear of the ground.

The rain had eased off and a badger moon shone through a break in the clouds. His dad and Brian were now talking about fishing – the best bait for carp at this time of year. Bored now and in need of a pee, Davey wandered off down the road, sucking on his roll-up, looking up in the sky for bats. He liked bats, mice, rats, voles, all those kinds of creatures. In fact he liked all animals. Animals never laughed at him the way humans used to, when he was at school. Maybe he'd go out to the badger sett when they got home. He liked to sit out there in the moonlight and watch them play.

Jigging the flashlight beam, he walked a short distance into the bushes, unzipped his fly and emptied his bladder onto a clump of nettles. Just as he finished, a voice called out, right in front of him, startling the hell out of him.

'Hey, hello?'

A crackly, disembodied voice.

Davey jumped.

Then he heard the voice again.

'Hello?'

'Shite!' He shone the beam ahead into the undergrowth but couldn't see anyone. 'Hello?' he called back. Moments later he heard the voice again.

'Hello? Hey, hello? Josh? Luke? Pete? Robbo?'

Davey swung the beam left, right, then further ahead. There was a rustling sound and a rabbit tail bobbed, for an instant, in the beam then was gone. 'Hello, who's that?'

Silence.

A hiss of static. A crackle. Then, only a few feet to his right, he heard the voice again. 'Hello? Hello? Hello?'

Something glinted in a bush. He knelt down. It was a radio, with an aerial. Inspecting it closer, with some excitement he realized it was a walkie-talkie.

He held the beam on it, studying it for a little while, almost nervous of touching it. Then he picked it up. It was heavier than it looked, cold, wet. Beneath a large green button he could see the word *talk*.

He pressed it and said, 'Hello!'

A voice jumped straight back at him. 'Who's that?'

Then another voice called out, from some distance away. 'Davey!'

His dad.

'OK, coming!' he yelled back.

Walking on to the road he pressed the green button again. 'This is Davey!' he said. 'Who are you?'

'DAVVVEEEEEYYYY!'

His dad again.

In his panic, Davey dropped the radio. It hit the road hard, the casing cracked and the batteries spilled out.

'COMING!' he shouted. He knelt, picked up the walkie-talkie and crammed it furtively into his jacket pocket. Then he scooped up the batteries and put them in another pocket.

'COMING, DAD!' he shouted again. 'JUST HAD TO TAKE ME A PISS!'

Keeping his hand in his pocket so the bulge wouldn't show, he hurried back towards the truck.

5

Michael pressed the *talk* button. 'Davey?'

Silence.

He pressed the button again. 'Davey? Hello? Davey?'

White-satin silence. Complete and utter silence, coming down from above, rising up beneath him, pressing in from each side. He tried to move his arms, but as hard as he pushed them out, walls pressed back against them. He also tried to spread out his legs, but they met the same, unyielding walls. Resting the walkie-talkie on his chest, he pushed up against the satin roof inches from his eyes. It was like pushing against concrete.

Then, raising himself up as much as he could, he took hold of the red rubber tube, squinted down it, but could see nothing. Curling his hand over it, he brought it to his lips and tried to whistle down it; but the sound was pathetic.

He sank back down. His head pounded and he badly needed to urinate. He pressed the button again. 'Davey! Davey, I need to pee. Davey!'

Silence again.

From years of sailing, he'd had plenty of experience with two-way radios. *Try a different channel,* he thought. He found the channel selector, but it wouldn't move. He pushed harder, but it still wouldn't move. Then he saw the reason why – it had been superglued, so that he couldn't change channels – couldn't get to Channel 16, the international emergency channel.

'Hey! Enough you bastards, come on, I'm desperate!'

With only the most local of movements possible, he held the walkie-talkie close to his ear and listened.

Nothing.

He laid the radio down on his chest, then slowly, with great difficulty, worked his right hand down and into his leather jacket pocket and pulled out the rugged waterproof mobile Ashley had given him for sailing. He liked it because it was different to the common mobiles everyone else had. He pressed a button on it and the display lit up. His hopes rose – then fell again. No signal.

'Shit.'

He scrolled through the directory until he came to his business partner Mark's name.

Mark Mob.

Despite the lack of a signal he pressed the dial button.

Nothing happened.

He tried Robbo, Pete, Luke, Josh in turn, his desperation increasing.

Then he pressed the walkie-talkie button again. 'Guys! Can you hear me? I know you can fucking hear me!'

Nothing.

On the Ericsson display the time showed 11.13.

He raised his left hand until he could see his watch: 11.14.

He tried to remember the last time he'd looked at it. A good two hours had passed. He closed his eyes. Thought for some moments, trying to figure out exactly what was going on. In the bright, almost dazzling light from the torch he could see the bottle wedged close to his neck and the shiny magazine. He pulled the magazine up over his chest, then manoeuvred it until it was over his face and he was almost smothered by the huge glossy breasts, so close to his eyes they were blurred.

You bastards!

He picked up the walkie-talkie and pressed the *talk* button once more. 'Very funny. Now let me out, please!'

Nothing.

Who the hell was Davey?

His throat was parched. Needed a drink of water. His head was swimming. He wanted to be home, in bed with Ashley. They'd be along in a few minutes. Just had to wait. Tomorrow, he would get them.

The nausea he had been feeling earlier was returning. He closed his eyes. Swimming. Drifting. He lapsed back into sleep.

6

In a crappy end to a crappy flight, the whole plane shook with a resounding crash as the wheels thumped the tarmac, exactly five and a half hours later than its scheduled time. As it decelerated ferociously, Mark Warren, worn out and fed up, in his cramped seat, safety belt digging into his belly, which was already aching from too many airline pretzels and some vile moussaka that he was regretting eating, took a final look at the pictures of the Ferrari 360 featured in the road test of his *Autocar* magazine.

I want you, baby, he was thinking. *Want you SO bad! Oh yes I do!*

Runway lights, blurred by driving rain, flashed past his window as the plane slowed down to taxiing speed. The pilot's voice came over the intercom, all charm, and apologies once more, laying the blame on the fog.

Goddamn fog. Goddamn English weather. Mark dreamed of a red Ferrari, a house in Marbella, a life in the sunshine and someone to share it with. One very special lady. If the property deal he had been negotiating up in Leeds came off, he'd be a step nearer both the house and the Ferrari. The lady was another problem.

Wearily, he unclipped his belt, dug his briefcase out from under his legs and shoved his magazine inside it. Then he stood up, mixing with the scrum in the cabin, leaving his tie at half mast, and pulled his raincoat down from the overhead locker, too tired to care how he looked.

In contrast to his business partner, who always dressed

sloppily, Mark usually was fastidious over his appearance. But like his neat, fair hair, his clothes were too conservatively cut for his twenty-eight years, and usually so pristine they looked brand new, straight off the rail. He liked to imagine the world saw him as a gentrified entrepreneur, but in reality, in any group of people, he invariably stood out as the man who looked as if he was there to sell them something.

His watch read 11.48 p.m. He switched on his mobile, and it powered up. But before he could make a call, the battery warning beeped and the display died. He put it back in his pocket. Too damned late now, far too late. All that he wanted now was to go home to bed.

An hour later he was reversing his silver BMW X5 into his underground parking slot in the Van Alen building. He took the lift up to the fourth floor, and let himself into his apartment.

It had been a financial stretch to buy this place, but it took him a step up in the world. An imposing, modern Deco-style building on Brighton seafront, with a bunch of celebrities among the residents. The place had class. If you lived in the Van Alen you were a somebody. If you were a *somebody,* that meant you were rich. All his life, Mark had had just that one goal – to be rich.

The voicemail light was winking away on the phone as he walked through to the large, open-plan living area. He decided to ignore it for a moment as he dumped his briefcase, plugged his mobile into the charger, then went straight to the drinks cabinet and poured himself a couple of fingers of Balvenie whisky. Then he walked over to the window, stared down at the promenade below, still buzzing with people despite the weather and the hour. Beyond that he could see the bright lights of the Palace Pier and the inky darkness of the sea.

All of a sudden his mobile beeped sharply at him. A message. He stepped over and looked at the display. *Shit.* Fourteen new messages!

Keeping it connected to the charger, he dialled his voicemail box. The first message was from Pete, at 7 p.m., asking where he was. The second was from Robbo at 7.45, helpfully telling him they were moving on to another pub, the Lamb at Ripe. The third was at 8.30 from a very drunken-sounding Luke and Josh, with Robbo in the background. They were moving on from the Lamb to a pub called the Dragon, on the Uckfield Road.

The next two messages were from the estate agent concerning the deal in Leeds, and from their corporate lawyer.

The sixth was at 11.05 from a very distressed-sounding Ashley. Her tone startled him. Ashley was normally calm, unflappable.

'Mark, please, please, *please* call me as soon as you get this,' she urged in her soft, distinctive North American accent.

He hesitated, then listened to the next message. It was from Ashley again. Panicky now. And the next, and the next one after that, each at ten-minute intervals. The tenth message was from Michael's mother. She also sounded distraught.

'Mark, I left a message on your home phone, too. Please call me as soon as you get this, doesn't matter what time.'

Mark paused the machine. *What the hell had happened?*

The next call had been Ashley again. She sounded close to hysterics. 'Mark, there's been a terrible accident. Pete,

Robbo and Luke are dead. Josh is on life support in Intensive Care. No one knows where Michael is. Oh God, Mark, please call me just as soon as you get this.'

Mark replayed the message, scarcely able to believe what he had heard. As he listened to it again he sat down, heavily, on the arm of the sofa. 'Jesus.'

Then he played the rest of the messages. More of the same from Ashley and from Michael's mother. *Call. Call. Please call.*

He drained his whisky, then poured out another slug, three full fingers, and walked over to the window. Through the ghost of his reflection he stared down again at the promenade, watching the passing traffic, then out at the sea. Way out towards the horizon he could see two tiny specks of light, from a freighter or tanker making its way up the Channel.

He was thinking.

I would have been in that accident, too, if the flight had been on time.

But he was thinking beyond that.

He sipped the whisky, then sat down on the sofa. After a few moments, the phone rang again. He walked over and stared at the caller display. Ashley's number. Four rings, then it stopped. Moments later, his mobile rang. Ashley again. He hesitated, then hit the *end-call* button sending it straight to voicemail. Then he switched the phone off, and sat down, leaned back, pulling up the footrest, and cradled the glass in his hands.

Ice cubes rattled in his glass; his hands were shaking, he realized; his whole insides were shaking. He went over to the Bang and Olufsen and put on a Mozart compilation CD. Mozart always helped him to think. Suddenly, he had a lot of thinking to do.

He sat back down, stared into the whisky, focusing intently on the ice cubes as if they were runes that had been cast. It was over an hour before he picked up the phone and dialled.

7

The spasms were getting more frequent now. By clenching his thighs together, holding his breath and squeezing his eyes shut, Michael was still just able to ward off urinating in his trousers. He couldn't do this, could not bear the thought of their laughter when the bastards came back and found he had wet himself.

But the claustrophobia was really getting to him now. The white satin seemed to be shrinking in around him, pressing down closer and closer to his face.

In the beam of the torch, Michael's watch read 2.47.

Shit.

What the hell were they playing at? Two forty-seven. Where the hell were they? Pissed out of their brains in some nightclub?

He stared at the white satin, his head pounding, his mouth parched, his legs knocking together, trying to suppress the pains shooting up through him from his bladder. He didn't know how much longer he could hold off.

In frustration, he hammered with his knuckles on the lid, and hollered, 'Hey! You bastards!'

He looked at his mobile again. No signal. Ignoring that, he scrolled down to Luke's number then hit the dial button. A sharp beep from the machine, and the display on the screen read out *no service.*

Then he fumbled for the walkie-talkie, switched that on and called out the names of his friends again. And then that other voice he dimly remembered.

'Davey? Hello, Davey?'

Only the crackle of static came back to him.

He was desperate for water, his mouth arid and furry. Had they left him any water? He lifted his neck up just the few inches that were available before his head struck the lid, saw the glint of the bottle, reached down. Famous Grouse whisky.

Disappointed, he broke the seal, unscrewed the cap and took a swig. For a moment just the sensation of liquid felt like balm in his mouth; then it turned to fire, burning his mouth, then his gullet. But almost instantly after that he felt a little better. He took another swig. Felt a little better still, and took a third, long swig before he replaced the cap.

He closed his eyes. His headache felt a tiny bit better now. The desire to pee was receding.

'Bastards . . .' he murmured.

8

Ashley looked like a ghost. Her long brown hair framed a face that was as colourless as the patients' in the forest of drip lines, ventilators and monitors in the beds in the ward behind her. She was leaning against the reception counter of the nursing station in the Intensive Care Unit of the Sussex County Hospital. Her vulnerability made her seem even more beautiful than ever, to Mark.

Muzzy from a sleepless night, in a sharp suit and immaculate black Gucci loafers, he walked up to her, put his arms around her, and held her tight. He stared at a vending machine, a drinking water fountain, and a payphone in a perspex dome. Hospitals always gave him the heebie-jeebies. Ever since he'd come to visit his dad after his near fatal heart attack and saw this man who had once been so strong now looking so frail, so damned pathetic and useless – and scared. He squeezed Ashley as much for himself as for her. Close to her head, a cursor blinked on a green computer screen.

She clung to him as if he were a lone spar in a storm-tossed ocean. 'Oh, Christ, Mark, thank God you're here.'

One nurse was busy on the phone; it sounded like she was talking to a relative of someone in the unit, the other one behind the counter, close to them, was tapping out something on a keyboard.

'This is terrible,' Mark said. 'Unbelievable.'

Ashley nodded, swallowing hard. 'If it wasn't for your meeting, you would have been—'

'I know. I can't stop thinking about it. How's Josh?'

Ashley's hair smelled freshly washed, and there was a trace of garlic on her breath, which he barely noticed. The girls had had a hen party last night, arranged in some Italian restaurant.

'Not good. Zoe's with him.' She pointed and Mark followed the line of her finger, across several beds, across the hiss-clunk of ventilators, and the blinking of digital displays, to the far end of the ward, where he could see Josh's wife sitting on a chair. She was dressed in a white T-shirt, tracksuit top and baggy trousers, body stooped, her straggly blonde ringlets covering her face.

'Michael still hasn't turned up. Where is he, Mark? Surely to God you must know?'

As the nurse finished her call, the phone beeped and she started talking again.

'I've no idea,' he said. 'I have absolutely no idea.'

She looked at him hard. 'But you guys have been planning this for weeks – Lucy said you were going to get even with Michael for all the practical jokes he played on the others before they got married.' As she took a step back from him, tossing hair from her forehead, Mark could see her mascara had run. She dabbed at her eyes with her sleeve.

'Maybe the guys had a last-minute change of mind,' he said. 'Sure, they'd come up with all kinds of ideas, like lacing his drink and putting him on a plane to some place, but I managed to talk them out of it – at least I thought I had.'

She gave a wan smile of appreciation.

He shrugged. 'I knew how worried you were, you know, that we'd do something dumb.'

'I was, desperately worried.' She glanced at the nurse, then sniffed. 'So where is he?'

'He definitely wasn't in the car?'

'Absolutely not. I've rung the police – they say that – they say – they—' She began sobbing.

'What did they say?'

In a burst of anger she blurted, 'They won't do anything.'

She sobbed some more, struggling to contain herself. 'They say they've checked all around at the scene of the accident and there's no sign of him, and that he's probably just sleeping off a mighty hangover somewhere.'

Mark waited for her to calm down, but she carried on crying. 'Maybe that's true.'

She shook her head. 'He promised me he wasn't going to get drunk.' Mark gave her a look. After a moment, she nodded. 'It was his stag night, right? That's what you guys do on stag nights, isn't it? You get smashed.'

Mark stared down at grey carpet tiles. 'Let's go and see Zoe,' he said.

Ashley followed him across the ward, trailing a few yards behind him. Zoe was a slender beauty, and today she seemed even more slender to Mark, as he laid his hand on her shoulder, feeling the hard bone beneath the soft fabric of her designer tracksuit top.

'Jeez, Zoe, I'm sorry.'

She acknowledged him with a faint shrug.

'How is he?' Mark hoped the anxiety in his voice sounded genuine.

Zoe turned her head and looked up at him, her eyes raw, her cheeks, almost translucent without make-up, tracked with tears. 'They can't do anything,' she said. 'They operated on him, now we just have to wait.'

He was hooked up to two IVAC infusion pumps, three syringe drivers and a ventilator, which made a steady, soft, eerie hissing sound. A range of data and waveform lines changed constantly on the machine's monitor.

The exit tube from Josh's mouth ended in a small bag, with a tap at the bottom, half filled with a dark fluid. There was a forest of cannulated lines, tagged yellow where they left the pumps and drivers, and tagged with white handwritten labels at the distal end. Wires ran out from the sheets and from his head, feeding digital displays and spiking graphs. What flesh Mark could see was the colour of alabaster. His friend looked like a laboratory experiment.

But Mark was barely looking at Josh. He was looking at the displays, trying to read them, to calculate what they were saying. He was trying to remember, from when he had stood in this same room beside his dying father, which were the ECG, the blood oxygen, the blood pressure readings, and what they all meant. And he was reading the labels on the drip lines. *Mannitol. Pentastarch. Morphine. Midazolam. Noradrenaline.* And he was thinking. Josh had always had it made. Smooth good looks, rich parents. The insurance loss adjuster, always calculating, mapping out his life, forever talking about five-year plans, ten-year plans, life goals. He was the first of the gang to get married, as he wanted to have kids early, so he would still be young enough to enjoy his life after they'd grown up. Marrying the perfect wife, darling little rich girl Zoe, totally fertile, allowed him to fulfil his plan. She'd delivered him two equally perfect babies in rapid succession.

Mark shot a glance around the ward, taking in the nurses, the doctors, marking their positions, then his eyes dropped to the drip lines into Josh's neck and into the back of his hand, just behind the plastic tag bearing his name.

Then they moved across to the ventilator. Then up to the ECG. Warning buzzers would sound if the heart rate dropped too low. Or the blood oxygen level.

Josh surviving would be a problem – he'd lain awake most of the night thinking about that, and had come to the reluctant conclusion it wasn't an option he could entertain.

9

Courtroom One at Lewes Crown Court always felt to Roy Grace as if it had been deliberately designed to intimidate and impress. It didn't carry any higher status than the rest of the courtrooms in this building, but it felt as if it did. Georgian, it had a high, vaulted ceiling, a public gallery up in the gods, oak-panelled walls, dark oak benches and dock, and a balustraded witness stand. At this moment it was presided over by a bewigged Judge Driscoll, way past his sell-by date, who sat, looking half asleep, in a vivid red-backed chair beneath the coat of arms bearing the legend. '*Dieu et mon droit*'. The place looked like a theatre set and smelled like an old school classroom.

Now as Grace stood in the witness stand, dressed neatly as he always was for court, in a blue suit, white shirt, sombre tie and polished black lace-ups, looking good outwardly, he felt ragged inside. Part lack of sleep from his date last night – which had been a disaster – and part nerves. Holding the Bible with one hand, he rattled his way through the oath, glancing around, taking in the scene as he swore for maybe the thousandth time in his career, by Almighty God, to tell the truth, the whole truth and nothing but the truth.

The jury looked the way all juries did, like a bunch of tourists stranded in a coach station. An untidy ragbag of a group, gaudy pullovers, open-throat shirts and creased blouses beneath a sea of blank faces, all white, ranked in two rows, behind water jugs, tumblers and a mess of loose-leaf jottings. Haphazardly stacked beside the judge were a video player, a slide projector and a huge tape recorder. Below him, the female stenographer peered primly from behind a battery of electronic equipment. An electric fan on a chair swivelled right then left, not having much impact on the muggy late-afternoon air. The public galleries were heaving with press and spectators. Nothing like a murder trial to pull the punters in. And this was the local trial of the year.

Roy Grace's big triumph.

Suresh Hossain sat in the dock, a fleshy man with a pockmarked face, slicked-back hair, dressed in a brown, chalk-striped suit and purple satin tie. He observed the proceedings with a laconic gaze, as if he owned the place and this whole trial had been laid on for his personal entertainment. Slimeball, scumbag, slum landlord. He'd been untouchable for the past decade, but now Roy Grace had finally banged him to rights. Conspiracy to murder. His victim an equally unsavoury business rival, Raymond Cohen. If this trial went the way it should, Hossain was going down for more years than he would survive, and several hundred decent citizens of Brighton and Hove would be able to enjoy their lives in their homes freed from the ugly shadow of his henchmen making every hour a living hell for them.

His mind drifted back to last night. *Claudine. Claudine bloody Lamont.* OK, it hadn't helped that he'd arrived for his date an hour and three-quarters late. But it hadn't helped either that her photograph on the U-Date website was, charitably, a good ten years out of date; nor that she'd omitted to put on her details that she was a non-drinking, cop-hating vegan, whose sole interest in life appeared to be her nine rescue cats.

Grace liked dogs. He had nothing in particular against cats, but he'd never yet met one that he'd connected with, in the way he almost instantly bonded with any dog. After two and a half hours in a dump of a vegetarian restaurant in Tunbridge Wells, being lectured and grilled alternately about the free spirits of cats, the oppressive nature of the British police and men who viewed women solely as sex objects, he had been relieved to escape.

Now, after a night of troubled, intermittent sleep and a day of hanging around waiting to be called, he was about to be grilled again. It was still raining this afternoon, but the air was much warmer and clammy. Grace could feel perspiration walking down the small of his back.

The defence silk, who had surprised the court by summoning him as a witness, had the floor now, standing up, arrogant stature, short grey wig, flowing black gown, lips pursed into a grin of rictus warmth. His name was Richard Charwell QC. Grace had encountered him before and it had not been a happy experience, then. He detested lawyers. To lawyers, trials were a game. They never had to go out and risk their lives catching villains. And it didn't matter one jot to them what crimes had been committed.

'Are you Detective Superintendent Roy Grace, stationed at CID headquarters, Sussex House, Hollingbury, Brighton?' the silk asked.

'Yes,' Grace answered. Instead of his usual confident voice, his reply came out of the wrong part of his throat, more like a croak.

'And have you had some dealings with this case?'

'Yes.' Another choked, dry-mouthed sound.

'I now tender this witness.'

There was a brief pause. No one spoke. Richard Charwell QC had the ear of the entire court. A consummate actor with distinguished good looks, he paused deliberately for effect before speaking again, in a sudden change of tone that suggested he had now become Roy Grace's new best friend.

'Detective Superintendent, I wonder if you might help us with a certain matter. Do you have any knowledge about a shoe connected with this case? A brown crocodile-skin slip-on loafer with a gold chain?'

Grace eyeballed him back for some moments before answering. 'Yes, I do.' Now, suddenly, he felt a stab of panic. Even before the barrister spoke his next words, he had a horrible feeling about where this might be going.

'Are you going to tell us about the person to whom you took this shoe, Detective Superintendent, or do you want me to squeeze it out of you?'

'Well, sir, I'm not exactly sure what you are getting at.'

'Detective Superintendent, I think you know very well what I'm getting at.'

Judge Driscoll, with the bad temper of a man disturbed from a nap, intervened: 'Mr Charwell, kindly get to the point, we haven't got all day.'

Unctuously, the silk responded, 'Very well, your honour.' Then he turned back to Grace. 'Detective Superintendent, is it not a fact that you have interfered with a vital piece of evidence in this case? Namely this shoe?'

The silk picked it up from the exhibits table and held it aloft for the entire court to see, the way he might have been holding up a sporting trophy he had just won.

'I wouldn't say I had interfered with it all,' Grace responded, angered by the man's arrogance – but, equally, aware this was the silk's game plan, to wind him up, wanting to rile him.

Charwell lowered the shoe, pensively. 'Oh, I see, you

don't consider that you have interfered with it?' Without waiting for Grace to answer, he went on. 'I put it to you that you have abused your position by removing a piece of evidence and taking it to a dabbler in the dark arts.'

Turning to Judge Driscoll, he continued. 'Your honour, I intend to show this court that the DNA evidence that has been obtained from this shoe is unsafe, because Detective Superintendent Grace has affected the continuity and caused possible contamination of this vital exhibit.'

He turned back to Grace. 'I am correct, am I not, Detective Superintendent, that on Thursday, March 9th of this year, you took this shoe to a so-called medium in Hastings named Mrs Stempe? And presumably we are going to hear from you that this shoe has now been to another world? A rather ethereal one?'

'Mrs Stempe is a lady of whom I have a very high opinion,' Grace said. 'She—'

'We are not concerned with your opinions, Detective Superintendent, just the facts.'

But the judge's curiosity seemed piqued. 'I think his opinions are perfectly relevant in this issue.'

After a few moments of silent stand-off between the defence silk and the judge, Charwell nodded reluctant assent.

Grace continued. 'She has helped me on a number of enquiries in the past. Three years ago Mary Stempe gave me sufficient information to enable me to put a name to a murder suspect. It led directly to his arrest and subsequent conviction.'

He hesitated, aware of the intense gazes of everyone in the room, then went on, addressing the silk. 'If I may respond to your concerns over continuity of the exhibit, sir. If you had checked through the records, which you are entitled to do, and looked at the packaging, you would have seen the label was signed and dated when I removed it and when I returned it. The defence have been aware of this exhibit from the start, which was found outside Mr Cohen's house on the night he disappeared, and have never asked to examine it.'

'So you regularly turn to the dark arts in your work as a senior police officer, do you, Detective Superintendent Grace?'

An audible snigger rippled round the courtroom.

'I wouldn't call it the *dark arts,*' Grace said. 'I would call it an alternative resource. The police have a duty to use everything at their disposal in trying to solve crimes.'

'So would it be fair to say you are a man of the occult? A believer in the supernatural?' the silk asked.

Grace looked at Judge Driscoll, who was staring at him as if it was he himself who was now on trial in this court. Desperately trying to think of an appropriate response, he shot a glance at the jury, then the public gallery, before he faced the silk again. And suddenly it came to him.

Grace's voice notched up a gear, more strident, more confident, suddenly. 'What is the first thing this court required me to do when I entered the witness stand?' he asked.

Before the silk could respond, Grace answered for him. 'To *swear on the Holy Bible.*' He paused for it to sink in. 'God is a supernatural being – the *supreme* supernatural being. In a court that accepts witnesses taking an oath to a supernatural being, it would be strange if I and everyone else in this room did not believe in the supernatural.'

'I have no more questions,' the silk said, sitting back down.

The prosecution counsel, also in a wig and silk gown,

stood up and addressed Judge Driscoll. 'Your honour, this is a matter I want to raise in chambers.'

'It's rather unusual,' Judge Driscoll responded, 'but I'm satisfied that it has been dealt with properly. However,' and now his eyes turned to Grace, 'I would hope cases that come before my court are based on evidence rather than the utterings of Mystic Megs.'

Almost the whole court erupted into laughter.

The trial moved on, and another defence witness was called, a bagman for Suresh Hossain called Rubiro Valiente. Roy Grace stayed to listen while this piece of Italian low-life told a pack of lies, which were exposed in rapid succession by the prosecution counsel. By the afternoon recess, the court was so agog with the audacity of the lies that Roy Grace began to hope the business of the shoe might have been overshadowed.

His hopes were dashed when he went outside into Lewes High Street to get some fresh air and a sandwich. Across the street, the news banner headline of the local paper, the *Argus*, shouted to the world:

POLICE OFFICER ADMITS TO OCCULT PRACTICES

Suddenly, he felt badly in need of a drink and a fag.

10

The hunger wouldn't go away no matter how hard Michael tried to block it from his mind. His stomach reminded him with a steady dull ache as if something were chafing away inside it. His head felt light and his hands shaky. He kept thinking of food, of meaty burgers with thick-cut fries and ketchup. When he pushed those from his mind, the smell of broiling lobsters replaced it; then barbecued corn; grilled garlicky mushrooms; eggs frying; sausages; sizzling bacon.

The lid was pressing down against his face and he began to panic again, snatching at the air, gulping it greedily. He closed his eyes, tried to imagine he was fine, he was somewhere warm, on his yacht – in the Med. Lapping water all around, gulls overhead, balmy Mediterranean air. But the sides of the coffin were pushing in. Compressing him. He fumbled for the torch resting on his chest and switched it on, the battery feeble and rapidly failing now. Carefully unscrewing the cap of the whisky bottle with trembling fingers, he brought the neck to his lips. Then he took one miserly sip, swilling the liquid around his parched, sticky mouth, stretching every drop out as far as it would go, savouring every second. The panic subsided and his breathing slowed.

Only some minutes after he had swallowed, after the warm burning sensation that spread down his gullet and through his stomach had faded away, did he turn his concentration back to the task of screwing the lid back on. Half a bottle left. One sip per hour, on the hour.

Routine.

He switched the torch off to conserve the last dregs of juice. Every movement was an effort. His limbs were stiff and he shivered with cold one moment, then broke out in a clammy, feverish sweat the next. His head pounded and pounded – he was desperate for some paracetamol. Desperate for noise above him, for voices. To get out.

Food.

By some small miracle, the batteries in the walkie-talkie were the same as those in the torch. At least he still had those in reserve. At least there was one bit of good news. The only good news. And the other bit was that in an hour he could have another sip of whisky.

Routine kept the panic attacks at bay.

You kept sane if you had a routine. Five years back he had crewed on a thirty-eight-footer sloop across the Atlantic, from Chichester to Barbados. Twenty-seven days at sea. For fifteen of them they'd had a gale on the nose that not once dropped below a force seven, and at times gusted up to ten and eleven. Fifteen days of hell. Watches four hours on and four hours off. Every wave shook every bone in his body, as they crashed down again and again, every chain rattling, every shackle smacking against the decking or the rigging, every knife, fork and plate clattering in its locker. They had got through that by routine. By measuring each day into groups of hours. And then by spacing those hours with small treats. Bars of chocolate. Sips of drink. Pages of a novel. Glances at the compass. Taking turns pumping the bilges.

Routine gave you structure. Structure gave you perspective. And perspective gave you a horizon.

And when you looked at the horizon, you felt calmer.

Now he measured each hour with a small sip of whisky. Half a bottle left, and his horizon was the hour hand of his watch. The watch Ashley had bought him, a silver-rimmed Longines with luminous Roman numerals. It was the classiest watch he had ever owned. Ashley had great taste. She had class. Everything about her was classy, the kink in her long, brown hair, the way she walked, the confidence with which she talked, her classically beautiful features. He loved walking into a room with her. Anywhere. Eyes turned, stared. Jesus, he loved that! There was something special about her. Totally unique.

His mother said that too, and usually she never approved of his girlfriends. But Ashley was different. Ashley had worked on his mum and charmed her. That was another thing he loved about her, she could charm anyone. Even the most miserable damned client. He fell in love with her the day she walked into the office he shared with Mark, for a job interview. Now, just six months later, they were getting married.

His crotch and thighs itched like hell. Nappy rash. Long back he'd given up on his bladder. Twenty-six hours had passed now.

Something must have happened, but he had no idea what. Twenty-six fucking hours of shouting into the walkie-talkie, dialling his mobile and getting the same damned message. *No service.*

Tuesday. Ashley wanted the stag night to be well before the wedding. *You'll get drunk and feel like shit. I don't want you feeling like that on our wedding day. Have it early in the week to give yourself time to recover.*

He pushed up with his hands for the hundredth time. Maybe the two hundredth time. Maybe even the thousandth time. It made no difference. He had already tried grinding a hole in the lid with the only hard implement he had, the casing of his walkie-talkie. The mobile and the torch were both plastic. But the casing still wasn't tough enough.

He switched on the walkie-talkie again. 'Hello? Is anyone there? Hello?'

Static was there.

A dark thought occurred to him. Was Ashley in on this? Was this why she'd been so insistent that he should have the stag party early in the week, on Tuesday? So he could be locked in here – wherever *here* was – for a whole twenty-four hours, longer, without it causing any problem?

Never. She knew he was claustrophobic, and she didn't have a cruel bone in her body. She always put everyone else first, was always thinking about other people's needs.

The number of presents she had bought for his mother and himself had staggered him. And everything exquisitely appropriate. Her favourite perfume. A CD of her favourite singer, Robbie Williams, a cashmere jumper she had been hankering after. A Bose radio he had coveted. How did Ashley find out all these things? It was a knack, a gift, just one of the endless list of attributes that made her such a special person.

And made him the luckiest man in the world.

The torch beam dimmed, noticeably. He switched it off again to conserve the battery and lay still in the darkness again. He could hear his breathing getting faster. What if?

If they never came back?

It was nearly 11.30. He waited, listening for a gaggle of voices that would tell him his friends were back.

Jesus, when he got out of there they weren't half

going to regret this. He looked at his watch again. Twenty-five to midnight. They would be along soon, any minute now.

They *had* to be.

11

Sandy stood over him, grinning, blocking the sunlight, deliberately provoking him. Her blonde hair swung down either side of her freckled face, brushing his cheeks.

'Hey! I have to read – this report – I—'

'You're so boring, Grace, you always have to read!' She kissed his forehead. 'Read, read, read, work, work, work!' She kissed his forehead again. 'Don't you still fancy me?'

She was wearing a skimpy sun dress, her breasts almost falling out the top; he caught a glimpse of her long, tanned legs, her hem riding up her thighs, and suddenly he felt very horny.

He reached up his arms to cup her face, pulling her down to him, staring into those trusting blue eyes, feeling so incredibly – intensely – deeply – in love with her.

'I adore you,' he said.

'Do you, Grace?' Flirting. 'Do you really adore me more than your work?' She pulled her head back, pouted her lips quizzically.

'I love you more than anything in—'

Darkness suddenly. As if someone had pulled out a plug.

Grace heard the echo of his voice in cold, empty air.

'Sandy!' he shouted, but the sound stayed trapped in his throat.

The sunlight faded into a weak orange glow; street lighting leaking in around the bedroom curtains.

The display on the digital clock said 3.02 a.m.

He was sweating, eyes wide open, his heart tossing around in his chest like a buoy in a storm. He heard the clatter of a dustbin – a scavenging cat or a fox. Moments later it was followed by the rattle of a diesel – probably his neighbour three doors down, who drove a taxi and kept late hours.

For some moments he lay still. Closed his eyes, calmed his breathing, tried to return to the dream, clinging as hard as he could to the memory. Like all the recurring dreams he had about Sandy it felt so real. As if they were still together but in a different dimension. If he could just find some way of locating the portal, crossing the divide, they really would be together again, they'd be fine, they'd be happy.

So damned happy.

A huge swell of sadness rolled through him. Then it turned to dread as he started to remember. The newspaper. That damned headline in the *Argus* last night. It was all coming back. Christ, oh Christ. What the hell were the morning papers going to say? Criticism he could cope with. Ridicule was harder. He already got stick from a number of officers for dabbling in the supernatural. He'd been warned by the previous Chief Constable, who was genuinely intrigued by the paranormal himself, that to let his interests be known openly could harm his promotion prospects.

'Everyone knows you're a special case, Roy – having lost Sandy. No one's going to criticize you for turning over every stone on the damned planet. We'd all do the same in your shoes. But you have to keep that in your box, you can't bring it to work.'

There were times when he thought he was getting over her, when he was getting strong again. Then there were moments like now when he realized he had barely progressed at all. He just wished so desperately he could have put an arm around her, cuddled up against her, talked through the problem. She was a glass-half-full person, always positive, and so savvy. She'd helped steer him through a disciplinary tribunal in his early days in the Force which could have ended his career, when he'd been accused by the Police Complaints Authority of using excessive force against a mugger he'd arrested. He'd been exonerated then, largely through following Sandy's advice. She would have known exactly what he should do now.

He wondered sometimes if these dreams were attempts by Sandy to communicate with him. From wherever she was.

Jodie, his sister, told him it was time to move on, that he needed to accept that Sandy was dead, to replace her voice on the answering machine, to remove her clothes from the bedroom and her things from the bathroom, in short – and Jodie could be very short – to stop living in some kind of a shrine to Sandy, and start all over again.

But how could he move on? What if Sandy was alive, being held captive by some maniac? He had to keep searching, to keep the file open, to keep updating the photographs showing how she might look now, to keep scanning every face he passed in the street or saw in a crowd. He would go on until—

Until.

Closure.

On the morning of his thirtieth birthday, Sandy had woken him with a tray on which was a tiny cake with a single candle, a glass of champagne and a very rude birthday card. He'd opened the presents she had given him, then they had made love. He'd left the house later than usual, at 9.15, and reached his office in Brighton shortly after half past, late for a briefing on a murder case. He'd promised to be home early, to go out for a celebratory meal with another couple – his best friend at the time, Dick Pope, also a detective, and his wife, Lesley, who Sandy got on well with – but it had been a hectic day and he'd arrived home almost two hours later than he had intended. There was no sign of Sandy.

At first he'd thought she was angry with him for being so late and was making a protest. The house was tidy, her car and handbag were gone, there was no sign of a struggle.

Then, twenty-four hours later, her car was found in a bay of the short-term car park at Gatwick Airport. There were two transactions on her credit card on the morning of her disappearance, one for £7.50 at Boots, and £16.42 for petrol from the local branch of Tesco. She had taken no clothes and no other belongings of any kind.

His neighbours in this quiet, residential street just off the seafront had not seen a thing. On one side of him was an exuberantly friendly Greek family who owned a couple of cafes in the town, but they had been away on holiday, and on the other side was an elderly widow with a hearing problem, who slept with the television on, volume at maximum. Right now, at 3.45 a.m., he could hear an American cop drama through the party wall between their semi-detached houses. Guns banged, tyres squealed, sirens *whup-whupped*. She'd seen nothing.

Noreen Grinstead, who lived opposite, was the one person he might have expected to have noticed something. A hawk-eyed, jumpy woman in her sixties, she knew everyone's business in the street. When she wasn't tending to her husband, Lance, who was steadily going downhill with

Alzheimer's, she was forever out front in yellow rubber gloves, washing her silver Nissan car, or hosing and scrubbing the driveway, or the windows of the house, or anything else that did or did not need washing. She even brought stuff out of the house to clean it in the driveway.

Very little escaped her eye. But, somehow, Sandy's disappearance had.

He switched the light on and got out of bed, pausing to stare at the photograph of himself and Sandy on the dressing table. It had been taken in a hotel in Oxford during a conference on DNA fingerprinting, a few months before she disappeared. He was lounging back in a suit and tie, on a chaise longue. Sandy, in an evening dress, was lying back against him, hair up in blonde ringlets, beaming her constant irrepressible grin at a waiter they had sequestered to take the picture.

He went over, picked up the frame, kissed the photo then set it down again, and went into the bathroom to urinate. Getting up in the middle of the night to pee was a recent affliction, a result of the health fad he was on, drinking the recommended minimum eight glasses of water a day. Then he padded, clad only in the T-shirt he slept in, downstairs.

Sandy had such great taste. Their house itself was modest, like all the ones in the street, a three-bedroom mock-Tudor semi, built in the 1930s, but she had made it beautiful. She loved browsing the Sunday supplements, women's magazines and design magazines, ripping out pages and showing him ideas. They'd spent hours together, stripping wallpaper, sanding floors, varnishing, painting.

Sandy got into Feng Shui, and built a little water garden. She filled the house with candles. Bought organic food whenever she could. She thought about everything, questioned everything, was interested in everything, and he loved that. Those had been the good times, when they were building their future, cementing their life together, making all their plans.

She was a good gardener, too. She understood about flowers, plants, shrubs, bushes, trees. When to plant, how to prune. Grace liked to mow the lawn but that was about where his skills ended. The garden was neglected now and he felt guilty about that, sometimes wondering what she would say if she returned.

Her car was still in the garage. Forensics had been through it with a toothcomb after it had been recovered, then he'd brought it back home and garaged it. For years he kept the battery on trickle charge, just in case . . . The same way he kept her slippers out on the bedroom floor, her dressing gown hanging on its peg, her toothbrush in its mug.

Waiting for her return.

Wide awake, he poured himself two fingers of Glenfiddich, then sat down in his white armchair in the all-white lounge with its wooden floor and pressed the remote. He flicked through three movies in succession, then a bunch of other Sky channels, but nothing grabbed his attention for more than a few minutes. He played some music, switching restlessly from the Beatles to Miles Davis to Sophie Ellis-Bextor, then back to silence.

He picked one of his favourite books, Colin Wilson's *The Occult*, from the rows of books on the paranormal that filled every inch of his bookshelves, then sat back and turned the pages listlessly, sipping his whisky, unable to concentrate on more than a couple of paragraphs.

That damned defence barrister strutting around in court today had got under his skin, and was now strutting around inside his mind. Richard bloody Charwell. Pompous sodding bastard. Worse, Grace knew he had been outsmarted by the man. Outmanoeuvred and outsmarted. And that really stung.

He picked up the remote again and punched up the news on Teletext. Nothing beyond the same stories that had been around for a couple of days now and were getting stale. No breaking political scandal, no terrorist outrage, no earthquake, no air disaster. He didn't wish ill on anyone, but he had been hoping for something to fill up the morning's headlines and airwaves. Something other than the murder trial of Suresh Hossain.

His luck was out.

12

Two national tabloids and one broadsheet led with front-page splashes on the murder trial of Suresh Hossain, and all the rest of the British morning papers had coverage inside.

It wasn't the trial itself that was the focus of their interest, but the remarks in the witness box made by Detective Superintendent Roy Grace, who at 8.30 in the morning found himself on the carpet in front of his boss, Alison Vosper, feeling as if the clock had been wound back three decades, and he was back at school, trembling in front of his headmistress.

One of Grace's colleagues had nicknamed her 'No. 27', and it had stuck. No. 27 was a sweet and sour dish on the local Chinese takeaway menu. Conversely, when ordering the dish, it was always referred to as an Alison Vosper. That's exactly what she was, sweet and sour.

In her early forties, with wispy blonde hair cut conservatively short, and framing a hard but attractive face, Assistant Chief Constable Alison Vosper was very definitely sour this morning. Even the powerful floral scent she was wearing had an acrid tinge.

Power-dressed in a black two-piece with a crisp white blouse, she sat behind an expanse of polished rosewood desk, in her immaculate ground-floor office in the Queen Anne police headquarters building in Lewes, with its view out across a trimmed lawn. The desk was bare except for a slim crystal vase containing three purple tulips, framed photographs of her husband (a police officer several years older but three ranks her junior) and her two children, an ammonite pen holder and a stack of the morning's newspapers fanned out like a triumphant poker hand.

Grace always wondered how his superiors kept their offices – and their desks – so tidy. All his working life, his own work spaces had been tips. Repositories of sprawling files, unanswered correspondence, lost pens, travel receipts and out-trays that had long given up on the struggle to keep pace with the in-trays. To get to the very top, he decided, required some kind of paperwork management skill for which he was lacking the gene.

Rumour was that Alison Vosper had had a breast cancer operation three years ago. But Grace knew that's all it would ever be, just rumour, because the Assistant Chief Constable kept a wall around herself. Nonetheless, behind her hard-cop carapace, there was a certain vulnerability that he connected to. In truth, at times he fancied her, and there were occasions when those waspish brown eyes of hers twinkled with humour, and when he sensed she might almost be flirting with him. This morning was not one of them.

No handshake. No greeting. Just a curt nod for him to sit in one of the twin high-backed chairs in front of her desk. Then she launched straight in, with a look that was part reproach, part pure anger.

'What the hell is this, Roy?'

'I'm sorry.'

'*Sorry?*'

He nodded. 'I – look, this whole thing got taken out of context—'

She interrupted him before he could continue. 'You

realize this could bring the whole case crashing down on us?'

'I think we can contain it.'

'I've had a dozen calls from the national press already this morning. You've become a laughing stock. You've made us look like a bunch of idiots. Why have you done this?'

Grace was silent for some moments. 'She's an extraordinary woman, this medium; she's helped us in the past. It never occurred to me anyone would find out.'

Vosper leaned back in her chair, staring at Grace, shaking her head from side to side. 'I had great hopes for you. Your promotion was because of me. I put myself on the line for you, Roy. You know that, don't you?'

Not strictly true, but this wasn't the moment to start splitting hairs. 'I know,' he said, 'and I appreciate it.'

She pointed at the newspapers. 'And this is how you show it? This is what you deliver?'

'Come on, Alison, I've delivered Hossain.'

'And now you've given his defence counsel a crack big enough to drive a coach and horses through.'

'No,' he said, rising to this. 'That shoe had already been through forensics, signed out and signed back in. They can't lay an exhibits contamination charge on me. They might be trying to take a pop at my methods, but this won't have any material effect on the case.'

She raised her manicured fingers and started examining them. Roy could see the tips were black from newsprint ink. Her scent seemed to be getting stronger, as if she were an animal excreting venom. 'You're the senior officer, it's your case. If you let them discredit you it could have a very big effect on the outcome. Why the hell did you do it?'

'We have a murder trial and we don't have a body. We *know* Hossain had Raymond Cohen murdered, right?'

She nodded. The evidence Grace had amassed was impressive and persuasive.

'But with no body there's always a weak link.' He shrugged. 'We've had results in the past from mediums. Every police force in the nation's used them at one time or another. Lesley Whittle, right?'

Lesley Whittle was a celebrated case. Back in 1975 the seventeen-year-old heiress had been kidnapped and vanished into thin air. Unable to find any clues to her whereabouts, the police finally acted on information from a clairvoyant using dowsing techniques, who led them to a drainage shaft, where they discovered the unfortunate girl tethered and dead.

'Lesley Whittle wasn't exactly a triumph of police work, Roy.'

'There have been others, since,' he countered.

She stared at him in silence. Then dimples appeared in her cheeks as if she might be softening; but her voice remained cold and stern. 'You could write the number of successes we've had with clairvoyants on a postage stamp.'

'That isn't true, and you know it.'

'Roy, what I know is that you are an intelligent man. I know that you've studied the paranormal and that *you* believe. I've seen the books in your office, and I respect any police officer who can think *out of the box.* But we have a duty to the community. Whatever goes on behind our closed doors is one thing. The image we present to the public is another.'

'The public *believe,* Alison. There was a survey taken in 1925 of the number of scientists who believed in God. It was forty-three per cent. They did that same survey again in 1998, and guess what? It was still forty-three per cent. The only shift was that there were fewer biologists who believed, but more mathematicians and physicists. There was another survey, only last year, of people who had had some kind of paranormal experience. It was ninety per cent!' He leaned forwards. 'Ninety per cent!'

'Roy, the Great Unwashed want to believe the police spend ratepayers' money on solving crimes and catching villains through established police procedures. They want to believe we are out scouring the country for fingerprints and DNA, that we have labs full of scientists to examine them, and that we are trawling fields, woods, dredging lakes, knocking on doors and interviewing witnesses. They don't want to think we are talking to Madame Arcata on the end of Brighton Pier, are staring into crystal balls or are shifting upturned tumblers around rows of letters on a bloody Ouija board! They don't want to think we are spending our time trying to summon up the dead. They don't want to believe their police officers are standing on the ramparts of castles like Hamlet talking to his father's ghost. Understand what I'm saying?'

'I understand, yes. But I don't agree with you. Our job is to solve crimes. We have to use whatever means are at our disposal.'

She shook her head. 'We're never going to solve every crime, and we have to accept that. What we have to do is inspire public confidence. Make people feel safe in their homes, and on the streets.'

'That's such bullshit,' Grace said, 'and you know that! You know fine well you can massage the crime statistics any way you want.' No sooner had he said it than he regretted his words.

She gave him a thin, wintry smile. 'Get the Government

to give us another hundred million pounds a year and we will eradicate crime in Sussex. In the absence of that all we can do is spread our resources as thinly and as far as they will go.'

'Mediums are cheap,' Grace said.

'Not when they damage our credibility.' She looked down at the papers. 'When they jeopardize a court case they become more than we can afford. Do you hear me?'

'Loudly, if not clearly.' He couldn't help it, the insolence just came out. She was irritating him. Something chauvinistic inside him that he couldn't help, made it harder for him to accept a dressing-down from a woman than from a man.

'Let me spell it out. You're lucky to still have a job this morning. The Chief is not a happy bunny. He's so angry he's threatening to take you out of the public arena for ever, and have you chained to a desk for the rest of your career. Is that what you want?'

'No.'

'Then go back to being a police officer, not a flake.'

13

For the first time since he had joined the Force, Roy Grace had recently begun wondering whether he should ever have become a policeman. From earliest childhood it was all he had wanted to be, and in his teens he had scarcely even considered any other career.

His father, Jack, had been a desk Sergeant till his retirement, and some of the older officers around still talked about him, with great affection. Grace had been in thrall to him as a child, loved to hear his stories, to go out with him – sometimes in a police car, or down to the station. When he was a child, his father's life had seemed so much more adventurous and glamorous than the dull lives most of his friends' dads lived.

Grace had been addicted to cop shows on television, to books about detectives and cops of every kind – from Sherlock Holmes to Ed McBain. He had a memory that bordered on photographic, he loved puzzles, and he was physically strong. And from all he saw and heard from his father, there seemed to be a teamwork and camaraderie in police life that really appealed.

But now, on a day like this, he realized that being a police officer was less about doing things to the best of your abilities and more about conforming to some preordained level of mediocrity. In this modern politically correct world you could be a law enforcement officer at the peak of your career one moment and a political pawn the next.

His latest promotion, making him the second-youngest Detective Superintendent ever in the Sussex Police Force, and which just three months ago had so thrilled him, was fast turning out to be a poisoned chalice.

It had meant moving from the buzz of Brighton police station in the heart of the town, where most of his friends were, out to the relative quiet of the former factory on an industrial estate on the edge of the city, which had recently been refurbished to house the headquarters of Sussex CID.

You could retire from the force on a full pension after thirty years. No matter how tough it got, if he just stuck it out he would be financially set up for life. That was not how he wanted to view his job, his career. At least, not normally.

But today was different. Today was a real downer. A reality-check day. Circumstances changed, he was thinking, as he sat hunched over his desk, ignoring the pinging of incoming emails on his computer screen, munching an egg and cress brown sandwich, and staring at court transcripts of the Suresh Hossain trial in front of him. Life never stands still. Sometimes the changes were good, sometimes less than good. In little over a year's time he would be forty. His hair was going grey.

And his new office was too small.

The three dozen vintage cigarette lighters that were his prize collection hunched together on the ledge between the front of his desk and the window which, unlike the fine view from Alison Vosper's office, looked down onto the parking lot and the cell block beyond. Dominating the wall behind him was the large, round wooden clock that had been a prop in the fictitious police station in *The Bill*. Sandy had bought him it for his twenty-sixth birthday.

Beneath it was a stuffed seven-pound, six-ounce

brown trout which he kept beneath the clock and used to give him a joke he could crack to detectives working under him, about patience and big fish.

Lined up on either side and slightly cramping it were several framed certificates, and a group photograph captioned 'Police Staff College Bramshill. Management of Serious and Series Crimes. 1997', and two cartoons of him in the police ops room, drawn by a colleague who had missed his true vocation. The opposite wall was taken up by bookshelves bulging with part of his collection of books on the occult, and filing cabinets.

His L-shaped desk was cluttered by his computer, overflowing in- and out-trays, BlackBerry, separate piles of correspondence, some orderly, most less so, and the latest edition of the magazine with a bad pun of a title, *Fingerprint Whorld.* Rising from the mess was a framed quotation: 'We don't rise to the level of our abilities, we fall to the level of our excuses.'

The rest of the floor space was occupied by a television and video player, a circular table, four chairs and piles of files and loose paperwork, and his leather go-bag, containing his crime-scene kit. His briefcase sat open on the table; his mobile, dictating machine and a bunch of transcripts he had taken home with him last night all lay beside it.

He dropped half his sandwich in the bin. No appetite. He sipped his mug of coffee, checked the latest emails, then logged back on to the Sussex Police site and stared at the list of files he had inherited as part of his promotion.

Each file contained the details of an unsolved murder. It represented a pile of about twenty boxes of files, maybe even more, stacked on an office floor, or bulging out of cupboards, or locked up, gathering mould in a damp police garage in a station in the area where the murder happened. The files contained scene-of-crime photographs, forensic reports, bagged evidence, witness statements, court transcripts, separated into orderly bundles and secured with coloured ribbon. This was part of his new brief, to dig back into the county's unsolved murders, liaise with the CID division where the crime happened, looking for anything that might have changed in the intervening years that could justify reopening the case.

He knew most of their contents by heart – the benefit of his near photographic memory which had propelled him through exams both at school and in the Force. To him each stack represented more than just a human life that had been taken – and a killer who was still free – it symbolized something very close to his own heart. It meant that a family had been unable to lay its past to rest, because a mystery had never been solved, justice had never been done. And he knew that with some of these files being more than thirty years old, he was the last hope the victims and their relatives probably had.

Richard Ventnor, a gay vet battered to death in his surgery twelve years ago. Susan Downey, a beautiful girl raped and strangled and left in a churchyard fifteen years back. Pamela Chisholm, a rich widow found dead in her wrecked car – but with the wrong kind of injuries for a car accident. The skeletal remains of Pratap Gokhale, a nine-year-old Indian boy found under floorboards at the flat of a suspected paedophile – long vanished. These were just a few of the many cases Grace remembered.

Although they were interred, or their ashes had been scattered a long time ago, circumstances changed for them too. Technology had brought in DNA testing, which threw up new evidence and new suspects. The internet had brought new means of communication. Loyalties had changed. New witnesses had emerged from the woodwork. People had divorced. Fallen out with their friends. Someone who wouldn't testify against a mate twenty years ago now hated him. Murder files never closed. *Slow time*, they called it.

The phone rang. It was the management support assistant he shared with his immediate boss, the Assistant Chief Constable, asking if he wanted to take a call from a detective. The whole political correctness thing irritated him more and more, and it was particularly strong in the Police Force. It hadn't been so long ago when they called them *secretaries*, not bloody *management support assistants.*

He told her to put him through, and moments later heard a familiar voice. Glenn Branson, a bright Detective Sergeant he'd worked with several times in the past, fiercely ambitious and razor sharp – as well as being a walking encyclopedia on movies. He liked Glenn Branson a lot. He was probably the closest friend he had.

'Roy? How you doing? Seen you in the papers today.'

'Yup, well you can fuck off. What do you want?'

'Are you OK?'

'No, I'm not OK.'

'Are you busy right now?'

'How do you define busy.'

'Ever given an answer in your life that isn't a question?'

Grace smiled. 'Have you?'

'Listen, I'm being pestered by a woman – about her fiancé. Seems like some stag-night prank has gone seriously wrong, and he's been missing since Tuesday night.'

Grace had to do a mental check on the date. It was Thursday afternoon now. 'Tell me?'

'Thought you'd be in court today. Tried your mobile, but it's off.'

'I'm having lunch. Got a break from court – Judge Driscoll's having a day in chambers dealing with submissions from the defence.'

One of the major drawbacks of bringing a prosecution to trial was the time it consumed. Grace, as the senior officer, had to be either in court or in close touch during the whole trial. This one was likely to last a good three months – and much of that time was just hanging around.

'I don't feel this is a normal missing persons enquiry – I'd like to pick your brains. You free this afternoon by any chance?' Glenn Branson asked.

To anyone else, Grace would have said no, but he knew Glenn Branson wasn't a time waster – and hell, right now he was pleased to have an excuse to get out of the office, even into this shitty weather. 'Sure, I can make some time.'

'Cool.' There was a moment's pause, then Glenn Branson said, 'Look, could we meet at this guy's flat – I think it would be helpful if you saw it for yourself – I can get the key and meet you there.' Branson gave him the address.

Grace glanced at his watch, then at the diary on his BlackBerry. 'How about meeting there at half five? We could go on for a drink.'

'It won't take you three hours to get – oh – I guess a man of your age has to start taking it slowly. See you later.'

Grace winced. He didn't like reminders of his looming big four-O birthday. He didn't like the idea of being forty – it was an age when people took stock of their lives. He'd read somewhere that when you reached forty you'd reached the shape your life was going to be for good. Somehow, being thirty-eight was OK. But thirty-nine meant you were very definitely nudging forty. And it wasn't so long ago that he'd considered people who were forty to be old. Shit.

He looked again at the list of files on the screen. Sometimes he felt closer to these people than to anyone else. Twenty murder victims who were dependent on him to bring their killers to justice. Twenty ghosts who haunted most of his waking thoughts – and sometimes his dreams, as well.

14

He had the use of a pool car, but he chose to drive his own Alfa Romeo 147 saloon. Grace liked the car; he liked the hard seats, the firm ride, the almost spartan functionality of the interior, the fruity noise the exhaust made, the feeling of precision, the bright, sporty dials on the dash. There was a sense of exactness about the vehicle that suited his nature.

The big, meaty wipers swung across the screen, clopping the rain from the glass, the tyres hissing on the wet tarmac, a wild Elvis Costello song playing on the stereo. The bypass swept up over a ridge and down into the valley. Through the mist of rain he could see the buildings of the coastal resort of Brighton and Hove sprawling ahead, and beyond the single remaining landmark chimney from the old Shoreham power station, the shimmering strip of grey, barely distinguishable from the sky, that was the English Channel.

He'd grown up here among its streets and its villains. His dad used to reel off their names to him, the families that ran the drugs, the massage parlours, the posh crooked antique dealers who fenced stolen jewels, furniture, the fences who handled televisions and CD players.

It had been a smugglers' village, once. Then George IV had built a palace just a few hundred yards from his mistress's house. Brighton had somehow never managed to shake off its criminal antecedents nor its reputation as a place for dirty weekends. But these gave the city of

Brighton and Hove its edge over any other provincial resort in England, he thought, flicking his indicator and turning off the bypass.

Grassmere Court was a red-brick block of flats about thirty years old, in an upmarket area of Hove, the city's genteel district. It fronted onto a main road and overlooked a tennis club at the rear. The residents were a mixture of ages, mostly twenty- and thirty-something career singles and comfortably off elderly people. On an estate agent's brochure it would probably have rated *highly des res.*

Glenn Branson was waiting in the porch, wrapped in a bulky parka, tall, black, and bald as a meteorite, talking into his mobile. He looked more like a drug dealer than a copper at this moment. Grace smiled – his colleague's massive, muscular frame from years of serious body-building reminded him of the broadcaster Clive James's description of Arnie Schwarzenegger: that he looked like a condom filled with walnuts.

'Yo, old wise man!' Branson greeted him.

'Cut it out, I'm only seven years older than you. One day you'll get to this age too and you won't find it funny.' He grinned.

They slapped high fives, then Branson, frowning, said, 'You look like shit. Really, I mean it.'

'Not all publicity agrees with me.'

'Yup, well I couldn't help noticing you grabbed yourself a few column inches in the rags this morning . . .'

'You and just about everyone else on the planet.'

'Man, you know, for an old-timer you're pretty dumb.'

'Dumb?'

'You don't wise up, Grace. Keep sticking your head above the parapet and one day someone's going to shoot it clean off. There are some days when I think you are just about the biggest dickhead I know.'

He unlocked the front door of the block and pushed it open.

Following him in, Grace said, 'Thanks, you really know how to cheer someone up.' Then he wrinkled his nose. Blindfolded you would always know if you were in an ageing apartment building. The universal smell of worn carpets, tired paint, vegetables boiling behind one of the closed doors. 'How's the missus?' he asked as they waited for the lift.

'Great.'

'And your kids?'

'Sammy's brilliant. Remi's turning into a terror.' He pressed the button for the lift.

After a few moments, Grace said, 'It wasn't how the press made it seem, Glenn.'

'Man, I know that because I know you. The press don't know you, and even if they did, they don't give Jack Shit. They want stories and you were stupid enough to give them one.'

They emerged from the lift on the sixth floor. The flat was at the end of the corridor. Branson unlocked the door and they went in.

The place was small, with a lounge/diner, a narrow kitchen with a granite worktop and a circular steel sink, and two bedrooms, one of which was used as a study, with an iMac computer and work-desk. The rest of this room/office was filled with bookshelves crammed mostly with paperbacks.

In contrast with the dull exterior and drab common parts of the building, the flat felt fresh and modern. The walls were painted in white, very lightly tinged with grey, and the furnishings were modernistic, with a distinct Japanese influence. There were low sofas, simple prints on the walls, a flat-screen television, with a DVD player beneath, and a sophisticated hi-fi system with tall, slender speakers. In the master bedroom there was an unmade futon bed, with handsome louvred doors on the wardrobe, another flat-screen television, and low bedside tables with starkly modern lamps. A pair of Nike trainers sat on the floor.

Grace and Branson exchanged a glance. 'Nice pad,' Grace said.

'Uh huh,' Branson said. *'Life is Beautiful.'*

Grace looked at him.

'I missed it in the cinema. Caught it on Sky. Incredible film – have you ever seen it?'

Grace shook his head.

'All set in a concentration camp. About a dad who convinces his kid that they're playing a game. If they win the game, they get a real tank. I tell you, it moved me more than *Schindler's List* and *The Pianist.*'

'I've never heard of it.'

'I wonder what planet you're on sometimes.'

Grace stared at a framed photograph by the bed. It showed a good-looking man, in his late twenties, with fair hair, black T-shirt and jeans, arm around a seriously attractive woman also in her late twenties, with long, dark hair.

'This him?'

'And her. Michael Harrison and Ashley Harper. Nice-looking couple, right?'

Continuing to stare at them, Grace nodded.

'Getting married on Saturday. At least, that's the plan.'

'Meaning?'

'Meaning, *if* he shows up. Doesn't look too good right now.'

'You said he hasn't been seen since Tuesday night?' Grace looked out of the window. The view down was across a wide, rain-lashed street backed up with traffic. A bus hove into view. 'What do you know about him?'

'Local boy made good. Property developer. Serious player. Double-M Properties. Has a partner called Mark Warren. Recently built a fuck-off development – an old warehouse on Shoreham Harbour. Thirty-two flats, all sold before they were finished. They've been in business for seven years, done a bunch of stuff in the area, some conversions, some new builds. The chick's Michael's secretary, smart bird, seriously gorgeous.'

'You think he's done a runner?'

Branson shook his head. 'Nope.'

Grace picked up the photograph and stared more closely at it. 'Bloody hell, I'd marry her.'

'That's my point.'

Grace frowned. 'Sorry, I'm slow, had a long day.'

'You'd marry her! If I was a single man, I'd marry her. *Anyone in their right mind would marry her*, right?'

'She's seriously gorgeous.'

'She is, seriously gorgeous.'

Grace stared at him blankly.

In mock exasperation, Branson said, 'Jesus, old timer, you losing your touch or something?'

'Maybe I am,' Grace said, blankly. 'What is your point?'

Branson shook his head. 'My point is exactly that. If you were going to marry this babe on Saturday, would you do a runner?'

'Not unless I was nuts.'

'So if he hasn't done a runner, where is he?'

Grace thought for a moment. 'You said on the phone something about a stag-night prank that might have gone wrong?'

'That's what his fiancée said to me. That was my first thought. Stag nights can be brutal. Even when he didn't show up all of yesterday, that's what I still thought then. But to stay out two nights?'

'Cold feet? Another bird?'

'All possible. But I'd like to show you something.'

Grace followed him into the living area. Branson sat down in front of the computer and tapped the keyboard. He was a wizard on computers. Grace had a good technical mind and was pretty well up to speed with most modern technology, but Branson was light years ahead of him.

A password command came up on the screen. Branson tapped furiously, and within a few seconds, the screen filled with data.

'How did you do that?' Grace asked. 'How did you know the password?'

Branson gave him a sideways look. 'There was no password. Most people see a password request and try to put one in. Why would he need one if he wasn't sharing his computer with anyone else?'

'I'm impressed. You really are a closet geek.'

Ignoring the remark, Branson said, 'I want you to take a close look at this.'

Grace did what he was told, and sat down in front of the screen.

15

Just a couple of miles away, Mark Warren was also hunched in front of his computer. The clock on the flat screen showed 6.10 p.m. His shirt sleeves were rolled up, a neglected Starbucks cappuccino beside him, the froth sunken into a wrinkled skin. His normally tidy desk, in the office he'd shared with Michael for the past seven years, was swamped with piles of documents.

Double-M Properties occupied the third floor of a narrow five-storey Regency terraced townhouse, a short distance from Brighton station, which had been their first property development together. Apart from the office he was in, there was a boardroom for clients, a small reception area and a kitchenette. The furnishings were modern and functional. On the walls were photographs of the three racing yachts they owned together, and through which their success could be charted – from their first boat, a Nicholson-27, to a more substantial Contessa-33, to the distinctly upmarket Oyster-42 which was their current toy.

There were also pictures of their developments. The waterfront warehouse at Shoreham Harbour which they had converted into thirty-two apartments. An old Regency hotel in Kemp Town, overlooking the seafront, which they had converted into ten apartments, and two mews houses at the rear. And their latest, and most ambitious development, an artist's impression drawing of a site in five acres of forest land where they had permission to build twenty houses.

His eyes were raw from two sleepless nights, and, taking a moment's respite from the screen, Mark stared out of the window. Directly opposite were a law firm and a discount bedding store. On sunny days it was a perfect spot to ogle the pretty girls walking down the street – but right now it was pelting with rain, people were hurrying, huddled under umbrellas or wrapped in coats, collars turned up, hands in pockets. And Mark was in no mood for thinking about anything except the task in front of him.

Every few minutes, as he had done all day long, he dialled Michael's mobile number. But each time it went straight to voicemail. Unless the phone was either switched off, or the battery was dead, this indicated Michael was still down there. No one had heard anything. Judging from the time of the accident, they would have buried him about 9 p.m. the night before last. About forty-five hours so far.

The main phone line was ringing. Mark could hear the muted warble and saw the light flashing on his extension. He answered it, trying to mask the nervous quaver that was in his voice each time he spoke.

'Double-M Properties.'

A man's voice. 'Oh, hello, I'm calling about the Ashdown Fields development. Do you have a brochure or prices?'

'I'm afraid not, sir, not yet,' Mark said. 'Be a couple of weeks yet. There is some information up on our website – ah – OK, you checked that already. If you want to leave me your name, I'll have someone get back to you.'

Ordinarily he'd have been pleased to have had such an early enquiry about a development, but sales were the last thing on his mind at the moment.

It was important not to panic, he knew. He'd read

enough crime novels, and seen enough cop shows, to know that it was the guys who panicked that got caught. You just had to keep calm.

Keep deleting the emails.

Inbox. Sent Items. Deleted Folder. All other folders.

It wasn't possible to erase emails totally, they would still be out there, stored on a server somewhere in cyberspace, but surely no one was going to look that far, or were they?

He typed keyword after keyword, doing an Advanced Find on each of them. *Michael. Stag. Night. Josh. Pete. Robbo. Luke. Ashley. Plans! Operation revenge!* Checking every email, deleting any that needed deleting. Covering all the bases.

Josh was on life support, his condition critical, and he almost certainly had severe brain damage. Likely to be a vegetable if he survived. Mark swallowed, his mouth dry. He'd known Josh since they were thirteen, at Varndean School. Luke and Michael, too, of course. Pete and Robbo came later: they'd met in a pub in Brighton one boozy night in their late teens. Like Mark, Josh was methodical and ambitious. And he was good-looking. Women always flocked around Josh the same way they went for Michael. Some people had natural gifts in life, others like himself had to struggle every inch of the way. But even at the young age of twenty-eight, Mark had seen enough of life to know that nothing stays the same for very long. If you were patient, if you bided your time, sooner or later you'd get a lucky break. The best predators were the most patient ones.

Mark had never forgotten a wildlife documentary he'd seen on television, filmed in a bat cave in South America. Some tiny micro-organism fed on the bat guano on the floor of the cave; a maggot ate the micro-organism; a beetle ate the maggot; a spider ate the beetle; then a bat ate the spider. It was a perfect food chain. The bat was smart, all it had to do was shit and wait.

His mobile rang. It was Michael's mother, her third call to him this afternoon and her umpteenth today. He remained as unfailingly polite and friendly as ever. There was still no news of Michael, he told her. It was terrible, he really had no idea what had happened to him, the plan had been simply to go on a pub crawl, he could not imagine where Michael might be now.

'Do you think he could be with another woman?' Gill Harrison asked in her timid, gravelly voice. He'd always got on quite well with her, in as much as it was possible. Her husband had gassed himself before he and Michael had met, and Michael said she had retreated into a shell and stayed there ever since. From the photos of her around the house she had been quite beautiful when younger, a blonde bombshell. But ever since Mark had known her, her hair was prematurely grey, her face dry and creased from chain smoking, her spirit withered.

'I guess anything is possible, Mrs Harrison,' Mark replied. He thought for a moment, choosing his words carefully. 'But he adored Ashley.'

'She's a lovely girl.'

'She is, could do with her back here – the best damned secretary we ever had.' He toyed with his mouse for a moment, moving the cursor idly around the screen. 'But you know drink sometimes makes men do irrational things—'

As the words came out he instantly regretted them. Hadn't Michael once told him that his father had been drunk when he killed himself?

There was a long silence, then she said, very placidly,

'I think he'd have had long enough to sober up by now. Michael's a good and a loyal person. Whatever he might have done drunk, he would never hurt Ashley. Something must have happened to him, otherwise he would have called. I know my son.' She hesitated. 'Ashley is in a terrible state. Will you keep an eye on her?'

'Of course.'

There was another silence then, 'How is Josh?'

'Unchanged. Zoe's staying in the hospital. I'll go back there and sit with her – as soon as I've finished in the office.'

'You'll call me the moment you hear anything?'

'Of course.'

He hung up, stared down at his desk, picked up a document, and something caught his eye beneath it. His Palm.

And as he stared at it, cold fear swept through him. *Oh shit,* he thought. *Oh shit, oh shit, oh shit.*

16

After leaving Detective Superintendent Grace, Glenn Branson headed back across town in the pool car he had taken, a blue Vauxhall that reeked of disinfectant – the result of someone either throwing up or bleeding in it last time it had been used. He parked it back in its space in the lot behind the bland edifice of Brighton police station, and walked into the rear entrance and up the stone staircase, to the office he shared with ten other detectives.

It was 6.20; his shift technically finished every day this week at 6, but he was swamped with paperwork after a major drugs bust on Monday, and had permission to do overtime – and he needed the extra cash. But he was going to do only one hour today, until 7. Ari was going out, on another of her self-improvement courses. Mondays she did evening classes in English literature, Thursdays she did architecture. Ever since their daughter Remi had been born she'd gone into panic mode about her perceived lack of education, and was scared she wasn't going to be able to answer their kids' questions when they grew older.

Although most of the computer screens were off, none of the desks were tidy. Every empty open-plan cubicle looked, as usual, as if its occupant had abandoned it in haste and would be returning shortly.

There were just two colleagues still at work in here, DC Nick Nicholl, late twenties, tall as a beanpole, a zealous detective and a fast football forward, and DS Bella Moy, thirty-five, cheery-faced beneath a tangle of brown hair.

Neither acknowledged him. He walked past Nick Nicholl, who was deep in concentration filling out a form, his lips pursed like a kid in an exam as he wrote in block capitals with a ballpoint. Bella was fixated by something on her screen, her left hand, like an automaton, plucking Maltesers from a box on her desk and delivering them to her mouth. She was a slim woman, yet she ate more than any human being Glenn Branson had ever seen.

As he sat down at his desk, the message light was blinking away, as usual. Ari, his wife, Sammy, his eight-year-old son and Remi, his three-year-old daughter, smiled out at him from a framed photo on his desk.

He glanced at his watch, needing to keep an eye on the time. Ari got mad if he was late and caused her to miss the beginning of her class. And besides, it was no hardship – there were few things he treasured more than spending time with his kids. Then his phone beeped.

It was the front desk. A woman had waited an hour to see him and wasn't leaving. Would he mind having a word with her? Everyone else was busy.

'Right, like I'm not busy?' Glenn said to the receptionist, letting irritation show in his voice. 'What does she want?'

'It's to do with the accident on Tuesday – the missing groom.'

Instantly he mellowed. 'Right. OK, I'll come down.'

Despite her bleached-out complexion, Ashley Harper looked every bit as beautiful in the flesh as she did in the photograph he had just seen of her in Michael Harrison's apartment. She was dressed in designer denims, with a bling belt, and carried a classy handbag. He led her into an interview room, got them each a coffee, closed the door and sat down opposite her. Like all the interview rooms it was small and windowless, painted a drab pea green, with a brown carpet and grey metal chairs and table, and reeked of stale cigarette smoke.

She placed her handbag on the floor. Beautiful grey eyes framed by smudged mascara stared out from a wan face, leaden with grief. Fronds of her brown hair fell across her forehead, the rest swooped in a single wave either side of her face and onto her shoulders. Her nails were perfect, as if she had come straight from a manicure. She looked immaculate, and that surprised him a little. People in her state were usually careless about their appearance, but she seemed dressed to kill.

Equally he knew how hard it was to figure women out. Once, when their relationship was going through a rocky time, Ari had given him the book *Men are from Mars, Women are from Venus.* It had helped him go some way towards understanding the mental gulf between men and women (but not all the way).

'You're a hard man to get hold of,' she said, and tossed her head, flicking her long brown hair away from her eyes. 'I left four messages.'

'Yeah, I'm sorry.' He raised his hands. 'I've two of my team off sick and two away on holiday. I understand how you must feel.'

'Do you? Do you have any idea how I feel? I'm meant to be getting married on Saturday and my fiancé's been missing since Tuesday night. We have the church booked, I've got my dressmaker turning up for a fitting, two hundred guests invited, wedding presents pouring in. Do you have *any* idea how I feel?' Tears rolled down her cheeks. She sniffed, fumbled in her handbag and pulled out a tissue.

'Look, I'm sorry. I have been working on your – Michael

– your fianceé's disappearance since we spoke this morning.'

'And?' She dabbed her eyes.

He cradled his beaker of coffee, which was too hot to drink. Had to let it cool. 'I'm afraid I don't have anything to report, yet.' Not strictly true, but he wanted to hear what she had to say.

'What exactly are you guys doing?'

'Like I said this morning on the phone, ordinarily when someone goes missing—'

She cut him short. 'This isn't *ordinarily*, for God's sake. Michael's been missing since Tuesday night. When we're apart he rings me five, ten times a day. It's now two days. Two fucking days, for Christ's sake!'

Branson studied her face carefully, searching for give-aways. But he found nothing. Just a young woman desperate for news of her loved one. *Or* – ever the cynic – *a fine actress*. 'Hear me out, OK? Two days is not in ordinary circumstances enough for alarm. But I agree, in this situation, it is strange.'

'Something's happened to him, OK? This isn't some normal missing persons situation. His friends did something to him, put him somewhere, sent him somewhere, I don't know what the hell they did to him – I—' She lowered her head as if to hide her tears, fumbled for her bag, found it, pulled out a tissue and dabbed her eyes, still shaking her head.

Glenn was moved. She had no idea, and this wasn't the moment to tell her.

'We're doing everything we can to find Michael,' he said gently.

'Like what? What are you doing?'

Her grief lifted momentarily, as if she was wearing it

like a veil. Then another flood of tears and deep, gulping sobs.

'We've done a search around the immediate vicinity of the accident, and we still have people there – sometimes people get disoriented after an accident, so we're searching all the surrounding area – and we've now put out an all-points alert. All police forces have been informed. Airports and seaports—'

Again she cut him short. 'You think he's done a runner? Jesus! Why would he do that?'

Using a subtle technique he had learned from Roy Grace to tell if someone was lying, he asked her, 'What did you have for lunch today?'

She looked at him in surprise. 'What did I have for lunch today?'

'Yes.' He watched her eyes closely. They moved to the right. *Memory* mode.

Human brains are divided into left and right hemispheres. One contains long-term memory storage, and in the other the creative processes take place. When asked a question, people's eyes almost invariably move to the hemisphere they are using. In some people the memory storage is in the right hemisphere and in some the left; the creative hemisphere the opposite one.

When people are telling the truth, their eyes swing towards the memory hemisphere; when they lie, towards the creative one. Branson had learned to tell which by tracking their eyes in response to a simple *control* question such as the one he had just asked, where there would be no need for a lie.

'I didn't have lunch today.'

Now he judged it was time to tell her. 'How much do

you know about your fiancé's business dealings, Miss Harper?'

'I was his secretary for six months, OK? I don't think there's much I don't know.'

'So you know about his Cayman Islands company?'

Genuine surprise in her face. Her eyes shot to the left. Construct mode. She was lying. 'Cayman Islands?' she said.

'He and his partner' – he paused, pulled out his notebook and flipped through several pages – 'Mark Warren. You're aware of this company they have there? HW Properties International?'

She stared at him in silence. 'HW Properties International?' she echoed.

'Uh huh.'

'No, I know nothing about this.'

He nodded. 'OK.'

The tone of her voice had shifted subtly. Thanks to Roy Grace's teaching he knew what it meant. 'Tell me more?'

'I don't know much more, I was hoping you could tell me.'

Her eyes shot to the left again. Construct mode again. 'No,' she said, 'I'm sorry.'

'It's probably not significant anyway,' he said. 'After all, who doesn't want to avoid the tax man?'

'Michael is shrewd. He's a clever businessman. But he would never do anything illegal.'

'I'm not suggesting that, Miss Harper. I'm trying to establish that perhaps you don't know the full picture about the man you are marrying, that's all.'

'Meaning what?'

Again he raised his hands in the air. It was five to seven.

He needed to go. 'It doesn't necessarily mean anything at all. But it's something we have to be aware of.' He gave her a smile.

It was not returned.

17

On the unstable television screen in the chaotically untidy Portakabin annexed to his dad's house on the edge of Lewes, with its view out on to the yard filled with car wrecks, Davey was watching the American cop show, *Law and Order*. His favourite character, a sharp cop called Detective Reynaldo Curtis, was eyeballing a low-life, holding him by the dewlaps with a clenched fist. 'I'm in your face, know what I'm saying?' Reynaldo Curtis snarled.

Davey, in his baggy jeans, and baseball cap tugged tight over his head, lay back on his beat-up sofa munching a Twinkie bar from a supply that was delivered to him weekly from the States by mail order and shouted out, 'Yeah, scumbag! I'm in your face, know what I'm saying?'

The detritus of Davey's quarterpounder and fries dinner lay on the curled carpet tiles at his feet amid the piles of junk – much of it salvaged during his work with his dad – that covered just about every inch of the floor, shelf and table space of his domain.

Beside him sat the pieces of the walkie-talkie he had found a couple of nights back. He'd been meaning to try to fix it, but hadn't got around to it yet. Idly, he picked the main body of it up and peered at it.

The casing was badly cracked. There was a loose bit of plastic with flanges and two AAA batteries that he had retrieved from the road when he had dropped it. He'd really meant to put it back together but somehow it had slipped his mind. Lots of stuff slipped his mind. Just as fast as most things came into his head, they went out again.

Stuff.

There was stuff all the time that made no sense.

Life was like a jigsaw puzzle where bits were always missing. The important bits. Now there were four bits to the walkie-talkie jigsaw. The cracked box, two batteries and the thing that looked like a lid.

He finished his Twinkie, licked the wrapper, then tossed it onto the floor.

'Know what I'm saying?' he announced to no one. Then he leaned forward, picked up the burger's polystyrene box and rummaged around through the mess of ketchup with his finger. 'Yeah! I'm in your face, know what I'm saying?'

He chuckled. There was a commercial break. Some smarmy media fuckwit talking about building society rates. Growing impatient, Davey said 'Come on, baby, let's get back to the show.'

Instead, another commercial came on. On the screen a baby crawled across the carpet talking in a deep male adult voice. Davey watched for some moments, transfixed, wondering how a baby could learn to speak that way. Then his attention drifted back to the walkie-talkie. There was a telescopic aerial, which he pulled out as far as it would go, then pushed back in again. 'Kerloink!' he said. Then out again. 'Kerloink!'

He pointed it at the television screen, staring down its length, taking aim as if it were a rifle. Then the show came back on.

He looked at his brand new watch, which his dad had given him for his birthday yesterday. It was for timing motor races, and had all kinds of buttons, dials and digital displays that he hadn't quite figured out yet from the instruction book. His dad promised to help him read it, get through the tough words. He needed to have it all working OK for this Sunday, the Monaco Grand Prix, it was important he had it ready for that.

There was a knock on his door, then it opened a few inches. His dad stood there, dressed up in a hunting cap with ear flaps, battered old windcheater and wellington boots. 'Five minutes, Davey.'

'Awww. It's *Law and Order*. Could we make it fifteen?'

Cigarette smoke drifted into the room. Davey saw the red glow as his dad took a drag. 'If you want to come shooting rabbits, we have to leave in five minutes. You must have seen every show of *Law and Order* they ever made.'

The ads ended, the show was coming back on. Davey raised a finger to his lips. Grinning in mock despair, Phil Wheeler backed out of the room. 'Five minutes,' he said, closing the door.

'Ten!' Davey shouted after him, American accent now. 'Compromise! Know what I'm saying?'

Davey turned his focus back on the walkie-talkie, thinking it might be cool to take it out rabbit shooting with him. He peered closely into the battery compartment, figured out which way they were supposed to go in, and inserted the batteries. Then he pushed one of two buttons on the side. Nothing happened. He tried the second button and instantly there was a crackle of static.

He held the speaker part to his ear, listening. Just static. And then, suddenly, a male voice so loud he could have been in the room with him.

'Hello?'

Startled, Davey dropped the walkie-talkie on the floor.

'Hello? Hello?'

Davey stared down at it, beaming with delight. Then

there was another knock on his door and his father called out, 'I've got your gun, let's go!'

Then suddenly afraid his father might get mad if he saw the walkie-talkie – he wasn't supposed to take anything they found around wrecks – Davey crouched down on the floor, pressed the other button, which he assumed to be the *talk* one, and hissed furtively, in his American accent, 'Sorry, can't talk, he's in my face – know what I mean?'

Then he shoved the walkie-talkie under the bed and hurried from the room, leaving the television, and Detective Reynaldo Curtis, having to cope without him.

18

'Hey! Hello! Hello! Hello!'

Silence came back at him from the ivory satin.

'Hey, please, help me!'

Michael, sobbing, stabbed the *talk* button repeatedly. 'Please, help me, please help me!

Just static crackle.

'Sorry, can't talk, he's in my face – know what I mean?'

A strange voice, like some ham actor playing an American gangster. Was this all part of the joke? Michael guided the salty tears down to his dry, cracked lips, and for one fleeting, taunting instant savoured the moisture, before his tongue absorbed them like blotting paper.

He looked at his watch. More hours had gone past: 8.50. For how many more hours was this nightmare going to go on? How could they be getting away with it? Surely to God Ashley, his mother, *everyone*, for Christ's sake, must be on to the boys by now. He'd been down here for – for—

A sudden panic hit him. Was it 8.50 in the morning or evening?

It had been afternoon just a while ago, hadn't it? He'd watched each hour on the hour go past. Surely he could not have been so careless to lose track of a whole twelve-hour chunk? It had to be evening now, night, tonight, not tomorrow morning.

Almost forty-eight hours.

What the hell are you all doing?

He pressed his hands down, pushing himself up for a

moment, trying to get some circulation going into his numb backside. His shoulders hurt from being hunched, every joint in his body ached from lack of movement – and from dehydration – he knew about the dangers of that from sailing. His head throbbed incessantly. He could stop it for a few seconds by levering his hands up to his head and digging his thumbs into his temples, but then it came back just as bad as before.

'*Christ*, I'm getting married on Saturday, you fuckwits! Get me out of here!' he shouted as loudly as he could, then pounded the roof and walls with his feet and hands.

The imbeciles. Friday tomorrow. The day before the wedding. He had to get his suit. Haircut. They were going away on honeymoon on Saturday night to Thailand – he had a ton of stuff to do in the office before then, before going away for two weeks. Had to write his wedding speech.

Oh, come on, guys, there's so much I have to do! You've paid me back now, OK? For all the shit I ever did to you lot? You'd paid me back with interest. Big time!

Dropping his hand to his crotch, he located the torch and switched on for a few precious seconds, rationing the battery. The white satin seemed to be ever closer to him; last time he looked it seemed a good six inches above his face, now no more than three, as if this box, coffin, or whatever it was, was slowly, steadily caving in on him.

He took hold of the tube, dangling limp in front of his face, again squinted, trying to peer up into it, but could see nothing. Then he checked he was pushing the right button on the walkie-talkie. He pressed each one in turn. Listened first to static, then pressed *talk* and shouted as loudly as he could, then pressed the *listen* button again. Nothing.

'*Nada!*' he said out aloud. 'Not a fucking sausage.'

Then an image of a frying pan on his mother's stove came into his mind. A frying pan filled with sausages, eggs, bacon, tomatoes, crackling, fizzing, popping, hissing. He could smell them, dammit, smell the bread too, frying in another pan, the tin of baked beans heating up.

Oh Jesus, I'm so hungry.

He turned his mind away from food, from the pain in his stomach that was so bad it felt its own stomach acids were eating their way through his stomach lining. Somewhere inside his pounding skull his brain was reminding him of something he had read; it was about a breed of frogs – or toads – he couldn't remember which right now, which gestated its babies in its stomach rather than womb. For some reason the stomach acids didn't harm the babies.

What's to stop us humans digesting our own stomachs? he thought, suddenly. His brain was racing now, remembering bits of all kinds of stuff.

He remembered reading some years back a theory about Circadian rhythms. All other living organisms on this planet lived a twenty-four-hour cycle, but not humans – our average was twenty-five and a quarter. Tests had been done putting human beings down into dark places for weeks on end, with no clocks. Invariably they thought they had been down there for a shorter period of time than was the case.

Great, I could be one of their fucking lab rats now.

His mouth was so dry his lips stuck together and it hurt to part them. It felt as if their skin was ripping.

Then he shone the torch straight up, looked at the ever-deepening groove he had made in the wood above his face, picked up his leather belt and again began to rub the corner of the metal buckle backwards and forwards against the hard teak – he knew enough about wood to know this was teak – and that teak was just about the hardest wood – closing his eyes tight, in pain, as specks of sawdust struck them, and gradually the buckle became hotter and hotter until he had to stop to let it cool down.

'Sorry, can't talk, he's in my face – know what I mean?'

Michael frowned. Who the hell was this putting on the fake American voice?

How could any of them think this was funny? What the hell had they told Ashley? His mother?

After a few minutes, he stopped scraping, exhausted. Had to keep going, he knew. Dehydration made you tired. Had to fight the tiredness. Had to get the hell out of this damned box. Had to get out and at those bastards, and there was going to be hell to pay.

He struggled on for a few more minutes, scraping, sometimes catching his knuckles, trying to keep his eyes screwed tight against the sawdust that fell and tickled his face, until he was too tired to go on. His hand dropped down and his clenched neck muscles relaxed their grip. Gently his head dropped back.

He slept.

19

The evening was prematurely dark. Mark parked his car just beyond a bus stop a short way up the road, then waited for some moments. The wide street, lacquered black by the torrential rain, was quiet, a trickle of cars passing. No one seemed to be out walking; no one to notice him.

He pulled on a baseball cap low over his face, then, turning up his anorak collar, ran to the sheltered porch of Michael's apartment block, glancing at each of the parked cars in turn, looking for someone seated in there in the dark. Michael was always telling people that Mark was the detail man in their partnership. Then he would qualify that with a remark that Mark hated. *Mark is incredibly anal.*

But Mark knew that he was right, that was exactly why Double-M Properties was so successful, because he was the one who did all the real work. It was his role to scrutinize every line of the builder's estimates, to be there on site, to approve every single material that was purchased, to watch the schedules and to cost everything down to the last penny. While Michael spent half his time swanning around, womanizing, rarely taking anything too seriously. The success of the business was his, he believed, and his alone. Yet Michael had the majority shareholding, just because he'd had more cash to put in when they had started up.

There were forty-two bells to choose from on the entry-phone panel. He pressed one at random, deliberately on a different floor to Michael's. There was no answer. He tried another, with the name 'Maranello'.

After a few moments a crackly male voice in a thick Italian accent said, 'Hello? Yes? Hello?'

'Delivery,' Mark shouted.

'Delivery what?'

'FedEx. From America, for Maranello.'

'You what? Delivery? I – I not – I – I no—'

There was a moment's silence. Then the sharp buzz of the electric latch.

Mark pushed the door and walked in. He went straight to the lift and took it to the sixth floor, then walked down the corridor to Michael's flat. Michael kept a spare key under the doormat in case he locked himself out – which he had done once, drunk and naked. To Mark's relief it was still there. A single Yale key, covered in fluff.

As a precaution he rang the doorbell and waited, watching the corridor, anxious in case anyone should appear and see him. Then he opened the door, slipped in and quickly closed it behind him, and pulled a small torch from his pocket. Michael's apartment looked out onto the street. There was another apartment block opposite. It was probably safe to turn the lights on, but Mark didn't want to take chances. There *might* be someone out there watching.

Pulling off his sodden cap and coat, he hung them on pegs on the wall, then waited some moments, listening, nervous as hell. Through the party wall he could hear what sounded like marching music, from a television turned up too loud. Then with the aid of the flashlight, he began his search.

He went first into the main room, the lounge/dining area, shining the beam onto every surface. He looked at the pile of unwashed dishes on the sideboard, a half-drunk bottle of Chianti with the cork pushed back in, then the coffee table, with the television remote lying next to a glass bowl containing a large candle, partially burnt. A pile of magazines – *GQ, FHM, Yachts and Yachting.* Beside them a red light winked busily on the answering machine.

He listened to the messages. There was one, left just an hour ago, from Michael's mother, her voice nervy.

'Hello, Michael, I'm just checking in case you are back.'

Another was from Ashley, sounding as if she was on her mobile in a bad reception area. 'Michael darling, just calling to see if by chance you're back. Please, please call me the moment you get this. I love you so much.'

The next was from a salesman asking Michael if he would like to take advantage of a new loan facility Barclays Bank was offering to its card holders.

Mark continued playing the messages right through, but there was nothing of interest. He checked the two sofas, the chairs, the side tables, then went into the study.

On the desk in front of the iMac was just the keypad, cordless mouse, a fluorescent mouse pad, a heart-shaped glass paperweight, a calculator, a mobile charger and a black jar crammed with pens and pencils. What he was looking for was not there. Nor was it on the bookshelves or anywhere in Michael's untidy bedroom.

Shit.

Shit, shit, shit.

He left the apartment, walked down the fire-escape steps and went through the rear exit into the dark of the car park. *Bad news,* he thought to himself as he furtively made his way back to the street. *This was really bad news.*

*

Fifteen minutes later he drove his BMW X5 up the steep hill alongside the huge sprawling complex of the Sussex County Hospital, and pulled into the car park for the Accident and Emergency department. He hurried past a couple of waiting ambulances and into the brightly lit reception and waiting area, familiar to him from his visit the previous day.

He walked past the dozens of people waiting forlornly on the plastic seats, beneath a sign which read 'WAITING TIME – THREE HOURS', and along a series of corridors to the lift, and took that to the fourth floor.

Then he followed the signs to the ICU, the smells of disinfectant and hospital food in his nostrils. He rounded a corner, walked past a vending machine, and a payphone in a perspex dome, then saw ahead of him the reception desk of the Intensive Care Unit. Two nurses stood behind the counter, one on the phone, the other talking to a distressed-looking elderly woman.

He made his way across the ward, past four occupied beds, to the corner where Josh had been last night, expecting to see Zoe at his bedside. Instead, he saw a wizened old man, with wild white hair, sunken, liver-spotted cheeks, cannulated and intubated, with a ventilator beside him.

Mark scanned the rest of the beds, but there was no sign of Josh. Panicking that his health had improved and that he had now been moved to another ward, he hurried back to the reception desk and positioned himself in front of the nurse who was on the phone, a plump, cheery-looking woman of about thirty, with a pudding-basin haircut, and a badge that said 'ITU Staff Nurse, MARIGOLD WATTS'. From her demeanour she seemed to be chatting to her boyfriend.

He waited impatiently, resting his arms on the wooden

counter, staring at the bank of black and white monitors showing every bed, and the colour digital displays beneath each of them. He shifted his position a couple of times in rapid succession, trying to catch her eye, but she seemed to be mainly concerned about her dinner.

'Chinese, I think I fancy Chinese. Peking Duck. Somewhere that does Peking Duck, with the pancakes and—'

Then finally she seemed to notice him for the first time. 'Listen, I have to go. Call you back. Love you too.' She turned to Mark, all smiles. 'Yes, can I help you?'

'Josh Walker.' He pointed across the ward. 'He was over there – ah – yesterday. I'm just wondering which ward he's been moved to?'

Her face froze as if she'd suffered a massive infusion of Botox. Her voice changed, also, suddenly becoming tartly defensive. 'Are you a relative?'

'No, I'm his business partner.' Instantly Mark kicked himself for not saying he was his brother. She would never have known.

'I'm sorry,' she said, as if regretting she had terminated her call for him. 'We can only give information to relatives.'

'You can't just tell me where he has been transferred to?'

A buzzer sounded. She looked up at the screens and a red light was flashing beside one of them. 'I have to go,' she said. 'I'm sorry.'

She rushed from her station across the ward.

Mark took out his mobile. Then he saw a large sign: 'THE USE OF MOBILE PHONES IS STRICTLY FORBIDDEN IN THIS HOSPITAL'.

He backed away, hurriedly retracing his steps to the lift, then took it to the ground floor. Totally gripped with fear he raced through a labyrinth of corridors until he reached the main entrance.

Just as he walked up to the reception desk he heard a loud, near-hysterical voice, and saw Zoe, eyes raw, tears streaming down her cheeks, blonde ringlets totally unkempt.

'You and your friend Michael and all your stupid bloody jokes,' she shouted. 'You stupid, bloody immature jerks.'

He stared at her in silence for some moments. Then she collapsed in his arms, sobbing uncontrollably. 'He's dead, Mark, he just died. He's dead. Josh is dead. Oh God, he's dead. Please help me, what am I going to do?'

Mark put his arms around her. 'I – I thought he was OK, that he was going to pull through,' he said, lamely.

'They said there was nothing they could do for him. They said if he had lived he would have been a vegetable. Oh God. Oh God, please help me, Mark. What am I going to say? How do I tell the children their daddy's never coming home? What do I say to them?'

'Do you – do you want a – a cup of tea or something?'

Through deep gulping sobs she said, 'No I don't want a fucking cup of tea. I want my Josh back. Oh God, they've taken him down to the mortuary. Oh Christ. Oh God, what am I going to do?'

Mark stood in silence, holding her tightly, stroking her back, hoping to hell his relief did not show.

20

Michael woke with a start from a confused dream, tried to sit up, and his head instantly crashed against the coffin lid. Crying out in pain he tried to move his arms, and his shoulders met the unyielding satin first on the left and then the right. He tossed and thrashed in a sudden claustrophobic panic.

'Get me out of here!' he screamed, turning, thrashing, gulping air, sweating and shivering at the same time.

'Oh, please, get me out of here!'

His voice was deadened. Flat. It wasn't going anywhere, it was trapped in here just the same as he was.

His hands fumbled for the torch, unable to locate it for several seconds in his panic. Then he found it, switched it on, stared up and then sideways at the walls of his prison. He looked at his watch: 11.15.

Night?

Tomorrow?

Night, it must still be night, Thursday night.

Rivulets of sweat were running down his body. Making a puddle underneath him. He craned his neck to look over his shoulder, shone his torch down and a reflection shone back. Water.

A whole fucking inch.

He looked down in shock. There was no way. No, absolutely no way that he had sweated this much.

Two fucking inches.

He put his hand down again. Shone the torch. Held his

pinkie upright, like a dipstick. The water came up to just below the second joint. There was no way he had sweated that much. Cupping his hands he scooped some up and drank it greedily, oblivious to its salty, muddy taste. He drank more and more; for several minutes it seemed to him that the more he drank, the thirstier he was.

Then when he had finally finished, a new aspect of the rising water came into the equation. He grabbed the belt buckle and began frantically grinding away at the lid, but within minutes, the buckle became so hot it was burning his fingers.

Shit.

He picked up the whisky bottle. Still a third of its contents left. He struck the top of the bottle hard against the wood above him. Nothing happened. He tried again, heard the dull thud. A tiny sliver of glass sheared off. Tragic to waste it. He put the neck into his mouth, tilted it, swallowed a mouthful of the burning liquid. God, it tasted good, so good. He lay back, up-ended the bottle into his mouth and let it pour in, swallowing, swallowing, swallowing until he choked.

He held the bottle up, squinting at it in the beam, having difficulty focusing now, his head swimming. Only a small amount of whisky remained. Just about—

There was a thump right above his head. He felt the coffin move!

Then another thump.

Like a footstep.

Like someone standing on the lid of the coffin right above him!

Hope sprang every nerve in his body. *Oh Jesus Christ, they are getting me out of here at last!*

'OK, you bastards!' he yelled, his voice more feeble than

he had intended. He took a breath, heard another scrape above him. *At fucking last!*

'What the fuck kept you?'

Silence.

He banged his fist against the lid, slurring his words. 'Hey! What fucking kept you? Josh? Luke? Pete? Robbo? Have you any idea how long I've been down here? This is just so not funny, this really is just so not funny. You hear me?'

Silence.

Michael listened.

Had he imagined it?

'Hello! Hey, hello!'

Silence.

No way had he imagined it. There had been footsteps. A wild animal? No, they had been heavier than that. Human heavy.

He knocked frantically with the bottle and then with his fists.

Then very suddenly, very silently, as if he were watching a magic show on television, the breathing tube slid upwards and disappeared.

A few grains of soil fell down through the hole it vacated.

21

Mark could barely see. The red mist of panic that seized him was blurring his vision, fogging his brain. Michael's voice, he had heard Michael's goddamn muffled voice. Oh Jesus!

He closed the door of his BMW in the darkness of the forest, in the lashing rain, jabbed at the ignition, and tried to get the key in. His boots were heavy and tacky with cloying mud, water was streaming down from his baseball cap onto his face.

With his gloved hands he twisted the key and the headlamps came on in a brilliant white glare as the engine turned over and fired. In their beam he saw the grave and the trees beyond. An animal scurried off into the undergrowth, leaves and plants swayed in the wind and rain, for a moment almost surreally like plants in a current on the ocean floor.

He kept staring at the grave, at the corrugated sheet he had carefully pulled back over, and the shrubbery he had uprooted and laid over it to camouflage it. Then he saw the second spade still sticking in the ground and cursed. He climbed down from the car, ran across and grabbed it, and shoved it inside the tailgate. Then he climbed back in, slammed the door, scanning the scene, checking it as well as his blurred vision could.

He was thinking. No construction was due to start here for at least another month, there were still planning issues to be sorted and finalized. No reason for anyone to come here. The planning committee had made their inspection, everything now was on hold for the formal rubber stamp.

Shaking uncontrollably, he put the car in gear and headed back down the track, over the two cattle grids again that had been put there, presumably by the Forestry Commission, to stop deer getting out onto the road.

As he pulled out onto the road he switched on the radio, hitting button after button in search of some music. There was news. Talking. A commercial. He hit the CD button, surfed each of the CDs in turn, but none of them worked for him. He switched the machine off.

Minutes later, as he drove around a curve, the beam of the headlights picked up a row of wreaths on the verge. The sight churned his stomach. Headlights came the other way, passed. Then more headlights. He gripped the wheel tightly, his head swimming, trying to concentrate, trying to think clearly. Then he came to another curve, even sharper, and he was going much too fast. Panicking, he braked sharply, too sharply, felt the judder as the ABS anti-skid kicked in and heard a thump as the breathing tube shot forward off the passenger seat beside him and into the footwell.

Somehow he got around the bend, then saw a lay-by ahead and pulled in. He pressed the SatNav command button, then dialled in *Arlington Reservoir*. After a few moments the system's disembodied female voice announced, 'The route is being calculated.'

Twenty-five minutes later he pulled up at the start of the wooden jetty on the deserted hard of the yacht club of the five-mile-long reservoir and switched off the engine. Grabbing his flashlight, he climbed down and stood in the darkness, listening. The only sound was the clacking of rigging flailing in the wind. No lights on anywhere. The clubhouse was silent. He glanced at his watch. Ten after midnight.

He took the breathing tube from the footwell, then the two shovels from inside the tailgate and walked down to the end of the jetty. He and Michael had begun their sailing here, as kids, before they had become more adventurous and started ocean sailing. From his memory the water here was about twenty feet deep. Not perfect, but it should be adequate. He dropped the breathing tube and then the shovels into the inky, rippled surface and watched them disappear. Then he pulled off his boots and dropped them in too. They sank instantly.

Then he padded back to the car, pulled on the moccasin loafers he had brought and headed home, feeling suddenly very weary. He drove slowly, carefully, not wanting to get clocked by any speed cameras, nor attract the attention of any cop car.

His first task in the morning was going to be to drive straight to a car wash he knew, near Hove station. A place that was always busy, that local cab drivers used, where filthy cars were the norm, where there was always a queue, where no one would take the slightest notice of a BMW X5 caked in mud.

22

Grace took the smouldering stub of his cigar out of his mouth, yawned, then replaced the stub, gripping it with his teeth in a sudden burst of concentration as he scooped up his five cards off the rumpled green baize cloth. A small pile of fifty-pence chips lay in the centre of the table, the antes from each player. In front of him were tumblers of whisky, glasses of wine, piles of cash and chips, and a couple of overflowing ashtrays, surrounded by fragments of crisps and sandwich crumbs. There was a fug of smoke in the room, and outside rain and wind lashed the tall windows, which overlooked the English Channel and the lights of the Palace Pier.

They always played Dealer's Choice, and each time it was his turn, Bob Thornton, a long-retired Detective Inspector, always chose Draw – the poker game Grace liked least of all. He glanced at his watch: 12.38 a.m. Following the tradition of their weekly Thursday-night poker games, the last full round had started at half past midnight, and there would be just two more hands after this one.

It had not been a good night for him; despite wearing his lucky turquoise socks and his lucky blue-striped shirt, he'd had unremittingly lousy cards, made a couple of bad calls, and had been seen on an expensive bluff. The whole game had gone the same way as just about everything else this week: south. One hundred and fifty quid down so far, and the last round was often the most vicious.

He glanced fleetingly at his cards, while concentrating

on the reactions of his five colleagues to their own, and suddenly perked up a little. Three tens. The first decent hand he'd picked up in at least two hours. But a dangerous hand too – good enough that he'd be daft not to play it, but it was no slam-dunk.

Bob Thornton was a hard guy to read. In his mid-seventies, he was a big, energetic man who still played regular squash, with a hawkish face and liver-spotted hands that looked almost reptilian. He wore a green cardigan over a tartan open-neck shirt, corduroy trousers and tennis plimsolls. By a wide margin he was the oldest of the hard core of ten regular players, from whom enough to cobble together a game turned up to play every Thursday, week in, week out, year in, year out, each player taking it in turn to host the evening.

The game had been going on long before Grace had joined the Force. Bob had told them, more than once, that when he had joined the group decades ago he had been the youngest player. Thinking about his looming thirty-ninth birthday, Grace wondered if, like Bob, he would one day end up himself as the old fart of the group.

But age clearly brought some advantages. Bob was sharp as a tack, hard to read and a wily and very aggressive player. Grace could not remember many occasions over the years when Bob had not gone home with a profit – and true to form there was mountain of chips and cash in front of the man right now. Grace watched him hunch his shoulders as he inspected and sorted his cards, keeping them close to his chest, peering at them through his glasses with alert, greedy eyes. Then he opened and shut his mouth, flicking his tongue along his lips in a serpent-like manner, and Grace knew immediately he didn't have to worry about Bob's hand – unless he got lucky in the pick-up.

It was Grace's turn to open the betting. He eyed the rest of his companions.

Tom Allen, thirty-four years old, a detective in Brighton CID, with a serious, boyish face and a mop of curly hair. Dressed in a sweatshirt over a T-shirt, he peered at his cards impassively. Grace always found him hard to read.

Next to Tom sat Chris Croke, a motorcycle cop in Traffic – or *Road Policing*, as the department was now called. With lean and wiry good looks, short blond hair, blue eyes and a quick-fire charm, Croke was a consummate ladies' man, who seemed to live the lifestyle more of a playboy than of a cop. He was hosting tonight's game in his flash, fifth-floor apartment in the coolest apartment block in Brighton, the Van Alen. Ordinarily a cop living such a ritzy lifestyle would have aroused suspicions in Grace, but it was well known that Croke's ex-missus was a socialite heiress to a vast football pools fortune.

Croke had met her when he'd stopped her for speeding and it was his boast that, despite giving her a ticket, she had still married him. Whatever the truth, that was now history, but there was no question he had done well out of the marriage, because when she had finally got tired of the erratic hours that were the lot of any cop's spouse, she had settled a pile of loot on him.

Croke was reckless and unpredictable. In seven years of playing with him, Grace found his body language hard to decipher. He never seemed to care whether he won or lost; it was much easier to read people who had something at stake.

Grace turned his focus on Trevor Carter, a quiet, balding man who worked in IT at Brighton police station. Dressed conservatively in a grey shirt, sleeves rolled up, unfashionably large glasses and drab brown trousers,

Carter was a frugal, family man, who played the game as if the welfare of his four children depended on it. He rarely bluffed, rarely raised and as a result rarely finished any evening up. Carter's giveaway was a nervous twitch of his right eye – the sure-fire signal that he had a strong hand. It was twitching now.

Lastly he looked at Geoff Panone, a Drugs Squad detective of thirty, dressed in a black T-shirt, white jeans and sandals, with near-shoulder-length black hair and a gold earring, who was puffing away on a massive cigar. Grace had learned from watching him over the past couple of years that when he had a good hand at Draw poker, he systematically rearranged the cards in his hand, and when he had a lousy hand, he didn't. Worryingly, he was now rearranging his cards.

'Your bet, Roy,' Bob Thornton told him.

The limit was always the pot on the table. No one could bet higher, which kept the stakes to an affordable level. With six of them putting in a total ante of three pounds, that was the opening ceiling. Not wanting to give anything away, and at the same time wanting to keep everyone in, Grace opened with one pound. All of them came in until Trevor Carter, who raised by three pounds, the twitching of his eye even more pronounced now.

Geoff tossed in a further two pounds. Bob Thornton hesitated just for a fraction, just enough for Grace to know that he definitely did not have a good hand so far and was taking a chance because it was the last round. He decided to press his opportunity and raised by a further three pounds.

Everyone looked at him. They knew he'd had a bad night and this was a giveaway. But it was already too late to do anything about that.

Tom threw his cards down and shook his head. Chris hesitated for some moments, then tossed in five pounds. Trevor and Geoff upped their bets to match also. Bob Thornton followed.

'How many cards?' Bob asked Grace.

Changing two would have revealed he had three of a kind. But changing two would have given him better odds. Grace decided his strategy and changed just one, dumping his three of clubs, retaining a seven of spades. He picked up a seven of hearts.

His heart leapt. *A full house!* Not a top one, but a seriously strong hand. Tens on sevens. Now he was in business!

Certain from watching the change of cards of the others that he had the strongest hand, Grace decided to seize his opportunity and bet the ranch. To his dismay, each of the next three players in turn dropped out and he realized he'd pushed it too hard. But then to his relief Trevor Carter came in and raised him.

Confidently pulling out his wallet, Grace raised him further. Trevor then raised him several more times in succession, until Grace finally lost his nerve, peeled some more banknotes from his wallet and saw him.

Then he puffed nervously on his cigar as Carter flipped over his cards, one by one.

Oh shit, oh shit, oh shit.

A running flush – 7,8,9,10, Jack on the bounce.

'Bloody brilliant!' Croke said.

''Well played!' Bob Thornton exclaimed. 'My God, that was well hidden!'

'I picked them up,' a near-ecstatic Trevor Carter said. 'I picked them up!'

Grace sat back in dismay. It was a hand in a million – maybe even longer odds than that. Impossible to have predicted. And yet he should have realized, from the uncharacteristic strength of Trevor's betting, that Trevor knew he had him beat – and seen him much sooner.

'I reckon your supernatural powers need a bit of topping up, Roy,' chirped Croke.

Everyone laughed.

'Fuck off!' retorted Grace more good-naturedly than he felt. Assistant Chief Constable Alison Vosper was right. People *were* laughing at him. Here it was light-hearted, among friends. But there were others in the Force for whom there was no joke. If he wasn't careful his career could be stalled and he could find himself sidelined.

And right now he was down the best part of three hundred quid.

And by the time the remaining three games had been played, Grace had managed to increase his losses for the evening to four hundred and twenty-two pounds and fifty pence.

He was not a happy bunny as he took the lift down to the underground car park of the block. As he walked towards his Alfa Romeo parked in the visitors' section, he was still so cross with himself and his friends that he barely noticed the mud-streaked BMW X5 that was driving in.

23

'Yeeha!' Davey, soaking wet, unlocked the door of his Portakabin, then kicked it wide open and strutted in. 'Yeeha!' he announced to the television screen, which was always on, to all his buddies who hung around on the screen. He paused, water trickling down his baseball cap and off his oilskins and muddy wellingtons onto the foam carpet, to check them out. James Spader was in an office, talking to some chick he did not recognize.

'Wasted 'bout two hundred of them darned vermin. Know what I'm saying?' Davey said to James Spader in his best Southern drawl.

But Spader simply ignored him, kept on talking to the chick. Davey picked the remote off his bed and pointed it at the television. 'Yeah, well, I don't need you either, know what I'm saying?' He changed channels. Now he saw two guys he did not know, face to face, arguing with each other. Click.

James Gandolfino was walking through the cars in a Mercedes-Benz dealership, towards a handsome woman with long black hair.

Davey zapped him and he was gone.

He surfed through a whole bunch of channels, but there didn't seem to be anyone interested in talking to him. So he walked over to the fridge. 'Just gonna git me a beer from the minibar,' he announced, pulled out a Coke, flipped it open with one hand, drained half the can, then sat on the bed and belched. His watch said 2.21.

He was wide awake. Wanted to talk to someone, to tell them about all the rabbits he and his dad had shot tonight.

'Here's the thing,' Davey said, then he belched again. He checked the pockets of his oilskins, pulled out a couple of live shotgun cartridges, then hung the oilskins on their hook on the door. He sat on the edge of his bed, wearily, the way he'd seen Clint sit when he was easing off his boots, and dropped his wellingtons one after the other onto the floor.

Then he fondled the two unspent cartridges. 'They've got your name on them,' he informed Sean Penn, who was walking towards him. But Sean Penn wasn't in the mood for conversation either.

Then Davey remembered. There was someone who would talk to him. He knelt down on the floor, reached under the bed for the walkie-talkie, then pulled out the aerial as far as it would go. *Kerloink!*

He pressed the *listen* button and heard the crackle of static. Then he tried the *talk* button.

24

Michael, wide awake, was crying. He did not know what to do, he felt so utterly helpless. It was after two in the morning, Friday morning, he was meant to be getting married tomorrow. There were a million things that needed to be done.

Who or what the hell had taken the breathing tube? Could it have been a badger taking something to its lair? What would a badger want with a length of rubber tubing? Besides, the footsteps had been too heavy. It had been a human, for sure.

Who?

Why?

Where was Ashley, his beloved, darling, gorgeous, caring Ashley? What was she thinking right now, what was going through her mind?

He kept hoping, every moment, that this was some terrible nightmare and in a minute he would wake and be in his bed with Ashley beside him. It just did not make any sense.

There was a sudden sharp hiss, stark and clear. The walkie-talkie!

Then a voice, in a thick Southern drawl said: 'You have any idea how much damage they do? Huh? You got yourself any idea?'

Frantically, Michael scrabbled in the darkness for his torch.

The voice continued, 'Y'know, most folk ain't got no

idea. You git them durn conservationalists talking 'bout protecting the wildlife, but them guys, they don't know shit, know what I'm saying?'

Michael found the torch, switched it on, located the walkie-talkie and pressed the *talk* button. 'Hello?' he said. 'Hello? Davey?'

'Uh huh, I'm talking to ya! Bet you don't have no idea, right?'

'Hello, who are you?'

'Hey dude, you don't need to worry 'bout who I am. Thing is five danged rabbits eat near enough the same amount of grass as one sheep. Go figure.'

Michael gripped the black box, totally confused, wondering if he was hallucinating. What the hell was going on? 'Can I speak to Mark? Or Josh? Or Luke? Or Pete? Robbo?'

There was silence for some moments.

'Hello?' Michael said. 'Are you still there?'

'Ma friend, I ain't going nowhere.'

'Who are you?'

'Maybe I'm the Man With No Name.'

'Listen, Davey, this joke's gone on too long, OK? Too fucking long. Please get me out of here.'

'You gotta be impressed with two hundred rabbits, right?'

Michael stared at the walkie-talkie. Had everyone gone totally insane? Was this the lunatic who had just taken out the breathing tube? Michael tried desperately to think clearly.

'Listen,' he said. 'I've been put here as a joke by some friends. Can you get me out of here, please?'

'You in some kind of bad shit?' the American voice said.

Still unsure whether this was some kind of game, Michael said, 'Bad shit, you got it.'

'What do you think about two hundred rabbits?'

'What do you want me to think about two hundred rabbits?'

'Well dude, what I want you to think is that any dude wastes two hundred rabbits, he's gotta be an OK kind of a dude, know what I'm saying?'

'Totally,' Michael said. 'I totally agree with you.'

'OK, we're on the same page, that's cool.'

'Sure is. Cool.'

'Don't get much cooler, right, dude?'

'You got it,' Michael said, trying to humour him. 'So maybe you could lift the lid off for me and we could have a discussion about this face to face?'

'I'm kinda tired now. Think I'm going to hunker down, get me some shut-eye, know what I'm saying?'

Panicking, Michael said, 'Hey, no, don't do that, let's keep talking. Tell me more about the rabbits, Davey.'

'Told ya, I'm the Man With No Name.'

'OK, Man With No Name, you don't happen to have a couple of Panadols, because I've one mother of a headache?'

'Panadols?'

'Yes.'

There was silence. Just the crackle of static.

'Hello?' Michael said. 'You still there?'

There was a chuckle. 'Panadol?'

'Come on, please get me out of here.'

After another long silence the voice said, 'Guess that depends where *here* is.'

'I'm in the goddamn coffin.'

'You're shittin' me.'

'No shit.'

Another chuckle. 'No shit, Sherlock, right?'

'Right! No shit, Sherlock.'

'I have to go now, it's late. Shut-eye!'

'Hey, please wait – please—'

The walkie-talkie went silent.

In the fading beam of the flashlight Michael saw that the water had risen considerably just in the past hour. He tested the depth again with his hand. An hour ago it had reached the knuckle of his index finger.

Now it covered his hand completely.

25

Roy Grace, in a white short-sleeved shirt and sombre tie, his collar loose, stared at the text message on his phone, and frowned:

Can't stop thinking about you! Claudine xx

Claudine?

Sitting in his office shortly after 9 a.m., in front of his computer screen, which was pinging with new emails every few moments, feeling dog tired and with a blinding headache, he was cold. It was tipping down with rain outside and there was an icy draught in the room. For some moments he watched rain running down his window, staring at the bleak view of the alley wall beyond, then he unscrewed the cap of a bottle of mineral water he'd bought at a petrol station on his way in, rummaged in a drawer of his desk and took out a packet of Panadol. He popped two capsules from the foil, swallowed them, then checked the time the message had been sent: 2.14 a.m.

Claudine.

Oh God. Now it registered.

His cop-hating, vegan blind date from U-Date of Tuesday night. She'd been horrible, the evening had been a disaster, and now she was texting him. Terrific.

He held his mobile phone in his hand, toying with whether to reply or just delete it, when his door opened and Branson walked in, dressed in a crisp brown suit, a violent tie and two-tone brown and cream co-respondent's shoes, holding a capped Starbucks coffee in one hand and two paper bags in the other.

'Yo, man!' Branson greeted him, breezily, as usual, plonking himself in the chair opposite Grace and setting the coffee and paper bag down on his desk. 'Still own a shirt, I see.'

'Very funny,' Grace said.

'You win last night?'

'No, I did not sodding well win.' Grace was still smarting at his loss. Four hundred and twenty quid. Money wasn't a problem for him, and he had no debts, but he hated losing, especially losing heavily.

'You look like shit.'

'Thanks.'

'No, I mean, really. You look like absolute shit.'

'Nice of you to come all this way to tell me.'

'You ever see *The Cincinatti Kid*?'

'I don't remember.'

'Steve McQueen. Got wiped out in a card game. Had a great ending – you'd remember, the kid in the alley challenging him to a bet, and he tosses his last coin at him.' Branson peeled the lid off, spilling coffee onto the desk, then removed an almond croissant, dropping a trail of icing sugar next to the coffee spill. He proffered it to Grace. 'Want a bite?'

Grace shook his head. 'You should eat something more healthy for breakfast.'

'Oh really? So I get to look like you? What did you have? Organic wheat grass?'

Grace held up the Panadol packet. 'All the nourishment I need. What are you doing here in the sticks?'

'Got a meeting in ten minutes with the Chief. I've been drafted onto the Drugs Performance committee.'

'Lucky you.'

'It's all about profile, isn't that what you told me? Stay visible to your chiefs?'

'Good boy, you remembered. I'm impressed.'

'But actually that's not why I'm here to see you, old-timer.' Branson pulled a birthday card out of the second bag and laid it in front of Grace. 'Getting everyone to sign – for Mandy.'

Mandy Walker was in the Child Protection Unit in Brighton. At one time Grace and Branson had both worked with her.

'She's leaving?' Grace said.

Branson nodded, then mimed a pregnant belly. 'Actually, thought you'd be in court today.'

'Adjourned to Monday.' Grace signed alongside a dozen other names on the card; the coffee and pastry suddenly smelled good. As Branson took a bite of croissant he reached out a hand, took the other croissant from its bag and tore a mouthful off, savouring the instant hit of sweetness. He chewed slowly, peering at Branson's tie, which had such a sharp geometric pattern it almost made him dizzy, then handed back the card.

'Roy, that flat we went to on Wednesday, right?'

'Down The Drive?

'There's something I don't get. I need the wisdom of your years. You got a couple of minutes?'

'Do I have any choice?'

Ignoring him, Branson said, 'Here's the thing.' He took another bite of his croissant, icing sugar and crumbs falling onto his suit and tie. 'Five guys on a stag night, right? Now—'

There was a rap on the door, then it opened, and Eleanor Hodgson, Grace's management support assistant, brought in a sheaf of papers and files. A rather prim, efficient middle-aged woman, with neat black hair and a plain, slightly old-fashioned face, she always seemed nervous of just about everything. At the moment she looked nervous of Glenn Branson's tie.

'Good morning, Roy,' she said. 'Good morning, DS Branson.'

'How you doing?' Glenn replied.

She put the documents down on Roy's desk. 'I've got a couple of forensics reports back from Huntingdon. One's the one you've been waiting for.'

'Tommy Lytle?'

'Yes. I've also got the agenda and briefing notes for your budget meeting at eleven.'

'Thanks.' As she was leaving the room he quickly sifted through the pile and pulled the Huntington report to the top. Huntingdon, in Cambridge, was one of the forensic centres that Sussex Police used. Tommy Lytle was Grace's oldest 'cold case'. At the age of eleven, twenty-seven years ago, Tommy had set out from school on a February afternoon, to walk home. He'd never been seen again. The only lead at the time had been a Morris Minor van, seen by a witness who had had the presence of mind to write down the number. But no link to the owner, a weirdo loner with a history of sex offences on minors, had ever been established. And then, two months ago, by complete coincidence, the van had showed up on Grace's radar, when a classic car enthusiast who now owned it got stopped for drunken driving.

The advances in forensics from twenty-seven years back were beyond quantum. With modern DNA testing, police forensic scientists boasted, not without substance, that if a human being had ever been in a room, no matter how long ago, given time, they could find evidence. Just one skin cell that had escaped the vacuum cleaners, or a hair, or a clothing fibre. Maybe something one hundred times smaller than a pinhead. There would be a trace.

And now they had the van. And the original suspect was still alive. And forensics had been through that van with microscopes!

Despite his fondness for Branson, suddenly Grace could not wait for him to leave, so he could read the report. If he solved this, it would be the oldest cold case ever solved in the country.

Popping the remains of the croissant in his mouth and talking while he chewed, Branson said, 'Five guys go on a stag night, right? The groom is a real joker – he's pulled a stunt on each of the guys in the past – handcuffed one poor sod to a seat on the night train to Edinburgh when he was meant to be getting married in Brighton the next morning.'

'Nice guy,' Grace said.

'Yes, just the kind of fun bloke you want for your best friend. So. Let's look at what we have: Five of them start out. Somewhere along the line they lose the groom, Michael Harrison. Then they are in an RTA, three of them dead at the scene, the fourth in a coma and he died last night. Michael has vanished, no one has heard a word. It is now Friday morning and he's due to be married in a little over twenty-four hours.'

Branson sipped some coffee, stood up for a moment and walked around the office. He stopped and stared for a moment at the SASCO flip chart, on which a draft rota for something had been written in blue ink. He flipped it over, then picked up a pen and drew on the board.

'We got Michael Harrison.' He wrote his name and drew a circle around it. 'We got the four dead mates.' He drew a second circle. 'Then we have the fiancée, Ashley Harper.' He drew a third circle around her. 'Then the business partner, Mark Warren.' He drew a fourth circle. 'And . . .'

Grace looked at him quizzically.

'We have what we dug out of his computer yesterday, yeah?'

'A bank account in the Cayman Islands.'

Still holding the pen, Branson sat down in front of Grace again.

Grace continued. 'The business partner wasn't at the stag do, you said.'

Branson never failed to be impressed by Grace's memory for detail. He always seemed to retain everything. 'Correct.'

'Because he was stuck out of town on a delayed flight.'

'That's the story so far.'

'So what does he say? Where does he think Michael Harrison went? Did he fuck off to the Cayman Islands?'

'Roy, you have seen his bird. And we agreed no bloke in his right mind would ditch her and run away – she is drop-dead gorgeous, and smart with it. And . . .' Branson pursed his lips.

'And what?'

'She lies. I did your NLP stuff on her, the eye trick. I asked her if she knew about the Cayman Islands account and she said she didn't. She was lying.'

'She was probably just being protective. Covering her boss – and fiancé's arse.' Grace was distracted for an instant by the ping of another incoming email. Then he thought hard. 'What is your take so far?'

'The following possible scenarios: could be his mates have been paying him back and they've tied him up somewhere. Or he might have had an accident. Or he's got cold feet and done a runner. Or the Cayman Islands features in this somewhere.'

Grace clicked open one of the emails that was flagged as urgent and was from his boss, Alison Vosper. She asked if he was free for a brief meeting at 12.30. He typed back that he was, while he talked to Branson. 'The guy's business partner, Mark Warren, he'd know if they had been planning a prank, like tying him to a tree, or something.'

'Ms Harper says he knows they were planning something, but doesn't know what they decided on.'

'Have you checked out the pubs they visited?'

'Doing that today.'

'CCTV footage?'

'Starting on that, too.'

'Have you checked out the van?'

From the look of sudden panic on Branson's face, Grace saw he hadn't. 'Why the hell not? Isn't that the first place to look?'

'Yeah, you're right. I haven't got fully into gear on this yet.'

'Have you done an all-ports?'

'Yeah, his picture's being circulated this morning. We've put out a missing persons alert.'

Grace felt as if a dark cloud had slipped overhead. *Missing persons.* Every time he heard the phrase it affected him, brought it all right to the front of his mind again. He thought of this woman, Ashley, Branson had described. The day before her wedding and her man gone missing. How must she feel?

'Glenn, you said this guy is a joker – any chance this a prank he's pulling and he's about to turn up, with a big grin on his face?'

'With four of his best mates dead? He'd have to be pretty sick.' Branson looked at his watch. 'What you doing for lunch?'

'Unless I get a call from Julia Roberts, I may be free – oh – subject to No. 27 not detaining me for more than half a hour.'

'How is the delightful Alison Vosper?'

Grace gave him a bleak stare and raised his eyebrows. 'More sour than sweet.'

'Ever thought of shagging her?'

'Yes, for about one nano-second – or perhaps even a femto-second – isn't that the smallest unit of time that exists?'

'Could be a good career move.'

'I can think of a better one.'

'Like?'

'Like not trying to shag the Assistant Chief Constable.'

'Did you ever see Susan Sarandon in *Moonlight Mile*?'

'I don't remember it.'

'She reminds me of Susan Sarandon in that movie. I liked that movie, it was good. Yeah. Want to take a ride out to the car pound with me, lunchtime – talk some more on the way? I'll buy you a pint and slap-up sandwich.'

'Lunch at the car pound? Wow, proves what I thought the moment I saw that tie. You really do have style.'

26

The water was still rising, Michael calculated, at one inch every three hours. It was now just below his ears. He was shivering from cold, getting feverish.

He had worked frantically through the night, sawing with the glass, and he was now on the last fragment of the whisky bottle and his arms ached with exhaustion. He had made a deep groove in the lid, but had still not yet broken through to the outside of it.

He was pacing himself now, two hours on, half an hour off, imagining he was sailing. But he was losing. The water was rising faster than the hole was widening. His head would be underwater before the hole was wide enough to get through.

Every fifteen minutes he pressed the *talk* button on the walkie-talkie. Each time all he got was static back.

It was now 11.03 a.m. Friday.

He ground away, powdered glass and wet soil pouring steadily down, the last fragment of glass shrinking with every minute he worked, thinking, all the time thinking. When the glass was finished he still had the belt buckle. And when that was finished what other instruments did he have to grind away at the wood with? The lens of the torch? The batteries?

A sharp hiss as the walkie-talkie came to life, then a phoney American accent again. 'Hi, buddy, how ya doin'?' This time he recognized it.

Michael pressed the *talk* button. 'Davey?' he said. 'Is that you?'

'Just watching the news on TV,' Davey informed him. 'They're showing an auto wreck I went to with my dad on Tuesday! Boy that was some accident! All of 'em dead – and there's one guy missing!'

Michael suddenly gripped the walkie-talkie with deep intensity. 'What was it, Davey? What was the car?'

'Ford Transit. Boy was it trashed!'

'Tell me more, Davey.'

'There was one guy sticking right out through the windshield, half his head missing. Jeez, could see his brains coming out. Knew right away he was a goner. Only one survivor, but he died too.'

Michael began shaking uncontrollably. 'This guy who is missing. Do you know who he is?'

'Uh huh!'

'Tell me who he is?'

'I have to go in a minute, help my dad.'

'Davey, listen to me. I may be that guy.'

'You shittin' me?'

'What's his name, Davey?'

'Uh – dunno. They're just saying he's meant to be getting married tomorrow.'

Michael closed his eyes. *Oh no, oh Christ, oh no.* 'Davey, was this accident – ah – this auto wreck – about nine o'clock on Tuesday night?'

'That's about the size of it.'

With new urgency, Michael held the walkie-talkie up close to his mouth. 'Davey, I'm that guy! I'm that guy who is getting married tomorrow!'

'You shittin' me?'

'No, Davey. Listen to me carefully.'

'I have to go – can talk to you later.'

Michael shouted at him, 'DAVEY, DON'T GO, PLEASE DON'T GO. YOU ARE THE ONLY PERSON WHO CAN SAVE ME.'

Silence came back at him. Just the crackle of static to tell him Davey was still on the other end.

'Davey?'

'I have to go, know what I'm saying?'

'Davey, I need your help. You are the only person in the world who can help me. Do you want to help me?'

Another long silence. Then, 'What did you say your name was?'

'Michael Harrison.'

'They just said your name on television!'

'Do you have a car, Davey? Can you drive?'

'My dad has a truck.'

'Can I speak to your dad?'

'Uh – I dunno. He's pretty busy, you know, we have to go out and tow in a wreck.'

Michael thought, desperately hard, how to get through to this character. 'Davey, would you like to be a hero? Would you like to be on television?'

The voice became giggly. 'Me on television? You mean like, me be a movie star?'

'Yes, you could be a movie star! Just get your dad to speak to me and I'll tell him how you could be a movie star. Why don't you get him, put him on the walkie-talkie? How about that?'

'I dunno.'

'Davey, please get your dad.'

'Like here's the problem. My dad don't know I have this walkie-talkie, you see he'd be pretty mad at me if he knew I had this.'

Humouring him, Michael said, 'I think he'd be proud of you, if he knew you were a hero.'

'You reckon?'

'I reckon.'

'I have to go now. See ya! Over and out!'

The walkie-talkie fell silent again.

Pleading with all his heart, Michael was calling: 'Davey, please, Davey, don't leave me, please get your dad, please, Davey!'

But Davey had gone.

27

Ashley, sitting bleakly in an old, deep armchair in the tiny sitting room of Michael's mother's bungalow, stared blankly ahead through a blur of tears. She looked with no appetite at the untouched plate of assorted biscuits on the coffee table, then across at the colour photograph, on the mantelpiece above the fake-coal electric fire, of Michael, aged twelve, on a bicycle, then out through the net curtains at the view across the rain-lashed street to playing fields just below Brighton racecourse.

'I have the dressmaker coming at two,' she said. 'What do you think I should do?' She sipped her coffee then dabbed her eyes with a tissue. Bobo, Gill Harrison's tiny white shih-tzu dog with a bow on its head, looked up at Ashley and gave a begging whine for a biscuit. She responded by stroking the soft hair of its belly.

Gill Harrison sat on the edge of the sofa opposite her. She was dressed in a shapeless white T-shirt, shell-suit trousers and cheap white trainers. A thin ribbon of smoke trailed from a cigarette gripped between her fingers. Light glinted off a diamond engagement ring that was far too large to be real, next to a thin gold wedding band. A bracelet hung loose on her wrist.

She spoke in a gravelly voice, tinged with a coarse Sussex accent, and her strain showed through it. 'He's a good boy. He never let anyone down in his life – that's what I told the policeman what came round. This is not him, not Michael.' She shook her head and took a heavy drag on her cigarette. 'He likes a joke—' She gave a wry laugh. 'When he was a kid he was a terror at Christmas with a flippin' whoopee cushion. Always giving people a fright. But this is not him, Ashley.'

'I know.'

'Something's happened to him. Them boys done something to him. Or he's had an accident as well. He hasn't run out on you. He was round here Sunday evening, we had tea together. He was telling me how much he loved you, how happy he was, bless him. You've made him so happy. He was telling me about this house you've found out in the country that you want to buy, all his plans for it.' She took another drag on her cigarette, then coughed. 'He's a resourceful boy. Ever since his dad—' She pursed her lips, and Ashley could see this was really difficult for her. 'Ever since his dad – he told you?'

Ashley nodded.

'He stepped into his dad's shoes. I couldn't have coped without Michael. He was so strong. A rock, to myself and Carly – you'll like Carly. He sent her the money for her ticket back from Australia so she could be here for the wedding, bless him. She should be arriving here any minute. She phoned me from the airport a couple of hours ago.' She shook her head, in despair.

Ashley, in baggy brown jeans and a ragged white shirt, smiled at her.

'I met Carly just before she went to Australia – she came into the office.'

'She's a good girl.'

'If she's your daughter she must be!'

Gill Harrison leaned forward and stubbed out her cigarette. 'You know, Ashley, all his life Michael has worked so hard. Doing a newspaper round when he was a child to help me and Carly, and then his business with Mark. Nobody ever appreciates him. Mark's a nice boy but—'

'But what?'

Gill shook her head.

'Tell me?'

'I've known Mark since he was a child. Michael and he were inseparable. But Mark's always hung on to his coat tails. I sometimes think Mark's a bit jealous of him.'

'I thought they made a good team,' Ashley said.

Gill pulled a pack of Dunhills from her handbag, shook another cigarette out and stuck it in her mouth. 'I've always told him to watch out for Mark. Michael's innocent, he trusts people too easily.'

'What are you saying?'

She pulled a cheap plastic lighter from her bag and lit the cigarette. 'You have a good influence on Michael. You'll make sure he's all right, won't you?'

Bobo started whining again for a biscuit. Ignoring it, Ashley responded, 'Michael's strong. He's all right, he's fine.'

'Yeah, course he is.' She shot a glance across at the telephone on a table in the corner. 'He's all right. He'll call any time now. Those poor boys. They were so much a part of Michael's life. I can't believe—'

'I can't either.'

'You have your appointment with your dressmaker, dear. You should keep it. The show must go on. Michael will turn up, you do believe that, don't you?'

After a brief hesitation, Ashley said, 'Of course I do.'

'Let's speak later.'

Ashley stood up, walked over to her future mother-in-law, and hugged her hard. 'It's all going to be OK.'

'You're the best thing that ever happened to him. You

are a wonderful person, Ashley. I was so happy when Michael told me that – that—' She was struggling now, emotion choking her words. 'That you – the two of you—'

Ashley kissed her on the forehead.

28

Grace sat, tight-lipped, in the blue Ford, holding the edges of his seat, watching the unfolding country road ahead nervously through the wipers and the heavy rain. Oblivious to his passenger's fear, Glenn Branson swept tidily through a series of bends, proudly demonstrating the skill he had recently acquired from a high-speed police driving course. The radio, tuned to a rap station, was far too loud for Grace.

'Doing it right, aren't I?'

'Uh – yep,' Grace said, deciding the less conversation, the less distraction to Branson, which in turn meant longer life expectancy for both of them. He reached forward and turned the volume down.

'Jay-Z,' Branson said. 'Magic, isn't he?'

'Magic.'

They entered a long right-hander. 'They tell you to keep hard to the left, to open up the view; that's a good tip, isn't it.'

A left-hander was coming up and in Grace's view they were going too fast to get round it. 'Great tip,' he said, from somewhere deep in his gullet.

They got round it, then down into a dip.

'Am I scaring you?'

'Only slightly.'

'You're a wuss. Guess it's your age. Do you remember *Bullitt*?'

'Steve McQueen? You like him, don't you?'

'Brilliant! Best car chase ever in a movie.'

'It ended in a bad car smash.'

'Brilliant, that film,' Branson said, missing his point – or more likely, Grace thought, deliberately ignoring it.

Sandy used to drive fast too. That was part of her natural recklessness. He used to be so scared that Sandy would have a bad accident one day, because she never seemed to be able to get her head around the natural laws of physics that determined when a car would make it around a corner and when it would not. Yet in all the seven years they were together she never once crashed, or even scratched, her car.

Ahead of them, to his relief, he saw the sign – 'BOLNEY CAR POUND' – fixed to tall sheet-metal fencing, topped with barbed wire. Branson braked hard and turned in, past a guard dogs warning sign, into the forecourt of a large modern warehouse building.

Grabbing an umbrella from the boot, and huddling beneath it, they rang the bell on the entryphone beside a grey door. Moments later it was opened by a plump, greasy-haired man of about thirty, wearing a blue boiler suit over a filthy T-shirt, and holding a half-eaten sandwich in a tattooed hand.

'Detective Sergeant Branson and Detective Superintendent Grace,' Branson said. 'I rang earlier.'

Chewing a mouthful, the guy looked blank for a moment. Behind him, several badly wrecked cars and vans sat in the warehouse. His eyes rolled pensively. 'The Transit, yeah?'

'Yup', Branson said.

'White? Came in Tuesday from Wheeler's?'

'That's the one.'

'It's outside.'

They signed in, then followed him across the warehouse floor and out through a side door, into an enclosure that was a good acre in size, Grace estimated, filled with wrecked vehicles as far as the eye could see. A few were under tarpaulins, but most were exposed to the elements.

Holding the umbrella high, just clearing the top of Branson's head, he looked at a Rentokil van that was burnt out after a bad frontal collision – it was hard to imagine anyone had survived in it. Then he noticed a Porsche sports car, compacted to little more than ten feet in length. And a Toyota saloon with its roof cut off.

The place always gave him the heebie-jeebies. Grace had never worked in the Traffic Division, but in his days as a beat copper he'd attended his share of traffic accidents and it was impossible not to be affected by them. It could always happen to anyone. You could set out on a journey, happy, full of plans, and moments later, in the blink of an eye, maybe through no fault of your own, your car was turned into a monster that smashed you to pieces, cut your limbs off and maybe even broiled you alive.

He shuddered. The vehicles that ended up in this place, under secure lock and key, were the ones in the region that had been involved in serious or fatal accidents. They were kept here until the Crash Investigation Unit and sometimes Crime Scene Investigators had obtained all the information they required, before going to a breaker's yard.

The fat man in the boiler suit pointed at a twisted mass of white, with part of its roof cut away, the cab, with the windscreen gone, sheared jaggedly away from the rest of the van, and much of the interior was covered in white plastic sheeting. 'That's the one.'

Both Grace and Branson stared at it in silence. Grace couldn't help his mind dwelling for several uncomfortable moments on the sheer horror of the image. The two of them walked around the van. Grace noticed mud caked on the wheel hubs, and more, heavy mud on the sills and splashes of it up the paintwork, slowly dissolving in the rain.

Handing the umbrella to his colleague, he wrenched open the buckled driver's door, and immediately was hit by the cloying, heavy stench of putrefying blood. It didn't matter how many times he experienced it, each new occasion was just as bad. It was the smell of death itself.

Holding his breath to try to block it out, he pulled back the sheeting. The steering wheel had been hacked off and the driver's part of the front bench seat was bent right back. There were blood stains all over the front seat, the floor and the dash.

Covering them with the sheeting, he climbed in. It felt dark and unnaturally silent. It gave him the creeps. Part of the engine had come through the flooring and the pedals were raised in an unnatural position. Reaching across, he opened the glove compartment, then pulled out an owner's manual, a pack of parking vouchers, some fuel receipts and a couple of unlabelled tape cassettes. He handed the cassettes to Glenn.

'Better have a listen to these.'

Branson pocketed them.

Ducking under the jagged cut in the roof, Grace climbed into the back of the van, his shoes echoing on the buckled floor. Branson pulled open the rear doors, letting more light in. Roy stared down at a plastic fuel can, a spare tyre, a wheel-wrench and a parking ticket in a plastic bag. He took the ticket out, and saw it was dated several days before the accident. He handed it to Branson for bagging. There was a solitary, left-foot Adidas trainer which he also passed to Branson, and a nylon bomber jacket. He felt in the pockets, pulling out a pack of cigarettes, a plastic lighter and a dry-cleaning ticket stub with an address in Brighton. Branson bagged each item.

Grace scanned the interior carefully, checking he had missed nothing, thinking hard. Then climbing back out and sheltering under the umbrella, he asked Branson, 'So who owns this vehicle?'

'Houlihan's – the undertakers in Brighton. One of the boys who died worked there – it was his uncle's firm.'

'Four funerals. Should get a nice quantity discount,' Grace said grimly.

'You're a real sick bastard sometimes, you know that?'

Ignoring him, Grace was pensive for a moment. 'Have you spoken to anyone at Houlihan's?'

'Interviewed Mr Sean Houlihan, the owner, himself yesterday afternoon. He's pretty upset as you can imagine. Told me his nephew was a hard-working lad, eager to please.'

'Aren't they all? And he gave him permission to take the van?'

Branson shook his head. 'No. But says it was out of character.'

Roy Grace thought for a moment. 'What's the van ordinarily used for?'

'Collecting cadavers. Hospitals, hospices, old folk's homes, places like that where they'd be spooked to see a hearse. You hungry?'

'I was before I came here.'

29

Ten minutes later they sat at a wobbly corner table in an almost deserted country pub, Grace cradling a pint of Guinness and Branson a Diet Coke, while they waited for their food to come. There was a cavernous inglenook fireplace beside them piled with unlit logs, and a collection of ancient agricultural artefacts hung from the walls. It was the kind of pub Grace liked, a genuine old country pub. He loathed the theme pubs with their phoney names that were insidiously becoming part of every town's increasingly characterless landscape.

'You've checked his mobile?'

'Should have the records back this afternoon,' Branson said.

'Number twelve?'

Grace looked up to see a barmaid holding a tray with their food. Steak and kidney pudding for him, swordfish steak and salad for Glenn Branson.

Grace pierced the soft suet with his knife and instantly steam and gravy erupted from it.

'Instant heart attack on a plate that is,' Branson chided. 'You know what suet is? Beef fat. Yuk.'

Spooning some mustard onto his plate, Grace said, 'It's not what you eat, it's worrying about what you eat. Worry is the killer.'

Branson forked some fish into his mouth. As he started chewing, Grace continued. 'I read that the levels of mercury in sea fish, from pollution, are at danger level. You shouldn't eat fish more than once a week.'

Branson's chewing slowed down and he looked uncomfortable. 'Where did you read that?'

'It was a report from *Nature*, I think. It's about the most respected scientific journal in the world.' Grace smiled, enjoying the expression on his friend's face.

'Shit, we eat fish like – almost every night. *Mercury*?'

'You'll end up as a thermometer.'

'That's not funny – I mean—' Two sharp beeps in succession silenced him.

Grace tugged his mobile from his pocket and stared at the screen.

Why no reply to my text, Big Boy? Claudine XX

'God, this is all I need,' he said. 'A frigging bunny boiler.'

Branson raised his eyebrows. 'Healthy meat, rabbit. Free range.'

'This one isn't healthy and she doesn't eat meat. I mean bunny boiler as in that old movie with Glenn Close.'

'*Fatal Attraction?* Michael Douglas and Anne Archer, 1987. Great movie – it was on Sky on Sunday.'

Grace showed him the text.

Branson grinned. '*Big Boy,* eh?'

'It never got that far and it's never going to.'

Then Branson's mobile rang. He pulled it from his jacket pocket and answered. 'Glenn Branson. Yeah? OK, great, I'll be there in an hour.' He ended the call and left his phone on the table. Looking at Grace, he said, 'The Vodafone log from Michael Harrison's phone just came in. Want to come to the office and help me with it?'

Grace thought for a moment, then checked his diary on his BlackBerry. He'd kept the afternoon free, intending to clear up some paperwork relating to the Suresh Hossain trial that Alison Vosper had requested at their 12.30 meeting, then read the report on the Tommy Lytle case. But that had waited twenty-seven years, and another day would not make much difference either way. Whereas Michael Harrison's disappearance was urgent. Although he did not know the characters, he felt for them. Particularly for the fiancée; he knew just how wrenching it was when a loved one went missing. At this moment, if there was any way he could be of help, he should do it.

'OK,' he said. 'Sure.'

Branson ate his salad, and left the rest of his fish untouched, while Grace tucked into his steak and kidney pudding with relish. 'I read a while ago,' he told Branson, 'that the French drink more red wine than the English but live longer. The Japanese eat more fish than the English, but drink less wine and live longer. The Germans eat more red meat than the English, and drink more beer, and they live longer, too. You know the moral of this story?'

'No.'

'It's not what you eat or drink – it's speaking English that kills you.'

Branson grinned. 'I don't know why I like you. You always manage to make me feel guilty about something.'

'So let's go find Michael Harrison. Then you can enjoy your weekend.'

Branson pushed his fish to the side of his plate and drained his Diet Coke.

'Filled with Aspartame, that stuff,' Grace said, looking disapprovingly at his glass. 'I read a theory on the web that it can give you Lupus.'

'What's Lupus?'

'It's far worse than mercury.'

'Thanks, Big Boy.'

'Now you're just jealous.'

*

As they entered the tired-looking, six-storey building that housed Brighton police station from the parking lot at the rear, Grace felt a pang of nostalgia. This building had a reputation as being the busiest police station in Britain. The place hummed and buzzed and he had loved his time – almost fifteen years – working here. It was the buzz that he missed most about his recent posting to the relatively quiet backwater of the CID headquarters building on the outskirts.

As they climbed up the cement stairs, blue walls on either side of them, the familiar noticeboards with events and procedures pinned to them, he could smell that he was still in a busy police station. It wasn't the smell of hospitals, or schools, or a civil service building, it was the smell of energy.

They went on up past the third floor, where his old office had been, and then along a corridor on the fourth floor, past a large sign dominating an entire noticeboard, with the wording 'OVERALL CRIME DETECTION RATE. APRIL. 27.8%'. Then he followed Branson into the long, narrow office his colleague was setting up as the incident room for Michael Harrison. Six desks, each with a computer terminal. Two of them were occupied, both by detectives he knew and liked – DC Nick Nicholl and DS Bella Moy. There was a SASCO flip chart on an easel and a blank whiteboard on the wall, next to a large-scale map of Sussex, on which was a pattern of coloured pins.

'Coffee?' Branson offered.

'I'm fine for the moment.'

They stopped at Bella's desk, which was covered in neat wodges of paper, among which stood an open box of Maltesers. Pointing at the papers, she said, 'I have Michael Harrison's Vodafone log from Tuesday morning up until nine o'clock this morning. I also thought it would be a good idea to get the ones of the other four with him.'

'Good thinking,' Branson said, impressed with her initiative.

She pointed at her computer screen, on which there was a map: 'I've plotted here all the masts of the mobile networks the five of them used, Orange, Vodafone and T-Mobile. Orange and T-Mobile operate on a higher frequency than Vodafone – which Michael Harrison is on. The last signal from his mobile came from the base station at the Pippingford Park mast on the A22. But I've found out we cannot rely on the fact that this is the nearest, because if the network is busy it will hand off signals to the next available mast.'

She was going to go far, this young lady, Grace thought. Studying the map for a moment, he asked, 'What's the distance between the masts?'

'In cities it is about five hundred metres. But out in the country, it is several miles.'

From previous experience, Grace knew that the mobile phone companies used a network of radio masts that acted as beacons. Mobiles, whether on *standby* or *talk* mode, sent constant signals out to the nearest beacon. It was a simple task to plot the movements of any phone user from this information. But this was obviously a lot easier in cities than in the countryside.

Bella stood up and walked across to the map of Sussex on the wall. She pointed at a blue pin in the centre of Brighton, surrounded by green, purple, yellow and white pins. 'I've marked Michael Harrison's phone with blue pins. The other four with him have different colours.'

Grace followed her finger as she talked. 'We can see all five pins remained together from seven in the evening until nine.' She pointed to three different locations. 'There is a pub in each of these places,' she said. 'But this is where it gets interesting.' She pointed to a location some miles north of Brighton. 'All five pins close together here. Then we only have four. Here.'

Branson said, 'Green, purple, yellow and white. No blue.'

'Exactly,' she said.

'What movement on the blue pin after that?'

'None,' she said, emphatically.

'So they parted company,' Grace said, 'at – about – eight forty-five?'

'Unless he dropped his phone somewhere.'

'Of course.'

'So we're talking about a radius of five miles, about fifteen miles north of Brighton?' Glenn Branson said.

'Is his phone still giving off signals?' Grace said, distracted by Bella's combination of smart mind and good looks. He'd met her before but had never really *noticed* her before. She had a really pretty face, and unless she was wearing rocks inside her bra, she had seriously large breasts – something that had always turned him on. He switched his mind off her and back to business. Then he shot a glance at her hand to see if she was wearing any rings. One sapphire band, but not on the marriage finger. He filed it away.

'The last signal was at eight forty-five Tuesday night. Nothing since.'

'So what's your view, Bella?' Grace asked.

Bella thought for a moment, fixing him with alert blue eyes. But her expression bore nothing more than businesslike deference to a superior. 'I spoke to a technician at the phone company. He says his mobile is either switched off, and has been since Tuesday night, or it is in an area of no signal.'

Grace nodded. 'This Michael Harrison is an ambitious and busy businessman. He's due to get married tomorrow morning to a very beautiful woman, by all accounts. Twenty minutes before a fatal car smash that killed four of his best friends, his phone went dead. During the past year he has been stealthily transferring money from his company to a Cayman Islands bank account – at least one million pounds that we know about. And his business partner, who should have been on that fatal stag night, for some reason was not there. Are my facts right so far?'

'Yes,' Glenn Branson said.

'So he could be dead. Or he could have pulled a smart vanishing act.'

'We need to check out the area Bella has ring-fenced. Go to all the pubs he might have visited. Talk to everyone who knows him.'

'And then?'

'Facts, Glenn. Let's get all the facts first. If they don't lead us to him, then we can start to speculate.'

The phone on Bella's desk rang. She answered it, and almost instantly her expression conveyed that it was significant.

'You're certain?' she said. 'Since Tuesday? You can't be sure it was Tuesday? No one else could have taken it?' After a few moments, she said, 'No, I agree. Thank you, that could be very significant. May I take your number?'

Grace watched while she wrote down on a pad '*Sean*

Houlihan', followed by a number. 'Thank you, Mr Houlihan, thank you very much, we'll get back to you.'

She hung up and looked at Grace then Branson. 'That was Mr Houlihan, the owner of the undertakers where Robert Houlihan, his nephew, worked. They've just discovered that they are missing a coffin.'

30

'Missing a coffin?' Glenn Branson said.

'Not something people ordinarily steal, is it?' Bella Moy said.

Grace was silent for a moment, distracted by a bluebottle that buzzed noisily around the room for a moment, then batted against a window. Forensics was on the floor below. Bloodstained clothes and artefacts were a magnet for bluebottles. Grace hated them. Bluebottles – or *blowflies* – were the vultures of the insect world. 'This character, Robert Houlihan, borrowed the undertaker's van without permission. Seems possible he might have borrowed a coffin without permission too.' He looked quizzically at Branson then Bella, then at Nick Nicholl. 'Do we have one very sick prank on our hands?'

'Are you suggesting his mates might have put him in a coffin?' Glenn Branson said.

'Do you have a better theory?'

Branson smiled, edgily. 'Work on the facts. Right?'

Looking at Bella, subconsciously thinking how attractive she was, Grace said, 'How sure is this Houlihan fellow that his coffin has been taken and they haven't just misplaced it?'

'People misplace their front door keys – I don't think people misplace coffins,' Branson said, a tad facetiously.

Bella interrupted, 'He's very sure. It was the most expensive coffin in his range, Indian teak, says it would last for hundreds of years – but this one had a flaw – the wood had warped or something – wasn't sealing tight at the bottom – he was having a ding-dong with the manufacturers in India about it.'

'I can't believe we have to import coffins from *India*! Don't we have carpenters in England?' Branson said.

Grace was staring at the map. He traced a circle with his finger. 'This is a pretty big area.'

'How long could someone survive in a coffin?' Bella asked.

'If the lid was on properly it would depend on if they had air, water, food. Without air, not long. A few hours, maybe a day,' Grace replied.

'It's now three days,' Branson said.

Grace remembered reading about a victim who had been pulled out alive from the ruins of his home twelve days after an earthquake in Turkey. 'With air, at least a week, maybe longer,' he said. 'We'd have to assume if they have done some damned stupid prank on him they would have left him with air. If they didn't, then we're looking for a body.'

He looked at the team. 'Presumably you've talked to Mark Warren, the business partner?'

'He's also his best man,' Nicholl said. 'Says he has no idea what happened. They were going on a stag-night pub crawl and he was stuck out of town and missed it.'

Grace frowned, then glanced at his watch, acutely aware of time slipping away. 'There's one thing going on a stag-night pub crawl, there's another thing taking a coffin with you. You don't decide to take a coffin with you on the spur of the moment – do you?' He stared pointedly at each of them in turn.

All three shook their heads.

'Someone's talked to all the girlfriends, wives?'

'I did,' Bella said. 'It's hard because they're in shock, but one of them was very angry – Zoe . . .' She picked up her notepad and flipped over some pages. 'Zoe Walker – widow of Josh Walker. She said that Michael was always playing stupid pranks, and she was certain they had been planning revenge.'

'And the best man didn't know anything about it? I don't buy that,' Grace said.

'I'm pretty convinced he didn't know anything. Why would he have any reason to lie?' Nicholl said.

Grace was worried by the young detective's naivety. But he always believed in giving juniors opportunities to show their abilities. He let it ride for the moment, but logged it firmly in his mind to come back to later today.

'This is one hell of an area to search,' Branson said. 'It's heavily wooded; it could take a hundred people days to comb this.'

'We have to try to narrow it down,' Grace responded. He picked up a marker pen from Bella's desk, and drew a blue circle on the map, then turned to DC Nicholl. 'Nick, we need a list of every pub in this circle. This is where we need to start.' He turned to Branson. 'Do you have photographs of the lads in the van?'

'Yes.'

'Good boy. Two sets?'

'I have a dozen sets.'

'We'll divide in two, DS Branson and I will take one half of the pubs, you two take the other. I'll see if we can get the helicopter to cover the area – although it's very wooded, they've a better chance of seeing something from the air.'

*

An hour later, Glenn Branson pulled his car up on the deserted forecourt of a pub called the King's Head, on the Ringmer Road, on the perimeter of the circle. They climbed out of the car and went up to the door. Above it was a sign saying, 'John and Margaret Hobbs, landlords'.

Inside, the saloon bar was deserted and so was the drab restaurant area off to the left. The place smelled of furniture polish and stale beer. A fruit machine flashed and winked away in a far corner, near a dartboard.

'Hello?' Branson called out. 'Hello?'

Grace leaned over the bar and saw an open trap door. He lifted a flap in the counter, went behind it, kneeled and shouted down into the cellar, which was illuminated by a weak bulb. 'Hello? Anyone there?'

A gruff voice came back. 'Be up in a moment.'

He heard a rumbling sound, then a grey beer barrel, with 'HARVEY'S' stamped on the side, gripped by a pair of massive, grimy hands, appeared, followed by the head of a burly, red-faced man, in a white shirt and jeans, sweating profusely. He had the bulk and the broken nose of an ex-boxer. 'Yes, gents?'

Branson showed him his warrant card. 'Detective Sergeant Branson and Detective Superintendent Grace of the Sussex Police. We're looking for the landlord. Mr Hobbs?'

'You've found him,' he wheezed, climbing out, then hauling himself up on to his feet and staring at them warily. He stank of body odour.

'Wonder if you'd mind taking a look at these photographs and see if you recognize any of the faces. They might have come in here last Tuesday night.' Branson laid the photographs on the counter.

John Hobbs studied each of the photographs in turn. Then he shook his head. 'No, never saw them before.'

'Were you working here on Tuesday night?' Grace asked him.

'I'm here every sodding night,' he said. 'Seven days a week. Thanks to your bloody lot.'

'Our lot?' Grace said.

'Your Traffic Division. Not easy to make a living running a rural pub, when your chums in Traffic sneak around outside, breathalysing all my customers.'

Ignoring the comment, Grace said, 'Are you absolutely sure you don't recognize them?'

'I get ten people in here on a mid-week night, it's Fat City. If they'd been here, I'd have seen them. I don't recognize them. Any reason why I should?'

It was moments like this that made Roy Grace very angry at the Traffic Division. For most people, being stopped for speeding, or to take a breathalyser check, was the only contact they ever had with the police. As a result, instead of viewing the police as their friends and guardians of the peace, they regarded them as an enemy.

'Do you watch television? Read the local papers?' Grace asked.

'No,' he said. 'I'm too busy for that. Is that a crime?'

'Four of these boys are dead,' Glenn Branson said, riled by the man's attitude. 'They were killed in a traffic accident on Tuesday night.'

'And you walk in here with your big swinging dicks, looking for some poor sodding landlord to blame for plying them with drink?'

'I didn't say that,' Grace replied. 'No, I'm not. I'm looking for this lad who was with them.' He pointed at Michael's photograph.

The landlord shook his head. 'Not in here,' he said.

Looking up at the walls, Branson asked, 'Do you have CCTV?'

'That meant to be a joke? Like I have money to buy fancy security gizmos? You know the CCTV I use?' He pointed at his own eyes. 'These. They come free when you're born. Now, if you'll excuse me, I have a barrel to change.'

Neither of them bothered to reply.

31

Michael shivered. Something was crawling through his hair. It was progressing steadily, determinedly, towards his forehead. It felt like a spider.

In panic, dropping the belt buckle, he jerked his hands up, sweeping furiously at his hair, fingers raw and bloody from scraping away at the lid.

Then it was on his face, crossing his cheek, mouth, chin.

'Jesus, get off, you fuckwit!' He smacked at his face with both hands, then felt something small and sticky. It was dead, whatever it had been. He wiped what remains he could feel off the thick, itchy growth of his stubble.

He had always been fine with most creatures, but not spiders. When he was a kid, he'd read a story in the local newspaper about a greengrocer who got bitten by a tarantula that was concealed in a bunch of bananas and had nearly died.

The beam of the torch was very faint now, giving a dark amber glow to the interior of the coffin. He was having to hold his head up to stop the rising water washing over his cheeks and into his eyes and mouth. Something else had bitten him on the ankle a while back, some insect, and it was stinging.

He shook the torch. For a moment the bulb died altogether. Then a tiny strip of filament glowed for a few seconds.

He was freezing cold. Working away at the lid was the

only thing stopping him from getting even colder. He still hadn't broken through. He had to, *had to*, before the water – he tried to shut the unthinkable from his mind, but he couldn't. The water kept rising, it covered his legs and part of his chest. With one hand he was having to cradle the walkie-talkie in the gap between his chest and the lid to prevent it from getting immersed.

Despair, like the water, was steadily enveloping him. Davey's words went round and round inside his mind.

There was one guy sticking right out through the windshield, half his head missing. Jeez, could see his brains coming out. Knew right away he was a goner. Only one survivor, but he died too.

A Transit van in a smash at a time and place that fitted. Pete, Luke, Josh, Robbo – could they really all be dead? And that was the reason no one had come to find him? But Mark must have known what they were planning, he was his best man, for Christ's sake! Surely Mark was out there, leading a team looking for him? Unless, he thought bleakly, something had happened to him, too. Maybe he'd joined them at the next pub and been in the van with them?

It was ten past four, Friday afternoon. He tried to imagine what was happening right now. What was Ashley doing? His mother? Was everything still going forward for tomorrow as planned?

He raised his head, so his mouth was up a few precious inches closer to the lid, and shouted, as he did regularly, 'Help! Help me! Help!'

Nothing but numbing silence.

I have to get out.

There was a fizz, then a crackle that for a moment

Michael thought was splintering wood, until he heard the familiar hiss of static. Then a disembodied Southern drawl: 'You mean that, what you said, 'bout me being on television?'

'Davey?'

'Hey pal, we just got back – that was a real wreck, boy! You didn't want to be in that automobile, I tell you. Took 'em two hours to cut the driver out, he was in pretty bad shape. Better shape than the woman in the other car, though, you know what I'm saying?'

'Yes I do,' Michael said, trying the tack of humouring him.

'Not sure about that. I'm saying she's dead. Y'all understand?'

'Dead? Yes, I understand that.'

'You can tell y'know, just by looking, who the dead ones are and who the ones gonna survive are. Not all the time. But wow, I'm tellin' you something!'

'Davey, that wreck you went to on Tuesday night, can you remember how many young men were in it?'

After some moments of silence, Davey said, 'Just counting the ambulances. Bad accidents you get one ambulance for each person. There was one leaving when we arrived, one still there.'

'Davey, you don't by any chance know the names of the victims?'

Almost instantly, surprising Michael, Davey rattled them off to him. 'Josh Walker, Luke Gearing, Peter Waring, Robert Houlihan.'

'You have a good memory, Davey,' Michael said, trying to encourage him. 'Was there anyone else? Was someone called Mark Warren in that wreck, also?'

Davey laughed. 'Never forget a name. If Mark Warren

had been in that wreck, I'd have known about it. Remember every name I ever heard, remember where I heard it, and the time. Ain't ever been a shitload of use.'

'Must have been good for history at school.'

'Mebbe,' he said noncommittally.

Michael fought the temptation to shout at him from sheer frustration. Instead, keeping his patience, he said, 'Do you remember where the accident happened?'

'A26. Two point four miles south of Crowborough.'

Michael felt a ray of hope brightening inside him. 'I don't think I'm very far from there. Can you drive, Davey?'

'You mean like an automobile?'

'Yup, that's exactly what I mean.'

'Guess that would depend on how you define *drive*.'

Michael closed his eyes for some moments. There had to be some way to connect properly with this character. *How?* 'Davey, I need help, really badly. Do you like games?'

'You mean like computer games? Yeah! Do you have a Play-Station-2?'

'No not here, not actually with me.'

'We could connect online maybe?'

Water slopped into Michael's mouth. He spat it out, panicking. Christ it was rising quickly now. 'Davey, if I give you a phone number, could you dial it for me? I need you to tell someone where I am. Could you get someone on the line while you are talking to me?'

'Houston, we have a problem.'

'Tell me the problem?'

'The phone's in my dad's house, you see. He doesn't know I have this walkie-talkie – I shouldn't have it. It's our secret.'

'It's OK, I can keep a secret.'

'My dad would be pretty mad at me.'

'Don't you think he'd get even madder if he knew you could have saved my life and you let me die? I think you might be the only person in the world who knows where I am.'

'It's OK, I won't tell anyone.'

More water lapped into Michael's mouth; filthy, muddy, brackish water. He spat it out, his arms, shoulders, neck muscles all aching from trying to keep his head clear of the rising level. 'Davey, I'm going to die if you don't help me. You could be a hero. Do you want to be a hero?'

'I'm going to have to go,' Davey said. 'I can see my dad outside – he needs me.'

Michael lost it, and screamed at him. 'No! Davey, you are not fucking going anywhere. You have to help. YOU HAVE TO FUCKING HELP ME.'

There was another silence, a very long one this time, and Michael worried he'd pushed too far. 'Davey?' he said, more gently. 'Are you still there, Davey?'

'I'm still here.' Davey's voice had changed. His voice suddenly was meek, chastised. He sounded like a small, apologetic boy.

'Davey, I'm going to give you a phone number. Will you write this down and make the call for me? Will you tell them that they need to speak to me on your walkie-talkie – and that it is very, very urgent. Will you do that for me?'

'OK. Tell them it's very, *very* urgent.'

Michael gave him the number. Davey told him he would go and make the call then radio him back.

Five agonizingly long minutes later, Davey's voice

came back on the walkie-talkie. 'I just got voicemail,' he said.

Michael clenched his hands in frustration. 'Did you leave a message?'

'No. You didn't tell me to do that.'

32

The landlady of the Friars, in Uckfield, was a tall, blowsy lady in her late forties, with spiky blonde hair, who looked like she'd been around the block a few times. She greeted Grace and Branson with a friendly smile and studied the photographs Grace laid on the counter carefully.

'Uh huh,' she said. 'They were in here, all five of them. Let me think . . . About eight o'clock on Tuesday.'

'You're sure?' Glenn Branson said.

She pointed at the photograph of Michael. 'He was looking a bit wrecked, but was very sweet.' She pointed at Josh's photograph. 'He was the one buying the drinks. He ordered a round of beers, I think, and some chasers. This chap' – again she pointed at Michael – 'told me he was getting married on Saturday. He said I was the most beautiful woman he had ever seen, and if he'd met me sooner, he'd have been marrying me.'

She grinned at Branson, then gave Grace a distinctly flirtatious smile. She clearly knew how to play the police, he thought. No doubt she had the local law in her pocket. No problems over staying open beyond closing time here.

'Did you by any chance hear them talking about their plans?' Grace asked.

'No, love. They were all in a sunny mood. We weren't busy, they were all sitting in that corner.' She pointed across the empty lounge to an alcove table and chairs, above which hung several horse brasses. 'I didn't pay much attention, had one of my regulars talking about his marital problems. You know how it is.'

'Yep,' said Grace.

'So you don't know where they were going next?' Branson asked.

She shook her head. 'Seemed like they were on a bender. Downed their drinks and were off.'

'Do you have closed-circuit television here?'

She gave Grace another deeply flirtatious smile. 'No, love. Sorry.'

As they left the pub, and hurried across the forecourt to their car, ducking against the teeming late-afternoon rain, Grace heard the distant sound of a helicopter. He looked up but could see nothing, as Branson unlocked the car. He sat inside and slammed the door shut against the elements, then called up Bella and Nick.

'How are you guys doing?'

'Goose eggs,' Nicholl said. 'No joy. We've two pubs to go. You?'

'Three more,' Grace said.

Branson started the car. 'Bit of a tasty old slapper,' he said to Grace. 'Think you could be in there.'

'Thanks,' Grace said. 'After you.'

'I'm a happily married man. You ought to go with the flow a bit.'

Roy Grace looked down at his mobile. At the text messages from Claudine, the cop-hating vegan from Tunbridge Wells. 'You're lucky,' he said. 'Seems to me that half the women who aren't married are insane.'

He fell silent for some moments, then he said, 'The accident happened just after nine. This might have been the last pub they went to before they put him in the coffin.'

'They could have fitted in one more.'

They went to the next three pubs, but no one remembered the boys. Nick and Bella had found one more publican who recognized them. They left at around 8.30. All apparently very drunk. That pub was about five miles away. Grace was despondent at the news. From the information they had received, they were no nearer to pinpointing where Michael Harrison might be than when they had started.

'We should go and talk to his business partner,' Grace said. 'If he's the best man he *has* to know something. Don't you think?'

'I think we should organize a search of the area.'

'Yes, but we need to narrow it down.'

Branson started the car. 'You said to me some while back that you know a geezer who does some kind of thing with a pendulum?'

Grace looked at him in surprise. 'Yes?'

'Don't remember his name. You said he can find things that are lost, just by swinging a pendulum over a map.'

'I thought you didn't believe in that? You're the one who always tells me I'm an idiot for dabbling in that terrain. Now you are suggesting I go and see someone?'

'I'm getting desperate, Roy. I don't know what else to do.'

'We press on, that's what we do.'

'Maybe he's worth a try.'

Grace smiled. 'I thought you were the big sceptic.'

'I am. But we have a guy meant to be walking down the aisle in church tomorrow at two – and we have – ' he checked his watch ' – just twenty-two hours to get him there. And about fifty square miles of forest to search, with about four hours of daylight left. What say you?'

Privately, Grace believed that Harry Frame was worth a

try. But after the fiasco in court on Wednesday, he wasn't sure it was worth risking his career over it if Alison Vosper were to find out. 'Let's exhaust all our other avenues, first, then we'll see, OK?'

'Worried what the boss might say?' Branson taunted.

'You get to my age, you start thinking about your pension.'

'I'll bear that in mind, in about thirty years' time.'

33

Ashley Harper's address was a tiny Victorian terraced house close to a railway line in an area that had once been a working-class area of Hove, but now was an increasingly trendy – and expensive – enclave for singles and first-time buyers. The quality of the cars parked in the street and the smart front doors were the giveaway.

Grace and Branson climbed out of the car, walked past a Golf GTI and a convertible Renault, and rang the doorbell of number 119, which had a silver Audi TT parked outside.

After a few moments the door was opened by a very beautiful woman in her mid-twenties. She gave Branson a sad smile of recognition.

'Hello, Ashley,' Branson said. 'This is my colleague, Detective Superintendent Grace. Can we have a chat?'

'Of course, come in. Do you have any news?' She looked at Grace.

Grace was struck by the contrast of the interior of the house with the outside. They had entered an oasis of cool minimalism. White carpet, white furniture, grey metal Venetian blinds, a large framed Jack Vettriano print of four dudes in sharp suits on the wall, which Grace recognized, pin-pricks of coloured lights jigging on a wall-mounted sound system. The hands of a faceless clock on a wall read 6.20 p.m.

She offered them drinks. Branson was given a mineral

water in a smart glass tumbler and Grace, seated beside him on a long sofa, a black coffee in an elegant white mug.

'There were three confirmed sightings of your fiancé on Tuesday night at pubs in the Ashdown Forest area,' Glenn Branson told her. 'Each of them also confirmed he was with four companions – the ones you know. But we have no information on what they were up to, other than getting drunk.'

'Michael isn't a drinker,' she said bleakly, holding a large glass of red wine in both hands.

'Tell me about Michael,' Grace asked, watching her intently.

'What sort of things?'

'Anything. How did you meet him?'

She smiled, and for an instant visibly relaxed. 'I came for a job interview to his firm. Michael and his partner.'

'Mark Warren?' quizzed Grace.

A fleeting hesitation, so small it was barely noticeable. But Grace had seen it. 'Yes.'

'Where did you work before? he asked.

'I was working for a real estate firm in Toronto, Canada. I only came back to England just before I got this job.'

'Back?'

'I'm from England originally – my roots are here.' She smiled.

'What firm in Toronto?'

'You know Toronto?' she asked, a little surprised.

'I did a week there with the RCMP about ten years ago – at their murder lab.'

'Right. It was a small firm – part of the Bay group.'

Grace nodded. 'So Michael Harrison and Mark Warren hired you?'

'Uh huh, that was last November.'

'And?'

'It was a great job – good pay – I wanted to learn about the property business, and they seemed like really nice guys. I – um – I' – she blushed – 'I thought Michael was very attractive, but I was sure he was married or had a girlfriend.'

'Excuse me for being personal,' Grace said, 'but when did you and Michael become an item?'

After a brief pause she said, 'Very quickly – within a couple of months. But we had to keep it secret, because Michael was concerned about Mark finding out. He thought it would be difficult for Mark if he was – you know – having a thing with me.'

Grace nodded. 'So when did Mark find out?'

She reddened. 'He came back to the office one day when we weren't expecting him.'

Grace smiled. He felt for her, she had a vulnerability about her that he knew would make almost all men feel protective towards her. He felt the same way himself, already, and he'd only known her for a few minutes. 'And then?'

'It was a little bit awkward for a while. I told Michael I thought I should quit, but he was very persuasive.'

'And Mark?'

Grace noticed the minutest flinch. A barely visible tightening of her facial muscles. 'He was OK about it.'

'So it didn't affect your business relationship?'

'No.'

Watching her eyes closely, Grace asked, 'Did you know they have a business offshore, in the Cayman Islands?'

Her eyes shot to Branson then back to Grace. 'No – I – I don't know about it.'

'Did Michael ever talk to you about tax shelters for himself and Mr Warren?'

Anger flashed in her face, so harshly and so suddenly that Grace was startled. 'What is this? Are you policemen or are you from the Inland Revenue?'

'If you want to help us find your fiancé, you have to help us get to know him. Tell us everything, even the stuff you think is totally irrelevant.'

'I just want you to find him. Alive. Please God.'

'Your fiancé didn't talk about his stag night with you?' Grace questioned, thinking back to his own stag night, when he'd given Sandy a detailed itinerary and she'd rescued him, in the early hours of the following morning, when he'd been abandoned in a back street of Brighton, stark naked apart from a pair of socks, on top of a pillar box.

She shook her head. 'They were just going out for a few drinks, that's all he told me.'

'What are you going to do if he hasn't turned up by the time of your wedding tomorrow?' Branson asked.

Tears rolled down her cheeks. She went out of the room and returned holding an embroidered handkerchief, which she used to dab her eyes. Then she started sobbing. 'I don't know. I really don't know. Please find him. I love him so much, I can't bear this.'

After waiting for her to calm down, and watching her eyes again intently, Grace asked, 'You were secretary to both of them. Didn't Mark Warren tell you what they had planned?'

'Just a boys' night out. I was having a girls' night out, you know, a hen party. That was all.'

'You know that Michael has a reputation as a practical joker?' Grace asked.

'Michael has a great sense of humour – that's one of the things I love about him.'

'You don't know anything about a coffin?'

She sat bolt upright, almost spilling her wine. 'A coffin? What do you mean?'

Gently, Branson explained. 'One of the boys, Robert Houlihan – you knew him?'

'I met him a few times, yes. A bit of a loser.'

'Oh really?'

'That's what M – Michael said. He sort of hung on to their crowd but wasn't really part of it.'

'But part of it enough to be included in the stag night?' Branson persisted.

'Michael hates to hurt anyone. I think he felt Robbo had to be included. I suppose because he'd made the other guys ushers, but not Robbo.'

Grace drank some coffee. 'You didn't have any falling-out with Michael? Nothing to make you think he might have got cold feet about the wedding?'

'Christ,' she said. 'No. Absolutely not. I – he—'

'Where are you going on your honeymoon?' Grace asked.

'The Maldives. Michael's booked a fantastic place – he loves water – boats, scuba diving. It looks like paradise.'

'We have a helicopter out looking for him. We have drafted in one hundred special constables, and if he hasn't turned up by tonight we are going to start a full search of the area where he was last seen. But I don't want to tie up hundreds of valuable police man-hours only to find he's sunning himself in the Cayman Islands, courtesy of the British taxpayer. Do you understand?'

Ashley nodded. 'Loud and clear,' she said bitterly. 'This is about money, not about finding Michael at all.'

'No,' Grace said, softening his tone. 'This is not about money. I'm prepared to authorize whatever it costs to find Michael.'

'Then please start now.' Hunching her thin shoulders, she stared pitifully down at her glass of wine. 'I recognize you, from the *Argus* piece on you. And the *Daily Mail* yesterday. They were trying to ridicule you for going to a medium, right?'

'Yes.'

'I believe in all that. Don't you know somebody? You know – with your contacts? Aren't there mediums, psychics – who can locate missing people?'

Grace shot a glance at Branson, then looked at Ashley. 'There are, yes.'

'Couldn't you go to someone – or put me in touch with someone you can recommend?'

Grace thought carefully for a moment. 'Do you have anything belonging to Michael?' He was aware of Glenn Branson's eyes boring into him.

'Like what?'

'Anything at all. Some object. An item of clothing? Jewellery? Something he would have been in contact with?'

'I can find something. Just give me a couple of minutes.'

'No problem.'

34

'Are you out of your tree?' Branson said as they drove away from Ashley's house.

Holding the copper bracelet Ashley had given him in his hand, Grace replied, 'You suggested it.' There was a deep bass boom, boom, boom from the radio. Grace turned the volume down.

'Yeah, but I didn't mean for you to ask her.'

'You wanted us to nick something from his pad?'

'*Borrow*. Man, you live dangerously. 'What if she talks to the press?'

'You asked me to help you.'

Branson gave him a sideways look. 'So what do you make of her?'

'She knows more than she's telling us.'

'So she's trying to protect his arse?'

Grace turned the bracelet over in his hands. Three thin bands of copper welded together, each ending in two small roundels. 'What do you think?'

'There you go again – your usual, answering a question with a question.'

Grace said nothing for a while, thinking. In his mind he was recalling the scene inside Ashley Harper's house. Her anxiety, her answers to the questions. Nineteen years in the Police Force had taught him many lessons. Probably the most important one was that the truth is not necessarily what was immediately apparent. Ashley Harper knew more than she was saying, of that he was certain. The reading of her eyes told him that. Probably, he assessed, in her grief-stricken state she was concerned about whatever tax scam Michael Harrison might be involved with in the Cayman Islands getting out in the open. And yet he felt this was not the whole story.

*

Twenty minutes later they parked on a yellow line on the Kemp Town promenade, elevated above the beach and the English Channel, and climbed out of the car.

Rain was still pelting down, and, apart from the grey smudge of a tanker or freighter on the horizon, the sea was empty. A steady stream of cars and lorries sluiced past them. Over to the right, Grace could see the Palace Pier with its white domes, tacky lights and the helter-skelter rising like a pillar at the end.

Marine Parade, the wide boulevard that ran along a mile of handsome Regency facades with sea views, teemed with traffic sluicing past in both directions. The Van Alen was one of its few modern apartment buildings, a twenty-first-century take on Art Deco. A beady voice answered the bell of apartment 407 on the high-security entry panel within moments. 'Hello?'

'Mark Warren?' Glenn Branson said.

'Yes, who is this?'

'The police – may we have a word with you about Michael Harrison?'

'Sure. Come up – the fourth floor.' There was a sharp buzz and Grace pushed the front door open.

'Weird coincidence,' he said to Branson as they entered the lift. 'I was here last night on one of my poker nights.'

'Who do you know here?'

'Chris Croke.'

'Chris Croke – that git in Traffic?'

'He's all right.'

'How can he afford a pad in a place like this?

'By marrying money – or rather, by divorcing money. He had a rich missus – her dad was a lottery winner he told me once – and a good divorce lawyer.'

'Smart bastard.'

They stepped out on the fourth floor, walked down a plushly blue carpet and stopped outside 407. Branson pressed the bell.

After a few seconds the door was opened by a man in his late twenties, dressed in an open-neck white business shirt, pin-stripe suit trousers and black loafers with a gold chain. 'Gentlemen,' he said, affably, 'please come in.'

Grace looked at him with faint recognition. He had seen this man before, somewhere, recently. Where? Where the hell had he seen him?

Branson dutifully showed him his warrant card, but Mark Warren barely glanced at it. They followed him through a small hallway into a huge open-plan living area, with two red sofas forming an L-shape and a long, narrow black lacquer table acting as a border for a kitchen and dining area.

The place was similar in its minimalistic style, Grace noted, to Ashley Harper's, but considerably more money had been lavished here. An African mask sat on top of a tall black plinth in one corner. Classy, if impenetrable, abstract paintings lined the walls, and there was a picture window looking directly out at the sea with a fine view of the Palace Pier. A news programme, muted, played on a flat screen Bang and Olufsen television.

'Can I get you a drink?' Mark Warren asked, wringing his hands.

Grace observed him carefully, watching his body language, listening to the way he spoke. The man exuded anxiety. Unease. Hardly surprising, considering what he must be going through. One of the biggest problems for survivors of any disaster, Grace knew from past experience, was coping with guilt.

'We're fine, thanks,' Branson said. 'We don't want to keep you long – just a few questions.'

'Do you have any news of Michael?'

Grace told him about their trawl of pubs, and about the missing coffin. But there was something about the way he responded that ran up a flag in Grace's mind. Just a small flag, barely more than a minuscule fluttering pennant.

'I can't believe they'd do anything like taking a coffin,' Mark Warren said.

'You should know,' Grace retorted. 'Isn't it the role of the best man to organize the stag night?'

'So I read in the stuff I downloaded from the net,' he replied.

Grace frowned. 'So you weren't involved in the plans? At all?'

Mark looked flustered. His voice was awkward as he started speaking, but rapidly calmed. 'I – no, that's not what I'm saying. Like I mean – you know – we – Luke – wanted to organize a strippergram, but that's kind of so yesterday – we wanted something more original.'

'To pay back Michael Harrison for all his practical jokes?'

Flustered again for a moment, Mark Warren said, 'Yes, we did discuss that.'

'But you didn't talk about a coffin?' Roy Grace asked, locked on to his eyeballs.

'Absolutely not.' There was indignation in his voice.

'A teak coffin,' Grace said.

'I – I don't know anything about any coffin.'

'You're saying to me that you were his best man, but you didn't know anything about the plans for his stag night?'

A long hesitation. Mark Warren shot long glances at each of the police officers in turn. 'Yes,' he answered finally.

'I don't buy that, Mark,' Grace said. 'I'm sorry, but I don't buy it.' Instantly he detected the flash of anger.

'You're accusing me of lying to you? I'm sorry, gentlemen, this meeting is over. I need to talk to my lawyer.'

'That's more important to you than finding your business partner?' Grace quizzed. 'He's meant to be getting married tomorrow. You are aware of that?'

'I'm his best man.'

Watching Mark Warren's face closely, Grace suddenly remembered where he had seen him before. At least, where he *thought* he had seen him before. 'What car do you drive, Mark?' he asked.

'A BMW.'

'Which model? A 3-Series? 5-Series? 7-Series?'

'An X5,' Mark said.

'That's a four-wheel drive?'

'Yes, it is.'

Grace nodded and said nothing; his brain was churning.

35

Standing in the corridor, waiting for the lift, Branson watched Mark Warren's front door, making sure it was shut, then he said, 'What was that about – the business with the car?'

As they stepped inside the lift, Grace pressed the bottom button, marked 'B'. Still deep in thought, he didn't reply.

Branson watched him. 'Something's not right with that dude. You read that?'

Still Grace said nothing.

'You should have pressed "G" for the ground floor – that's the way we came in.'

Grace stepped out into the underground garage and Branson followed. The place was dry, dimly lit, with a faint smell of engine oil. They walked past a Ferrari, a Jaguar saloon, a Mazda sports car and a small Ford saloon, then a couple of empty bays until Grace stopped in front of a gleaming silver BMW X5 off-roader. He stared hard at the car. Droplets of rainwater still lay on the paintwork.

'Cool machines, these,' Branson said. 'But they don't have much room in the rear. Much more in a Range Rover or a Cayenne.'

Grace peered at the wheels, then knelt down and looked under a door sill. 'When I was here last night,' he said, 'and came down here for my car about quarter to one in the morning, this BMW drove in, covered in mud. I noticed it because it seemed a little unusual – you don't often see a dirty four-wheel drive in the centre of Brighton, they're mostly used by mothers doing the shopping run.'

'You sure it was *this* car.'

Grace tapped the side of his own head. 'The number plate.'

'Your photographic memory – still working at your advanced age . . .'

'Still working.'

'So what's your take?'

'What's yours?'

'A missing coffin. A forest. A mud-caked car. A best man who is the only survivor, who wants to speak to his lawyer. A bank account in the Cayman Islands. Something smells.'

'It doesn't smell, it stinks.'

'So what happens next?'

Grace pulled the copper bracelet out of his pocket and held it up. 'This happens next.'

'Is that what you really think?'

'You have a better idea?'

'Take Mark Warren in for questioning.'

Grace shook his head. 'The guy's smart. We need to be smarter.'

'Going to a flaky pendulum dowser is smarter?'

'Trust me.'

36

You had to stay awake. That was how you survived. Hypothermia made you sleepy, and when you fell asleep you would sink into a coma and then you died.

Michael was shivering, near-delirious. Cold, so, so cold; he heard voices, heard Ashley whispering into his ear; reached up to touch her and his knuckles struck hard teak.

Water slopped into his mouth and he spat it out. His face was squashed tight against the lid of the coffin. The flashlight didn't work any more, he tried keeping the walkie-talkie above the water, but his arm was hurting so much it was not going to be possible for much longer.

He wedged his mobile phone, which was useless, into the back pocket of his jeans. It made it uncomfortable, but it gave him another inch and a half height. For whatever good that would do. He was going to die; he did not know how much longer he had but it wasn't long.

'Ashley,' he said weakly. 'Ashley, my darling.'

Then more water filled his mouth.

He rubbed away at the ever-widening and deepening groove in the lid with the casing of the flashlight. He thought of the wedding tomorrow. His mum showing him the dress she had bought, and the hat and the shoes and the new handbag, wanting his approval, wanting to know she looked good for his special day, wanting him to be proud of her, wanting Ashley to be proud of her. He remembered the phone call from his kid sister, from

Australia, so excited by the ticket he had paid for. Carly would be here now, staying with his mother, getting ready.

His neck hurt so badly, he didn't know how much longer he could stand the pain; every few minutes he had to relax, sink back, holding his breath, let the water wash over his face, then push himself up. Soon that would not be possible any more.

Crying with frustration and terror he lashed out at the lid, pummelled it. He pressed the *talk* button again. 'Davey! Davey! Hey, Davey?'

He spat more water out.

Every molecule in his body shivered.

Static came back at him.

His teeth clicked in his mouth. He swallowed a mouthful of the muddy water, then another mouthful. 'Please, oh please, somebody, please, please, oh please, help me.'

He tried to calm himself down, to think about his speech. Had to thank the bridesmaids. Propose a toast to them. Must remember to thank his mother first. Finish with the toast to the bridesmaids. Tell funny stories. There was a great joke Pete had given him. About a couple going on honeymoon and—

Honeymoon.

It was all booked. They were flying tomorrow night, at nine o'clock, to the Maldives. First class – Ashley didn't know about that bit, that was his secret treat.

Oh get me out of here, you idiots. I'm going to miss my wedding, my honeymoon. Come on! Now!

37

The clock on the dash of the Ford read 7.13 p.m. as Branson drove Grace along past the elegant Regency townhouse faces of Kemp Town, then onto open road, high above the cliffs, past the vast neo-Gothic buildings of Roedean girls' school and then past the Art Deco building of St Dunstan's Home for the Blind. The rain lashed down and the wind buffeted the car, crazily. It hadn't stopped for days now. Branson turned the radio up, drowning out the intermittent crackle of the police two-way radio, swaying to the beat of a Scissor Sisters track.

Grace tolerated it for some moments, then turned the volume down again.

'What's the matter, man? This group is so cool,' Branson said.

'Great,' Grace said.

'You want to pull a bird, yeah? You need to get with the culture.'

'You're my culture guru, right?'

Branson shot him a sideways glance. 'I ought to be your style guru, too. Got a great hairdresser you should go to – Ian Habbin at The Point. Get him to sharpen up your hair – I mean, like, you are looking so *yesterday*.'

'It's starting to feel like yesterday,' Grace responded. 'You asked me to have lunch with you. It's now past teatime and heading for supper. At this rate we'll be having breakfast together.'

'Since when did you have a life?' Almost as the words

came out, Branson regretted saying them. He could see the pain in Grace's face without even turning to look at him. 'Sorry, man,' he said.

They drove through the smart, cliff-top village of Rottingdean, then along a sweeping rise, dip, followed by another rise, past the higgledy-piggledy suburban sprawl of post-war houses of Saltdean, then Peacehaven.

'Take the next left,' Grace said. Then he continued to direct Branson through a maze of hilly streets, crammed with bungalows and modest detached houses, until they pulled up outside a small, rather shabby-looking bungalow, with an even shabbier-looking camper van parked outside.

They hurried through the rain into a tiny porch, with wind chimes pinging outside, and rang the doorbell. After a few moments it was answered by a diminutive, wiry man well into his seventies, with a goatee beard, long grey hair tied back in a pony tail, wearing a kaftan and dungarees, and sporting an ankh medallion on a gold chain. He greeted them effusively in a high-pitched voice, a bundle of energy, taking Grace's hand and staring at him with the joy of a long-lost friend. 'Detective Superintendent Grace! So good to see you again.'

'And you, my friend. This is DS Branson. Glenn, this is Harry Frame.'

Harry Frame gripped Glenn Branson's hand with a strength that belied both his years and his size and stared up at him with piercing green eyes. 'What a pleasure to meet you. Come in, come in.'

They followed him into a narrow hallway lit by a low-watt bulb in a hanging lantern and decorated in a nautical theme, the centrepiece of which was a large brass porthole on the wall, and through into a sitting room, the shelves crammed with ships in bottles. There was a drab three-piece suite, its backs covered in antimacassars, a television, which was switched off, and a round oak table with four wooden chairs by the window, to which they were ushered. On the wall Branson clocked a naff print of Anne Hathaway's cottage and a framed motto which read, 'A mind once expanded can never return to its original dimensions.'

'Tea, gentlemen?'

'Thank you,' Grace said.

Looking at Grace for his cue, Branson said, 'That would be very nice.'

Harry Frame hurried busily out of the room. Branson stared at a lit, solitary white candle in a glass holder on the table, then at Grace, giving him a *What is this shit?* expression.

Grace smiled back at him. *Bear with it.*

After a few minutes a cheery, dumpy, grey-haired lady, wearing a heavy-knit roll-neck, brown polyester trousers and brand new white trainers, carried out a tray containing three mugs of tea and a plate of Bourbon biscuits, which she set down on the table.

'Hello, Roy,' she said familiarly to Grace, and then to Branson, with a twinkle in her eye she said, I'm Maxine. *She Who Must Be Obeyed!*

'Nice to meet you. Detective Sergeant Branson.'

She was followed by her husband, who was carrying a map.

Grace took his mug, and noticed the tea was a watery-green colour. He saw Branson eyeing his dubiously.

'So, gentlemen,' Harry said, seating himself opposite them, 'you have a missing person?'

'Michael Harrison,' Grace said.

'The young man in the *Argus*? Terrible thing, that accident. All so young to be called over.'

'Called over?' Branson quizzed.

'Obviously the spirits wanted them.'

Branson shot Grace a glance which the Detective Superintendent resolutely ignored.

Moving the biscuits and the candle over to one side, Frame spread out an Ordnance Survey map of East Sussex on the table.

Branson ate a biscuit. Grace fished in his pocket and gave the medium the copper bracelet. 'You asked me to bring something belonging to the missing person.'

Frame took it, held it tight and closed his eyes. Both police officers stared at him. His eyes remained closed for a good minute, then, finally, he started to nod. 'Umm,' he said, his eyes still closed. 'Umm, yes, umm.' Then he opened his eyes with a start, looking at Grace and Branson as if surprised to find them still in the room. He moved closer to the map, then pulled a length of string, with a small lead weight attached, from his trouser pocket.

'Let's see what we can find,' he said. 'Yes, indeed, let's see. Is your tea all right?'

Grace sipped his. It was hot and faintly sour-tasting. 'Perfect,' he said.

Branson sipped his too, dutifully. 'Good,' he said.

Harry Frame beamed, genuinely pleased. 'Now, now . . .' Resting his elbows on the table, he buried his face in the palm of his hands as if in prayer, and began to mutter. Grace avoided Branson's eye.

'Yarummm,' Frame said to himself. 'Yarummmm. Brnnnn. Yarummm.'

Then he sat bolt upright, held the string over the map

between his forefinger and thumb, and let the lead weight swing backwards and forwards, like a pendulum. Then, pursing his lips in concentration, he swung it vigorously in a tight circle, steadily covering the map inch by inch.

'Uckfield?' he said. 'Crowborough? Ashdown Forest?' He looked quizzically at each man. Both nodded.

But Harry Frame shook his head. 'No, I'm not being shown anything in this area, sorry. I'll try another map, smaller scale.'

'We're pretty sure he is in this area, Harry,' Roy Grace said.

Frame shook his head determinedly. 'No, the pendulum is not telling me that. We need to look wider.'

Grace could *feel* Branson's scepticism burning like a furnace. Staring at the new map, which showed the whole of East and West Sussex, he saw the pendulum swinging in a narrow arc over Brighton.

'This is where he is,' Frame murmured.

'Brighton? I don't think so,' Grace responded.

Frame produced a large-scale street map of Brighton and set the pendulum swinging over it. Within moments it began to make a tight circle over Kemp Town. 'Yes,' he said. 'Yes, this is where he is.'

Grace stared at Branson now, as if sharing his thoughts. 'You are wrong, Harry,' he said.

'No, I don't think so, Roy. This is where your man is.'

Grace shook his head. 'We've just come from Kemp Town – we've been to talk to his business partner – are you sure you aren't picking up on that?'

Harry Frame picked up the copper bracelet. 'This is his bracelet? Michael Harrison?'

'Yes.'

'Then this is where he is. My pendulum is never wrong.'

'Can you give us an address?' Branson asked.

'No, not an address – the housing is too dense. But that's where you must look, that is where you will find him.'

38

'Fucking weirdo,' Branson said to Grace as they drove away from Harry Frame's house.

Grace, deep in thought, did not say anything for a long while. In the past hour the rain had finally stopped, and streaks of late-evening sunlight pierced the net of grey cloud that sagged low over the sea. 'Let's assume he's right for a moment.'

'Let's get a drink and something to eat,' Branson said. 'I'm starving; I'm about to keel over.'

The clock read 8.31 p.m.

'Good idea.'

Glenn called his wife on his mobile. Grace listened to Branson's end of the conversation. It sounded pretty heated and finished with him hanging up in mid-call. 'She's well pissed off.'

Grace gave him a sympathetic smile. He knew better than to make an uninformed comment on someone else's domestic situation.

A few minutes later, in the bar of a cliff-top pub called the Badger's Rest, Grace cradled a large Glenfiddich on the rocks, noticing that his companion was making short work of a pint of beer, despite the fact he was driving.

'I went into the Force,' Branson said, 'so I'd have a career that would make my kids proud of me. Shit. At least when I was a bouncer, I had a life. I'd get to bath my Sammy and put him to bed and had time to read him a story before I went off to work. Do you know what Ari just said to me?'

'What?' Grace stared at the specials on the blackboard.

'She said Sammy and Remi are crying 'cause I'd promised to be home and read them stories tonight.'

'So go home,' Grace said gently, meaning it.

Branson drained his pint and ordered another. 'I can't do that, you know I can't. This isn't a fucking nine-to-five job. I can't just walk out of the office like some dickhead civil servant, and do a Piss Off Early Tomorrow's Saturday stunt. I owe it to Ashley Harper and to Michael Harrison. Don't I?'

'You have to learn when to let go,' Grace said.

'Oh really? So when exactly do I let go?'

Grace drained his whisky. It felt good. The burning sensation first in his gullet, then in his stomach. He held his glass out to the barman, ordered another double, then put a twenty-pound note down and asked for change for the cigarette machine. He hadn't had a cigarette for several days, but tonight his craving for one was too strong.

The pack of Silk Cut dropped into the tray of the machine. He tore off the cellophane and asked the barman for some matches. Then he lit a cigarette and drew the smoke deeply, gratefully, down into his lungs. It tasted beyond exquisite.

'I thought you'd quit,' Branson said.

'I have.'

He received his new drink and clinked glasses with Glenn. 'You don't have a life and I'm destroying mine. Welcome to a career in the police.'

Branson shook his head. 'Your friend Harry Frame is one weird dude. What a flake!'

'Remember Abigail Matthews?'

'That kid a couple of years ago? Eight years old, right?'

'Right.'

'Kidnapped outside her folks' home. You found her in a crate in a hangar at Gatwick Airport.'

'Nigerian. She'd been sold into a child sex ring in Holland.'

'That was great detective work. Wasn't that part of the reason you got promoted so fast?'

'It was. Except I never told anyone the truth about how I found her.' The whisky was talking now, rather than Roy Grace. 'I never told anyone, because—'

'Because?'

'It wasn't great detective work, Glenn, that's why. It was Harry Frame who found her, with his pendulum. OK?'

Branson was silent for some moments. 'So that's why you believe in him.'

'He's been right in other cases, too. But I don't shout about him. Alison Vosper and her brass cronies don't like anything that doesn't fit into their boxes. You want a career in the police, you have to be seen to play by the rules. You have to be *seen*, OK? You don't actually have to play by them, just so long as they *think* you are playing by them.' He drained the second whisky far faster than he had intended. 'Let's get some grub.'

Branson ordered scampi. Grace chose a distinctly unhealthy gammon steak with two fried eggs and French fries, lit another cigarette and ordered another round of drinks.

'So what do we do next, old wise man?'

Grace squinted at Branson. 'We could get smashed,' he said.

'That's not exactly going to help us find Michael Harrison, is it? Or have I missed something?'

'You haven't missed anything – not that I can see. But it is now about . . .' Grace checked his watch. 'Nine on a

Friday night. Short of heading out into Ashdown Forest with a shovel and a flashlight, I'm not sure what else we can achieve.'

'There must be something that we're missing.'

'There's always something, Glenn. What very few people understand is the importance of serendipity in our job.'

'You mean luck?'

'You know the old joke about the golfer?'

'Tell me.'

'He says, "It's a strange thing . . . the more I practise, the luckier I get."'

Branson grinned. 'So maybe we haven't practised enough.'

'I think we've practised enough. Tomorrow's the big day. If Mr Michael Harrison is playing the joke of all jokes, then tomorrow will be the moment of truth.'

'And if he's not?'

'Then we go to Plan B.'

'Which is what?'

'I have no idea.' Grace squinted at him across the top of his glass. 'I'm just your lunch date. Remember?'

39

Ashley, in her white towelling dressing gown, was slouched on her bed watching a *Sex in the City* repeat playing on the plasma television screen, when the telephone rang. She sat up with a start, nearly spilling some of the Sauvignon Blanc in the glass she was holding. Her alarm clock said 11.18 p.m. It was late.

She answered it with a nervous, near-breathless, 'Yeshello?'

'Ashley? I hope I haven't woken you, love?'

Ashley put her wine glass down on her bedside table, grabbed the remote and muted the sound. It was Gill Harrison, Michael's mother. 'No,' she said. 'Not at all. I can't sleep anyhow. I haven't slept a wink since – Tuesday. I'm going to take a pill in a little while – the doctor gave me some – said they would knock me out.' In the background she heard Bobo, Gill's little white shih-tzu, barking.

'I want you to think again, Ashley. I really think you must cancel the reception tomorrow.'

Ashley took a deep breath. 'Gill – we discussed it all yesterday and today. We can't get anything refunded cancelling this late; we have people coming from all over the place – like my uncle from Canada who's giving me away.'

'He's a nice man,' Gill said. 'Poor fellow's come all this way.'

'We adore each other,' Ashley said. 'He took the whole week off just so he could be at the rehearsal on Monday.'

'Where's he staying?'

'In London – at the Lanesborough. He always stays at the best.' She was quiet for a moment. 'Of course, I've told him, but he said he would come down anyway to give me support. I've managed to stop my other girlfriends in Canada – four of them were coming over – and I have other friends in London I've convinced not to come – the phone's been ringing off the hook for the past couple of days.'

'Here, too.'

'The problem is Michael has friends and colleagues invited from all over England – and the Continent. I've tried to contact as many people as possible, and so has Mark – but – we need at least to look after those who do turn up. And I still think Michael might.'

'I don't think so, love, not now.'

'Gill, Michael played all kinds of pranks on his friends when they got married – two of them only made it to the church minutes before the wedding began, because of what he did to them. Michael could still be somewhere, locked up or tied up, not knowing anything about what has happened. He *might* still be planning – or trying – to make it.'

'You're a lovely girl, and you are a kind person – it's going to be devastating for you to be at the church and he doesn't arrive. You have got to accept that something has happened to him. Four people are dead, love. Michael must have heard about them – if he is OK.'

Ashley sniffed, then began to sob. For some moments she cried inconsolably, dabbing her eyes with a tissue she had plucked from a box on her bedside table. Then, sniffing hard, she said, 'I'm trying so damned hard, but I'm not coping. I just – I – keep – praying he's going to turn up – every time the phone rings I think it's going to be him –

you know – that he'll be laughing, explaining it's all been some dumb joke.'

'Michael's a good boy,' Gill said. 'He's never been cruel – this is too cruel. He wouldn't do this; it's not in him.'

There was a long silence. Finally Ashley broke it. 'Are you OK?'

'Apart from being worried sick about Michael, yes, I'm OK, thanks. I've got Carly here.'

'She's arrived?'

'Yes, a couple of hours ago from Australia. I think she'll be a bit jet-lagged tomorrow.'

'I should come over to say hello.' She was silent for a moment. 'You see what I mean – all these people coming from all over the place – we just have to at least be at the church to meet them – and offer them some food. Can you imagine if we weren't there and Michael then turned up?'

'He would understand – that you cancelled out of respect for the boys who died.'

Sobbing even harder, Ashley said, 'Please, Gill, please let's go to the church and see.'

'Take that pill and get some sleep, love.'

'I'll call you in the morning.'

'Yes. I'll be up early.'

'Thanks for calling.'

'Night night.'

'Night!' Ashley said.

She replaced the receiver then, charged with a burst of energy, rolled over, her breasts spilling out of the open front of her dressing gown, and gazed down at Mark, who was lying naked under the bedclothes beside her. 'Stupid cow, doesn't have a clue!' Her lips burst into a massive grin, her whole face alight with joy. 'Not a clue!'

She put her arms around his neck, held him tightly and kissed him passionately, on the mouth at first, before working her way slowly, steadily, with maximum possible torture, further and further down his body.

40

He was sweating under the duvet. Too hot, far too hot, somehow it had worked its way right over his head and he could barely breathe. Rivulets of water ran down his face, down his arms, legs, the small of his back. He pushed the duvet off, sat up, felt a numbing crack to his skull, sank back.

Splash.

Oh Jesus.

Water slopped all around him. And felt as if it were inside him too, as if the blood in his veins and the water in which he lay were interchangeable. Some word for it. Some word he grasped for, and it eluded him, slipped from his grasp each time he closed on it. *Like soap in a bathtub*, he thought.

Cold now. Unbearably hot an instant ago, now cold. So cold. Oh so teeth-chattering-cold-cold-cold. His head was splitting. 'Just going to check and see if there are any paracetamol in the bathroom cabinet,' he announced. To the silence that came back at him he said, 'Won't be long. Just popping out to the chemist.'

The hunger had gone away some hours ago, but now it was back with a vengeance. His stomach burned as if the acids had now turned on the lining for want of anything else to break down. His mouth was parched. He put a hand out and scooped water into his mouth, but despite his thirst it was an effort to drink it.

Osmosis!

'OSMOSIS!' In a burst of elation he shouted the word out at the top of his voice, repeating it over and over. 'Osmosis! Gotcha! *Osmosis!*'

Then suddenly he was hot again. Perspiring. 'Someone turn the thermostat down!' he shouted out in the darkness. 'For Christ's sake, we're all boiling down here; what do you think we are, lobsters?'

He started giggling at his remark. Then, right above his face, the lid of the coffin began to open. Slowly, steadily, noiselessly, until he could see the night sky, alive with comets racing across it. A beam of light shone out from him, dust motes drifted lazily through it, and he realized all the stars in the firmament were projected there from the light. The sky was his screen! Then he saw a face drift across, through the beam, through the dust motes. Ashley. As if he were looking up at her from the bottom of a swimming pool, and she was drifting face-down over him.

Then another face drifted over – his mother. Then Carly, his kid sister. Then his father, in the sharp brown suit, cream shirt and red silk tie that Michael remembered him in best. Michael did not understand how his father could be in the pool but his clothes were dry.

'You're dying, son,' Tom Harrison said. 'You'll be with us soon now.'

'I don't think I'm ready yet, Dad.'

His father gave a wry smile. 'That's the thing, son, who is?'

'I found that word I was looking for,' Michael said. '*Osmosis.*'

'That's a good word, son.'

'How are you, Dad?'

'There are good deals to be had up here, son. Terrific deals. Heck of a lot better. You don't have to fart around trying to hide your money in the Cayman Islands up here. What you make is what you keep – like the sound of that?'

'Yes, Dad—'

Except it wasn't his father any more he was talking to, but the vicar, Reverend Somping, a short, supercilious man in his late fifties, with greying wavy hair and a beard that only partially masked the ruddy complexion of his cheeks – ruddy not from a healthy outdoors lifestyle, but from broken veins from years of heavy boozing.

'You're going to be very late, Michael, if you don't haul yourself out of there. You do realize that, if you don't reach the church by sunset, I cannot marry you, by law?'

'I didn't, no – I—'

He reached up to touch the vicar, to seize his hand, but he struck hard, impenetrable teak.

Darkness.

The slosh of water as he moved.

Then he noticed something. Checking with his hands, the water was no longer up to his cheeks; it had subsided to the top of his neck. 'I'm wearing it like a tie,' he said. 'Can you wear water like a tie?'

Then the shivers gripped him, clenched his arms so that his elbows banged against his ribs, his feet knocked, his breathing got faster, faster until he was hyperventilating.

I'm going to die, I'm going to die, here, alone, on my wedding day. They are coming for me, the spirits, they are coming down here into the box and—

He put his jerking hands together over his face. He could not remember the last time he had prayed – it was sometime long before his dad had died. Tom Harrison's death had been the final confirmation to him that there was no God. But now the words of the Lord's Prayer poured into his head and he whispered them into his hands, as if not wanting to be overheard.

A crackle of static broke his concentration. Then a burst of twangy country and western music. Followed by a voice. 'Well, good morning, sports fans, this is WNEB Buffalo bringing you the latest in sports, news and weather on this rainy ole Saturday morning! Now last night in the play-offs . . .'

Frantically, Michael fumbled for the walkie-talkie. He knocked it off his chest and into the water. 'Oh shit, no, oh shit, shit shit!'

He fished it out, shook it as best he could, found the *talk* button and pressed it. 'Davey? Davey, is that you?'

Another hiss and crackle. 'Hey, dude! You the dude with the friends in the wreck on Tuesday, right?'

'Yes.'

'Hey, good to talk to you again!'

'Davey, I really need you to do something for me. Then you could make a big announcement on your radio station.'

'Depends what other news there is on the day,' Davey said, dismissively.

'OK.' Michael fought the urge to snap at him. 'I need you either to get someone on the phone that I can speak with via your walkie-talkie, or for you and your dad to come and rescue me.'

'I guess that would depend on whether y'all are in an area we cover, know what I'm saying?'

'I do, Davey. I know exactly what you are saying.'

41

Later, lying naked in bed with a dozen scented candles burning around them in the room, and Norah Jones singing on the stereo, Ashley lit a cigarette, then held it up to Mark's lips. He took a deep drag.

'Gill's right,' Mark said. 'I don't think you should go to the church, and you definitely should not go ahead with the reception.'

Ashley shook her head vigorously. 'We absolutely should. Don't you see? I'll turn up there at the church . . .' She paused to take a drag, then blew the smoke out slowly, deliciously, towards the ceiling. 'Everyone will see me, the poor abandoned bride, and they'll all feel so sorry for me.'

'I'm not sure I agree; it could backfire.'

'How?'

'Well – they might think you're insensitive, insisting on going ahead – that you're not respecting Pete, Luke, Josh and Robbo. We both need to be seen to be acting as if we care about them.'

'You and I have been in touch with their families. We've both written them all letters, we're doing all the right things there. But we've been discussing the wedding for the past three days. *We are going ahead!* We have to pay the bloody caterers whatever we do, so we might as well look after those people who make the effort to turn up. It probably won't be many – but surely that's the least we can do?'

Mark took the cigarette from her and drew hard, inhaling the smoke deep into his lungs. 'Ashley, people would understand. You've battered me with your logic for three days and you haven't listened to me. I think this is a huge mistake.'

'Trust me,' Ashley said. She gave him a fierce look. 'Don't start wimping out on me now.'

'Christ, I'm not wimping out – I just—'

'Want to bottle out?'

'This is not about bottling out. Come on, partner, be strong!'

'I am being strong.'

She wormed her way down his body, nuzzling her face in his pubic hairs, his penis limp against her cheek. 'This is not what I call strong,' she said mischievously.

42

Grace started his weekend the way he liked, with an early-Saturday-morning six-mile run along Brighton and Hove seafront. Today it was again raining hard, but that did not matter; he wore a baseball cap with the peak pulled down low to shield his face, a lightweight tracksuit and brand new Nike running shoes. Powering along at a good, fast pace, he soon forgot the rain, forgot all his cares, just breathed deep, went from cushioned stride to cushioned stride, a Stevie Wonder song, 'Signed, Sealed, Delivered', playing over in his head, for some reason.

He mouthed the words as he ran past an old man in a trenchcoat walking a poodle on a leash, and then was passed by two Lycra-clad cyclists on mountain bikes. It was low tide. Out on the mudflats a couple of fishermen were digging lugworms for bait.

With the tang of salt on his lips, he ran alongside the promenade railings, on past the burnt-out skeleton of the West Pier, then down a ramp to the edge of the beach itself, where the local fishermen left their day boats dragged up far enough to be safe from the highest of tides. He clocked some of their names – *Daisy Lee, Belle of Brighton, Sammy* – smelled bursts of paint, tarred rope, putrefying fish as he ran on past the still-closed cafes, amusement arcades and art galleries of the Arches, past a windsurfing club, a boating pond behind a low concrete wall, a paddling pool, then underneath the girdered mass of the Palace Pier – where seventeen years back he and

Sandy had had their first kiss, and on, starting to tire a little now, but determined to get to the cliffs of Black Rock before he turned round.

Then his mobile phone beeped with the message signal.

He stopped, pulled it from his zipped pocket and looked at the screen.

You can't tease a girl like this, Big Boy. Claudine XX

Jesus! Leave me alone. You spent the whole evening attacking me for being a cop, now you're driving me nuts. So far his only experience of internet dating wasn't working out too well. Were they all like Claudine? Aggressive, lonely women with a screw loose? Surely not, there had to be some normal women out there. Didn't there?

He pocketed the phone and ran on, knowing he owed her a reply, but wondering if it was better to just continue ignoring her. What could he say? *Sod off and stop bothering me? It was nice meeting you but I've decided I'm gay?*

Eventually he decided he would send her a text when he got back. He would take the coward's route: *Sorry, I've decided I'm not ready for a relationship.*

His relaxing mind turned to work, to the paper mountain that seemed to be forever building and building. The Nigerian trafficking of young women; the trial of Suresh Hossain; the cold case of little Thomas Lytle; and now the disappearance of Michael Harrison.

This really bugged him. And one thought in particular had woken him during the night and stayed with him. He reached the under-cliff walk, ran along below the white chalk bluffs, high above the Marina with its rows of pontoons and forest of masts, its hotels and shops and restaurants, and on for two more miles.

Then he turned, feeling the burn in his lungs, his legs high from the exertion, and ran back until he reached the point where he was near the Van Alen building. He ran up the ramp onto the promenade, waited for a gap in the busy traffic of Marine Parade and crossed over. He made his way down the narrow street along the side of the building, and stopped by the entrance to the underground car park.

His luck was in. Within moments, the gates swung open and a dark blue Porsche Boxster drove out, a predatory-looking blonde in dark glasses – despite the dull, wet day – at the wheel. He slipped in before the gates closed. It was good to be out of the rain.

He breathed in the dry, engine-oil-laced air as he ran down the hard concrete, past a red Ferrari he remembered from before, and several other cars he recalled, and then stopped in front of the gleaming, mint-clean BMW X5 off-roader.

He stared at the number plate. W796 LDY. Then he looked around, scanning the area. It was deserted. He walked up closer, knelt beside the front nearside wheel, then lay down on his back, wormed himself under the sill and peered up at the inside of the wheel arch. It was covered in mud.

He pulled his handkerchief out of his pocket, opened it out in the palm of his left hand, then with his right hand scraped at the dry mud until several pieces of it fell into his handkerchief.

Carefully he closed it, knotted it and replaced it in his pocket. Then he hauled himself back up, walked to the garage entrance and waved his hand across the infra-red beam. Moments later, with a loud clank and a busy whirr, the doors opened for him.

He walked out, checked the street in both directions, then resumed his homeward run.

43

At 9.30, showered and after a relaxed breakfast of scrambled eggs and grilled organic tomatoes – organic was a current fad he was going through at home, to counteract all the junk food he often had to eat when working, along with drinking quantities of mineral water – he enjoyed a leisurely read of the *Daily Mail*, followed by a drool over a road test of the latest Aston Martin in *Autocar*. Then Grace went into the study he had created in a small back room of the house overlooking his tiny, increasingly overgrown garden, and the almost embarrassingly neat gardens of his neighbours on either side, sat down at his desk in front of his computer screen and rang Glenn Branson's home phone number. His handkerchief, containing the soil he had scraped from Mark Warren's car, lay on the desk inside a small plastic bag.

Ari, Branson's wife, answered. Although he had clicked with Glenn from the day he had met him, Grace found Ari quite hard to get on with. She was often brittle with him, almost as if she suspected that, because he was single, he might be trying to lead her husband astray.

Over the years Grace had worked hard to charm her, always remembering their kids' birthdays with cards and generous presents, and taking her flowers on the few occasions he had been invited round for a meal. There were moments when he thought he was making progress with her, but this morning was not one of them. She sounded less than pleased to hear him. 'Hi, Roy', she said curtly, 'you want to speak to Glenn?'

No, actually, I want to speak to the Man in the Moon, he nearly said, but didn't. Instead, a tad lamely, he asked, 'Is he around?'

'We're in rather a hurry,' she said. In the background he heard the sound of a kid screaming. Then Ari shouting, 'Sammy! Give it to her, you've had your turn, now give it to your sister!' Then the screaming got louder. Finally Branson came on the line.

'Yo, ole wise man, you're up early.'

'Very funny. What was it you said you were doing today?'

'Ari's sister's thirtieth birthday party – in Solihull. Seems I have the choice – find Michael Harrison or save my marriage. What would you do?'

'Save your marriage. Be grateful for your sad-old-git friends who have no life and can spend their weekends doing your work for you.'

'I'm grateful. What are you doing?'

'I'm going to a wedding.'

'You're such a sentimentalist. 'Top hat? Tails? All cleaned and pressed?'

'Anyone ever tell you what a bitch you are?'

'The wife I nearly don't have any more.'

Grace felt a twinge of pain. He knew that Glenn did not mean any malice, but the words stung. Every night, even if it was late, and even if it meant hassle, Glenn at least went home to loving kids and to a beautiful warm woman in his bed. People who had that were incapable of understanding what it meant to live alone.

Solitude.

Solitude could be crap.

Was crap.

Grace was tiring of it – but did not know what to do about it. What if he found someone? Fell in love with a woman, big time? And then Sandy turned up? What then?

He knew in his mind she wasn't ever going to turn up, but there was a part of his heart that refused to go there, as if it was stuck like some old-fashioned record needle, in an eternal groove. Once or twice every year, when he was low, he would go to a medium, trying to make contact with her, or at least trying to prise out some clue about what might have happened to her. But Sandy remained elusive, a photographic negative that lay for ever black and featureless in the hypo fluid of the developing tray.

He wished Branson a good weekend, envying him his life, his demanding wife, his gorgeous kids, his damned normality. He washed up his breakfast things, staring out of his kitchen window at Noreen Grinstead across the street, in a brown polyester trouser suit, apron and yellow rubber gloves, a plastic hat over her head to shield her from the rain, busily soaping her silver Nissan on the driveway. A black and white cat darted across the road. On the radio the presenter, on *Home Truths*, was interviewing a woman whose parents had not spoken one word to each other throughout her childhood.

Nineteen years in the police had taught him never to underestimate the weirdness of the human species. Yet barely a day went by when it didn't seem to be getting even weirder.

He went back into the study, dialled Brighton police station and asked if any of the Crime Scene Investigators were in. Moments later he was put through to Joe Tindall, a man he rated highly.

Tindall was meticulous, hard-working and endlessly

resourceful. A short, thin, bespectacled, man, with thinning wiry hair, he could have been a mad professor drawn straight from Central Casting. Before joining the police, Tindall had worked for several years for the British Museum as a forensic archaeologist. Joe was the man he was working with on the Tommy Lytle cold case.

'Hey, Joe!' Grace said. 'No weekend off?'

'Ha! I'm having to do the ballistics testing on the jewellery shop raid – everyone else has buggered off. And I've got the stabbing on Wednesday to deal with, thank you very much.'

Grace remembered there had been a man stabbed to death in Brighton late on Wednesday night. No one knew yet whether it was a mugging or a tiff between two gay lovers.

'Joe, I need some help. I have a sample of soil I've taken from a suspect vehicle. How can I find out, very quickly, what part of Sussex this soil is from? How specific could anyone get for me?'

'How specific do you need?'

'Within a few square feet.'

'Very funny, Roy.'

'I'm not smiling.'

'Do you have a sample from the suspect area? I could get tests run and see if they match. We have chalk, clay, gravel and sand in Sussex.'

'The suspect area is Ashdown Forest.'

'The soil there is predominantly sand and clay. We can get matches from pollen, fossils, seeds, animal droppings, grasses, water, all kinds of stuff. How specific can you get?'

'Within a few square miles.'

'You'd have to do a lot better than that. There are areas all over England that would match Ashdown Forest.'

'How long would it take you to get a match without a sample from the specific area?'

'We're talking weeks – and I'd need a huge team – and one hell of a budget.'

'But you could do it?'

'Given unlimited resources and enough time, I could give you a match in a small area.'

'How small?'

'That would depend. A few hundred square feet, perhaps.'

'OK, thanks. I have something I want to bring over to you – are you in the office for a while?'

'All day, Roy.'

44

An hour later, dressed in a blue suit, white shirt and a bright tie, Grace drove onto the sprawling, hilly Hollingbury industrial estate on the outskirts of Brighton, past an ASDA store, an ugly 1950s low-rise, and then slowed as he reached the long, low Art Deco Sussex House, headquarters of Sussex CID.

Originally built as a factory, it had been bought by the police a few years back and transformed. If it wasn't for the dominant police insignia on the facade, a passer-by could have mistaken it for a swanky, hip hotel. Painted gleaming white against red brickwork, with a long grass bank running its full length, it wasn't until you passed the security guard and drove through the high, railed gates into the rear car park, filled with police vehicles, skips and with a formidable cell block beyond, that it became less glamorous.

Grace parked underneath the building between a police off-roader and a police van, walked up to the rear entrance, held his ID card against the electronic panel to open the door and entered the building. He flashed his card at the security officer behind the front desk and made his way up the plushly carpeted stairs, past ancient truncheons in patterns mounted on blue boards and two more large blue boards halfway up the stairs on which were pinned photographs of some of the key police personnel working in this section of the building.

He knew all the faces. Ian Steel and Verity Smart, of

the Specialist Investigations Branch, David Davison of the Crime Policy and Review Branch, Will Graham and Christopher Derricott in the Scientific Support Branch, James Simpson in the Operations and Intelligence Branch, Terrina Clifton-Moore of the Family Liaison Unit, and a couple of dozen more.

Then he walked through a wide open-plan area filled with desks, few of them attended today, and offices on either side labelled with their occupants' names and the Sussex Police badge.

He passed the large office of Detective Chief Superintendent Gary Weston, who was the Head of Sussex CID. Reaching another door, he held his card up against the security panel and entered a long, cream-painted corridor lined with red noticeboards on either side, to which were pinned serious crime detection procedures. One was labelled 'Diagram – Common Possible Motives', another, 'Murder Investigation Model', another, 'Crime Scene Assessment'.

The place had a modern, cutting-edge feel, which he liked. He had spent much of his career in old, inefficient buildings that were like rabbit warrens; it was refreshing to feel that his beloved Police Force, to which he had dedicated his life, was truly embracing the twenty-first century. Although it was marred with one flaw that everyone here moaned about – there was no canteen.

He walked further along, past door after door flagged with abbreviations. The first was the Major Incident Suite, which housed the incident room for serious crimes. It was followed by the Disclosure Officers Room, the CCTV Viewing Room, the Intelligence Office Room, the Outside Enquiry Team Office, and then the stench hit him, slowly at first, but more powerful with every step.

The dense, cloying, stomach-churning reek of human putrefaction, which had become too familiar to him over the years. Much too familiar. There was no other stench like it; it enveloped you like an invisible fog, seeping into the pores of your skin, deep into your nostrils and your lungs and your stomach, and the fibres of your hair and clothes, so that you carried it away with you and continued on smelling it for hours.

As he pushed open the door of the small, pristine Scene of Crimes Office, he saw the cause: the Crime Scene Investigators' photographic studio was in action. A Hawaiian shirt, torn and heavily bloodstained, lay under the glare of bright lights, on a table, on a sheet of brown background paper. Nearby, in plastic bags, he could see trousers and a pair of camel loafers.

Peering further into the room, Grace saw a man, dressed in white overalls, who he did not recognize for a moment, staring intently into the lens of a Hasselblad mounted on a tripod. Then he realized Joe Tindall had had a makeover since he'd last seen him a few months back. The mad-professor hairstyle and large tortoiseshell glasses had gone. He now had a completely shaven head, a narrow strip of hair running from the centre of his lower lip down to the centre of his chin and hip rectangular glasses with blue-tinged lenses. He looked more like a media trendy than a scientific boffin.

'New woman in your life?' Grace asked, by way of a greeting.

Tindall looked up at him in surprise. 'Roy, good to see you! Yes, as a matter of fact – who told you that?'

Grace grinned, looking at him more closely, almost expecting to spot an earring as well. 'Young, is she?'

'Actually – yes – how do you know?'

Grace grinned again, staring at his newly shaven pate, his trendy glasses. 'Keeping you young, isn't she?'

Then Tindall understood and grinned sheepishly. 'She's going to kill me, Roy. Three times a night every night.'

'You *try* three times a night or succeed?'

'Oh, fuck off!' He stared Grace up and down. 'You're looking sharp, for a Saturday. Hot date yourself?'

'A wedding, actually.'

'Congratulations – who's the lucky girl?'

'I have a feeling she's not that lucky,' Grace retorted, placing a small plastic bag containing the earth he had retrieved from Mark Warren's BMW down on the table, next to the shirt. 'I need you to pull out some stops.'

'You always need me to pull out some stops. Everyone does.'

'Not true, Joe. I gave you the Tommy Lytle material and told you there was all the time you need. This is different. I have a missing person – how fast you get this analysed might determine whether he lives or dies.'

Joe Tindall held the bag up and peered at it. He shook it gently, peering at it all the time. 'Quite sandy,' he said.

'What does that tell you?'

'You mentioned Ashdown Forest on the phone?'

'Uh huh.'

'This might be the kind of soil you'd find there.'

'*Might?*'

'The UK is knee-deep in sandy soil, Roy. There's sandy soil in Ashdown Forest – but there's sandy soil in a million other places, too.'

'I need an area that's about seven foot long and three foot wide.'

'Sounds like a grave.'

'It is a grave.'

Joe Tindall nodded, peering closely at the earth again. 'You want me to locate a grave in the middle of Ashdown Forest from this little bag of earth?'

'You're catching on.'

The SOCO officer removed his glasses for some moments, as if that would give him clarity of vision, then put them on again. 'Here's the deal, Roy. You locate the grave and I'll get you an analysis on whether this soil matches or doesn't.'

'Actually, I need it to be the other way around.'

Tindall held up the plastic bag. 'I see. Who do you think I am? David Blaine? Derren Brown? I swing this in the air and somehow magic up a grave in the middle of a ten-thousand-hectare forest?'

'You have a problem with that?'

'Actually, yes, I do have a problem with that.'

45

A few hours later, Grace cruised slowly up a steep hill past All Saints' church in Patcham Village, where a certain wedding had been scheduled to happen at two o'clock this afternoon – in exactly three-quarters of an hour.

This was his own personal favourite church in the area. A classic Early English parish church, intimate, simple, with unadorned grey stonework, a small tower, a fine stained-glass window behind the altar and tombstones going back centuries in the overgrown graveyard out the front and along the sides.

The heavy rain had eased to a light drizzle as he sat in his Alfa, parked close to the entrance, on a grass bank opposite the church, giving him a commanding view of all the arrivals. No sign of anyone yet. Just a few pieces of sodden confetti on the wet tarmac, from an earlier wedding, probably this morning.

He watched an elderly woman in a hooded PVC raincoat wheel a shopping basket down the pavement and pause to exchange a few words with a huge man in an anorak with a tiny dog on a leash, who was walking up in the opposite direction. The dog cocked its leg on a lamppost.

A blue Ford Focus pulled up and a man with a couple of cameras slung around his neck climbed out. Grace observed him, wondering whether he was the official wedding photographer, or press. Moments later a small brown Vauxhall pulled up behind it, and a young man in an anorak emerged, carrying a distinctive reporter's notebook. The two men greeted each other and began chatting, both looking around, waiting.

After ten minutes he saw a silver BMW off-roader pull up. Because of its tinted glass windows and the rain, he could not make out who was inside, but he recognized immediately Mark Warren's number plate. Moments later, Warren, in a dark raincoat, jumped down and hurried up the path to the main entrance of the church. He disappeared inside, then came out almost immediately and hurried back to his car.

A taxi pulled up, and a tall, distinguished-looking man with silver hair, dressed in a morning suit with a red carnation in the buttonhole, and holding a grey top hat, closed the rear door and walked towards the church. The taxi had evidently been paid to wait. Then a silver Audi TT sports car pulled up. Grace remembered seeing one like it parked in front of Ashley Harper's house.

The driver's door opened, and Ashley, holding a small umbrella, emerged, in a smart white, wedding dress, her hair up. An older woman appeared from the passenger door, in a white-trimmed blue dress and neatly coiffed silver-grey hair. Ashley waved acknowledgement to the BMW, then huddled under the umbrella. The pair hurried up the path and disappeared into the church. Mark Warren followed.

Then, at five to two, Grace saw the vicar cut across the graveyard and enter, and decided it was time to make his move. He left his car, tugging on his Tommy Hilfiger blue and yellow anorak. As he crossed the road the young man with the notebook approached him. He was in his mid-twenties, sharp-faced, wearing a cheap grey suit with his tie knotted massively but slackly, so the top button of his white shirt showed above it, and chewing gum.

'Detective Superintendent Grace, isn't it?'

Grace eyeballed him, used to being recognized by the press, but wary all the same. 'And you are?'

'Kevin Spinella, the *Argus.* Just wondering if you have any update on Michael Harrison for us?'

'Nothing yet, I'm afraid. We'll be waiting to see if he turns up to his wedding.'

The reporter glanced at his watch. 'Cutting it a bit fine, isn't he?'

'It wouldn't be the first time a groom has been late.' Grace smiled and eased past Spinella.

Hurrying after him, the reporter asked, 'Do you think Michael Harrison is alive or dead, Detective Superintendent?'

Stopping for one moment, Grace said, 'We're regarding this as a missing persons enquiry.'

'For the moment?'

'I don't have any further comment, thank you.' Grace pushed open the heavy door, stepped into the gloom of the porch and closed the door behind him.

Whenever he entered a church, Grace always felt a sense of conflict. Should he unhook a kneeler, get down on the floor and pray, the way most people did? The way he did as a kid alongside his mother and father, most Sunday mornings of his childhood. Or should he just sit down on a pew, letting the God he was no longer sure he believed in know his anger? For a long time after Sandy's disappearance he had gone to church and had prayed for her return. Sometimes he had attended services, but mostly he had gone into an empty church. Sandy had never been a believer, and during the past few years, with his prayers unanswered, he had increasingly become an agnostic. It no longer felt right, praying.

Give me Sandy back, then I'll pray my heart out to you. But not until then, Mr God, OK?

He walked past a row of dripping umbrellas, a criss-crossed noticeboard and a stack of service sheets with *Michael John Harrison and Ashley Lauren Harper* printed on the front, then into the church itself, instantly breathing in the familiar smells of dry, old wood, old cloth, dust and a hint of burning wax. The place was beautifully bedecked with flowers, but there was no hint of their perfume.

About a dozen people stood in the aisle and nave, all of them silent, expectant, as if they were extras on a film set waiting for the director's command to move.

Grace took in the group rapidly, nodding at Ashley, who was sheet-white and clutching the arm of the tall man in the black morning coat, presumably her father. Next to her stood the woman he had seen emerging from the car with Ashley, a handsome woman in her fifties but with the strained look of someone who has been through a sustained rough time. Mark Warren, in a navy suit, sporting a white carnation, stood beside a good-looking young couple in their early thirties.

He realized everyone was looking at him. In a faltering voice Ashley broke the ice by thanking him for coming and introduced him first to Michael's mother, who seemed distraught, and then to the handsome, distinguished-looking man he had thought was her father, but turned out to be her uncle. He gave Grace a warm handshake, introducing himself as Bradley Cunningham, staring Grace straight back in the eye and saying, 'Good to meet you, Detective Superintendent.'

Picking up on his North American accent, Grace asked, 'Whereabouts in the States are you from?'

The man frowned as if insulted. 'Actually, I'm Canadian, from Ontario.'

'I apologize.'

'No problem, it's a common mistake you Limeys make.'

'I guess you might have problems differentiating regional accents across Britain,' Grace said.

'Actually, you are right.'

Grace smiled, eyeing his morning coat approvingly. 'It's good to see someone properly dressed for a wedding.'

'Actually the pants are killing me,' Cunningham confessed. 'Rented this lot from your wonderful Moss Bros, but I think I got given the wrong pants!' Then his face became grave. 'Still, this is a terrible thing, isn't it?'

'Yes,' Grace said, distracted suddenly. 'Terrible.'

Ashley interrupted them, introducing Grace to the vicar, the Reverend Somping, a short, bearded man in white robes and a dog collar, with rheumy, bloodshot eyes, who looked distinctly angry.

'I told Miss Harper we should have cancelled this completely,' the Reverend Somping said. 'It is ridiculous to put someone through this agony – and what about the guests? This is such a nonsense.'

'He *will* turn up,' Ashley blubbed. 'He will, I know he will.' She looked imploringly at Grace. 'Please tell him that Michael is on his way.'

Grace stared at the bride, so sad and vulnerable-looking, and almost had to restrain himself from reaching out his arms and hugging her. She looked so forlorn, so desperate. He felt like punching the arrogant vicar in the face.

'Michael Harrison might yet turn up,' he said.

'He's going to have to turn up pretty smartly,' the vicar said, coldly. 'I have another wedding here at four.'

'I thought this was a church,' Grace said, angry at his insensitivity to Ashley. 'Not a supermarket.'

The Reverend Somping attempted, without success, to glare Grace out. Then he said, defensively, 'I work for the Lord. He gives me his timetable.'

After a few moments Grace snapped back, 'In that case I suggest you ask your boss to produce the groom, pronto.'

46

At twenty past two, quite unnecessarily considering the small number of people present, the Reverend Somping climbed up the steps into the pulpit with all the labour of a man scaling Everest the hard way. He placed his palms on the wooden rails, leaned forward with an expression leaden with gravitas and announced:

'I have been asked by the bride, Miss Ashley Harper, and by the mother of the groom, Mrs Gillian Harrison, to inform you that this wedding is delayed, indefinitely, pending the presence of Michael Harrison. What should be a joyous occasion, the union of two young, loving people, in the eyes of our Lord, has been curtailed by the absence of Michael. None of us knows what has happened to him, but our thoughts and prayers are with him, his family and with his bride-to-be.'

He paused, staring challengingly at the group of people, before continuing. 'Miss Harper and Mrs Harrison have generously suggested that even though no wedding has taken place, you should at least enjoy the refreshments which have been laid on for the reception, in the Queen Mary Room of the Brighton Pavilion. They would appreciate it if you would join them there after we have said a prayer for Michael's well-being.'

He launched into a brief, hurried prayer. Then someone opened the church doors.

Grace watched the people filing out in silence. It had all the atmosphere of a funeral. Sometime in the next week several of the guests here would be attending four funerals. And he hoped that the no-show by Michael Harrison didn't mean it could be five. But it was not a good sign, it was a very bad sign indeed. Any prospect that Michael Harrison was playing a prank could now be discounted.

And there was something else bothering him.

*

An hour later at the reception, in the Queen Mary Room at the Royal Pavilion, with fine oil paintings in gilded frames hung on its pink walls, there was none of the cheery buzz of a party, but instead a number of stilted conversations punctuated the silence. Only a few of the twenty tables, beautifully laid for 200 guests, and decorated with orchids, were being used. Two chefs in white coats and toques manned the laden buffet tables with an army of waiters and waitresses, and the tiered wedding cake sat in a space of its own, an almost unwelcome reminder of the reason everyone was here. All the same, several people seemed to be tucking into platefuls of food and swigging down the champagne and wines.

Grace, who had been invited by Ashley, had been delayed talking on his phone to DC Nicholl and DS Moy about increasing the team. There was a rookie female detective constable Bella rated highly and who was free, called Emma-Jane Boutwood. Grace backed Bella's judgement by suggesting Emma-Jane be brought into the team immediately.

Now at the reception, he watched Ashley and Mark Warren keenly. Despite her eyes being tear-stained and streaked with mascara, she was putting on a brave face, seated at a table, with a young man on one side and a woman the other that Grace did not recognize from the church. It seemed several more people had turned up here, told by Ashley that the reception was still on for anyone who would like to come.

'He'll turn up,' Grace heard her saying. 'There's a reason behind this.' Then she continued, 'This is just so bizarre – isn't your wedding day meant to be the happiest day of your life?' before breaking down in a flood of tears.

On another table, Grace singled out Michael's mother and Ashley's uncle seated next to each other. He watched Bradley Cunningham for some moments, thoughtfully. Then he was interrupted by Mark Warren, sporting a white carnation in his buttonhole, holding an empty champagne flute, his voice slurred. He pushed his face close up against Grace's.

'Detective Sergeant Grace?' he quizzed.

'Detective *Superintendent*,' Grace corrected him.

'S-shorry – didn't realize you'd been promoted.'

'I haven't, Mr Warren.'

Mark stood back a moment, then squared up to him, eyeballing him as levelly as he could, except the alcohol was making him squint. His presence was clearly making Ashley uncomfortable – Grace saw her look up from her table.

'Can't sh'you leave thish young lady alone? Do you have any idea what she is going through?'

'That's why I'm here,' Grace said calmly.

'You should be out, trying to find Michael, not hanging around, freeloading here.'

'Mark!' Ashley cautioned.

'Fuck it,' Mark said, brushing her aside, and eyeballing Grace again. 'What the fuck are you doing about this situation?'

Angered by his attitude, but remaining calm, Grace said, 'My team are doing everything they can.'

'Doesn't much look like it to me. Should you be drinking on duty?'

'It's mineral water.'

Mark squinted at Grace's glass.

Standing up and joining them, Ashley said, 'Why don't you circulate, Mark?'

Grace clocked the edge in her voice. Something very definitely did not feel right but he couldn't place quite what.

Then Mark Warren jabbed him in the chest. 'You know your problem? You don't give a fuck, do you?'

'Why do you think that?'

Mark Warren gave him an asinine grin, raising his voice. 'Come on. You don't like rich people, do you? We can go fuck ourselves, can't we? You're too busy looking at speed cameras, trapping motorists. Why should you give a fuck about some poor rich sod who's the victim of some prank that's gone wrong, hey? When you could be out earning a fat bonus from trapping motorists?'

Grace deliberately lowered his voice, almost to a whisper, which he knew would force Mark Warren to lower his voice, also. 'Mr Warren, I don't have any connection with the Traffic Division. I'm here to try to help you.'

Mark leaned closer, straining to hear him. 'Sorry, I missed that. What did you say?'

Still speaking deliberately quietly, Grace said, 'When I was at Police Training College we had to do a parade and be inspected. I'd buffed my belt buckles to a shine like a mirror. The Chief made me take the belt off and held up the back for everyone to see. I hadn't polished that at all and I felt ashamed. It taught me a lesson – it's not just what you can see that matters.' He gave Mark a quizzical look.

'What exshacktly ish that meant to mean?'

'I'll leave you to think about that, Mr Warren – next time you have your BMW washed.'

Grace turned and walked away.

47

Back in his car, with the rain pattering down on the windscreen, Grace was deep in thought. So deep, it was several moments before he even noticed the parking ticket tucked under the wiper.

Bastards.

He climbed out of the car, grabbed the ticket and tore it from its cellophane wrapping. Thirty-quid fine for being five minutes over the time on his voucher – and no chance of putting it through expenses. The Chief had clamped down firmly on that.

Hope you appreciate this, Mr Branson, having your nice weekend break in Solihull. He grimaced, tossing the ticket into the passenger footwell in disgust. Then he turned his mind back to Mark Warren. Then back five years to the fortnight's course in forensic psychology he had done at the FBI training centre in Quantico in the USA. It had not been enough to make him an expert, but it had taught him the value of his instincts, and it had taught him how to read certain aspects of body language.

And Mark Warren's body language was all wrong.

Mark Warren had lost four close friends. His business partner was missing, maybe dead. Very likely dead. He ought to be in shock, numb, bewildered. Not angry. It was too soon for anger.

And he had noticed the reaction to his remark about the car wash. He had touched a nerve there very definitely.

I don't know what you are up to, Mr Mark Warren, but I'm making it my business to find out.

He picked up his phone, dialled a number, listened to it ringing. On a Saturday afternoon he was expecting to get the answering machine, but instead he got a human voice. Female. Soft and warm. Impossible for anyone to guess from her voice what she did for a living.

'Brighton and Hove City Mortuary,' she said.

'Cleo, it's Roy Grace.'

'Wotcher, Roy, how you doing?' Cleo Morey's ordinarily quite posh voice was suddenly impish.

Involuntarily, Grace found himself flirting with her over the phone. 'Yes, OK. I'm impressed you're working on a Saturday afternoon.'

'The dead don't know what day of the week it is.' She hesitated. 'Don't 'spose the living care much, either. Most of them anyhow,' she added as an afterthought.

'*Most* of them?'

'Seems to me most living people don't really know what day of the week it is – they give the impression they do, but they don't really. Don't you think?'

'This is heavy philosophy for a wet Saturday afternoon,' Grace said.

'Well I'm doing my Open University degree in philosophy, so I've got to practise my arguments on someone – and I don't get much response from the lot in here.'

Grace grinned. 'So how are you?'

'OK.'

'You sound a bit – low.'

'Never felt better, Roy. I'm tired, that's all. Been here on my own all week – short-staffed – Doug's on holiday.'

'Those lads who were killed on Tuesday night – are they still in the mortuary?'

'They're here. And so is Josh Walker.'

'The one who died afterwards, in hospital?'

'Yes.'

'I need to come over, take a look at them. Would now be OK?'

'They're not going anywhere.'

Grace always enjoyed her dark humour. 'I'll be there in about ten minutes,' he said.

*

The Saturday-afternoon traffic was heavier than he had expected and it was nearly twenty minutes before he entered the busy gyratory system, then turned right, past a sign saying 'BRIGHTON & HOVE CITY MORTUARY' and through wrought iron gates attached to brick pillars. The gates were always open, twenty-four hours a day. Like a symbol, he reflected, that the dead didn't have much respect for business hours.

Grace knew this place far too well. It was a bland building with a horrible aura. A long, single-storey structure with grey pebbledash rendering on the walls and a covered drive-in on one side deep enough to take an ambulance or a large van. The mortuary was a transit stop on a one-way journey to a grave or a crematorium oven, for people who had died suddenly, violently or inexplicably – or from some fast-onset disease like viral meningitis, where a post-mortem might reveal medical insights that could one day help the living.

Yet a post-mortem was the ultimate degradation. A human being who had been walking, talking, reading, making love – or whatever – just a day or two before being cut open and disembowelled like a pig on a butcher's slab.

He didn't want to think about it, but he couldn't help

it; he'd seen too many post-mortems and knew what happened. The scalp would be peeled back, then the cap of the skull sawn off, the brain removed and sliced into segments. The chest wall would be cut open, all the internal organs taken out and sliced and weighed and some bits sent off for pathological analysis, the rest crammed into a white plastic bag and stitched back inside the cadaver like giblets.

He parked behind a small blue MG sports car, which he presumed was Cleo's, and hurried through the rain over to the front entrance and rang the bell. The blue front door with its frosted glass panel could have come straight from a suburban bungalow.

Moments later, Cleo Morey opened it, smiling warmly. No matter how many times he saw her, he could never quite get used to the incongruity of this immensely attractive young woman, in her late twenties, with long blonde hair, dressed in a green surgical gown, with a heavy-duty green apron over the top and white wellington boots. With her looks she could have been a model, or an actress, and with her brains she could have probably had any career she set her mind to – and she chose this. Booking in cadavers, preparing them for post-mortems, cleaning up afterwards – and trying to offer crumbs of comfort to the families of the bereaved, invariably in shock, who came to identify the bodies. And for much of the time she worked alone here.

The smell hit Roy immediately, the way it always did, that sickly sweet reek of disinfectant that permeated the whole place and made something squirm in his guts.

They took a left off the narrow entrance hall into the undertaker's office, which doubled as reception. It was a small room with a blower heater on the floor, pink Artexed walls, a pink carpet, an L-shaped row of visitor chairs, and a small metal desk on which sat three telephones, a stack of small brown envelopes printed with the words 'PERSONAL EFFECTS', and a large green and red ledger bearing the legend 'MORTUARY REGISTER' in gold block lettering.

There was a light box on one wall, as well as a row of framed 'PUBLIC HEALTH AND HYGIENE' certificates, and a larger one from the 'BRITISH INSTITUTE OF EMBALMERS', with Cleo Morey's name inscribed beneath. On another wall was a closed-circuit television camera, which showed, in a continual jerky sequence, views of the front, back, then each side of the building, then a close-up on the entrance.

'Cup of tea, Roy?'

Her clear bright blue eyes engaged with his for just a fraction longer than was necessary for the question. Smiling eyes. Incredibly warm eyes.

'I'd love a cup of tea.'

'English breakfast, Earl Grey, Darjeeling, China, camomile, peppermint, green leaf?'

'I thought this was the mortuary, not Starbucks,' he said.

She grinned. 'We also have coffee. 'Espresso, latte, Colombian, mocha—'

He raised a hand. 'Builder's tea, perfect.'

'Full fat milk, semi-skimmed, with lemon—'

He raised both his hands. 'Whatever milk you have open. Joe not here yet?'

He had asked Joe Tindall, from SOCO, to attend.

'Not yet, do you want to wait until he gets here?'

'Yes, we should.'

She flicked a switch on the kettle and disappeared into the locker room opposite. As the kettle began burbling, she returned with a green gown, blue overshoes, a face mask and white latex gloves, which she handed to him.

While he pulled them on, she made his tea for him and opened a tin containing digestive biscuits. He took one and munched it. 'So you've been here on your own all week? Doesn't it get you down? No conversation?'

'I'm always busy – we've had ten admissions this week. Eastbourne was going to send over someone from their mortuary, but they got too busy as well. Must be something about the last week in May.'

Grace pulled the band of the mask over his head, then let the mask hang loose below his chin; the young men had not been dead long enough to smell too bad, in his experience. 'You've had the families of all the four young men up?'

She nodded. 'And has the guy who was missing, the groom, turned up yet?'

'I've just come from the wedding,' Grace said.

'I thought you were looking a bit smart for a Saturday, Roy.' She grinned. 'So at least that's resolved itself?'

'No,' he replied. 'That's why I'm here.'

She raised her eyebrows but didn't comment. 'Anything in particular you want to see? I can get you copies of the pathologist's reports to the Coroner's office.'

'What I want to start with when Joe gets here,' he replied, 'are their fingernails.'

48

Followed by Joe Tindall, who was tugging on his gloves, Grace followed Cleo along the hard, speckled floor, watching her streaked blonde hair swinging against the neck of her green gown, past the glass window of the sealed infection chamber, into the main post-mortem room.

It was dominated by two steel tables, one fixed, one wheeled, a blue hydraulic hoist and a row of fridges with floor-to-ceiling doors. The walls were tiled in grey and the whole room was surrounded by a drain gulley. Along one wall was a row of sinks and a coiled yellow hose. Along another was a wide work surface, a metal cutting board and a glass-fronted cabinet filled with instruments and some packs of Duracell batteries. Next to the cabinet was a chart itemizing the name of each deceased, with columns for the weights of their brain, lungs, heart, liver, kidneys and spleen. A man's name, Adrian Penny, with his grim recordings was written in blue chinagraph pen.

Seeing what Grace was looking at, she said cheerfully, 'A motorcyclist we did a PM on yesterday. Overtook a lorry and didn't notice a steel girder sticking out the side – sliced the poor sod's head clean off at the neck.

'How the hell do you remain sane?' he asked.

Grinning, she replied, 'Who said I'm sane?'

'I don't know how you do your job.'

'It's not the dead who harm people, Roy, it's the living.'

'Good point,' he said. He wondered what her views were about ghosts. But this was not the time to ask.

The room felt cold. There was a hum from the refrigeration system, and a sharp clicking sound from overhead, from one fluorescent light that hadn't come on properly. 'Any preference who you want to see first?'

'No, I'd like to see all of them.'

Cleo marched up to the door marked '4' and pulled it open. As she did so there was a blast of icy air, but it wasn't the cold that instantly sent a chill through Grace. It was the sight of the human form beneath the white plastic sheets on each of the four tiers of metal trays on rollers.

The mortician wheeled the hoist up close, cranked it up, then pulled the top tray out onto it and closed the fridge door. Then she pulled back the sheet to reveal a fleshy white male, with lank hair, his body and waxy white face covered in bruises and lacerations, his eyes wide open, conveying shock even in their glassy stillness, his penis shrivelled and limp lying in a thick clump of pubic hairs like some hibernating rodent. Grace looked at the buff tag tied around his big toe. The name read 'Robert Houlihan'.

Grace's eyes went straight to the young man's hands. They were big, coarse hands, with very grimy nails. 'You have all their clothes here?'

'Yes.'

'Good.' Grace asked Tindall to take scrapings from the nails.

The SOCO officer selected a sharp tool from the instrument rack, asked Cleo for a specimen bag, then carefully scraped part of the dirt from each of the nails into the bag, labelled and sealed it.

The hands of the next body, Luke Gearing, were badly mangled from the accident, but apart from blood under them, the nails, bitten to the quick, were reasonably clean. There was no grime on Josh Walker's hands either. But

Peter Waring's were filthy. Tindall took scrapings from his nails, and bagged them.

Next he and Grace carefully examined all their clothes. There was mud on all their shoes, and plenty of traces of it on Robert Houlihan and Peter Waring's clothes. Tindall bagged all of these items separately.

'Are you going back to the lab now with these?' Grace asked him.

'I was planning to go home – be quite nice to see it before the weekend is over and have a life – or some pretence of one.'

'I hate to do this to you, Joe, but I really need you to start work on these now.'

'Great! You want me to cancel my U2 concert tickets for tonight, which I paid fifty fucking quid each for, stand my date up and haul my sleeping bag out of the office cupboard?'

'U2 – she really is young, isn't she?'

'Yes, and you know what, Roy, she has a short fuse. She's high maintenance.'

'There might be a man's life at stake here.'

His anger rising, Tindall said, 'I want the price of my tickets back from your budget.'

'It's not my case, Joe.'

'Oh – so whose is it?'

'Glenn Branson's.'

'And where the hell is he?'

'At a birthday party in Solihull.'

'It gets better all the time.'

By the row of lockers Tindall peeled off and binned his protective clothing and said, 'Have a nice sodding evening, Roy – go and ruin someone else's weekend next time.'

'I'll come over and keep you company.'

'Don't bother.'

Tindall slammed the door behind him. Moments later Grace heard the angry revving of a car engine. Then he noticed that, in his pique, the forensic expert had left behind the black bin liner containing his bags of evidence. He debated whether to run out after him, then decided to drive it over himself and try to calm the man down. He could understand his being hacked off – he would have been too, in the same circumstances.

He ducked into the sitting area, helped himself to another digestive biscuit and drained the remains of his tea, which had gone cold. Then he picked up the bin liner and Cleo walked him to the door. As he was about to step out into the rain he turned to her.

'What time are you finishing work today?'

'Another hour or so, with luck – assuming no one dies this afternoon.'

Grace stared at her, thinking she really did look incredibly lovely – and suddenly feeling a bag of nerves as he glanced at her hands and saw no rings. Of course she could have taken them off for work. 'I—' he said. 'I – just wondered – do you – you know – I mean – have any plans for this evening?'

Her eyes lit up. 'Actually I have a date to go to the cinema,' she said. Then added, as if for reassurance, 'With a friend – an old girlfriend who's going through a traumatic divorce.'

All his usual confidence deserting him, Grace said, 'I didn't know – whether you were married – or had a fellow – I—'

'Neither,' she said, giving him a long, friendly, expectant gaze.

'Would you – sometime – maybe – like to have a drink one night?'

Continuing to gaze at him, her lips slowly breaking into a broad smile, she said, 'I'd like that a lot.'

He walked on air across the tarmac to his car, oblivious to the pelting rain. Just as he pressed the remote to unlock the doors, Cleo called out to him. 'Roy! I think you forgot something!'

He turned and saw she was holding the black bin liner in her hand.

49

'You idiot,' Ashley said to Mark, who was slumped raggedly in the back of the limousine beside her. 'I can't believe your behaviour – why the hell did you have to be so aggressive to that cop?' She leaned forward and checked the glass partition to the chauffeur was firmly shut.

Mark put a hand on her ankle, and worked his way up her leg, beneath her wedding dress. She pushed him away sharply.

'Behave!' she said, sharply. 'For Christ's sake.'

'He'sh a jerk.'

'You're pissed out of your skull. What the hell did you think you were doing, having a go at him about speed cameras?'

Mark squinted at her. 'Putting him off the scent.'

Through the window she could see they were approaching the Van Alen building. It was half past five. 'How exactly is that *putting him off the scent*?'

'Wouldn't expect me to be rude if I had someshing to hide, would he?'

'So what exactly did he mean about having your BMW washed?'

'No idea.'

'You must have some idea – what did he mean?'

The intercom suddenly clicked and the driver's voice said, 'Front entrance?'

'Sh'fine,' Mark said. Then he turned to Ashley. 'Want to come up for a drink?'

'I don't know what I want. I could kill you.'

'What a charade thash wash.'

'It was a good charade – until you almost blew it.'

Mark spilled out of the car, almost falling on his face onto the pavement. It was only Ashley's steadying hand that saved him. Several people walking past stared, but she ignored them, her one goal to get Mark inside before he did anything else incriminating.

She dismissed the driver and helped Mark up to the front entrance, where he stared, bleary-eyed, at the door panel then managed to punch in his entry code accurately.

A few minutes later they were inside his apartment. Mark closed the door and slid the safety catch in place.

'I can't stay, Mark,' she said.

He began pawing at her clothes. She pushed his hands away. 'Let's have some coffee, and then I want you to tell me what the detective meant about having your car washed.'

Mark stared at her. She was wearing her white lace wedding dress, the veil pushed up. He lunged forward and kissed her on the mouth. She allowed him to kiss her on the lips and gave him a half-hearted kiss back, then pulled away. 'I mean it, I can't stay. I have to go round to Michael's mother and play the role of the grieving stood-up bride – or whatever fucking role I'm meant to be playing. God, what an afternoon. What a nightmare.'

Mark staggered over towards the open-plan kitchen, opened a cupboard and pulled out a jar of coffee. He stared at it with a puzzled expression, put it back in the cupboard, opened the fridge and removed a bottle of Cristal champagne.

'I think we should have a proper toast to your wedding day,' he said.

'That's not amusing – and you've had more than enough to drink.'

Holding the unopened bottle, Mark slumped onto a sofa, then patted the cushion beside him, by way of an invitation.

After some moments of haughty hesitation, Ashley sat at the far end of the sofa, as far from Mark as possible, tugged off her veil, then crossed her legs and kicked her shoes off. 'Mark, I want to know what Grace meant about your having the BMW washed.'

'I have no idea.'

She was silent.

'Do you love me?'

Shaking her head in despair she stood up. 'Yes, I love you. I have no idea why at this moment, but I do. And Michael's mother is waiting for me to turn up and blub my bloody eyes out, which is what I am about to go and do.'

'Have a drink first.'

'Christ, Mark.'

He pushed himself up from the sofa, staggered towards her and took her in his arms. Then he nuzzled her neck. 'You know – if the accident hadn't happened – the wedding would've gone ahead. You'd be Mrs Michael Harrison now.'

She nodded, melting a fraction.

He stared into her eyes. 'You'd have been on your way to the Savoy in London. You'd have made love to him tonight, wouldn't you?'

'That's what wives are meant to do on their wedding night.'

'And how would you have felt?'

Cupping his face in her hands, she said, 'I would have imagined it was you.'

'Would you have gone down on him? Sucked his dick?'

She pulled away from him. 'Mark!'

'Would you?'

'No way.'

'Come on!'

'We had an agreement, Mark.'

He took the bottle over to the sink, removed the foil then took two glasses from the cabinet. He popped the cork then filled the glasses and handed one to her.

She took it reluctantly and chinked glasses with him. 'We had it all planned,' she said to him.

'We had Plan A. Now we're into Plan B.' He drank a large gulp, draining half his glass. 'Wash wrong wish shat?'

'The first is that you are pissed. The second is that I now don't happen to be Mrs Michael Harrison. Which means I don't get to participate in his half of Double-M Properties.'

'His two-thirds, actually,' Mark said.

'So?'

'So I do, under our shareholders' agreement, and our key man insurance policy.'

'Provided he's dead.'

'Why do you say that? *Provided?*'

'You plugged the air hole properly, didn't you? You used superglue like I told you?'

Squirming, he said, 'Yesh.'

She was staring hard at him, seeing through him. 'Are you sure?'

'Yesh. That lid was screwed down. I pulled the tube out and I put a ton more earth down on top. If he was alive he'd have made contact, wouldn't he?'

She gave him a strange look.

'You want me to go and stick a fucking stake through his heart?'

She drank some champagne, then walked over to the

stereo and looked at the CD rack. 'How much do you love me?'

'How much? More than I could ever put into words.'

She pulled a CD out of its container, put it on the player and pressed the *play* button. Moments later, 'Love is All Around' filled the room. She put her glass down, took Mark's and put that down, then put her arms around him and began to lead him in a dance to the music. Pressing her lips against his ear she said, 'If you love me, you'll always tell me the truth, won't you?'

They danced for some moments, then he said, 'There'sh shomething that's been bothering me for the past few daysh.'

'Tell me?'

'You know that Michael and I both use Palms for picking up email when we're out of the office. We've been careful not to copy him in on any emails about his stag night – but I think I might have messed up.'

'What do you mean?'

'I think I copied him on one by mistake. And he has it with him.'

She pulled back from him, her eyes sharp as tacks. 'Are you saying he has it with him?'

'Possibly.'

'How *possibly*?'

'I can't find it anywhere in his office – or in his flat.'

'It's in the grave with him?'

'It might be.'

'*Might* be?'

Mark shrugged.

'You'd better make bloody sure, Mark.'

He stared at her in silence. 'I'm just telling you because—'

'Because?'

'Because it could be a risk.'

'You'd better get it back, hadn't you?'

'We're OK so long as no one finds him.'

Ashley sat down on a sofa and drank some of her champagne. 'I don't believe what I'm hearing. Why didn't you tell me this before?'

Mark shrugged. 'I thought – I—'

'You what?'

Mark joined her and attempted to clink glasses. Ashley withdrew hers, sharply.

'You'd better get it back,' she said. 'Pretty damned sharply. Like tonight. *Capisce?*'

50

As he drove back out towards the CID headquarters, Grace plugged his mobile into the hands-free and rang Glenn Branson. 'How's Solihull?' he asked.

'Pissing with rain. How's Brighton?'

'Pissing with rain.'

'And Ari's sister's gone to bed with a migraine.'

'So it's going to be a great birthday party.'

'I've collected plenty of brownie points for turning up, though. How was the wedding?'

'A bit like your birthday party's going to be. No show from the host.'

'No surprise there. Tell me – how many of Ashley Harper's relatives turned up?'

'Just one that I saw,' Grace said. 'An uncle.' He halted at a traffic light. 'I wanted to ask you, have you checked on Michael Harrison's bank account and credit cards?'

'Got a constant monitor on them. Nothing since Tuesday afternoon. Same with his mobile. Any developments your end?'

'The helicopter's been up again but seen nothing. Nicholl and Moy are working over the weekend – they're getting Michael's photograph circulated to the press, and they're collecting all the CCTV camera footage in the suspect area – I have a team starting work viewing it. We're going to have to make a decision about calling in specials and getting a full-blown search of the area. And I'm getting unhappier by the minute with his business partner, Mark Warren.'

'Tell me?'

'Nothing specific yet, but I think he knows something he isn't telling. We need to run some background checks on him.'

'I have the Holmes team doing that already.'

'Good boy. Hang on—' Grace concentrated for a moment as he pulled away from the lights. 'I think we should take a close look at their company, Double-M Properties. See what their insurance policies are.'

'I have that under way, too – and I'm having their Cayman Islands company checked out. What do you make of Ashley?'

'I don't know,' Grace said. 'I don't have a view. She's giving a convincing performance. I think we should check her out, too. You know what's odd about her?'

'This no relatives thing? You ever see that movie *The Last Seduction,* with Linda Fiorentino?' The phone signal weakened suddenly and Branson's voice became crackly.

'I don't remember it.'

'Bill Pullman was in it, too.'

'Doesn't ring a bell.'

'She was in *Men in Black* too.'

'OK.'

'Worth seeing – *The Last Seduction.* Had a predatory woman. Dark ending. She kind of reminds me of Ashley.'

'I'll check it out.'

'Get it on DVD. Play.com – great value.'

'How many twenty-seven-year-olds do you know that don't have relatives? You're twenty-seven, you are getting married, the biggest day of your life, and you can only produce one relative to turn up to your big day.'

'She could be an orphan. We need to check her background out.'

'I'll go and talk to Michael's mother – she must know about her future daughter-in-law.'

'Mine knew more about Ari than I did before I got hitched.'

'Precisely,' Grace said.

*

Ten minutes later Grace was walking along the corridor of the Major Incident Suite of the CID headquarters, lugging the black plastic bag from the mortuary. He stopped by a white sheet pinned to a red board which was headed 'DIAGRAM – COMMON POSSIBLE MOTIVES'. It was helpful, sometimes, to refresh his mind from these charts, although most of it was ingrained in his brain. He read the chart:

> Sexual. Jealousy. Racism. Anger/fright. Robbery.
> Power control. Maintain active lifestyle. Gain.
> Payment. Homophobia. Hate. Revenge. Psychotic.

He moved on to the next board, which was headed, 'FAST TRACK'. Below was printed:

1. Identify suspects
2. Intelligence opportunities
3. Scene forensics
4. Crime scene enquiries
5. Witness search
6. Victim enquiries
7. Possible motives
8. Media
9. Post-mortems
10. Significant witness interview
11. Other critical actions

Media, he thought. This was a good story for the media. He would phone his contacts, start getting the story out. Maybe that would get the ball rolling. He walked on and entered the small, pristine SOCO Suite. He would phone the *Argus* reporter Kevin Spinella for starters, he decided.

Joe Tindall was ready for him in the first of the two rooms, known as the *wet room.* There was a cluster of brown paper sacks on the floor, each labelled, in black print 'Evidence Bag', a roll of brown paper on a worktop, a sink and a tall air box.

'Thanks,' Joe Tindall said, as he handed him the bag, his tone a lot less friendly than when they had met earlier, but at least he was calmer.

The SOCO officer opened the black bin liner and pulled out the individual bags of soil, then the bags of clothes. Most of the clothes were heavily bloodstained. The stench of putrefaction began to rise from the clothes bags. 'These soil samples taken from the victims' fingernails and shoes,' he said. 'You want to see if we can establish a match with the soil sample you brought in earlier?'

'From the suspect vehicle, yes. How quickly could you do this?'

'The person to do this is Hilary Flowers – appropriate name, don't you think?'

Grace smiled. 'I've used her before. She's good.'

'She's a genius on pollens. She's got me several results from pollen scrapings from victims' nostrils. But she's expensive.'

Grace shook his head in frustration. When he had first joined the police it was about solving crimes. These days, with everything farmed out to private companies, it was more about budgets. 'How quick is she?'

'She normally works on about two weeks' turnaround.'

'I don't have two weeks – we're talking about someone who might be buried alive. Every hour counts, Joe.'

Tindall looked at his watch. 'Twenty past six on a Saturday night. You're going to be lucky.' He picked up the phone and dialled. Grace watched his face, anxiously. After some moments, Tindall shook his head and whispered back, 'Voicemail.'

He left a message, asking her to call him back, urgently, then replaced the receiver. 'That's all I can do, Roy. If there's a match, she'll find it. Pollen, insect larvae, fossils, soil composition, you name it.'

'Nobody else you can think of?'

Joe Tindall looked at his watch again. 'It's Saturday night, Roy. If I leave now and drive like the clappers, I might just make the second half of the U2 concert – and get a shag afterwards. I think you're going to find that everyone else on this planet who might be able to identify soil samples also has plans for tonight.'

'My guy who's buried alive had plans for today, Joe. He was meant to be getting married.'

'Bummer.'

'You could say that.'

'I don't mean to be frivolous. But I have worked one hundred and ten hours this week, so far.'

'Join the club.'

'I can't do anything, Roy. Nothing. You know me well enough – if there was anything at all that I could suggest, I would tell you. If there was anyone, anywhere in England right now who could give us the analysis on this soil tonight, I'd get in the car and drive to them. But I don't know anyone else. Hilary is the woman. I'll give you her number and you can keep trying. That's all I can say.'

Grace wrote the number down.

51

As he climbed back into his Alfa, his mobile beeped with a text message.

Who's talking about a relationship?
I'm just talking about sex. XXX

Grace shook his head, despairing of ever understanding women. On Tuesday night Claudine had been vile to him, berating him about the police for the best part of three hours. Now in response to his text this morning she wanted to sleep with him?

And the worst part of it was that he actually felt horny. For the first time in years. Claudine was no beauty, but she wasn't a paper-bag job either. With another empty Saturday night stretching out ahead of him, the prospect of driving to Tunbridge Wells and making out with this cop-hating vegan was almost appealing.

But not appealing enough. And at this moment, his head was full of more prosaic thoughts, listing everything he needed to do in the search for Michael Harrison.

*

Shortly after seven o'clock, with the rain easing, accompanied by Linda Buckley, a uniformed WPC in her mid-thirties with short blonde hair and a kind but alert face, he walked from his car up the path of the neat front garden of Gillian Harrison's bungalow and rang the doorbell. It triggered a loud yapping sound from within. Moments later the door opened and a small white dog, with a pink bow on its head, rushed out and began worrying his shoes.

'Bobo! Come here! Bobo!'

He flashed his warrant card at the woman he recognized from the aborted wedding this afternoon. 'Mrs Harrison? Detective Super-intendent Grace from Brighton CID, and this is the Family Liaison Officer we have assigned to you and Miss Harper, WPC Buckley. If there is anything you need, she will help you.'

Shoeless, her silvery blonde hair elegantly coiffed, wearing a smart blue dress with white trim and reeking of cigarette smoke, she gave a fleeting smile to the WPC, then a fearful look at Grace that instantly made him feel sorry for her. 'Yes, I remember you – you were at the reception this afternoon.'

'Is it possible to have a word with you?'

Her eyes were tear-stained and streaked with mascara. 'Have you found him? Have you found my son?'

He shook his head. 'I'm afraid not, no, I'm sorry.'

After a moment's hesitation she said, 'Would you like to come in?'

'Thank you.'

He followed her into the small sitting room, then sat down in the armchair she indicated, beside an unlit fake coal fire. 'Would you like something to drink? A glass of wine? Coffee?'

'A glass of water would be fine,' he said.

'Nothing at all for me,' said the WPC. 'Would you like me to help you?'

'No, thank you, that's kind of you.'

The dog looked up at him and gave a begging whine.

'Bobo, quiet!' Gill Harrison commanded. The dog followed her, slavishly, out of the room.

Grace stared around. There was a framed print of *The Haywain* on the wall and another print, of the Jack and Jill windmills at Clayton, a large framed photograph of Michael Harrison, in a tuxedo, with his arm around Ashley Harper, in a long evening dress, clearly taken at some function, another photograph of a much younger Michael Harrison, in short trousers, astride a bicycle and a black and white wedding photograph of Gill Harrison and her late husband, he presumed, from the information Glenn Branson had given him. He could see the resemblance between Michael Harrison and his father – a tall, good-looking man with long brown hair touching his shirt collar. From his huge lapels and wide trousers he guessed it was taken in the mid-seventies.

Gill Harrison returned, followed by the dog, with a tumbler of water in one hand and a wine glass in the other. She gave Grace the tumbler then sat down on the sofa opposite him.

'I'm very sorry about today, Mrs Harrison, it must have been very distressing for you,' he said, taking the glass, and sipping the cold water gratefully.

A young woman walked into the room. She had a sun-tanned, slightly beaky face, long, ragged blonde hair, and was dressed in a singlet and jeans. She sported rings on her lips and ears and a stud in her tongue.

'This is Carly, my daughter. Carly – this is Chief Inspector Grace of the CID, and WPC Buckley,' Gill Harrison said. 'Carly flew back from Australia for the wedding.'

'I saw you at the reception, but we didn't get a chance to speak,' he said, standing up to shake her reluctant hand, then sitting down again.

'Nice to meet you, Carly,' the WPC said.

Carly sat on the sofa right next to her mother and put a protective arm around her shoulder.

'Where were you in Australia?' Grace asked, trying to be polite.

'Darwin.'

'I haven't been there. I've been to Sydney.'

'I have a daughter who lives there,' said Linda Buckley breezily, trying to break the ice.

Carly shrugged, indifferently.

'I wanted to cancel the wedding and reception completely,' Gill Harrison said. 'It was Ashley who insisted. She felt—'

'She's a stupid bitch,' Carly said.

'Carly!' her mother exclaimed.

'Excuse me,' Carly said. 'Everyone thinks she's' – and she made a cutesy, Barbie doll flutter with her hands – 'so sweet. But I think she's a calculating little bitch.'

'Carly!'

Carly gave her mother a kiss on the cheek. 'I'm sorry, Mum, but she is.' Turning to Grace she said, 'Would you have insisted on the reception going ahead?'

Grace, watching them both, thought carefully before responding. 'I don't know, Carly. I guess she was caught between a rock and a hard place.'

'My brother is the sweetest guy in the world,' she said. 'Yeah.'

'You don't seem to like Ashley,' he said, seizing the chance.

'No, I don't like her.'

'Why not?'

'I think she's a lovely girl,' Gill Harrison butted in.

'Oh crap, Mum! You're just desperate to have grandchildren. You're just pleased that Michael isn't gay.'

'Carly – that's not a nice thing to say.'

'Yeah, well, it's the truth. Ashley's a manipulative ice queen.'

Grace, suddenly feeling excited, tried to remain impassive. 'What gave you that impression, Carly.'

'Don't listen to her,' Gill Harrison said. 'She's tired and emotional with jet-lag.'

'Bullshit,' Carly said. 'She's a gold-digger.'

'How well do either of you know her?' Grace asked.

'Met her once – that was once too often,' Carly said.

'I think she's a delightful girl,' Gill answered. 'She's intelligent, domesticated – you can talk to her, have a proper conversation with her. She's been very good to me.'

'Have you met her family?' Grace asked.

'Poor thing hasn't got any family apart from her very lovely Canadian uncle,' Gill said. 'Her parents were killed in a car crash on holiday in Scotland when she was three. She was brought up by foster parents who were complete bullies. In London at first, then they moved to Australia. Her foster father tried to rape her repeatedly during her teens. She left them when she was sixteen and went to Canada – Toronto – where her uncle and aunt took her in – her aunt died quite recently, I gather, and she's very upset about that. I think Bradley and his wife were the only people who ever showed her kindness. She's had to make her own way in the world. I really admire her.'

'Phoeey!' said Carly.

'Why do you say that?' Grace asked.

''Cause I didn't think she was real when I met her. And after seeing her today, I think she's even less real. I can't explain it – but she doesn't love my brother. I know that. She might have been desperate to get married to him, but that's not the same as loving him. If she genuinely loved him, she'd never have gone through this charade today, she'd have been too upset.'

Grace looked at her with growing interest.

'You see?' Carly said. 'That's a woman talking. Maybe a jet-lagged woman, like my mum says. But a woman. A caring woman who loves her bro. Unlike his bitch-queen-from-hell fiancée.'

'Carly!'

'Oh fuck off, Mum.'

52

After Ashley left the flat, still furious at him, Mark switched on the television, hoping to catch the local news. He tried the radio too, but it was just gone seven and he had missed it.

Changed into jeans, trainers, a sweatshirt and a light anorak, with a baseball cap tugged low over his forehead, he was shaking from nerves and from an overdose of caffeine. He'd already downed two mugs of strong coffee in his attempt to sober up and was now finishing off a third. He drained the last dregs, then walked to the front door of his apartment. Just as he reached it the phone rang.

Hurrying back into the living area, he looked at the caller display. *Private number.* After a moment's hesitation he picked up the receiver.

'This is Kevin Spinella from the *Argus*. I'd like to speak to Mr Mark Warren.'

Mark cursed. If he'd been thinking more clearly he might have told the man that Mark Warren was out, but instead he found himself saying, 'Yes, speaking.'

'Mr Warren, good evening, sorry to trouble you on a Saturday evening. I'm calling about your business partner, Michael Harrison. I went along to the wedding that should have taken place this afternoon at All Saints' church, Patcham. You were the best man – I didn't feel it appropriate to intrude at the church – but I wonder if I could have a few words with you now?'

'Um – yes – yes, of course.'

'I understand Michael Harrison disappeared on his stag night, when there was that terrible accident. I'm curious to know why you, as best man, weren't there?'

'On the stag night?'

'Exactly.'

'I should have been, of course,' Mark said, calmly, trying to sound friendly, to make it all sound perfectly natural. 'I was out of town – up north on a business meeting – had it all scheduled to be back in good time, but my flight was delayed by fog,' Mark said.

'Where was that?'

'Leeds.'

'Ah right. These things happen – that's the problem with this country.'

'Absolutely!' Mark said, feeling they were starting to bond.

'I understand from the police that you have no knowledge of what was planned for the stag night. Is that right?'

Mark was silent for a moment. Thinking. *Careful.* 'No,' he said. 'That's not strictly true. I mean – that's not true at all. We had planned to go on a pub crawl.'

'A pub crawl! Right, OK. But isn't it usual for the best man to arrange the stag night?'

'Yes, so I believe.'

'But you didn't organize this stag night?'

Mark tried to focus his thoughts. Alarm bells were ringing. 'Yes, I did – Michael didn't want anything too elaborate – just to go to a few pubs with his mates. I had fully intended to be there.'

'What exactly did you plan?'

'We – ah – were going to do the usual stuff, you know – a bunch of pubs, get Michael wrecked, then deliver him home. We were going to hire a minibus and have a designated driver, but one of our crowd said he had access to a van and that he didn't mind not drinking, so we went along with that.'

'Where did the coffin fit into this plan?'

Shit. Mark felt himself getting deeper into mire. 'Coffin, did you say?'

'I understand you arranged for a coffin.'

'I don't know anything at all about a coffin!' Mark exclaimed. 'That's a new one on me.' Trying to sound really surprised he said again, for emphasis, '*Coffin?*'

'Do you think your friends organized this in your absence?' the journalist asked.

'Absolutely. Must have done. One of them, Robert Houlihan, works – worked – for his uncle, an undertaker – but we never discussed a coffin. Are you sure about this?'

'I'm informed by the police they believe there was a coffin in the van – before the accident. Can you think what might have happened to Michael Harrison?'

'No, I have no idea. I'm desperately worried.'

'I spoke yesterday to the widow of one of your friends. Mrs Zoe Walker. She said you were all planning to get revenge on Michael Harrison because he regularly played pranks on the rest of you. Might the coffin have something to do with that?'

'As I said, I don't know anything about the coffin. It sounds like some last-minute idea.'

'Do you think your mates might have put Michael Harrison into the coffin and that he's stuck somewhere?'

Mark thought hard before responding. 'Listen, you know how it is when a bunch of guys get drunk. Sometimes they do crazy things.'

'Been there myself.'

They both chuckled. Mark felt a tad relieved.

'Well, thank you for your time. If you hear anything, perhaps you'd be kind enough to let me know, if I give you my number?'

'Of course,' he said, looking around for a pen.

As Mark stood in the lift a few minutes later, he was thinking about the conversation, hoping to hell he hadn't said anything stupid, and worrying how Ashley would react if she saw him quoted in the paper. She'd be furious that he'd even spoken to them. But what choice did he have?

Driving up the ramp of the car park, he turned cautiously into the street, made a left turn, then eased out into the heavy Saturday-evening traffic, being careful to keep his speed down, knowing he must be over the legal limit. The last thing he needed was to be stopped and breathalysed.

Twenty minutes later he reached the car park of the garden centre at the back of Newhaven, the Channel port ten miles from his apartment. With little time to spare before its 8 p.m. closing time, he made a rapid dash through the store, buying a spade, screwdriver, hammer, chisel, small Maglite flashlight, rubber gardening gloves and a pair of gum boots. By eight he was back in his car, in the almost deserted lot. The sky was surprisingly clear and it would be a good couple of hours yet before it was completely dark – if then.

Two hours that he had to kill.

He knew he should eat something, but his stomach was all knotted up. He thought about a burger, a Chinese, an Indian. Nothing appealed. Ashley was angry at him; he'd never seen her angry before and it distressed and scared him. It was as if some connection between them had been switched off. He had to switch it back on and the only way was to appease her. Do what she said. Do what he had known for several days that he needed to do.

He wanted to call her, tell her he loved her, hear her tell him she loved him back. But she wasn't going to do that, not now, not yet. She was right to be mad at him; he'd been an idiot, nearly blown everything. Christ, why the hell had be been so stupid with that cop?

He started the engine and the radio came on. Eight o'clock. The local station news. First an international story, more bad stuff about Iraq. Then an item about Tony Blair and the European Union. Then his ears stiffened as the chirpy newscaster said, 'Sussex Police are stepping up their search for Brighton property developer Michael Harrison. His fiancée, Ashley Harper, and their guests were tragically disappointed when he failed to turn up at All Saints' church, Patcham, this afternoon for his wedding, confirming suspicions that he is incapacitated following the stag night prank that left four of his best friends dead. Detective Superintendent Roy Grace of the Sussex CID, who is now leading the enquiry into Michael Harrison's whereabouts, said this morning that the police were upgrading their search from a missing persons enquiry into a Serious Incident Investigation.'

Mark turned the volume of the radio up louder, and caught the Detective Superintendent's voice.

'We believe that Michael Harrison may be the victim of a prank that has gone very tragically wrong, and we would like all persons who believe they may have information about the events surrounding last Tuesday evening to contact the Incident Suite at Sussex CID urgently.'

Mark's vision blurred; the whole parking lot seemed to be vibrating and there was a muzzy sound in his ears as if he were in an aircraft that was taking off, or diving deep underwater. He pinched his nostrils, blew and his ears popped. His hands were wet with perspiration – then he realized his whole body was wet; he could feel the droplets of water running down his skin.

Breathe deeply, he remembered. That was the way to deal with stress. Ashley had taught him that just before he'd been to see a particularly tricky client.

So he sat in his car in the falling light, listening to the rhythm of his pounding heart, and breathed deeply.

For a long while.

53

Once any investigation – such as a murder, kidnapping, rape, armed robbery, fraud or missing persons enquiry – was elevated to Major Incident status it was awarded a code word.

All major incidents were now being handled from CID headquarters at Sussex House, which was why at twenty past eight on Saturday night, when most normal people who had a life were either at home or out enjoying themselves, Roy Grace, now officially in charge of the investigation, found himself climbing the stairs of Sussex House, past the framed photographs of the key team members and the displays of truncheons on the walls.

He had taken the decision – and the appropriate action – to upgrade the Michael Harrison missing persons enquiry to a Major Incident within minutes of leaving Gill Harrison's house. It was a big decision, with huge cost and police time implications, one that he was going to be required to justify to the Chief Superintendent and to Alison Vosper. No doubt he'd have a tough time doing that – he could already imagine some of the withering questions she would throw at him.

DC Nick Nicholl and DS Bella Moy, their Saturday-night plans long in tatters anyway, were on their way over here, along with their new recruit to the team, Emma-Jane Boutwood, bringing everything that they'd had in the Incident Room at Brighton police station – which was not much, so far.

Entering the Major Incident Suite, he walked through the green-carpeted, open-plan area lined with desks that housed the support staff of the senior officers of the CID. Each senior officer had his own room flanking this area, with his or her name printed on blue and yellow photochromatic card on the door.

On his left, through a wide expanse of glass he could see into the impressive office of the man who was technically his immediate boss – although Alison Vosper in practice was – Detective Chief Superintendent Gary Weston. Gary Weston and Roy Grace went back a long way – they had been partnered up when Grace had first joined the CID as a rookie constable, and Weston had not been much more experienced.

There was only a month's age difference between the two men, and Grace wondered, a little enviously sometimes, how Gary had achieved quite such a meteoric rise compared to his own, and would doubtless end up as a Chief Constable somewhere in Britain very soon. But in his heart he knew the answer. It wasn't that Gary Weston was a better cop or academically any brighter – they'd sailed through many of the same advancement courses together – it was simply that Gary was a better political animal than he would ever be. He didn't resent his former partner for this – they had remained good friends – but he could never be like him, never keep his opinions to himself the way Gary so often had to.

No sign of Gary in his office now, at 8.30 on a Saturday night. The Detective Chief Superintendent knew how to live the good life, mixing home, pleasure and work with ease. The framed photographs of greyhounds and racehorses that lined his walls were evidence of his passion for the tracks, and the stand-up framed photographs of his attractive wife and four young children strategically placed on every flat surface left visitors to his office in no doubt about his priorities in life.

Gary would probably be at a greyhound track tonight, Grace imagined. Having a cheery meal with his wife and friends, placing bets, relaxing, looking forward to a family Sunday. He saw the spectral reflection of his own face in the glass and walked on across the deserted room, past winking message lights on desks, silent fax machines, screensavers playing their eternal loops. Sometimes – at moments like this when he felt so disconnected from the real world – he wondered if this was what it was like to be a ghost, drifting unseen past everyone else's lives.

Holding his security card up to the panel at the end of the room, he pushed open the door, entering a long, silent, grey-carpeted corridor that smelled of fresh paint. He passed a large red felt-faced noticeboard headed 'OPERATION LISBON' beneath which was the photograph of an oriental-looking man, with a wispy beard, surrounded by several different photographs of the rocky beach at the bottom of the tall cliffs of local beauty spot Beachy Head, each with a red circle drawn on it.

This unidentified man had been found dead four weeks ago at the bottom of the cliff. At first he was assumed to be another jumper, until the post-mortem had revealed to the pathologist that he was already dead at the time he took his plunge.

On the opposite wall was 'OPERATION CORMORANT', with a photograph of a pretty teenage brunette who had been found raped and strangled on the outskirts of Brighton.

Grace passed the Outside Enquiry Team office on his left, a large room where detectives drafted in on major incidents would base themselves for the duration, then entered the door immediately opposite, marked 'INTEL ONE'.

The Intelligence Office Room was the new nerve centre for all major incidents. As he entered it, everything about it felt new, smelled new, even the attitude of the people working in here – apart from a distinct odour of Chinese food tonight. Despite opaque windows too high to see out of, the room, with its fresh white walls, had an airy feel, good light, good energy, very different to the messy buzz of police station incident rooms that Grace had grown up with.

It had an almost futuristic feel, as if it could as easily have housed Mission Control at Houston, and was a large, L-shaped room, divided up by three principal work stations, each comprising a curved, light-wood desk with space for up to eight people to sit, and massive white-boards, one marked 'OPERATION CORMORANT', one marked 'OPERATION LISBON' and one 'OPERATION SNOW-DRIFT', each covered in crime scene photographs and progress charts. Another would shortly be labelled 'OPERATION SALSA', the random name the police headquarters computer in Scotland Yard had thrown out for his Michael Harrison investigation.

Mostly the names had nothing to do with the investigations themselves, and occasionally they had to be changed. He remembered one time when the name 'OPERATION CAUCASIAN' had been given to the investigation of a black man who had been found dismembered in the boot of a car. It had been changed to something less controversial. But with Operation Salsa, the dumb computer had by chance struck a right chord. Grace had the very definite feeling of being involved in a song and dance.

Unlike the work stations in most police offices, there was no sign of anything personal on the desks or up on the walls. No pictures of families, footballers, no fixture lists, no jokey cartoons. Every single object in this room, apart from the furniture and the business hardware, was related to the matters under investigation. Apart from the Pot Noodle a weary-looking, long-haired Detective Inspector Michael Cowan was tucking into with a plastic fork at the end of one of the work stations.

Heading another of the work stations, glued to a flat computer screen, with a beaker of Coke in his hand, sat Jason Piette, one of the shrewdest Detective Inspectors that Grace had ever worked with. He would have been happy to place money on Piette one day becoming head of the Met – the top police job in the country.

Each of the work stations was manned by a minimum team of an office manager, normally a Detective Sergeant or Detective Inspector, a system supervisor, normally a lesser-ranking police officer, an analyst, an indexer and a typist.

Michael Cowan, wearing a loose checked shirt over jeans, greeted Grace cordially. 'How you doing, Roy? You're looking a bit smart.'

'Thought I should dress up for you boys – obviously I didn't need to bother.'

'Yeah, yeah!'

'What crap are you eating?' Grace responded. 'You have any idea what's in that stuff?'

Michael Cowan rolled his eyes, grinning. 'Chemicals, they keep me going.'

Grace shook his head. 'Smells like a Chinese takeaway in here.'

Cowan jerked his head up at the whiteboard beside

him, headed ‘OPERATION LISBON’. ‘Yup, well, you can take my Chinese problem away from me any time you feel like. I’ve given up a hot date to be here.’

‘I’ll trade with you gladly,’ Grace said.

Michael Cowan looked at him inquisitively. ‘Tell me?’

‘You don’t want to know, believe me.’

‘It’s that bad?’

‘Worse.’

54

In the beam of the headlamps, Mark could see a whole cluster of wreaths at the roadside, on the apex of a right-hand curve. Some lay on the grass verge, some were propped against a tree and the rest against a hedge. There were several more than the last time he had passed here.

Taking his foot off the accelerator, he slowed to a crawl, a shiver rippling through him, deep inside him, deep inside his soul. He continued to watch them as they receded in the glow of his tail lights, until they vanished into the darkness, into the night, vanished, were gone, had never been there. *Josh, Pete, Luke, Robbo.*

Himself, too, if the plane had not been delayed.

Then of course the problem would have been different. Covered in goose pimples, he floored the accelerator, wanting to get away from here; it was giving him the creeps. His mobile beeped, then began to ring. Ashley's number on caller display appeared on the panel on the dash.

He answered it on the hands-free, glad to hear her, badly in need of human company. 'Hi.'

'Well?' She sounded as frosty as when she had left his apartment.

'I'm on my way.'

'Only now?'

'I had to wait for it to get dark. I don't think we should talk on mobiles – shall I come and see you when I get back?'

'That would be really stupid, Mark.'

''Yes. I – I – how is Gill?'

'Upset. How do you expect her to be?'

'Yup.'

'*Yup?* Are you OK?'

'Sort of.'

'Are you sober now?'

'Of course,' he said, tetchily.

'You don't sound good.'

'I don't feel good, OK?'

'OK. But you're going to do it?'

'That's what we agreed.'

'Will you call me after?'

'Sure.'

He hung up. It was misty ahead, and a film of moisture covered the windscreen. The wipers arced twice, the rubber blades were shrieking. He switched them off. The shrubbery at the edge of the forest was looking familiar, and he slowed down, not wanting to overshoot the turn-off.

Moments later he rattled over the first cattle grid then the second, the headlight beams stretching out ahead through the mist like twin lasers, the car lurching on the potholed track as he accelerated, driving too fast, scared of the trees that seemed to be pressing threateningly in on either side, and glancing in his mirror, just in case . . .

Just in case what, exactly?

He was getting close now. A low murmur of chatter from the radio distracted him, and he switched it off, dimly aware that his breathing was getting faster, that perspiration kept pouring down his temples, his back. The nose dipped steeply as the front wheels plunged into a puddle, and water, sounding as hard as pebbles, spattered the windscreen. Switching the wipers on again, he slowed right down. Jesus, it was deep; he hadn't realized how much rain there'd been since he was last here. And then – *shit, oh shit, no!*

The wheels had lost traction in the mire.

Pressing the accelerator harder made the BMW vibrate, slide a few feet sideways, then slip back again.

Oh, Christ, no!

He could not get stuck, could not, could not. How the hell could he explain this, half-ten at night, out here?

Breathe deeply . . .

He breathed in, peering out fearfully at the darkness, at every shadow in front of him, to the side of him, behind him, then pressed the central locking, heard the *clunk*, but felt no better. Then he switched on the dome light and looked down at the controls. There were settings for off-road conditions, a lower gear ratio, a differential lock; he'd seen them a hundred times and never bothered to read up about them.

Reaching over, he pulled the handbook out of the glove compartment, frantically scrambled through the index, then turned to the relevant pages. He pushed a lever, pressed a button, put the book down beside him, and tentatively tried the accelerator. The car lurched, then, to his relief, powered forwards.

He kept going at a steady ten miles per hour, the car much more surefooted now, moving forward through more puddles as if it was on a conveyor belt. Then he made the right fork which would take him to the clearing. A baby rabbit hopped out in front of him, turned and ran back, then scampered forward, right beneath him. He had no idea whether he hit it or not, didn't care, just wanted to press on, maintain his speed, his momentum, his grip on the mud.

The small glade of scrubby mosses and grasses was right ahead now, and to his relief the sheet of corrugated iron, beneath the camouflage of uprooted plants he had strewn over it, was still in place.

He drove up onto the relatively firm soil, not wanting to risk the car bogging itself down while it was parked, then, switching off the engine but leaving the headlamps on full beam, he tugged on his new gum boots, grabbed the Maglite and climbed down onto the squelchy soil.

There was an instant of total silence. Then a faint rustle in the undergrowth which made him turn, stabbing the beam of the Maglite into the forest in fear. Holding his breath, he heard a crackle, then a rattle like a coin in a tin, and a large pheasant careened clumsily off between the trees.

He swung the beam from right to left, sick with fear, opened the tailgate of the car, pulled on the rubber gloves, then pulled out the tools he had bought and carried them over to the edge of the grave.

He stood still for some moments, staring down at the corrugated iron sheet, listening. The car engine pinged. Droplets of water fell all around him in the forest, but otherwise silence. Total silence. A snail had attached itself to one section of the corrugated iron, its shell rising like a barnacle on a wreck. Good. This sheet looked like it had lain here undisturbed for years.

Placing his tools and the Maglite down in the wet grass, he grabbed an end of the sheet, and pulled it back. The grave appeared like a dark crevasse. Gripping the flashlight, he stood up, but remained rooted to the spot, trying to pluck up the courage to step forward.

As if Michael might be crouching in there, ready to grab him.

Slowly, small step by small step, he inched towards the edge, then in a panicky thrust he pointed the beam down into the long, rectangular hollow.

And breathed out.

Everything was as he had left it. The earth still heaped, undisturbed. For some moments he stared, guiltily. 'I'm sorry, partner,' he whispered. 'I—'

There wasn't anything to say. He went back to the car and turned the lights off. No sense in advertising his presence, just in case there was anyone out in the woods at this hour, which he doubted – but you never knew.

It took almost an hour of hard digging before the spade struck the wood of the coffin lid. There was much more earth than he had thought – OK, he had added quite a bit the other night, but even so . . . He continued to scrape away until he could see the whole lid clearly and the brass screws in each corner. The tiny hole where the breathing tube had been, which he had plugged with earth, had been widened; it seemed a little larger – or was it his imagination?

Reaching up, he put the spade on the ground, grabbed the screwdriver and set to work on each of the screws in turn. Then came the bit he hadn't quite worked out: the coffin fitted tightly into the hole, and there was no gap beside it – the only place to stand was on the lid, and that made it impossible to remove it.

He climbed out, then clenching the Maglite in his teeth, still holding the screwdriver, prostrated himself and wriggled forwards over the edge of the grave, and reached down. He could touch the lid of the coffin easily.

Then he began trembling. What the hell was he

going to find? Removing the flashlight from his mouth he called, softly, 'Michael?' Then louder. 'Michael? Hello? Michael?'

Then he rapped several times on the lid with the handle of the screwdriver – although he knew that if Michael was alive – and conscious – he would have heard his footsteps and the scraping of the shovel on the lid. Except he might be too weak to have responded.

If he was still alive.

A big *if.* It was four days now – and he clearly had no air. He stuck the barrel of the Maglite back in his mouth and clenched hard. *He had to do this. Had to do this fucking thing. Had to be here to get the goddamn Palm back from Michael.* Because one day someone was going to find this grave and open it up and find the corpse, and find the goddamn Palm with all the emails on it, and that cop, Detective Superintendent Graves or whatever his name was, would find the email he had sent Michael on Monday, telling him they all had a real treat in store for him, and giving him cryptic clues – too cryptic for Michael to have figured out in advance what they were going to do to him, but a total giveaway to the cop.

Mark eased the blade of the screwdriver under the lid, then levered it up a few inches, until he could get his fingers in. Taking the strain with his left hand, he put the screwdriver down on the ground above him, then lifted the heavy lid as high as he could, barely registering the deep, jagged groove that had been carved on the inside.

Inky water shimmered back at him, the soggy remnants of a magazine floating on the surface, large bare breasts just visible in the bright beam.

Mark screamed and the Maglite fell from his teeth, splashed into the water and struck the bottom of the coffin with a dull thud.

There was no one inside.

55

The lid fell down with a bang like a gunshot. Mark scrambled to his feet, tripped and went sprawling in the muddy soil. He hauled himself to his knees, swivelled in a complete circle, his eyes scanning the darkness, whimpering, panting, his brain seized up in his panic, wondering which way to run. To the car? Into the woods?

Oh sweet Jesus. Christ. Christ.

Still on all fours he backed away from the grave and spun around in a complete circle again. Was Michael out there, watching him, about to strike?

About to blind him with a flashlight beam?

He stood and ran to the car, wrenched open the door, climbed in and the bloody interior lights all came on, fucking floodlighting him! He slammed the door shut, hit the central locking button, twisted the ignition key, rammed the gear lever into *drive,* snapped on the lights and floored the accelerator, swinging the car round in a wide arc, the beam of the lights traversing the trees, shadows leaping, fading; he continued round in a circle, then another circle, then a third.

Oh Jesus.

What the hell had happened?

He hadn't got the fucking Palm. Had to go back and check. Had to.

How the hell could . . . ?

How could he have got out? Screwed the lid back down? Put the earth on top?

Unless?

He'd never been there?

But if he hadn't been there, why didn't he turn up to the wedding?

Thoughts hurtled round his brain. All jumbled. He wanted to call Ashley, and, oh sure, he knew the first thing she would ask him.

Did you get the Palm?

He drove up to the edge of the grave, sat in the car, waiting, watching. Then he opened the door, jumped down, flat on his stomach, and without bothering to roll up his sleeves plunged his hands into the cold water. Hit the soft, satin bottom. Felt the padded sides, then the bottom again. Found the torch and retrieved it. No longer working. His hands hit something small, round, metallic; his fingers clasped around it and pulled it out too, holding it up to the beam of the headlights. It looked like the cap of a whisky bottle.

He turned and stared fearfully at the woods all around. Then he plunged his arms back into the coffin, working his way from one end to the other. The sodden page of a magazine wrapped itself around his hand. Nothing else. Nothing at all. The damned thing was empty.

He stood up, replaced the corrugated iron sheet, half-heartedly throwing some grasses over it, then got back into the safety of his car. He slammed the door and hit the central locking button again, then turned and headed back down the track, accelerating hard, crashing through the ruts and puddles until he rumbled over the two cattle grids and reached the main road.

Then he switched the diff lock off and pushed the gear lever back to normal high-gear drive and turned back towards Brighton, staring into his rear-view mirror, fearful of every pair of headlights that appeared behind him, wanting desperately to call Ashley but too confused to know what to say to her.

Where the hell was Michael?

Where?

Where?

He drove back past all the wreaths, glancing at the orange glow of the dash, then at the road, then into his mirror. Had he imagined it? Hallucinated it? *Come on, guys, what's your secret? What do you know that I don't? You put an empty coffin in the ground? OK, so what did you do with Michael?*

As he drove on he began to calm down a fraction, starting to think more clearly, convincing himself it was unimportant now. Michael was not there. There was no dead body. No one had anything on him.

Clenching the steering wheel with his knees, he pulled his rubber gloves off and dropped them in the passenger footwell. Of course, this was Michael all over. It had all his hallmarks. Michael the joker. Had Michael set this whole damned thing up?

Missing his wedding day?

Wild thoughts began going through his mind now. Had Michael twigged about himself and Ashley? Was this part of his revenge? He and Michael had known each other for a long time. Since they were thirteen. Michael was a smart guy, but he had his own way of dealing with problems. Possible that he had twigged – although he and Ashley had been incredibly careful.

He thought back as he drove. To the day Ashley had first come to the office in response to an ad they had put in the *Argus* for a PA. She had walked in, so smart, so beautiful, streets ahead of all the others they had interviewed before and after her. She was in a whole different league.

Having just split up with a long-term girlfriend, and being free, he'd fancied her in a way he'd never fancied anyone before. They'd connected from that first moment, although Michael had seemed blind to it. By the end of her second week working for them, unknown to Michael, they started sleeping together.

Two months into their secret relationship, she told Mark that Michael had the hots for her and had invited her out to dinner. What should she do?

Mark had felt angry, but had not revealed that to Ashley. All his life, ever since he had met Michael, he had lived in his shadow. It was Michael who always pulled the best-looking girls at parties, and it was Michael who somehow charmed his bank manager into giving him a loan to buy the first run-down property that he had made a big return on, while Mark had struggled on a meagre salary in a small accountancy practice.

When they had decided to go into business together, it was Michael who had the cash to fund it – and took two thirds of the shares for doing that. Now they had a business worth several million pounds. And Michael had the lion's share.

When Ashley had walked in that day, it was the first time that a woman had looked at him first.

And then the shit had dared to ask her out.

What happened next had been Ashley's idea. All she had to do was marry Michael and then engineer a divorce. Just set him up with a hooker and have a hidden cameraman. She'd settle for half his shares – and with Mark's thirty-three per cent, that would give them a majority holding. Control of the company. Goodbye, Michael.

Dead simple, really.

Murder had never been on the agenda.

56

Ashley, in a white towelling dressing gown, her hair down and loose over her shoulders, opened the front door of her house and stared at the mud-spattered figure of Mark with a mixture of disbelief and anger.

'Are you insane, coming here?' she said as a greeting. 'And at this hour. It's twenty past twelve, Mark!'

'I have to come in. I couldn't risk phoning you. We have to talk.'

Startled by the desperate tone of his voice, she relented, first stepping out and looking carefully down the quiet street in both directions. 'You weren't followed here?'

'No.'

She looked down at his feet. 'Mark, what the hell are you doing? Look at your boots!'

He stared down at his filthy gum boots, pulled them off, then carried them inside. Still holding them, he stood in the open-plan living area, watching the winking lights from the silent wall-mounted stereo.

Closing the front door, she stared at him fearfully. 'You look terrible.'

'I need a drink.'

'I think you had enough earlier today.'

'I'm too bloody sober now.'

Helping him off with his anorak she asked, 'What would you like? A whisky?'

'Balvenie if you have some. Otherwise anything.'

'You need a bath.' She headed towards the kitchen. 'So, tell me, was it awful? Did you get the Palm?'

'We have a problem.'

Ashley spun round as if she'd been shot. 'What kind of a problem?'

Mark stared at her helplessly. 'He wasn't there.'

'Not there?'

'No – he – I don't know – he—'

'You mean *he* wasn't there? The *coffin* wasn't there?'

Mark told her what had happened. Ashley's first reaction was to go to each of the windows and draw the blinds tightly, then she poured him a whisky and made herself a black coffee. Then they sat down on opposite sofas.

'Is it possible you went to the wrong place?'

'You mean – like there's two different coffins? No. I was the one who suggested that spot in the first place. We were going to leave him with a porno magazine and a bottle of whisky – both of those are in there – well the cap of the bottle is.'

'And the coffin lid was screwed down – with earth on top?' Clasping her coffee with both hands, she blew steam away from the top and sipped it. Mark watched as her dressing gown opened and part of her large white breasts was visible through the gap. And they made him want her, now, despite everything, despite all his panic; he just wanted to seize her in his arms and make love to her.

'Yes – it was exactly how it was on Thursday when I—'

'Took the breathing tube?'

He gulped some whisky. She was giving him a sympathetic smile now. Maybe he could at least get to stay an hour or two. Make love. He needed some release from this nightmare.

Then her expression darkened. 'How sure are you that he was in there when you took the tube?'

'Of course he was bloody in there. I heard him shout. Christ!'

'You didn't imagine it?'

'Imagine him shouting?'

'You were in a pretty bad state.'

'You would have been too. He was my business partner. My best friend. I'm not a bloody murderer – I—'

She gave him a richly cynical look.

'I'm only doing this – because – because I love you, Ashley.' He drank some more whisky.

'He could be out there right now,' she said. 'Prowling in the dark, watching, couldn't he?'

Mark shook his head. 'I don't know. If he wasn't in the coffin, why didn't he come to the wedding? But he was – or someone was – there are marks inside the lid; someone had been trying to scrape their way out.'

Ashley took the news impassively.

'Maybe he knows about us – that's all I can think. That he fucking *knows* about us.'

'He doesn't,' Ashley said. 'He has no idea. He talked to me a lot about you, how much you wanted to settle down with the right woman and have kids, and that you never seemed to be able to find a steady girlfriend.'

'Oh great, he always gave my ego a real boost.'

'Not in a nasty way, Mark. He cares about you.'

'You're being very defensive about him.'

'He is my fiancé.'

'Very funny.' Mark set his glass down on the square coffee table, then buried his face in his hands.

'You need to pull yourself together. Let's look at this logically, OK?'

Still with his face in his hands, he nodded.

'Michael was there on Thursday night. You took the tube, plugged the air hole, right?'

Mark made no comment.

'We know he is a big practical joker. So, somehow he gets out of the coffin, and he decides to make it look as if he is still in there.'

Mark stared at her, abjectly. 'Great joke. So he's out and he knows I took the breathing tube – and there could only be one reason why I did that.'

'You're wrong. How would he know it was you? Could have been anyone out walking in the woods.'

'Come on, Ashley, get real. Someone walking in the woods stumbles across a grave, with a breathing tube sticking out of the coffin, removes the tube and heaps a ton more earth on top of the coffin?'

'I'm just trying to throw thoughts out.'

Mark stared at her, the thought suddenly going through his mind that perhaps Ashley and Michael had hatched something between them. To trap him.

Then he thought about all those days and evenings he had spent with Ashley over the past months, the things she had said to him, the way they had made love, planned – and the scornful way she always spoke about Michael, and he dismissed that thought completely.

'Here's another idea,' she said. 'The others – Pete, Luke, Josh and Robbo – all knew you were going to be arriving late. Perhaps they were setting up a practical joke on you – with Michael – and it backfired?'

'OK,' he said. 'Even supposing Michael wasn't in that coffin when I went there, and I imagined him calling out, then where the hell is he? Where has he been since

Tuesday night? Why hasn't he been in touch; why didn't he turn up to the wedding? Can you answer me that?'

'No. Unless the others were pulling a stunt on you and him – and he's tied up or locked up in some other place.'

'Or done a runner?'

'He hasn't done a runner,' Ashley said. 'I can tell you that.'

'How can you be sure?'

Her eyes rested on Mark's. 'Because he loves me. He really, genuinely loves me. That's why I know he hasn't done a runner. Did you put everything back as it was?'

Mark hesitated, then lied, not wanting to admit he'd fled in panic. 'Yes.'

'So either we have to wait,' she said. 'Or you go find him – and deal with him.'

'Deal with him?'

Her look said it all.

'I'm not a killer, Ashley. I might be a lot of things—'

'You might not have a choice, Mark. Think about it.'

'He won't be able to nail anything on me. Nothing that he can stick.' He fell silent, thinking. 'Can I wait here?'

She stood up and walked over to him, placed her hands on his shoulders and gently massaged his back. Then she kissed his neck. 'I would love you to stay,' she whispered. 'But it would be madness. How do you think it would look if Michael turned up? Or the police?'

Mark turned his head and tried to kiss her on the lips. She allowed him one quick peck then pulled away. 'Go,' she said. 'Vamoosh! Find Michael, before he finds you.'

'I can't do that, Ashley.'

'You can. You already did it on Thursday night. It might not have worked, but you proved you *can* do it. So *go* do it.'

He padded dejectedly across the floor to get his boots,

and Ashley brought over his sodden, muddy anorak. 'We need to be careful what we say over the phone – the police are getting nosy. We should start assuming the phones are tapped,' she said. 'OK?'

'Good thinking.'

'Talk to you in the morning.'

Mark opened the door warily, as if expecting to find Michael there with a gun or a knife in his hand. But there was just the glow of the streetlamps, the dull shine of silent cars and the still of the urban night punctuated only by the distant screech of two fighting cats.

57

Every couple of months, Roy Grace took his eight-year-old goddaughter, Jaye Somers, out for a Sunday treat. Her parents, Michael and Victoria, both police officers, had been some of his and Sandy's closest friends, and they had been hugely supportive in the difficult years following her disappearance. With their four children, aged two to eleven, they had become almost a second family to him.

Today he'd had to disappoint Jaye by explaining when he collected her that he could only spare a couple of hours, as he had to go back to work to try to help someone who was in trouble.

He never told Jaye in advance what the treat would be, so she always enjoyed the guessing game for the first few minutes of their car journey.

'I think we are going to see animals today!' Jaye said.

'Do you?'

'Yes.'

She was a pretty child, with long silvery blonde hair, a cherubic, happy face and an infectious laugh. Today she was smartly dressed, as usual, in a green frock with white lace trim and a tiny pair of pink trainers on her feet. Sometimes her expressions, and the things she said, could seem incredibly grown-up. There were moments when Grace felt he was out with a miniature adult, not a child.

'So what makes you think that?'

'Umm, let me see.' Jaye leaned forward and twiddled the dials on Grace's car radio, selected the CD and punched a number. The first track of a Blue album began to play. 'Do you like Blue?'

'Uh huh.'

'I like the Scissor Sisters.'

'Do you?'

'They're cool. Do you know them?'

Grace remembered that Glenn Branson was into them. 'Of course.'

'We're definitely going to see animals.'

'What sort of animals do you think we're going to see?'

She turned the music up, swaying her arms to the beat. 'Giraffes.'

'You want to see giraffes?'

'Giraffes don't dream much,' she informed him.

'Don't they? You talk to giraffes about their dreams?'

'We have a project in school about animals dreaming. Dogs dream a lot. So do cats.'

'But not giraffes?'

'No.'

He grinned. 'OK, so how do you know that?'

'I just do.'

'How about llamas?'

She shrugged.

It was a fine late-spring morning, the sun bright and warm and dazzling through the windscreen, and Grace pulled his sunglasses out of the glove compartment. There was a hint, today at any rate, that the long spell of bad weather might be over. And Jaye was a sunny person, he enjoyed her company a lot. He normally forgot his troubles during the few precious hours he was with her.

'So what else have you been up to at school?'

'Stuff.'

'What kind of stuff?'

'School's boring at the moment.'

Grace drove extra carefully with Jaye on board, slowly heading out of Brighton into the countryside. 'Last time we went out you said you were really enjoying school.'

'The teachers are so stupid.'

'All of them?'

'Not Mrs Dean. She's nice.'

'What does she teach?'

'Giraffe dreams.' She burst into giggles.

Grace pulled up as the traffic queued for a roundabout. 'That's all she teaches?'

Jaye was quiet for a moment, then said suddenly, 'Mummy thinks you should get married again.'

Surprised, he said, 'Does she?'

Jaye nodded very definitely.

'And what do you think?'

'I think you'd be happier if you had a girlfriend.'

They reached the roundabout. Grace took the second exit, onto the Brighton bypass. 'Well,' he said, 'who knows?'

'Why don't you have a girlfriend?' she asked.

'Because . . .' He hesitated. 'Well – you know – finding the right person is not always that easy.'

'I have a boyfriend,' Jaye announced.

'You do? Tell me about him.'

'His name is Justin. He's in my class. He told me he wants to marry me.'

Grace shot her a sideways glance. 'And do you want to marry him?'

She shook her head vigorously. 'He's yuck!'

'He's your boyfriend, but he's *yuck*? What kind of a boyfriend is that?'

'I'm thinking of ending it,' she said, deadly serious.

This was another reason why Grace loved his days out

with Jaye, because he felt she kept him in touch with the young world. Now, for a moment, he felt totally lost. Did he ever have a girlfriend at eight? No way . . .

His mobile, lying in his door pocket, rang. He picked it up and held it to his ear rather than use the hands-free in case it was bad news which might upset Jaye. 'Roy Grace,' he said.

A young female voice said, 'Hello? Detective Superintendent Grace?'

'Speaking.'

'It's DC Boutwood.'

'Emma-Jane? Hi, welcome to the team.'

She sounded nervous. 'Thank you. I'm at Sussex House – DC Nicholl asked me to call you – there's been a development.'

'Tell me?'

Even more nervous now, she said, 'Well, sir, it's not very good news. Some ramblers have found a body in Ashdown Forest, about two miles east of Crowborough.'

Right in the heart of the suspect area, Grace thought instantly.

'A young man,' she continued. 'Late twenties or early thirties. Sounds like he fits Michael Harrison's profile.'

Glancing at Jaye, he said, 'What condition is he in?'

'I don't have that information. Dr Churchman is on his way there now. DC Nicholl wants to know if you will be able to attend?'

Grace glanced at Jaye again. There was no option. 'I'll be there in an hour.'

'Thank you, sir.'

As he hung up, Jaye informed him, 'Mummy said that people mustn't use their mobile phones when they are driving. It is very dangerous.'

'Your mummy is quite right. Jaye, I'm sorry, I'm going to have to take you back home.'

'We haven't seen the giraffe yet.'

He switched on his indicator, to pull off the road at the next exit and turn back. 'I'm sorry. There is a young man who has gone missing and I have to help find him.'

'Can I help too?'

'Not this time, Jaye, I'm sorry.' He picked up his phone and dialled Jaye's home number. Fortunately her parents were in. Grace gave an edited version of the events to her mother and reversed the car. He promised to take her out again next Sunday, instead. They would go and see a giraffe, for sure.

Ten minutes later, holding his hand, she trotted back alongside him up to the front door of her house, her disappointment palpable.

He felt like a heel.

58

A mud-spattered police patrol car was waiting at the side of the main road, marking the start of the track into the forest for him. Grace pulled up alongside, then the constable at the wheel led the way for a good mile.

The waterlogged, potholed track was barely driveable in his car, the sump bottoming, the front wheels slithering and spinning as they lost traction. Mud exploded over the bonnet, spattering the windscreen with large brown flecks. Grace, who had just taken the Alfa to a pricey car wash before picking up Jaye, cursed. Then a clump of gorse scraped the side, sounding as hard as nails. He cursed again, more loudly, his nerves wound up, upset that he'd disappointed Jaye, but far more upset about the news of the body.

It wasn't necessarily Michael Harrison, he thought. But he had to admit it was hard to escape the coincidence. Michael Harrison was last seen in exactly this area. Now a body matching his age, height and build turns up.

Did not sound good.

As they rounded a bend he saw a cluster of vehicles ahead, and a strip of yellow crime-scene tape sealing off the area. There were two police cars, a white SOCO van, a plain green van – probably belonging to an undertaker – and a convertible Lotus Elise sports car which he knew belonged to Nigel Churchman, the local consultant pathologist who had a penchant for boy's toys. How had he got that up here?

He pulled up and opened his door, expecting the sickly stench of death to fill his nostrils. But all he smelled were pine, flowers, earth, the scents of the forest. Whoever it was had not been dead long, he thought, climbing out, his moccasin loafers instantly sinking into the boggy woodland soil.

He removed his white protective suit and overshoes from a bag in the boot of his car and pulled them on, then made his way over, ducking under the tape. Joe Tindall, also dressed in white protective clothing and white boots, turned towards him, holding a large camera.

'Hi!' Grace greeted him. 'You're having a great weekend!'

'You and me,' Tindall said sourly, nodding at the undergrowth yards behind him. 'You know my mother wanted me to be an accountant?'

'Never figured you for a bean counter,' Grace replied.

'Apparently, most accountants have a life,' he retorted. 'But what kind of a life?'

'One where they get to spend their Sundays at home with their wife and kids.'

'All the people I know with kids,' Grace replied, 'can't wait to get rid of them for the day. Especially on Sundays.' He patted his colleague on the back. 'One man's Sunday in his garden is another man's hell.'

Tindall jerked his head over at the body, barely visible in the dense undergrowth. 'Well, he's not having a great Sunday, whichever way you slice it.'

'Probably not the best metaphor under the circumstances,' Grace said, walking over towards the corpse, a dozen or more bluebottles hovering over it. Churchman, a handsome, fit-looking man with a boyish face, wearing a white oversuit, was kneeling beside it, holding a small tape recorder.

Grace saw a slightly overweight young man with short spiky fair hair, wearing a checked shirt, baggy jeans and brown boots, lying on his back, mouth open, eyes shut, his skin waxy white. There was a small gold earring in his right ear. The rounded face, frozen in death, had boyish looks.

He tried to recall the photographs of Michael Harrison that he had seen. The hair colouring was the same, the features could have been his, but he had seemed better-looking than this. Equally, Grace knew that people's looks changed after death, as the skin contracted and the blood dried.

Nigel Churchman looked up at him. 'Roy,' he said. 'Hi, how are you?'

'I'm OK, you?'

The pathologist nodded.

'What have we got?'

'I'm not sure yet – too early to tell.' With his rubber-gloved hands he gently lifted the young man's head. Grace swallowed as dozens of the small flies flew angrily off. There was a deep, uneven dent in the back of the cranium, covered in knotted hair and dark, congealed blood.

'He's had a violent blow from some blunt instrument,' Churchman said. Then with his typical dry humour he added, 'Wasn't good for his health.'

'You know, you get sicker every time I meet you.'

Churchman grinned broadly, as if it were a compliment. 'You sound like my wife.'

'I thought you got divorced?'

'I did.'

They were interrupted by a sharp fizz, crackle, then a burst of speech from the police radio of one of the constables behind him. Grace turned and saw the police officer talk into his two-way radio, giving a report. Then he looked down at the corpse, studying it carefully, noting again the face, the clothes, the cheap watch and the even cheaper-looking plastic strap. The green string bracelet on his right wrist. He swept his hand across the corpse's face, brushing away the hovering flies. Yes, the corpse was definitely in the right place, but could they be sure this was Michael Harrison?

'There's nothing on him at all? No credit card or paper?'

'Not that we've found.'

Looking down at the young man again, Grace wondered, was this how he would have dressed for his stag night? The image he had of Michael Harrison was altogether someone more classy-looking. This man looked like a spiv. But whoever he was, he did not deserve to be lying here, being pecked away by blowflies, with the back of his head stove in.

'Any sense of how long he's been here?' Grace asked.

Churchman stood up, to his full six-foot height. 'Tough one. Not long. No sign of first-generation larvae infestation; no discolouration on the skin – in the conditions we've had, several days of warm and damp air, we would expect rapid deterioration. He's been here twenty-four hours max, possibly less.'

Grace's brain was churning, thinking about all the young males aged twenty to thirty who had been reported missing in the past couple of weeks. He knew the statistics only too well, from all his years of searching for Sandy. Two hundred and fifty thousand people a year in England alone went missing. Of those, one-third were never seen again. Some were dead, their bodies disposed of so efficiently they would never be found. Others had run away, beyond the reach of the best efforts of the police. Or else they had gone overseas and changed their identities.

He only ever saw just a fraction of the missing person enquiries: those who had gone in suspicious circumstances; the ones the police were looking into and the tiny percentage of those he got asked to review.

The timescale fitted. The looks sort of fitted. *Sort of.* There was only one sure way to find out.

'Let's get him to the mortuary,' he said. 'See if we can get someone to identify him.'

59

Naked apart from the towel around his midriff, Mark padded out of the shower into the locker room of the sports club. He'd worked up a sweat, but it had been a lousy game of tennis. He had played badly against his regular Sunday-morning opponent, an olive-skinned half-Danish, half-American investment banker with a wiry determination called Tobias Kormind. He didn't usually beat Tobias, but he normally took one set off him. Today, distracted and unable to focus, he had only taken a couple of games in the entire match.

Mark liked Tobias because he had never been part of Michael's tight clique of old friends. And Tobias, who had a creative brain and was well connected in the London banking world, had given Mark some smart ideas on how to develop Double-M Properties beyond the confines of Brighton, and build it into an international property empire. But Michael had never wanted to know. He never saw the reason to take gambles; he just wanted to continue down the plodding path they were on, doing one development at a time, selling it, then moving to the next.

Tobias gave him a friendly pat on the back. 'Guess your mind wasn't on the game this morning, huh?'

'I guess not, I'm sorry.'

'Hey, you know, you've had terrible things happen to you this week. You lost four of your best friends, and your business partner has vanished.' Tobias, standing naked, towelled his hair vigorously. 'So what are the police doing?

You have to get behind them, you know, push them – like everybody else. They are probably all overworked and will respond best to the people who push them.'

Mark smiled. 'Ashley's a pretty tenacious girl – she's giving them hell.'

'How is she doing?'

'Bearing up – just about. It was tough for her yesterday – some people she hadn't been able to reach showed up for the wedding.'

Tobias had never met either Michael or Ashley, so he was not able to add much. 'Sounds bad, if he didn't show for the wedding.'

Mark nodded, inserting his key into his locker door. As he pulled it open his mobile, which he had left inside, beeped twice. The display informed him that he had four messages.

Apologizing to Tobias, and stepping a few paces away from him, he played them back. The first was from his mother, asking if there was any news, and reminding him not to be late for Sunday lunch today as she was going to a concert in the afternoon. The next was from Ashley, sounding worried. 'Mark? Mark? Oh, guess you are on court. Call as soon as you get this.' Then another one from Ashley. 'It's me, trying you again.' The fourth was also from Ashley. 'Mark – please call, it's really urgent.'

Moving further away from Tobias, he felt the blood draining from his head. *Had Michael turned up?*

All night he had been thinking, trying to figure out how Michael had got out of the coffin and what he would say to Michael if confronted by him. Would Michael believe that he did not know the plan? All it needed was one email on Michael's Palm. Mark – and the others – had sent him several, teasing him about the stag night.

He rang Ashley, fearing the worst. She sounded distressed, and at the same time strangely formal – he presumed for the benefit of anyone who might be tapping the phones.

'I – I don't know exactly what's going on,' she said. 'About half an hour ago I had a phone call from a young woman detective called Emma-Jane something – um . . .' She was silent for moment. Mark heard a rustle of paper and then her voice again. 'DC Boutwood. She asked me if Michael wore an earring. I told her he did when I first started going out with him, but I made him take it off because I thought it was bad for his image.'

'You were right,' Mark replied.

'Do you think he might have put it on for his stag night?'

'It's possible; you know he's always liked dressing up a bit wildly for an evening out. Why?'

'I've just had a call back from this Detective Constable. They've found a body that matches Michael's description – in the woods near Crowborough.' She began crying. It was a great performance if anyone was listening to their conversation.

'Oh Jesus,' Mark said. 'Are they sure it's him?'

In between deep, gulping sobs she said, 'I don't know. Michael's mother has been asked to go to the mortuary to identify the body. She's just rung to ask if I'll go with her. They want us to go over as soon as we can.'

'Do you want me to come? I could drive you both?'

'Would you mind? I – I don't think I could cope with driving, and Gill can't, she's on the floor. Oh God, Mark, this is so terrible.' Then she began crying again.

'Ashley, I'll be there as soon as I can. I'll pick Gill up first as she's nearest to me, then you. Be with you in half an hour.'

Ashley was crying so hard he wasn't even sure if she heard him.

60

Grace, driving back towards Brighton, phoned Jaye and apologized to her that he had had to cut short their day out.

'What's his name, the lost boy?' she asked.

Grace hesitated, then could see no harm in telling her. 'Michael.'

'Why is he hiding, Uncle Roy? Has he been naughty?'

He smiled; children saw the world so much more simply than adults. But it was a good question. He had learned a long time ago in police work never to take anything at face value; turn over every stone, open every door, always think out of the box. It was important to consider Michael Harrison as an active participant in his disappearance, as much as a passive one. Despite the corpse that should already be at the mortuary by now.

'I'm not sure,' he answered.

'What happens if you don't ever find Michael?'

It was an innocent question, but it hit home with his emotions. 'I think we will find him.' He didn't want to say anything about the corpse.

'But what happens if you don't?' she persisted. 'How long will you keep looking?'

He smiled sadly at her innocence. She'd been born a year after Sandy had disappeared and had no idea of the poignancy of her questions. 'For as long as it takes.'

'That could be a long time, if he's hidden really well. Couldn't it?'

'It's possible.'

'So that means we might not get to see a giraffe for years and years?'

After he had finished his conversation with her, he immediately dialled Emma-Jane Boutwood in the Incident Room. 'What did you find out about the earring?'

'Michael Harrison used to wear one all the time – a small gold ring, until his fiancée stopped him. But it's possible he was wearing it for his night out.'

Not good news, Grace thought. 'OK. Mobile phones. We should have the mobile phone numbers of Mark Warren and Ashley Harper on file by now – I want you to get on to the companies and get copies of their logs from – ' he thought for a moment, ' – last Saturday.'

'I might not get much joy until tomorrow, sir. I've had problems getting anything out of phone companies at weekends before.'

'Do your best.'

'Yes, sir.'

*

Ten minutes later, for the second time this weekend, Grace drove up to the long, low building that housed the Brighton and Hove City Mortuary. The bright May sunlight made no impact on its grim exterior, as if the grey pebbledash walls were there to ward off any therms of warmth that might dare try to enter. Only cold corpses and even colder souls were permitted inside.

Cleo Morey excepted.

He hoped she was on duty again today. *Very much* hoped, as he walked over to the entrance and rang the bell. Moments later, to his delight, Cleo opened the door. Dressed as usual in her uniform of green gown, green apron and white boots – the only kit he had ever seen her in – she greeted him with a bright smile, seeming genuinely pleased to see him.

And for a moment he stood, tongue-tied, like a kid on his first date with a girl he knows in his heart is out of his league. 'Hi!' he said, and then added, 'We can't go on meeting like this.'

'I prefer you walking in, than to have you come in feet first,' she said.

He shook his head, grinning. 'Thanks a lot.'

She ushered him in to her tiny office with its pink walls. 'Can I offer you some tea? Coffee? A cold drink?'

'Can you do a full Cornish cream tea?'

'Sure – scones with strawberry jam and clotted cream?'

'And toasted tea cakes?'

'Of course.' She tossed her blonde hair back, her eyes never leaving his, very definitely flirting with him. 'So, this is your idea of a relaxing Sunday afternoon?'

'Absolutely. Doesn't everyone take a Sunday afternoon drive out into the country?'

'They do,' she said, switching on the kettle. 'But most people go to enjoy the flowers and the wildlife – not to look at corpses.'

'*Really?*' he feigned. 'I knew there was something wrong with my life.'

'Mine too.'

There was a silence between them. An opportunity, he knew. The kettle made a faint hissing sound. He saw a trickle of steam from the plastic spout. 'You told me you weren't married – have you ever been?' he asked. 'Do you have a family?'

She turned to look at him, resting her eyes on his, a warm, friendly, relaxed gaze. 'You mean do I have an ex-husband, two-point-two children, a dog and a hamster?'

'That sort of thing.' Grace smiled at her, his colly-wobbles gone, feeling comfortable with her. Extremely comfortable.

'I have a goldfish,' she said. 'Does that count as family?'

'You do? Me too.'

'What's she called.'

'It's *he.* Marlon.'

She burst out laughing. 'That's an absurd name for a goldfish.'

'Luckily, he doesn't know that,' Grace responded.

She shook her head, grinning broadly as the kettle came to the boil. 'Actually, I think it's great.'

'So what's yours called?'

She teased him with her eyes for some moments, before saying, coyly, 'Fish.'

'*Fish?*' Grace echoed. 'That's its name?'

'*Her* name.'

'OK. Guess that's easy to remember. *Fish.*'

'Not as smart as *Marlon,*' she said.

'It's OK, I like it. It has a certain something about it.' Then he seized his chance, although the words came out clumsily. 'Don't suppose you'd like to meet up for that drink some time this week?'

The warmth of her reply took him by surprise. 'I would *love* to!'

'Great. OK. When's good – ah – I mean – how's tomorrow?'

'Monday's are good for me,' she said.

'Great. Terrific! Um . . .' He was racking his brains, thinking of somewhere to go. Brighton was full of cool bars, but right now he couldn't think of one. Should they go to a quiet bar? A buzzy place? A restaurant? Monday nights were quiet. Maybe just a pub first time, he thought. 'Whereabouts do you live?' he asked.

'Just up off the Level.'

'You know the Greys?'

'Of course!'

'How about there – about eight?'

'I'll see you there.'

The kettle shrieked and they both grinned. As she began pouring water into the pot, the doorbell rang. She went out of the room and came back in accompanied by the beanpole-tall frame of DC Nicholl, dressed in weekend casuals. 'Good afternoon, Roy,' he said, greeting his boss.

'Want some tea. Great service here today.'

'Earl Grey?' Cleo asked. 'Green leaf? Camomile? Darjeeling?'

Looking confused, the young DC, who was always very serious, very earnest, asked, 'Do you have any ordinary tea?'

'One builder's tea coming up,' Cleo said.

'So what do we think?' Grace asked, getting to the point.

'Gillian Harrison – Michael Harrison's mother – is on her way here to identify the body,' Nick informed him.

'I've made him look presentable,' Cleo said.

'It was one of her skills, to take a body – however badly marked or mangled – and make it look as intact and peaceful as possible for when a loved-one or relative came to identify someone. Sometimes it was never going to be possible. But as they walked through to the back of the mortuary, to the small, carpeted viewing room, with its perennial silver vase containing a small spray of plastic flowers, which doubled as a multidenominational chapel for the many people who wanted that solace, Grace could see she had done a good job on this body.

The young man had been placed on his back, his head resting on a plastic pillow which cleverly concealed the fact that the rear of his cranium was stove in. Cleo had washed the mud and grime off his face and hands, tidied his spiky hair and arranged his clothes. If it wasn't for his alabaster complexion, he could have been just another young man enjoying a quiet Sunday afternoon kip after a few jars in a boozer, Grace thought.

'Emma-Jane is on the case on the mobile phone numbers,' Nick Nicholl told him.

'We need to see which way the wind blows before deciding on any more action,' Grace said, looking at the body. 'Let's find out first if this is our man.' Then he heard the distant ring of the front entrance bell.

'I think we're about to find out now,' Cleo said, walking off.

Moments later she returned, followed by an ashen Gill Harrison, and Ashley Harper, stiff-faced, holding her hand. PC Linda Buckley, the Family Liaison Officer, stood a few steps behind. Michael Harrison's mother looked a wreck, as if she had just come in from gardening. Her hair was dishevelled; she wore a grubby windbreaker over a white sleeveless vest, brown polyester trousers and scuffed mules. Ashley, by contrast, in a navy suit and starchy white blouse, looked as if she was dressed in her Sunday best.

Both women acknowledged Grace with a silent nod, then he stepped aside to let them past. He watched them carefully as Cleo led them up to the viewing window, and for a moment his eyes were drawn to Cleo. She said few words to the two women, yet conveyed exactly the right balance of sympathy and professionalism. The more he saw of her, the more he liked her.

Gill Harrison said something and turned away, sobbing.

Ashley shook her head and turned away too, putting a comforting arm around her fiancé's mother.

'You are absolutely sure, Mrs Harrison?' Cleo asked.

'It's not my son,' she sobbed. 'It's not him, not Michael. It's not him.'

'It's not Michael,' Ashley confirmed to Cleo. Then she stopped in front of Grace and said, 'That's not Michael.'

Grace could see both women were telling the truth. Gill Harrison's bewildered expression was understandable. But he was surprised Ashley Harper did not look more relieved.

61

Two hours later, Grace, Glenn Branson, who had just arrived back from Solihull, Nick Nicholl, Bella Moy and Emma-Jane Boutwood sat at the work station which Operation Salsa had been allocated.

Grace smiled to reassure their new recruit, Emma-Jane, a slim, attractive girl with an alert face and long fair hair scooped up in a bun, then started to read out loud to them the report he had dictated since leaving the mortuary, and which Emma-Jane had just typed up. This was the way he liked to run all his investigations – keeping everything under constant review.

'The time is six-fifteen p.m., Sunday May 29th,' he read out. 'This is the first review of Operation Salsa, the investigation into the disappearance of twenty-nine-year-old male Michael Harrison, conducted on day five of his disappearance. I will now summarize the incident.'

For some minutes, Grace reviewed the events leading up to Michael's disappearance. Then he discussed possible suspects. 'At this time we have no evidence a crime has been committed. However, I am uncomfortable about Michael Harrison's business partner, Mark Warren, and his fiancée, Ashley Harper. I am also uncomfortable about Ashley's uncle from Canada, Bradley Cunningham, because I have a hunch he is not who he says he is – just a hunch at this stage.'

He paused to drink some water, then continued. 'Resourcing. East Downs Division has been very positive in offering manpower. We instigated a search of the vicinity of the accident last Tuesday night and have been upgrading the level of this further over the past few days. I'm now bringing in the Sussex Police Underwater Search Unit, and will have the USU team drag all local rivers, lakes and reservoirs. We will also request a further helicopter sweep – the visibility from the improved weather conditions may be helpful.'

He went on through the headings. 'Meeting cycles': Grace announced there would be a daily 8.30 a.m. and 6.30 p.m. briefing. He reported that the Holmes computer team had been up and running since Friday. He read out the list under the heading 'Investigative Strategies', which included 'Communications/Media', reporting that Michael Harrison's disappearance was scheduled to feature in this week's *Crimewatch* television programme if he hadn't turned up by then.

Next was 'Forensics'. Grace reported that soil samples from Mark Warren's car were being analysed along with soil samples recovered from the clothing and hands of the four dead boys. There should be an initial report some time tomorrow from Hilary Flowers, the forensic geologist they had consulted.

Then he reached the heading 'Any Concerns Raised by SIO', and there read out his detailed issues about the attitudes and anomalies in Mark Warren's and Ashley Harper's behaviour – and the disclosure of the Cayman Islands bank account of Double-M Properties.

When he reached the end of the report, he summed up: 'The alternative scenarios as I see them are as follows:

'One. Michael Harrison has been incarcerated somewhere and cannot escape.

'Two. Michael Harrison is dead – either as a result of his incarceration or has been unlawfully killed.

'Three. Michael Harrison has deliberately disappeared.'

Then he asked his team if they had any questions. Glenn Branson raised his hand and asked whether the body of the as yet unidentified man found in the woods had any bearing on the events.

'Unless there's a serial killer in Ashdown Forest targeting twenty-nine-year-old males, I don't think so.'

Grace's reply raised a titter despite the seriousness of the situation.

'Who's going to own this murder victim?' Branson asked.

'East Downs Division,' Grace said. 'We have enough on our plate.'

'Roy, any thoughts of putting tails on Ashley Harper and Mark Warren?' Branson asked.

It was an option he had been considering, but to put an effective twenty-four-hour surveillance watch on anyone could take as many as thirty people – three teams working in eight-hour shifts – on a simple job. More if it was complicated. The drain on manpower was astronomical, and Grace knew from experience that his chiefs would only sanction surveillance when absolutely necessary – such as on a potential major drugs bust or when there was a life at stake. If they made no headway soon, he might have to make the request.

'Yes,' he said. 'But park that for now. But what I do want is a scan on all the CCTV footage in Brighton and Hove last Thursday, from dawn until one a.m. Friday morning. Mark Warren was out in his car, a BMW off-roader – the details are on the file. I'd like to know where he went.' Then he added, 'Oh yes, and Michael Harrison has a yacht he keeps at the Sussex Motor Yacht Club. Someone should make sure it's still there. We'll look like dickheads organizing a manhunt if we find he's buggered off to sea on his boat.'

He looked at DC Boutwood. 'You can narrow the CCTV footage down from the mobile phone cell logs – you just need to pick the cameras in the area they throw up. Have you made any progress?'

'Not yet, sir. I'll be on it first thing in the morning – no one can help me today.'

Grace looked at his watch. 'I have to be in court tomorrow at ten – I may or may not be needed there all day. So we meet here at eight-thirty first.' He turned to Branson. 'Our liaison at the East Downs is Detective Inspector Jon Lamb. He's already got his team started – be good if you speak to him.'

'I'll call him in a few minutes.'

Grace fell silent, scanning the pages of the review, checking he had not missed anything. He needed to know more about the character of Michael Harrison and about his business relationship with Mark Warren, and also about Ashley Harper. Then he looked up at his team. 'It's now almost seven-thirty, on a Sunday evening. I think you should go home, get some rest – I think we're going to have a full week ahead of us. Thanks for giving up your Sunday.'

Branson, wearing fashionably baggy slacks and a sharp, zip-up cotton top, walked out to the car park with him. 'What's your sense, old wise one?' he asked.

Grace dug his hands in his pocket and said, 'I've been too close to this for the past couple of days – what's yours?'

Branson slapped his hands against his sides in frustration. 'Man! Why are you always doing this to me? Can't you just answer my questions?'

'I dunno. Tell me?'

'Shit, you really piss me off sometimes!'

'Oh, so you had a nice weekend away with your family, leaving me to do your job, and that pisses you off?'

Indignant, Branson exclaimed 'A *nice* weekend with my family. You call driving three hours up the M1 and three hours back, with a bolshy wife and two screaming kids, a *nice* weekend? Next time you drive them to Solihull, and I'll stay here and do whatever crap job you want me to do. Deal?'

'Bargain.'

Grace reached his car. Branson hovered. 'So, what is your sense?'

'It's not all as it seems, Horatio, that's my sense.'

'Meaning?'

'I can't put it any more clearly – yet. I have a bad feeling about Mark Warren and about Ashley Harper.'

'What kind of bad feeling?'

'A *very* bad feeling.'

Grace gave his friend a warm pat on the back, then climbed into his car and drove to the security gate. As he pulled out on the main road, with its panoramic view across Brighton and Hove, right down to the sea, with the sun still high above the horizon in the cloudless cobalt sky, he punched the CD button for Bob Berg's *Riddles*, and as he drove he began to chill. And for a few delicious moments his thoughts turned away from his investigations, to Cleo Morey.

And he smiled.

Then his thoughts turned back to work: to the long drive to south London and back he had ahead. If he was lucky, he might be home by midnight.

62

Mark, in sweatshirt, jeans and socks, paced around his apartment, a glass of whisky in his hand, unable to settle or to think clearly. The television was on, the sound mute, the actor Michael Kitchen striding, steely-faced, through a war-torn southern England landscape that looked vaguely familiar – somewhere near Hastings, he thought he recognized.

He had locked his door from the inside, bolted the safety chain. The balcony was safe, impenetrable, four floors up, and besides Michael had a fear of heights.

It was almost fully dark outside now. Ten o'clock. In just over three weeks it would be the longest day of the year. Through the glass doors to the balcony he watched a single light bobbing out at sea. A small boat, or yacht.

It had been weeks since he and Michael had taken out *Double-MM*, their racing sloop. He had planned to go to the Marina today and do some work on her. You could never leave a boat for long; there was always something leaking, corroding, tearing or peeling.

In truth, the boat was a damned chore for him. He wasn't even sure he needed the hassle, and rough seas petrified him. Sailing was a big part of Michael's life, always had been ever since Mark had known him. If he wanted to be Michael's business partner, then sharing the boat with him went with the territory.

And sure, they had fun, lots of fun; plenty of good, wind-blown days out sailing under a brilliant sky, plenty of weekends down the coast to Devon and Cornwall, and sometimes across to the French coast or the Channel Islands. But if he never stepped on a yacht again, it wouldn't bother him.

Where the fuck are you, Michael?

He drank some more whisky, sat on the sofa, leaned back, crossed his legs, feeling so damned confused. Michael and Ashley should have been jetting away on their romantic honeymoon today. He had not figured how he was going to cope with that, Ashley making love to Michael, loads of times probably. He would have expected that on a damned honeymoon, unless she feigned something – she had promised him she was going to feign something, but how could she keep that up for a fortnight?

And besides, he knew she and Michael had already slept together, it was part of their plan. At least she had told him Michael was lousy in bed.

Unless that was a lie.

He shook the ice cubes around in the glass and drank some more. He'd rung Pete's, Luke's and Josh's widows, and Robbo's father, each time on the pretext of finding out about the funeral plans – but in reality to pick their brains, to see if any of them had let anything slip before they'd gone out on Tuesday night. Anything that could incriminate him, or that could give him a clue to what they had been planning.

Michael had been there Thursday night, for sure. He had not imagined it. No way. So, he was there Thursday night, but not last night. The coffin lid was screwed down tight. And Michael was not Houdini.

So if Michael had been there Thursday and was not there now, someone must have let him out. And then screwed back the lid. But why?

Michael's humour?

And if he had got out why didn't he show up for the wedding?

Shaking his head he arrived back at his starting point. Michael was not in the coffin and he had imagined the voice. Ashley was convinced of that. There were moments when he convinced himself. But not strongly enough.

He needed to talk this through with Ashley some more. What if Michael had somehow got out and discovered their plans?

Then surely he would have confronted one or the other of them by now.

He stood up, wondering if he should go over to Ashley's. She was worrying him, behaving so damned coldly towards him, as if this whole thing was his bloody fault. But he knew what she would say to him.

He stood up and paced around the room again. If Michael was alive, if he had got out of the coffin, what could he find out from the emails on his Palm?

Mark suddenly realized in the panic of the past few days he had overlooked one very simple way of checking. Michael always backed up the contents of his Palm onto the office server.

He went into his study, flipped open the lid of his laptop and logged on. Then cursed. The damned server was down.

And there was only one way to get it back up and running.

63

Max Candille was almost impossibly good-looking, Roy Grace always thought on each occasion he met him. In his mid-twenties, with bleached blond hair, blue eyes and striking features, he was a modern Adonis. He could surely have been a top model, or a movie star. Instead, in his modest semi-detached house in the suburban town of Purley, he had chosen to make his *gift,* as he called it, his career. Even so, he was quietly becoming a rising media star.

The bland exterior of the house, with its mock-Tudor beams, neat lawn and a clean Smart parked in the driveway, gave few clues about the nature of its occupant.

The whole interior of the house – the downstairs at least, which was all Grace had ever seen – was white. The walls, the carpets, the furniture, the slender modern sculptures, the paintings, even the two cats which prowled around like bonsai versions of Siegfried and Roy's tigers, were white. And seated in front of him, in an ornate rococo chair, with a white frame and white satin upholstery, sat the medium, dressed in a white roll-neck, white Calvin Klein jeans and white leather boots.

He held his china demitasse of herbal tea delicately between his finger and thumb and spoke in a voice that was borderline camp.

'You look tired, Roy. Working too hard?'

'I apologize again for coming so late,' Grace said, sipping the espresso Candille had made for him.

'The spirit world doesn't have the same time frames as the human one, Roy. I don't consider myself a slave to any clock. Look!' He put down his tea, held up both his hands, and pulled each sleeve back to reveal he wore no watch. 'See?'

'You're lucky.'

'Oscar Wilde is my hero when it comes to time. He was always unpunctual. One time when he arrived exceptionally late for a dinner party the hostess angrily pointed at the clock on the wall and said, "Mr Wilde, are you aware what the time is?" And he replied, "My dear lady, pray tell me, how can that nasty little machine possibly know what the great golden sun is up to?"'

Grace grinned. 'Good one.'

'So, are you going to tell me what brings you here today, or should I guess? Might we be concerned with something to do with a wedding? Am I warm?'

'No prizes for that one, Max.'

Candille grinned. Grace rated the man. He didn't always get things right, but his hit rate was high. In Grace's long experience, he didn't believe that any medium was capable of always getting everything right, which is why he liked to work with several, sometimes cross-checking one against another.

No medium he had worked with so far had been able to tell him what had happened to Sandy – and he had been to many. In the months following her disappearance he visited every medium he could find who had any kind of a reputation. He had tried a few times with Max Candille, who had been honest enough at their very first meeting to tell him that he simply did not know, that he was unable to make a connection with her. Some people left a trail behind, all kinds of vibrations in the air, or in their belongings, Max had explained. Others, nothing. It was as if, Max told him, Sandy had never existed. He couldn't explain it. He couldn't say whether she had covered her own tracks, or if someone had done it for her. He didn't know whether she was alive or not.

But he seemed very much more definite about Michael Harrison. Taking the bracelet Ashley had given Grace, he thrust it back at the police officer within seconds, as if it was burning his hand. 'Not his,' he said, emphatically. 'Absolutely not his.'

Frowning, Grace asked, 'Are you sure?'

'Yes, I'm sure, absolutely.'

'It was given to me by his fiancée.'

'Then you need to ask her and yourself *why*. This absolutely does not belong to Michael Harrison.'

Grace wrapped the bracelet back in a tissue and carefully pocketed it. Max Candille was emotional – and *not* always accurate. However, combining his comments on the bracelet with Harry Frame's, something did not feel right about it.

'So what can you tell me about Michael Harrison?' Grace asked.

The medium sprang up from his chair, went out of the room, pausing to blow kisses at the cats, then returned moments later holding a copy of the *News of the World*. 'My favourite paper,' he informed Grace. 'I like to know who's screwing who. Far more interesting than politics.'

Grace enjoyed reading it himself, sometimes, but wasn't about to admit that now. 'I'm sure,' he said.

The medium folded back a couple of pages then held the paper up so Grace could see the headline, with Michael Harrison's photograph beneath. 'MANHUNT FOR AWOL FIANCE'.

Then the medium looked at it himself for some moments. 'Well, see, you are even quoted in here. "'We are now regarding Michael Harrison's disappearance as a Major Incident,' said Detective Superintendent Roy Grace of Sussex Police, 'And are stepping up police manpower to comb the area he is believed to be in . . .'"'

Then he looked up at Grace again. 'Michael Harrison's alive,' he said. 'Definitely alive.'

'Really? Where? I need to find him – that's what I need your help for.'

'I see him somewhere small, dark.'

'Could it be a coffin?'

'I don't know, Roy. It's too blurred. I don't think he has much energy.' He closed his eyes for some moments and slowly swivelled his head from left to right. 'No, very little there. The battery's almost flat, poor thing.'

'What do you mean?'

The medium closed his eyes again. 'He's weak.'

'How weak?' Grace asked, concerned.

'He's fading, his pulse is low, much too low.'

Grace watched him, wondering. *How did Max know this?* Was he connected across the ether? Just making a guess on a hunch? 'This small dark place – is it in the woods? In a town? Under ground or above ground? On water?'

'I can't see, Roy. I can't tell.'

'How long has he got?' Grace asked.

'Not long. I don't know if he's going to make it.'

64

'You see, here's the thing, Mike. Not everyone gets to have a lucky day on the same day. So we have a sort of irregular situation here – this is your lucky day and it's my lucky day. How lucky is that?'

Michael, weak, shivering from fever and near-delirious, stared up, but all he could see was darkness. He did not recognize the man's voice; it sounded a hybrid of Australian and south London, spoken quickly, with fast, nervy inflections. Davey with another of his accents? No, he did not think so. His brain swirled. Confused. He did not know where he was. In the coffin?

Dead?

His head pounded, his throat was parched. He tried to open his mouth, but his lips would not part. Ice squirmed through his veins.

I'm dead.

'You were in a horrible wet coffin, getting all soggy and rheumatoid, now you're in a nice, dry, cosy cot. You were going to die. Now maybe you aren't going to die – but I want to stress that's a pretty big *maybe*!'

The voice receded into the darkness. Michael was sinking, going down a lift shaft, down, down, the walls rushing past. He tried to call out, but his lips would not move. There was something pressing tightly around his mouth. All he could do was make a panicky grunt.

Then the voice again, really close, as if the man was in

the lift with him. 'Do you know about Schrödinger's Cat, Mike?'

They were still going down. How many floors? Did it matter?

'Did you study physics when you were at school?'

Who was this? Where was he? 'Davey', he tried to say, but all that came out was a murmur.

'If you know anything about science, Mike, you'd know about it. Schrödinger's Cat was inside a box, and was both alive and dead at the same time. That's like you now, my friend.'

Michael felt consciousness slipping away. The lift was swaying on ropes now; darkness seemed to be racing past him, round and round. He closed his eyes. Then felt a blast of heat and saw red through his eyelids. He opened his eyes, then immediately squeezed them shut against a blinding glare of light.

'I don't think you should be going to sleep; you need to keep awake now, Mike. Can't let you die on me, I went to a lot of trouble. I'll give you more water and glucose in a while, got to introduce foods to you slowly. I got trained in all this stuff, you're in good hands. Jungle training. I know how to survive, and help others survive. You're lucky it was me who came along. Need to keep you awake. We'll chat to each other for a while, get to know each other a little better – bond a little, OK?'

Michael tried to speak again. Just a murmur came out. He was trying to remember, the sensation of being lifted from the coffin, of being on something soft in a van – but was that on the stag night? Was this maybe one of his mates? Weren't they dead? Mark? He just wanted to close his eyes and sleep now.

Cold water lashed his face, startling him. His eyes sprang open, blinking into watery darkness.

'I'm just keeping you awake, no offence meant, mate.' The voice sounded more Australian than south London now.

Michael shivered; the water had sharpened him a fraction. He tried to move his arms, to see if he was still in the coffin, but he couldn't move them. He tried to move his legs, but they wouldn't move either; it was as if they were bound together. He tried to raise his head, to touch the lid, but he barely had the strength to raise it a couple of inches.

'Guess you're wondering who I am and where you are?'

Michael closed his eyes tightly again as a blast of light dazzled him, hurting his retinas like sunburn. He emitted another grunt.

'It's OK, Mike, don't bother to try to talk back. It's duct tape – hard to say anything through that. I'll do the talking and you just do the listening – until you're better, that is. We have a deal?'

Michael felt bewildered; but at the same time deeply apprehensive. Nothing was making any sense – he wondered if he was dreaming or hallucinating.

'First, Mike, I'm going to give you the house rules. You don't ask my name and you don't ask where we are. You got that?'

Michael grunted again.

'I'll remind you later, anyway. You ever see that Stephen King film, *Misery*?'

Michael heard the question through his drifting mind, but was unsure whether it was directed at him or someone else. *Misery*. He seemed to recall it. Kathy Bates. He tried to ask if Kathy Bates was in it, but his damned lips wouldn't move. 'Mnhhhh,' he said.

'That was some movie. Remember, James Caan got caught by his crazy fan, Kathy Bates, who smashed his legs with a sledgehammer so he couldn't run away? But that wasn't faithful to the novel, you know, Mike? Did you know that?'

'Mnhhhh.'

'In the novel she actually cut one leg off, then cauterized it with a blow torch. You got to be pretty weird to do that, wouldn't you think, Mike?'

Michael stared into the darkness, trying to make out his features, to put a face to the voice, to check if this voice was coming from above him, below him, inside him.

'You would, wouldn't you, Mike?'

'Mnhhhh.'

'I've been listening to you for five days, Mike. You and your buddy, Davey. Figured you were getting pretty frustrated with him – I would have been too, in your shoes.' The man laughed. 'I mean, that's pretty tough shit. You get trapped and the only person in the whole world who knows you're alive is a fucking moron!' He was silent for some moments, then he continued. 'Of course, I was there with you, Mike, as well, but I just didn't want to interrupt. Breakers' code, don't butt in on someone else's conversation. Well, that's my code anyway. How you doing?'

Michael's head was throbbing, darkness swirling all around him even faster now.

'You're doing OK. Another twenty-four hours in that grave and you might as well have stayed there. But you'll be OK now. I'll get your strength up; you're lucky, I was trained in the Australian SAS. Signals. I know all about survival; you couldn't be in better hands, Mike. I'd say that was worth a lot, wouldn't you? I'm talking about money, Mike. Big money! Moolah!'

'Mnhhhh.'

'But I'm afraid I'm going to need some bona fides, Mike. Understand what bona fides are? Proof it's you – are you on my bus?'

Michael squeezed his eyes shut against another burst of light. Then he opened them again and caught a glint of steel.

'This will hurt a little, but you don't have to worry, Mike. I'm not doing a Kathy Bates on you – I'm not crazy; I'm not about to cripple you. Just need some bona fides, that's all.'

Then Michael, through his delirium, felt an excruciating pain in his left index finger. He bellowed in agony, a tornado of air hurtling up his windpipe and screeching through the duct tape like a banshee.

65

Arriving back in Brighton shortly before midnight, Roy Grace was wide awake. The large espresso Candille had made him seemed to be having an effect like rocket fuel on his energy level. For no particular reason he decided to make a small detour and swing past the offices of Double-M Properties, in the street just below Brighton station.

As he approached he was surprised to see Warren's BMW parked right outside. He pulled up in front of it, climbed out and looked up. He could see on the third floor that the lights were on, and again, purely on a whim, he walked up to the front entrance and pressed the Double-M button on the panel.

After some moments he heard a crackly, very wary-sounding Mark Warren. 'Hello?'

'Mr Warren – Detective Superintendent Grace.'

There was a long silence. Then Mark Warren said, 'Come on up.' There was a sharp rasping sound from the lock, and Grace pushed open the door, then climbed three steep, narrow flights of stairs.

Mark opened the glass-panelled door into the reception area, looking sheet-white and, in Grace's opinion, very uneasy. 'This is a bit of a surprise, officer,' he said clumsily.

'I was just passing, saw the lights were on – wondered if we could have a quick chat. I thought you might like an update.'

'Um – yes, thank you.'

Mark shot a nervous glance at an open door behind

him, which led into an office where he was clearly working. He then steered Grace in a different direction, into a cold, windowless boardroom, switched on the lights and pulled out a chair for him at the highly polished conference table.

But before he sat down, Grace fished in his pocket and pulled out the bracelet he'd been given by Ashley. 'I found this on the staircase – does it belong to anyone who works here?'

Mark stared at it. 'On the staircase?'

Grace nodded.

'Actually, yes, this is mine – it has tiny magnets at each end – I wear it for my tennis elbow. I – I don't know how it got there.'

'Lucky I spotted it,' Grace said.

'Indeed – thank you.' Mark seemed very confused.

Grace noted a row of framed photographs on the walls: a warehouse at Shoreham Harbour, a tall Regency terraced house and a modern office block, which he recognized as being on the London Road, on the outskirts of Brighton. 'These all yours?' he asked.

'Yes.' Mark fiddled with the bracelet for some moments, then pulled it onto his right wrist.

'Impressive,' Grace said, nodding at the photographs. 'Seems like you have a good business.'

'Thank you. It's going well.'

Mindful of the blasting he'd had from Ashley after being rude to the Detective Superintendent yesterday at the wedding, Mark was now making a big effort to be polite. 'Can I get you a coffee or anything?'

'I'm fine, thanks all the same,' Grace said. 'Equal shares – you and Michael Harrison?'

'No – he has the majority.'

'Ah. He put up the money?'

'Yes – well, two thirds. I put up the rest.'

Watching his body language carefully, Grace asked, 'And there are no issues between you, over this imbalance?'

'No, officer – we get on well.'

'Good. Well . . .' Grace stifled a yawn. 'We're stepping up our search of the area in the morning. As you may have heard, we had a false alarm today.'

'The body of the young man. Who was he?'

'A local chap – a young man who I'm told was a bit backward. Quite a few of the local police knew him, apparently – his dad's got a tow-truck and crash repair business – does quite a lot of work for the Traffic Division.'

'Poor sod. He was murdered?'

'It seems likely,' Grace said guardedly. Then, watching Mark again closely, he said, 'Am I correct that you and Michael Harrison have a bank account in the Cayman Islands?'

Without flinching, Mark replied, 'Yes, we have a company there, HW Properties International.'

'Two-thirds – one-third split?'

'Correct.'

Grace remembered there was at least one million pounds in that account. More than a tidy sum. 'What kind of insurance do you and Michael have? Do you have life insurance policies on each other, as business partners?'

'We have the usual key-man insurance – do you want to see the policy?'

'Not at this moment, but at some point I'd like to, yes. Perhaps you could fax a copy over to the Incident Room for me tomorrow?'

'No problem.'

Grace stood up. 'Well, I won't trouble you any more tonight. Busy are you? Often work on a Sunday night?'

'I like to catch up on my paperwork at the weekend. Only chance I get when the phones aren't ringing.'

Grace smiled. 'I know the feeling.'

Mark watched the detective's head disappear down the stairwell, then closed the door, making sure the latch was down, then returned to his office, switched his computer back on, and began the arduous task he had started a couple of hours earlier, of reading every day's back-up of Michael's Palm, going back weeks, and deleting any references to the stag night.

Ashley had been spending this afternoon doing the same on the laptops of Peter, Luke, Josh and Robbo, on the pretext to their families that she was looking for clues about Michael's whereabouts.

Downstairs, Grace closed the front door behind him and walked across the pavement to his car. But it was some moments before he climbed back into it. Instead, he leaned against the passenger door, staring up at the third-floor window, thinking. Thinking.

He did not like Mark Warren. The man was a liar – and he was nervous as hell about something. Ashley Harper was a liar, also. She had deliberately given him a bracelet that did not belong to Michael.

And what exactly was Mark Warren's bracelet doing in her house?

66

Jesus, oh Jesus. Michael was crying in pain, holding up his left hand as far as the duct tape wound right around his body, pinioning both arms to his side, would allow. Blood gouted from the stump of his forefinger, cut off at the first joint. He stared up into the blinding lights. 'What is this; what the hell are you doing?'

'It's OK, Mike, relax!'

His arm was held by a thin, hairy hand with an iron grip, the wrist sporting a heavy diver's watch. And he could see his assailant's head now, shadowy against the dazzling lights, two eyes behind slits in a black hood.

Then he saw white cream oozing from the neck of a tube, and the next moment it felt as if ice had been put on his finger. He cried out again, the pain almost unbearable.

'I know what I'm doing, Mike. You don't have to worry; it won't go septic. I'd like you to call me Vic. Understand? Vic?'

'Vhrrrr,' Michael gasped.

'That's good, you and me on first-name terms. We're business partners, see? We should be on first-name terms.'

His assailant pulled out a long white bandage and wound it tightly around the bloody tip of the finger, then on down, tighter and tighter until it was acting as a tourniquet. Then he wound sticking plaster around it to hold it. 'See, Mike, the way I look at it, I saved your life – so that's got to be worth something, hasn't it? And from what I read in the papers and saw on television, it seems like you're loaded. I'm not, you see, that's the difference. Want some water?'

Michael nodded. He was trying to think straight but the numbing, throbbing pain in his finger made that hard.

'If you want to drink, I have to take the tape off your mouth. I do that on condition you don't shout. Is that a deal, Mike?'

He nodded his head.

'My word has always been my bond. Is it yours?'

Again Michael nodded.

An arm reached down. The next instant Michael felt as if half the skin on his face had been ripped away. His mouth gasped open, his chin and cheek stinging like hell. Then the man reached down again holding a plastic mineral water bottle with the top removed and tilted some of the contents into Michael's mouth. It tasted cold and good as he gulped it down greedily, some spilling over and dribbling down his chin and neck. Then some went down the wrong way and he began to choke.

The bottle was withdrawn. He carried on coughing. When the fit finally stopped, he felt more alert. He could smell dank air and engine oil as if he was in some kind of underground car park. Looking up at the eye slits he asked, 'Where am I?'

'You have a short memory, Mike. I told you never to ask where you are, or who I am.'

'You – you said Vic – your name.'

'I'm Vic to you, Mike.'

There was a silence between them.

In his rapidly clearing brain Michael was starting to feel

more scared of this man that he had been in the coffin. 'How – how did you find me?'

'I spend all week out in my camper van, Mike – see, I check on mobile phone masts around the south of England, for the phone companies. Listen to the old Citizens' Band radio, chat to a few mates around the globe. When there's no one to chat to, I scan all the radio bands, sometimes listen in to the police chatter. With my kit I can listen to just about any conversation I want – mobile phones, anything. Told you I was in Signals in the Australian Marines.'

Michael nodded.

'So, Wednesday, I was sitting around in the evening after work and I stumbled across Davey and you having a cosy chat. I stayed tuned to the channel and picked up some subsequent chats between you. Saw the news coverage, heard about the coffin. So I pulled on my thinking hat and I thought to myself, if I was going to take my best mate on a pub crawl why would I take a coffin? Maybe to hide you somewhere? Bit of a sick prank? So I went along to the local Planning Office in Brighton and looked up your company – and lo! – I discover you're applying for planning consent on forest land you bought last year, right in the area where you were having your pub crawl. I figured was that a coincidence, or was that a coincidence? And I also figured, out on a pub crawl, your mates would all be lazy bastards. They wouldn't want to carry you too far. You'd be close to a track you could get a vehicle down.'

'Is that where I was?' Michael asked.

'That's where you'd still be, mate. Now tell me about this money you have stashed away in the Cayman Islands.'

'What do you mean?'

'I told you, I pick up chatter on the police radios. You've

got money in the Cayman Islands, haven't you? North of a million, I understand. Wouldn't that be a reasonable reward for saving your life? Cheap at twice the price, Mike, if you ask me.'

67

At 7.20 the next morning, Grace arrived at Sussex House. The sky was dark blue, with wispy trails of cloud like strips of rags. One cop he'd been out on the beat with years back knew all about cloud formations and could predict the weather from them. From memory, the clouds up there this morning were cumulonimbus. Dry weather. Good for the search today.

In most police stations he could have got a good fry-up, which was what he needed for energy, he thought as he walked along the corridor to the bank of vending machines. He pushed a coin in the hot drinks dispenser, then waited for the plastic cup to fill with white coffee. Carrying it back to his office, he realized how weary he felt. All night he'd tossed and turned, switched the light on, made a note, switched it off, then back on again. Operation Salsa drip-fed its facts and anomalies to him relentlessly, drip by drip by drip, until grey light had begun to seep around the curtains, and the first tentative chatter of dawn birdsong had begun.

The bracelet. The BMW arriving back so late in the parking lot, covered in mud. Mark Warren working in his office at midnight on a Sunday. Ashley Harper's Canadian uncle, Bradley Cunningham. Ashley Harper's expression and behaviour at the mortuary today. Forensic results on the soil due today. CCTV results, possibly.

He looked at his in-tray, piled with post from last week he had not yet dealt with, then switched on his computer and looked at an even bigger stack of emails in his in-box. Then his door opened and he heard a chirpy, 'Good morning, Roy.'

It was Eleanor Hodgson, his management support assistant, who he had asked to come in especially early today. She held a sheet of paper in her hand.

'How was your weekend?' he asked.

'Very nice, I went to my niece's wedding on Saturday, then had a houseful of relatives yesterday. And you?'

'Managed to get out in the country yesterday.'

'Good!' she said. 'You needed a break and some fresh air.' She peered at him more closely. 'You look very pale, you know.'

'Tell me about it.' He took the sheet of paper, already knowing what it was – his agenda for the week. She had produced it every Monday morning for him, for as long as he could remember.

He sat down, the smell of the coffee tantalizing, but the liquid as yet too hot to drink, and scanned the agenda, needing to clear his diary of everything non-essential now he was the SIO on the case.

At ten this morning he was due to attend court for the continuation of the Suresh Hossain trial, and he would have to do that. At 1 p.m. he had a dentist's appointment in Lewes – which would have to be cancelled. At 3 o'clock tomorrow he had a meeting scheduled with South Wales CID for an exchange of information on a known Swansea villain found dead with a snooker cue sticking through his eye on a waste tip near Newhaven. That would have to be rescheduled. On Wednesday he was due at the Police Training College at Bramshill for an update on DNA fingerprinting. Thursday's highlight was the Sussex Police headquarters cricket team – of which he had landed himself the unwelcome headache of being Hon. Sec. – AGM. Friday was clear at the moment, and on Saturday there was a terrorist attack training exercise at Shoreham Harbour – in which he was not involved.

It would have been a nothing week, if it weren't for the Hossain trial and now Operation Salsa. But, then, in his experience, few weeks finished the way he expected them to.

He told Eleanor to reschedule everything except his trial attendances, then rummaged through his post, dictating replies to the most urgent on the pile. He scanned his emails and because time was short and he was a slow typist, dictated replies to those, too. Then he walked along the maze of corridors to the Incident Room. It was already beginning to feel like home to him.

*

The 8.30 a.m. Operation Salsa briefing meeting was short. There had been no new developments overnight – apart from what he had gleaned from Max Candille, which he kept to himself, and from his visit to Double-M's offices. Hopefully by their next meeting at 6.30 p.m. there might be some news.

Grace drove into Lewes, stopping at a petrol station on the way to buy an egg and bacon sandwich, which he was still munching as he walked up the courthouse steps at 9.50. It was already beginning to feel like a very long day.

The morning proceedings were taken up with in-camera submissions to the Judge by the prosecuting counsel, and all Grace could do was hang around in the waiting room, giving Eleanor some dictation over the phone and speaking to Glenn Branson a couple of times. There was not enough time to get to the office and back during the lunch recess, so instead he went along to his dental appointment after all, for his six-monthly check-up, and to his relief his teeth were fine, although he received a reprimand from the dentist about not brushing his gums carefully enough. But at least no fillings – he dreaded them, always had.

Returning to court at 2 p.m., he discovered he was not going to be needed for the rest of the day, and went back to his office. With the time Operation Salsa was now consuming, a massive backlog was building up on the rest of his paperwork, and he did his best to deal with the most urgent of it.

It was an uneventful afternoon for him, right up until his arrival at the 6 p.m. briefing in the Incident Room. He could tell instantly from the team's faces that there had been a development. It was Bella Moy who told him the news.

'I've just had a call from a Phil Wheeler, Roy – the father of the murdered lad found this afternoon.'

'Tell me?'

'He said he didn't know if it was significant, but apparently his son told him that he'd been chatting with Michael Harrison on a walkie-talkie radio – since – Thursday.'

68

Ashley walked up behind Mark, who was hunched over his desk in front of his computer screen, trying to catch up on his work. He badly owed the architect, the quantity surveyor and the construction company responses to a whole raft of emails on issues that had been raised by the Planning Department over the company's most ambitious project to date, the new Ashdown development of twenty houses.

She slipped her arms around his neck, leaned forward and nuzzled his cheek. He breathed in the heady scents of her fresh, summery cologne and the faint citrus tang of her hair.

Bleary-eyed, he lifted his arms up and cupped her cheeks in his hands. 'We're going to be OK,' he said.

'Of course. We don't do *not OK*, right?'

'Right.'

Leaning further over, she kissed him on the forehead.

Mark shot a glance across the office at the open doorway, wary every second of the day and night of who might walk through it.

She kissed him again. 'I love you,' she said.

'I love you too, Ashley.'

'Do you? You haven't shown me much affection the past few days,' she chided.

'Oh, right, like you've been all over me?'

'Let's put that behind us.' She nibbled his ear, then, unbuttoning his shirt front, slipped her hands inside and began to tease his nipples with her fingers and thumbs. She felt him react almost instantly, heard his sharp intake of breath, felt his chest tighten. Slipping her hands out, she reached around him, clicked his mouse to exit the program, then whispered into his ear, 'Fuck me.'

'Here?'

'Here, now!'

Mark stood up, a little panicky, and glanced at his watch. 'The cleaners come around six-thirty – they'll be—'

Ashley unbuckled his suit trousers, and jerked down his zip. Then she pulled down his trousers and underpants together in one swift tug. 'So we'll just have to have a quickie, won't we?' She stopped and stared for a moment, as if in appreciation, at his engorged penis, then said, 'Well, somebody seems pleased to see me!'

Then she took him in her mouth.

Mark stared out of the window. They were in full view of the windows across the street. He tried to step sideways and almost tripped over his trousers and pants. He leaned down, fumbled with the buttons on Ashley's blouse, got his hands inside, unhooked her bra. Within a couple of minutes, naked except for his shoes and socks, he was lying on top of her, deep inside, the dusty, nylon smell of the hard carpet mingling with Ashley's scents in his nostrils.

Then there was a sharp buzz from the intercom.

'Shit!' he said, panicking. 'Who the fuck's that?'

Ashley pulled him tighter into her, her nails raking his back. 'Ignore it,' she said.

'What if it's Michael? Checking if anyone is in?'

'You're such a wuss!' she said, releasing him.

Ignoring the remark, Mark hauled himself to his feet and hobbled out of the room and over to the reception desk which Ashley normally manned and stared at the small black and white CCTV monitor. He could see a man in a motorcycle helmet, holding a package, standing outside the front door in the street. Mark pressed the *speak* button. 'Hello?'

'Package for Mr Warren, Double-M Properties.'

'Do you want to just put it through the letter box?'

'I need a signature.'

Mark cursed. 'I'll be down in a moment.'

He pulled his clothes back on, stuffing his shirt tails into his trousers, and blew Ashley a kiss. 'Back in two secs.'

'Don't worry about me,' she said unsmiling. 'I'll carry on without you.'

He hurried downstairs, opened the door and took a small Jiffy bag, with a printed label addressed to him but no information where it was from, from a stocky hulk of a man in leathers with 'FAST TRACK COURIERS' embossed on the front. He signed the docket, was given a duplicate copy then closed the door and climbed back up the staircase.

The sender's handwritten name on the docket read, 'JK Contractors'. Mark had no idea what was inside it. There was so much damned paperwork on the planning applications that he was steadily sinking under the mountain. This was probably a bunch of technical drawings from the quantity surveyor. Typically extravagant to send them by courier when post would have been fine. He would open it later. Right now there was just one thing on his mind, Ashley, lying naked on his office floor. And he was feeling crazily, dizzily, rampantly horny.

Then, totally unexpectedly, within seconds of lying back on top of her it was all over.

'Sorry,' he said, taking his weight on his elbows. 'I—'

'Get turned on by motorcycle couriers, do you?' she asked, seemingly only partly in jest.

'Oh sure.'

'A lot of men are gay and don't realize it. You know, bikers in leather can be a pretty erotic thing for guys.'

'What is this?'

'What do you think it is? You leave me here naked and on the verge of coming; you go down and see a guy in leathers and the next moment you shoot your bolt before you've barely got back inside me.'

He rolled off and sat up beside her on the floor, a wave of gloom washing through him. 'I'm sorry,' he said. 'I just have a shitload of stuff going on in my head at the moment.'

'And I don't?'

'Maybe you're better at handling this than I am.'

'I don't know what you're capable of handling, Mark. I thought you were the strong guy and Michael was the weak one.'

He leaned forward and placed his face in his hands. 'Ashley, we're both tense, OK.'

'You shouldn't be tense, you just had a great orgasm.'

'OK, OK, OK. I have apologized. You want me to work on you? I'll make you come – you know – by hand.'

She stood up abruptly, picking up some of her clothes as she did. 'Forget it, I'm not in the mood any more.'

They both dressed in silence. It was Ashley, putting on some lipstick, who finally broke it. 'You know what they say, Mark? Good sex is one per cent of a relationship; bad sex is ninety-nine per cent.'

'I thought we had great sex – normally.'

She checked her lipstick in her compact mirror, as if she was about to go out on a date. 'Yes, well, I did, too.'

Mark walked over and put an arm around her. 'Ashley, darling, come on, I apologized – I'm so damned stressed. We should go away for a few days.'

'Sure, that would look good, wouldn't it.'

'I mean when this is all over.'

She gave him a sharp look. 'When exactly will it all be over?'

'I don't know.'

She put her mirror away in her handbag. 'Mark, darling, it can never be over while Michael is alive. We both know that. We burnt our bridges on Thursday night when you took out the breathing tube.' She gave him a peck on the cheek. 'See you in the morning.'

'Are you going?'

'Yes, I'm going. I always go at the end of the day; something wrong with that? I thought we were supposed to be keeping up appearances?'

'I guess, yes – I mean . . .'

She looked at him for a couple of seconds. 'Pull yourself together, for Christ's sake. Understand?'

He nodded lamely. Then she was gone.

He stayed on for another hour, working on his emails, then, with the noise of the cleaners driving him to distraction, he decided to quit for the day and take the rest of his work home.

On his way to the door, he picked up the package he had signed for earlier and tore it open. There was something inside, a small object, tightly wrapped in cellophane then bound with tape.

Frowning, he wondered what it was. A replacement sim card for a mobile? A computer part?

He pulled a pair of scissors out of the desk drawer and snipped one end open, squeezed it, and peered inside.

At first he thought it was a joke, one of those plastic fake fingers you can buy in novelty shops. Then he saw the blood.

'No,' he said, feeling giddy suddenly. 'No. NO.'

The severed fingertip fell from the pack and landed noiselessly on the carpet.

Stepping back away from it in horror, Mark saw there was an envelope inside the packet.

69

Grace turned off the main road and onto a country lane, barely beyond the outskirts of Lewes. He passed a farm-shop sign, a telephone booth, then saw a tall mesh fence topped with barbed wire, some of it erect, some in a state of collapse, ahead on his left. There were two gates, wide open, that didn't look as if they had been closed in a decade. Fixed to one of them was a faded, cracked painted sign which read 'WHEELER'S AUTO RECOVERY'. Beside it was another, much smaller warning sign, reading 'GUARD DOGS!'

The appearance of the place was about as near to a hillbilly homestead as Grace had ever experienced. It was beyond ramshackle; it was beyond the most untidy place he had ever seen in his life.

The yard was dominated by a large blue tow-truck, parked amidst a dozen or so partially or totally cannibalized carcasses of vehicles, some smashed, some badly rusted, and one, a small Toyota, just looking as if it had been parked and someone had nicked everything it was possible to nick from it.

There were piles of sawn and unsawn logs, a wooden trestle, a rusting bandsaw, a decrepit Portakabin, against which was a faded chalked sign which read 'XMAS TREES SALE', and a wood-framed bungalow that looked as if it could collapse at any moment.

As he drove in and switched the engine off, he heard the fierce, deep barking of a guard dog shattering the quiet stillness of the warm evening, and remained prudently in the car for some moments, waiting for a hound to appear. Instead, the front door of the bungalow opened, and a hulk of a man came out. In his fifties, he had thinning, greasy hair, a heavy five-o'clock shadow and a massive beer belly barely restrained by a string vest and bulging over the buckle of his brown dungarees like an overhang of snow about to avalanche.

'Mr Wheeler?' Grace said, approaching, still wary of the sound of the barking dog, which was getting even louder and deeper.

'Yes?' The man had a gentle face with big sad eyes, and massive, grimy hands. He smelled of rope and engine grease.

Grace pulled out his warrant card and held it up for him to see. 'Detective Superintendent Grace from Sussex CID. I'm very sorry to hear about your son.'

The man stood still, impassively, then Grace saw he was starting to tremble. His hands clenched tight, and a tear rolled down from the corner of each eye. 'You want to come in?' Phil Wheeler said, in a faltering voice.

'If you have a few minutes, I'd appreciate it.'

The inside of the house was pretty much like the outside and the reek of the place indicated a heavy smoker. Grace followed the man into a dingy sitting room with a three-piece suite and a large old television. Almost every inch of the floor and furniture was covered in motorbiking magazines, country and western magazines and vinyl record sleeves. There was a photograph of a fair-haired woman resting her hands on the shoulders of a small boy on a scooter, on the sideboard, and a few cheap-looking china ornaments, but nothing at all on the walls. A clock on the mantelpiece, set into the belly of a chipped porcelain racehorse, indicated the time at ten minutes past seven. Grace was surprised, checking it against his own watch, that it was more or less accurate.

Scooping several record sleeves off an armchair, Phil Wheeler said, by way of an explanation, 'Davey liked this stuff, used to play it all the time, liked to collect—'

He broke off and walked out of the room. 'Tea?' he called.

'I'm fine,' Grace said, unsure what kind of hygiene went on in the kitchen.

This level of interview would have been delegated to someone junior by most SIOs, but Grace had always been a firm believer in getting out in the field himself. It was his style of operating – and it was one of the aspects of police work that he found most interesting and rewarding if sometimes, like now, challenging.

After a couple of minutes, Phil Wheeler lumbered back into the room, swept a pile of magazines and some more record sleeves off the settee and eased himself down, then pulled a tobacco tin out of his pocket. He prised open the tin with his thumbnail, removed a packet of cigarette papers, then proceeded, one-handed, to roll himself a cigarette. Grace couldn't help watching; it had always fascinated him how people could do this.

'Mr Wheeler, I understand your son told you he had some conversations on a walkie-talkie radio with a missing person, Michael Harrison.'

Phil Wheeler ran his tongue along the paper and sealed the cigarette. 'I can't understand why anyone would want to hurt my boy. He was the friendliest person you could meet.' Holding his unlit cigarette, he bicycled his hand in the air. 'Poor kid had – you know – water on the brain, hydrocephalus. He was slow, but everyone liked him.'

Grace smiled in sympathy. 'He had a lot of friends in the traffic police.'

'He was a good lad.'

'So I understand.'

'He was my life.'

Grace waited. Wheeler lit the cigarette from a box of Swan Vesta matches and moments later the sweet smoke wafted across to Grace. He breathed in deeply, enjoying the smell, but not enjoying this task. Talking to the newly bereaved had always been, in his view, the single worst aspect of police work.

'Can you tell me a bit about the conversations he had? About this walkie-talkie?'

The man inhaled, smoke spurting from his mouth and nostrils as he spoke. 'I got pretty angry with him on – I don't know – Friday or Saturday. I didn't know he had the damned thing. He finally told me he'd found it near that terrible wreck on Tuesday night with the four lads.'

Grace nodded.

'He kept talking about his new friend. To be honest I didn't take much notice. Davey lived in – how do you put it – his own little world most of the time – always off having conversations with people inside his head.' He put the cigarette down in a tin ashtray, then blotted his eyes with a scrunched up handkerchief and sniffed. 'He was always chatting. I sometimes had to switch off, otherwise he could drive me nuts.'

'Can you remember what he said about Michael Harrison?'

'He was very excited – I think it was Friday – he'd been told he could be a hero. You see, he loved American cop shows on the telly – he always wanted to be a hero. He was going on about knowing where someone was, and that he was the only person in the world who knew, you see, and this was his chance to be a hero. But I didn't take much notice; had a busy day with two wrecks we had to bring in – I didn't make the connection.'

'Do you have the radio?'

He shook his head. 'Davey must have taken it with him.'

'Did Davey drive?'

He shook his head. 'No. He liked to steer the truck sometimes, I let him do that on a quiet road – you know – like one hand on the wheel? But no, he could never drive, didn't have the ability. He had a mountain bike, that was all.'

'He was found about six miles away from here – do you think he went off to find Michael Harrison? To try to be a hero?'

'I had to pick up a car on Saturday afternoon. He didn't want to come with me, told me he had important business.'

'Important business?'

Philip Wheeler gave a sad shrug. 'He liked to believe he mattered.'

Grace smiled, thinking privately, *we all do.* Then he asked, 'Did you glean anything from Davey about where Michael Harrison might be?'

'No, it didn't occur to me to make any connection – so I didn't take much notice of what he said.'

'Would it be possible to see your son's room, Mr Wheeler?'

Phil Wheeler jabbed a finger, pointing past Grace. 'In the Portakabin. Davey liked it there. You can go across – please don't mind if I don't – I—' He pulled his handkerchief out.

'That's fine, I understand.'

'It's not locked.'

Grace crossed the yard and walked up to the Portakabin. The dog which he had still not yet seen, which he thought had to be on the far side of the bungalow, began barking again, even more aggressively. Fixed to the wall beside the front door was a warning sign to intruders reading 'ARMED RESPONSE!'

He tested the door handle, then pulled the door open and stepped inside onto carpet tiles, several of which were curling at the edges, but most of which were covered in either socks, underpants, T-shirts, sweet wrappers, a McDonald's burger container lying open, the lid smeared with congealed ketchup, car instruments, hub caps, old American licence plates and several baseball caps. The room was even more untidy than the bungalow, and had a rank odour of cheesy feet, which reminded him of a school locker room.

Much of the space in the room was taken up by a bed and an unstable television flickering between colour and black and white, on which he saw the credits running for *Law and Order.* Grace never liked watching British cop shows – they always managed to irritate him by showing wrong procedures or stupid decisions by the investigating officers. US cop shows seemed more exciting, more together. But maybe that was because he didn't know US police procedures well enough to be critical.

Glancing around, he saw adverts which looked like they had been torn from magazines plastered all over the walls. Looking more closely, he identifed all of them as being for things American – cars, guns, food, drink, vacations.

Stepping past the burger container, he looked down at

a very old Dell computer, with a floppy disk protruding from the front of the processor, sharing a work surface that sufficed for a desk with a carton of Twinkie bars, a six-inch-tall plastic Bart Simpson and a large scrap of lined notepaper on which there were ballpoint jottings in child-like handwriting.

Grace looked carefully at the jottings and realized it was a crude diagram. Beside two sets of parallel lines was scrawled: '*A 26. NORTH KROWBURG. DUBBLE KATTLE GRYD. 2 MYLES. WITE COTIDGE.*'

It was a map.

Below it, he saw a sequence of numbers: *0771 52136.* It looked like a mobile number, and he tried dialling it, but nothing happened.

He spent another twenty minutes rummaging through everything in the room, opening every drawer, but he found nothing else of interest. Then he took the sheet of paper back to the bungalow and showed it to Phil Wheeler.

'Did Davey talk to you about this?'

Phil Wheeler shook his head. 'No.'

'Do the directions mean anything to you?'

'Double cattle grid, two miles, white cottage? No, don't mean anything.'

'The number? Do you recognize this?'

He looked at the number, reading out each digit aloud. 'No, not any number I know.'

Grace decided he had got about as much out of the man as he was going to get tonight. He stood up, thanked him, and told him again how sorry he was about his son.

'Just catch the bastard who did it, Detective Superintendent. Do that at least, for me and Davey, will you?'

Grace promised to do his best.

70

Mark Warren, dripping with perspiration, jigged the key in the front door lock of his apartment, panicking for a moment that the lock was jammed. Then he pushed the door open fearfully, stepped inside, closed it, locked it and engaged the safety chain.

Ignoring the bundle of post awaiting him, he set down his briefcase, ripped off his tie, unbuttoned his shirt collar, then slung both his jacket and the tie on the sofa. He poured himself four fingers of Balvenie, chinked some ice cubes out of the fridge straight into the glass, then gulped down some of the whisky.

He opened his leather laptop bag and removed the Jiffy bag that had arrived earlier, holding it at arm's length, hardly daring to look at it. He put it on a black lacquered table on the far side of the room, took out the note which he had already looked at earlier, in the office, then walked over to the coffee table, took another deep gulp of his whisky and sat down.

The note was short, printed off a computer on blank A4 paper. It said: 'Have the police check the fingerprints out and you'll find it is your friend and business partner. Every 24 hours I will cut an increasingly bigger bit off him. Until you do exactly what I tell you.'

There was no signature.

Mark drank some more whisky, draining the glass. He refilled it – another four fat fingers but the same ice cubes, and read the note again. Then again. He heard a siren somewhere outside and flinched. Then the door intercom buzzed, throwing him into a flat spin of panic. Marching across to the CCTV panel, he desperately hoped it was Ashley. Her phone had been off when he tried to call her from the office and it had still been off when he had called her again minutes ago coming up in the lift.

But it wasn't Ashley; it was the face of a man he was starting to see too much of, for his liking, Detective Superintendent Grace.

For some moments he wondered whether to ignore him, let him go away, come back some other time. But maybe he had news.

He picked up the receiver and told Grace to come in, then pressed the button for the electronic door catch.

It seemed only seconds later that Grace was knocking on his door, and he'd barely had time to scoop up the note and the Jiffy bag and stuff them in a cupboard.

'Good evening, officer,' Mark said as he opened the door, conscious suddenly that he was feeling a tad muzzy from the drink and that his voice was affected, too. He kept a full arm's length as he shook Grace's hand, so that the policeman wouldn't notice the alcohol on his breath.

'Mind if I come in for a few minutes, or are you busy?'

'Never too busy for you, officer – I'm around to help you seven-two-four. What news do you have? Can I get you a drink?'

'A glass of water, please,' Grace said, feeling parched.

They sat down opposite each other on the deep leather sofas, and Grace watched him for a little while. The man looked in a bad state of nerves; he seemed a little uncoordinated and smelled strongly of alcohol. Watching his eyes carefully, Grace asked him, 'What did you have for lunch today?'

Mark's eyes shot to the left momentarily and then back to the centre. 'I had a turkey and cranberry sandwich, from a deli just around the corner. Why?'

'It's important to eat,' Grace said. 'Particularly when you are stressed.' He gave Mark a smile of encouragement then sipped some water from the tall, expensive-feeling glass he had been given. 'Got a bit of a mystery, Mark, which I wonder if you could help me with?'

'Of course – I'll try.'

'A couple of CCTV cameras picked up a BMW X5 registered in your name, late Thursday night, heading into Brighton from the direction of Lewes . . .' Grace paused to pull his Blackberry out of his pocket. 'Yes, at 12.29 a.m. and again at 12.40 a.m.' Grace decided for the moment to say nothing about the results of the soil analysis that he'd been given at the briefing meeting, earlier. Like a lion closing in on a kill, he leaned forward. 'You went for a late-night drive in Ashdown Forest, perhaps?'

Now he watched Mark's eyes rigidly. Instead of going back to the left, to the same side as when Mark answered his question about the sandwich, to the memory side, they swung wildly, right, then left, then right again, very definitely settling right now. *Construct* mode. He was intending to lie his way out of this one.

'I may have done,' he replied.

'You *may* have done? Isn't driving in a forest at midnight a little bit of an unusual thing to do? Wouldn't you remember a bit more clearly?'

'It's not unusual for me,' Mark responded, seizing his drink, his entire body language changing suddenly. It was Grace's turn to feel uneasy now, wondering what was going on. Mark leaned back, swirled the whisky around in his glass, the ice cubes chinking. 'You see, that's where we are doing our new big property development. We got outline planning permission a couple of months back for twenty new houses on a five-acre site in the heart of the forest, and now we're working on the details – because we're getting a lot of hostility from the environmental groups. I go back and forward to the forest all the time, day and night – I have to check out the environmental factors, and a big part of that is the impact on the wildlife at night time. I'm working up a whole report to support our application.'

Grace's heart sank; he felt as if a rug had just been pulled away, quickly and very smartly, from beneath him. He'd just wasted the best part of a thousand pounds of his budget on the soil analysis, and he felt an idiot. Why hadn't he known this? Why hadn't Glenn or anyone on the team known it?

His brain was spinning and he tried to slow it down and get some traction on this thoughts. Mark Warren still looked a wreck and he just did not get the impression it was from worrying about his business partner. The aggression he had shown at the wedding indicated something else altogether, but he didn't know what.

Then, for about the third time in the past ten minutes, he saw Mark Warren's eyes flick across to a point on the far side of the room, as if someone was standing there. Grace deliberately dropped the cover of his BlackBerry on the floor and, in leaning down to get it, glanced back in the direction Mark kept looking at. But he couldn't see anything of significance. Just the smart hi-fi set, some interesting modern art and a few cupboards.

'I read about that young man – in the mortuary. Saw the piece in the paper today. Very sad,' Mark said.

'Might even have been on your land,' Grace said, testing.

'I don't know exactly where it happened.'

Fixing on his eyes again, and remembering the words on the sheet of notepaper in Davey's bedroom, Grace said, 'If you take the A26 outside Crowborough just past a white cottage, then over a double cattle grid. Is that where you are?'

Mark didn't need to respond. Grace could see all he needed to know from the rapid swivelling of his eyes, the furrowing of his forehead, the hunching of his entire frame and the change in tone of his face colour.

'It could be – possibly – yes.'

Now it was all starting to come clear to Grace. 'If a bunch of you were going to bury your mate alive in a coffin, it would make sense to do it on land you own, wouldn't it? Somewhere familiar to you?'

'I – I suppose . . .'

'You're still insisting you had no idea of any plan to bury Michael Harrison in a coffin?'

His eyes were all over the place for a few seconds. 'Absolutely. Nothing at all.'

'Good, thank you.' Grace studied his BlackBerry for a moment. 'I also have a number I wonder if you could help me with, Mark?'

'I'll try.'

Grace read out the number that had been written on the same diagram.

'0771 52136,' Mark repeated. His eyes shot instantly to the left. Memory mode. 'That sounds like Ashley's mobile with a couple of digits missing. Why do you ask?'

Grace drained his water and stood up. 'It was found in Davey Wheeler's home – the murdered boy. Along with the directions I just gave you.'

'What?'

Walking over to the window, Grace slid open the patio door and stepped out on to the teak decking that covered the balcony. Steadying himself on the metal guard rail, he looked down four floors at the bustling street below. It wasn't far, but it was enough for him; he had always suffered from vertigo, never had any head for heights.

'How did this boy get Ashley's phone number and the directions to our land?' Mark asked.

'I'd also like to know that very much.'

Once again Mark's eyes shot across the room. Grace wondered, was it the cupboard? Something in there? What?

Grace had such bad feelings about this man, and about Ashley Harper, that he wanted to get search warrants and take their homes – and office – apart. But to do that was not easy. Magistrates required convincing to sign warrants, and to convince them you needed evidence. The bracelet she had given him wouldn't be enough. Right now, on both Mark Warren and Ashley Harper all he really had were gut feelings. No evidence.

'Mark, is this land of yours easy to find? The directions – the white cottage, the cattle grid?'

'You have to know the turn-off – it's not marked, other than by a couple of stakes – we didn't want to draw attention to it.'

'Sounds to me that that's the place to look for your partner, pretty damned quick, wouldn't you say?'

'Absolutely.'

'I'll liaise with the Crowborough police, who are already doing a full search of the area, but it sounds like it would be vital for you to be there – at least point them to the right area. If I arrange to get you picked up in the next half-hour?'

'Fine. Thank you. Ah – how long do you think I'll be needed?'

Grace frowned. 'Well – all I need is for you to show us the entrance – the turn-off – and to take us to where your land begins. Maybe an hour altogether. Unless you want to join in the search yourself?'

'Sure – I mean – I'll do what I can.'

71

Mark closed the door on Grace, ran into the bathroom, knelt down and threw up into the toilet bowl. Then he threw up some more.

He stood up, pressed the flush lever, then rinsed his mouth with cold water; his clothes were wringing wet with perspiration, his hair plastered to his head. With the tap running, he nearly didn't hear the landline phone ringing.

Grabbing the receiver off the hook, he just caught it on the last ring before it would have diverted to voicemail. 'Hello?'

A male voice with an Australian accent said, 'Is that Mark Warren?'

Something about the voice made Mark instantly wary. 'This is an ex-directory number. Who am I speaking to?'

'My name's Vic – I'm with your friend, Michael – he gave me your number. Actually he'd like to have a quick word with you; shall I put him on?'

'Yes.' Mark gripped the receiver hard against his ear, trembling. Then he heard Michael's voice, very definitely Michael, but making a sound unlike Mark had ever heard before. It was a bellow of pain that seemed to start deep within Michael's soul then burst, like a train from a tunnel, into a crescendo of utter, unbearable agony.

Mark had to pull the phone away from his ear. The roar died away then he heard Michael whimpering then screaming again. 'No, please, no, no. NO NO NO NO!'

Then he heard Vic's voice again. 'Bet you're wondering

what I'm doing to your mate, don't you, eh Mark? Don't worry, you'll find out when it arrives in tomorrow's post.'

'What do you want?' Mark asked, straining his ears, but he could hear no sound from Michael now.

'I need you to transfer some money in your Cayman Islands bank to an account number I'm going to give you shortly.'

'It isn't possible – even if I was willing to do it. Two signatures are needed for any transaction, Michael's and mine.'

'In your safe in your company office you have documents signed by both of you, giving power of attorney to a lawyer in the Cayman Islands; you put it there last year when you both went off sailing for a week, and you were hoping to close on a property deal in the Grenadines that then didn't happen. You've forgotten to destroy those documents. Just as well, I'd say.'

How the hell did the man know this, Mark wondered.

'I want to speak to Michael – I don't want to hear him in pain, I'd just like to talk to him, please.'

'You've talked to him enough today. I'm going to leave you to think about this, Mark, and we'll catch up later, have a cosy chat. Oh, and Mark, not a word of this to the police – that could really make me angry.'

The line went dead.

Immediately Mark hit the last number recall button. But it was no surprise that the automated voice came up with, 'I'm sorry, we do not have the caller's number.'

He tried Ashley's number again. To his relief she answered.

'Thank God,' he said. 'Where have you been?'

'What do you mean, where have I been?'

'I've been trying to get hold of you.'

'I went to have a massage, actually. One of us has to keep a cool head, OK? Then I popped in to see Michael's mum and now I'm on my way home.'

'Can you swing by here – like now, this second?'

'Your voice is slurred – have you been drinking?'

'Something's happened, I *have* to speak to you.'

'Let's talk in the morning.'

'It can't wait.'

The imperative in his voice got through. Reluctantly she said, 'OK – I just don't know if it's a good idea coming to you – we could meet somewhere neutral – how about a bar or a restaurant?'

'Great, somewhere the whole world can hear us?'

'We'll just have to talk quietly, OK? It's better than me being seen coming over to your apartment.'

'Jesus, you are paranoid!'

'Me? You're a fine one to talk about paranoia. Name a restaurant.'

Mark thought for a moment. A police car would collect him in half an hour. It was about half an hour's drive out to the site. Maybe just ten minutes there, then half an hour back. It was eight o'clock on Monday night; places would be quiet. He suggested meeting at ten at an Italian restaurant near the Theatre Royal, which had a large upstairs dining area that would almost certainly be empty tonight.

*

It wasn't. To his surprise, the restaurant was heaving – he had forgotten that after the Brighton Festival the city was still in full swing, its bars and restaurants crowded every night. Most of the tables upstairs were taken as well, and he was squeezed into a cramped table behind a rowdy party table of twelve. Ashley wasn't there yet. The place was typically Italian: white walls, small tables with candles jammed in the top of Chianti bottles and loud, energetic waiters.

The ride out to Crowborough and back had been uneventful: two young detectives in an unmarked car, who had spent most of the way out there arguing about football players, and most of the way back discussing cricket. They showed no interest in him at all other than to tell him they should both have gone off duty an hour ago and were in a hurry to get back. Mark viewed that as good news.

He directed them to the start of the track, with the double cattle grid, then sat and waited as they radioed for the local search team to join them. After a short while several minibuses, headed by a police Range Rover, arrived in convoy.

Mark got out of the car, explained how far up they had to drive, but did not volunteer to join them. He did not want to be there when they found the grave – and they would find it for sure.

He needed a drink badly, but was not sure what he wanted. He was thirsty, so he ordered a Peroni beer to tide him over, then stared at the menu as a distraction from his thoughts. Moments later, Ashley arrived.

'Still drinking?' she admonished, by way of a greeting, and without kissing him, squeezed in opposite him, throwing a disapproving glance at the rowdy group beside them, who were guffawing at a joke, then put her very bling pink Prada handbag on the table.

She looked more beautiful than ever, Mark thought, dressed in a fashionably ragged cream blouse, which gave her breasts considerable, and very erotic, exposure, and a small choker; she had her hair up. She looked fresh and relaxed, and smelled of a gorgeous perfume he recognized but could not name.

Smiling at her, he said, 'You look stunning.'

Her eyes were darting around the room impatiently, as if seeking a waiter. 'Thanks – you look like shit.'

'You'll understand why in a moment.'

Semi-ignoring him, she raised a hand, and when a waiter finally scuttled over, she imperiously ordered a San Pellegrino.

'Want some wine?' Mark said. 'I'm going to have some.'

'I think you should have water, too – you're drinking far too much just recently. You need to stop, get a grip. OK?'

'OK. Maybe.'

She shrugged. 'Fine, you do what you want.'

Mark slipped his hand across the table towards hers, but she withdrew her hands, sitting bolt upright, arms firmly crossed.

'Before I forget, tomorrow is Pete's funeral. Two o'clock, the Good Shepherd, Dyke Road. Luke's is on Wednesday; I haven't got the time yet – and I don't know about Josh and Robbo yet. So what's this big latest thing you have to tell me?'

The waiter came with her water, and they ordered. Then when the waiter had moved away Mark began by telling her about the finger.

She shook her head, sounding shocked. 'This cannot be true, Mark.'

Mark had put the finger in the Jiffy bag into the fridge in his apartment, but he'd brought the note with him and gave it to her.

Ashley read it carefully, several times, mouthing the words as if in total disbelief. Then suddenly there was anger in her eyes and she looked at him accusingly. 'This isn't your doing, Mark?'

It was Mark's turn to be shocked. He mouthed the word before he said it. 'What? You think I have Michael hidden somewhere and I cut his finger off. I might not like him too much but—'

'You're happy to let him die of asphyxiation in a coffin – but you wouldn't ever do something nasty to him, like cut a finger off? Come on, Mark, what kind of bullshit is this?'

He glanced around, alarmed at the way she had raised her voice. But no one was taking any notice.

Mark could not believe the way she seemed to be turning on him. 'Ashley, come on, this is me. Jesus Christ, what's got into you? We're a team, you and I – isn't that the deal? We love each other; we're a team, right?'

She softened, glanced around, then reached forward, took his hand and brought it to her lips, planting a gentle kiss on it. 'My darling,' she said, her voice lowered. 'I love you so much – but I'm just in shock.'

'Me too.'

'I suppose we all handle shock, stress – you know – in different ways.'

He nodded, pulled her hand towards his mouth and kissed it tenderly. 'We have to do something for Michael.'

She shook her head. 'It's perfect, don't you see? We just do nothing! This man – Vic – he's going to think you care because you're Michael's partner.' She grinned. 'It's an incredible situation!'

'It's not; I haven't told you everything.' He drained his beer and looked around, wondering if the wine was on its way. Then he told her about the phone call from Vic and the sound of Michael screaming.

Ashley listened in silence. 'Christ, poor Michael – he—'

She bit her lip and a tear rolled down her cheek. 'I mean – oh shit, oh shit.' She closed her eyes for some moments, then opened them again, staring directly into Mark's. 'How – how the hell – how did this man find Michael?'

Mark decided not to mention the visit from Grace at this moment; Ashley was already distressed enough. 'All I can think is he must have stumbled across the grave – it wasn't exactly well concealed. Hell, the boys only planned to be away a max of an hour or two. I camouflaged it a bit – but it wouldn't have been hard – a rambler could easily have seen it.'

'A rambler's one thing,' she said bleakly. 'This guy's not a rambler.'

'He's a chancer, maybe. Finds Michael, figures out from all the press and media coverage that this is the rich guy everyone's looking for – it's the chance of a lifetime. He takes him off to another location and sends us a ransom note – and proof that he has Michael.'

Ashley said, her voice faltering, 'How – how do – you – we – anyone – I mean – how do we know it's Michael's finger?'

'About three weeks ago Michael and I were on the boat, doing some maintenance work on her, on a Saturday afternoon – remember?'

'Vaguely.'

'The heads door slammed shut on Michael's index finger. He was hopping around, cursing, running it under a cold tap. He showed me a few days later a black band right across the nail.' He paused. 'The finger that arrived has a black band. OK?'

A hearty plate of avocado, mozzarella and tomatoes arrived for Ashley. And a large bowl of minestrone was set down in front of Mark. When the waiter went away again,

Ashley said, 'Do you want to call the police, Mark? Tell the bloodhound Detective Superintendent about this?'

Mark churned that over in his mind, letting his soup cool while Ashley began eating. If they told the police and the man carried out his threat to kill Michael, that was one elegant solution to the situation. Except the bellow of pain from Michael had got to him. None of this had seemed quite real before. All the boys dead in the wreck. Going up to the grave and taking the air tube. Even when Michael had shouted out in the coffin, it hadn't affected him, not really. Not the way the sound of him in pain was affecting him now.

'Michael must have his Palm. If he gets out alive he is going to know that I knew where he was being buried.'

'Since the accident there's never been any question of him getting out alive,' she said. Then after a moment's hesitation added a testy, 'Has there?'

Mark was silent. His mind, normally so orderly and focused, was a messed-up jumble at this moment. They'd never intended to harm Michael with the stag-night prank – that was just the payback for all his jokes. And the original plan he'd hatched with Ashley had never involved hurting Michael either, surely? Ashley was going to marry him, and get half his shares in Double-M Properties. When the ink was dry on the certificates, Mark and she would have enough votes between them to take control of the company. They would vote Michael off the Board of Directors, and then he would be a minority shareholder – and wouldn't have much option but to let them buy him out at a low price.

Why the hell had he kept quiet the night he had arrived home from Leeds and heard about the accident? Why? Why?

But of course he knew the real reason why. Pure jealousy. It was because he had never been able to bear the thought of Ashley going off on honeymoon with Michael – and the solution had fallen into his lap.

'Has there, Mark?' Ashley's persistent voice cut through his thoughts.

'Has there what?'

'Duh! Hello! Has there ever been any question of him getting out alive?'

'No, of course not.'

She stared at him, a firm, steady gaze.

He stared back, replaying the terrible screams of pain over and over inside his head, thinking, *Ashley, you didn't hear them.*

72

Michael lay in the bitumen-black darkness, his heart thudding, his head pounding, his index finger throbbing, and excruciating spikes of pain from his balls shooting deep up into his belly. It was – he didn't know how long ago, maybe an hour, maybe more, maybe less – from when that hooded bastard had clipped callipers to them and fired electric shocks into them.

But the pain was nothing compared to the dark, cold fear that stalked his mind. He was remembering the movie, *The Silence of the Lambs,* which he had seen some years back, and again more recently on television with Ashley. A girl, a senator's daughter, had been kept in the bottom of a well by the serial killer, who skinned his victims. He couldn't help it; he was shivering, trying to focus his thoughts, determined, somehow, to survive.

To get back to Ashley. To take her down the aisle. That was all he wanted.

God, how he pined for her!

He couldn't move his arms or his legs. After spooning him tinned stew and bread, his captor had sealed his mouth again with duct tape and he had to breathe just through his nose, which was partially blocked. He sniffed, suddenly panicking that it was getting completely blocked. Sniffed again, harder, deep, rapid sniffs, setting his heart racing.

He tried to work out where he might be. The place smelled dank, musty, there was still a faint reek of engine oil. He was lying on a hard surface and something sharp was digging into the base of his spine, hurting like hell, getting worse by the minute.

He felt stronger, despite the pain, much stronger than he had earlier. The food was having an effect. *I am not fucking staying here and dying. I haven't done everything in life to end up here. No way. No absolutely no absolutely no, no no fucking way.*

He struggled against his bonds. Breathed in deeply, trying to shrink his body, then out, trying to expand. And felt something give. Some tiny hint of slack. In again, pulled his arms in tight, tight, tight, out, in, out. Oh sweet Jesus he could move his right arm. Only a tiny amount. But he could move it! He pushed against his bonds, constricted, pushed again, constricted. More slack for his right arm.

Then more still!

He rolled over onto his side, then his stomach. His nostrils filled with the reek of engine oil now; he was lying face down in the slimy stuff, but it didn't matter, because at least the pain in the base of his spine had stopped.

He wriggled his hand round, further round, and then touched something.

OhmyGod!

He was touching the top of his Ericsson mobile!

Got his hand on it, pulled, and it came out of the back pocket of his trousers.

His heart kicked into overdrive. It had been there in the coffin, underwater. Even though it was supposed to be waterproof he doubted it would work. All the same, he ran his fingers over its surfaces as if he was caressing the best friend he had ever had in his life. Found the power button at the top, pushed it. Listened.

There was the faintest beep. Then a dim glow of light, enough that he could see steep walls either side of him. He was in a space about six feet wide and maybe five feet high, covered with a door of some kind. And suddenly he was alert, his brain sharp and focused. He tried to move his hand, to slip it free of the bonds and bring the phone up to his face, but nothing he did succeeded. The bonds were too tight, too well wound around his arms.

Yet.

He had to think this through.

Text.

He could try to send a text.

Think! You switch the phone on and what happens? First is a request for the pin code. Like most people, he used a simple code: 4–4–4–4, his lucky number.

He ran his finger across the key pad – 4 was far left, second row. He tapped it and heard a beep; then another beep each time he tapped the next three. Incredible! The thing had been submerged in the coffin but it was working. Enough to send a text?

The next part was going to be much harder. He had to work out the letters on the keys. On key number 1 he remembered there were no letters. Key number 2 had ABC. He did some maths in his head – the whole alphabet was in groups of three letters except for two numbers, where there were four. Which numbers? Shit, he had used text so much, it must be imprinted in his brain, if he could just access it.

It had to be the least popular letters in the alphabet, Q and – X or Z?

Taking it slowly, counting very carefully, he tried to recall the sequence on his phone. The *menu* button was top left. One tap took you to *messages*. The second tap took you to *write message*. The third tap took you to the blank screen. Then he tapped out what he hoped were the right letters. *Alive. Call police.*

The next tap, he hoped he remembered correctly, took you to *send*.

The one after that to *phone number*.

He tapped in Ashley's number.

The one after that should be *send*.

He pressed, and to his incredible relief heard a confirmation beep. The message had gone!

Then he felt a stab of panic. Even if the message had gone successfully, what use would it be to her, or the police? How the hell would they be able to find him from a text? Within moments he was engulfed in despair darker than the blackness that surrounded him.

But he refused to give up. There had to be a way. *Think! Think!*

His fingers moved along the keys, counting, 1–2–3–4–5–6–7–8–9.

He pressed 9–9–9. Then he pressed the send button. Moments later he heard a faint ringing sound. Then a female voice, very faint also.

'Emergency, which service?'

He tried desperately to speak, but all he could make was his feeble grunting sound. He heard the voice say, 'Hello? Caller? Hello? Is everything all right? Hello, Hello, caller, can you identify yourself? Hello? Caller, are you in trouble? Can you hear me, caller?'

There was a silence.

Then her voice again. 'Hello, caller, are you there?'

He hung up, dialled again. Heard another female voice speak almost identical words. He hung up again. They would have to understand if he kept doing this. Surely they would understand?

73

In the saloon bar of the pub, Grace ordered Cleo Morey her second Polstar vodka and cranberry, and himself a Diet Coke. One large Glenfiddich had been enough – he was going to have to return to the Incident Room later this evening and needed all his wits.

They sat on cushioned seats at a corner table. With less than a dozen other people in the pub the place was not very busy. A one-armed bandit at the far end of the room winked and blinked away forlornly like an old tart in a windswept alley.

Cleo looked stunning. Her hair, freshly washed and shining, hung down over her shoulders. She wore a classy-looking light suede jacket over a beige tank top, white jeans of fashionable three-quarter length, revealing her slender ankles, and plain white mules.

Grace had dashed from Mark Warren's apartment to the Incident Room to get copies of Davey's diagram faxed out to the team, and from there went straight on to the pub, still arriving an hour and twenty minutes late. Of course he had had no time to change or even tidy himself up. He was wearing the plain navy suit he had put on early this morning in case he had to appear in court, with a white shirt and plain navy tie – now slackened and hanging at half mast with his top button open. Compared to Cleo he was feeling very dowdy.

'I've never seen you in civvies before,' he joked.

'Would you have felt more comfortable if I'd turned up in my green gown and wellies?'

'I guess it would have had a certain *je ne sais quoi* about it.'

She beamed at him, and raised her glass. 'Cheers!'

She had a great figure. He loved her blue eyes, her small, pretty nose, her almost rosebud lips, her dimpled chin, her lean body. And she smelled stunning too, as if she had been marinated in some very classy perfume. Some difference to the reek of Trigene disinfectant that he normally associated her with – tonight she radiated femininity, her eyes sparkled with fun, and every man in the pub was ogling her. Grace wondered if they would still be ogling if they knew what she spent her days doing.

He poured some more Coke over the ice cubes and lemon and raised his glass back. 'Good to see you.'

'And you, too. So, tell me about your day?'

'You don't want to hear about my day!'

She leaned closer, all her body language receptive to him. If she came any closer still she would be snuggling up to him. He felt very good, very comfortable sitting here with her, and for a moment all his cares were parked in another space. 'I do,' she said. 'I want a blow-by-blow account of every minute!'

'How about the edited version? I got up, had a shower, went out, met Cleo for a drink. That enough?'

She laughed. 'OK, that's a start. Now talk me through the bits you edited out.'

He gave her a brief summary, mindful of the time. It was a quarter past nine – in an hour he had to be back in the Incident Room. He shouldn't have come on this date at all, he ought to have cancelled because of everything he had to do, but hell, didn't he have the right to enjoy himself just once in a while?

'Must be tough, interviewing the bereaved,' she said. 'In seven years I should have got used to seeing people, often within a few hours of getting the news that their loved one is dead; but I still dread every single one of those moments.'

'It might sound callous,' Grace said, 'but catching the bereaved within a few hours is the best chance we have of getting them to talk. When people have just lost someone, their first automatic response is to go into shock. While they are in that state they will talk. But within twelve hours or so, with family and friends gathering around, they start to close ranks, and clam up. If you are going to get anything useful, in my experience, you have to do it in those first hours.'

'You like what you do?' she asked.

He sipped his Coke. 'I do. Except – when I run up against people in my organization with limited minds.'

Cleo poked around in her drink with a cocktail stick as if looking for something, and for a moment the intensity of her gaze reminded Grace of her at work in the post-mortem room, when she was taking a tissue sample. He wondered what it would be like if he ever made love to her. Would the sight of her naked body remind him of all the naked cadavers he had looked at with her? Would he be put off by knowing that beneath her beautiful skin were the same hideous, slimy, fat-coated internal organs that all humans – and all mammals – shared in common?

'Roy, there's something I've been wanting to ask you for a long time. And of course I saw that stuff in the papers last week. How did you get interested in the supernatural?'

It was his turn to probe his drink. With the plastic

cocktail stick he squeezed the lemon flesh, releasing some of the juice into the Coke. 'When I was a kid, my uncle – my dad's brother – lived on the Isle of Wight – in Bembridge. I used to go and stay every summer for a week – and loved it. They had two sons, one slightly older than me, the other slightly younger – I kind of grew up with them from about the age of six. I don't know if you've ever been to Cowes?'

'Yes, Daddy's taken me sailing there during Cowes Week lots of times.'

Mimicking her posh accent, Grace said, 'Ew, Deeaddy would.'

Grinning and blushing, she gave him a friendly prod in the arm. 'Don't be mean! Carry on with your story.'

'They had a tiny terraced cottage, but right opposite was quite a grand house – a townhouse, four storeys high. There were two very sweet old ladies who lived there, and they were always sitting in a big bay window on the top floor, and they'd wave at us every time we saw them. When I was fourteen my aunt and uncle sold their house and emigrated to New Zealand, and I didn't go back there for about eight years. Then, in the spring of the summer that Sandy and I got married, I was taking her on one of those kind of *meet the ancestors* tours – and I thought it would fun to show her Cowes and the place where I'd spent so many happy holidays as a kid.'

He paused to light a cigarette, clocking Cleo's frown of surprise, then continued. 'When we got to my uncle's house, the beautiful townhouse opposite was in the process of being demolished – to make way for an apartment building. I asked the workmen what had happened to the two old ladies and they introduced me to the property developer – he'd lived in Cowes all his life and knew just about everyone. He told me the house had been empty for over forty years.'

He paused to drag on his cigarette. 'There had been two old ladies, sisters – both had lost their husbands in the First World War, the story goes. They became inseparable, then one was diagnosed with cancer and the other decided she didn't want to go on living alone. So they both gassed themselves in that top room, sitting in the bay window. That was in 1947.'

Cleo sat for some moments, thinking. 'You never saw the old ladies outside?'

'No – I was young – just a kid. I suppose at the time it never occurred to me that they were always indoors. I supposed that some old people did just stay indoors.'

'And your uncle and aunt?'

'I spoke to them about it afterwards – called them in New Zealand. They said they used to wave at this blank window just to humour us – they thought these two old ladies were our imaginary friends!'

'And they were real to you?'

'I looked them up in the newspaper archives. There were photographs of both of them – unmistakable. Absolutely no question in my mind – these were the two old ladies I had waved at – and who had waved at me every day for a week, for ten years of my childhood.'

'Amazing! That's a pretty convincing story,' she said. 'So what is your explanation?'

He noticed her glass was empty. 'Another?'

'Oh, why not!' she said. 'But it's my turn to buy.'

'I kept you waiting and hour and twenty minutes – I'm buying the drinks. No argument!'

'So long as I can buy them on our next date – deal?'

They locked eyes, both smiling. 'Deal.'

Then she tapped the table impatiently with her manicured finger. 'So, come on, what is your explanation?'

Grace ordered Cleo Morey a third vodka and cranberry, then said, 'I have several theories about ghosts.' After a brief pause, he added, 'What I mean is, I believe there are different types of ghosts—'

He was interrupted by the beeping of his phone.

Apologizing to Cleo, he answered with a curter than usual, 'Grace speaking.'

It was DC Boutwood in the Incident Room. 'Sorry to bother you, sir. There has been a development. Are you on your way back yet?'

He looked at Cleo Morey, loath to tear himself away, and said with more than a trace of reluctance, 'Yes, I'll be there in fifteen minutes.'

74

In the studious atmosphere of the Incident Room time barely intruded. At five past ten, when Grace walked back in, all the desks were almost fully manned. At the Operation Salsa work station, Nick forked his way through a Chinese takeaway, Bella munched on an apple, and Emma-Jane sat glued to her computer screen, sipping a carton of Ribena through a straw. For a moment none of them noticed him.

'Hi,' he said. 'What's up?'

Immediately all three of them looked up. Bella Moy said, through a mouthful of apple, 'Glenn's had to rush home – some problem with the babysitter. He'll be back shortly.'

'Great! Is that the development you wanted to tell me about?'

DC Boutwood looked at him nervously; the junior on the team, she hadn't yet spent enough time with him to know when he was being funny and when he was in a temper. She was wise to be cautious – at this moment it was borderline and he was very tired. 'Sir, they've found a coffin in a concealed grave on land owned by Double-M Properties – from the diagram you brought in.'

'Brilliant! Fantastic news!'

Then he was aware of all three pairs of eyes on him, and that there was something wrong. 'Yes?'

'I'm afraid it's not such good news, sir. There's no one in it.'

'Just an empty coffin? In a proper grave?'

'As I understand, sir, yes.' She was getting increasingly nervous.

'Was there anyone in it – I mean – had there been anyone in it?'

'Apparently on the lid – the inside – there were signs of it, yes – sir.'

'Cut the *sir*, OK? Call me Roy.'

'Yes, sir – I – I – mean – *Roy*.'

He gave her a fleeting smile of reassurance. 'What kind of signs inside the lid?'

'Evidence of someone trying to scrape – cut – their way out of it.'

'And Michael Harrison, or whoever it was, succeeded?'

'The lid was off, sir – Roy – but apparently the grave was covered with a corrugated iron sheet and someone had put shrubs and mosses on top. Sounds like they were trying to conceal it.'

Grace leaned his arms wearily on the work-station surface. 'So who the hell are we dealing with here? Houdini?'

'It doesn't make much sense,' added Nicholl.

'The guy – Michael Harrison – has a reputation as a practical joker. It makes plenty of sense,' Grace retorted testily. He was starting to feel very tired and very grumpy and wished he wasn't here at all, but back in the pub, chatting with the warm and lovely Cleo Morey.

Realizing his blood sugar must be running low – he'd not eaten anything since a sandwich at lunchtime, and was now starving – he went out, down the corridor to a vending machine, and bought himself a double espresso, a bottle of water and a Mars Bar.

When he returned to the Incident Room, already

munching on the Mars, Emma-Jane was holding a telephone receiver up for him.

'Ashley Harper – she's insisting on speaking to you and says it is very urgent.'

Grace swallowed his mouthful, and took the receiver. 'This is Detective Superintendent Grace,' he said.

'It's Ashley Harper,' she said, sounding frantic. 'I've just had a text message from Michael. He's alive!'

'What does he say?'

'*Alive, call police.* I think that's what it says.'

'You think?'

'The spelling's a bit strange – text messages come out a bit oddly sometimes, don't they?'

'That's all it says?'

'Yes.'

Thinking fast, Grace asked, 'From his own mobile?'

'Yes, his normal number.'

He could have dispatched Nick or Bella over to her, but he decided he wanted to see Ashley himself.

'Stay there. I'm coming over right now.'

75

Mark stared at his gloomy reflection in the smoked-glass mirror in the lift that was sweeping him up to the fourth floor of the Van Alen building. Everything seemed to be unravelling around him.

Less than a week ago he'd sat on the aeroplane flying back from Leeds, reading the road test on the Ferrari 360 and trying to decide whether he would buy one in red or in silver, and whether it should have Formula-One-style gear-shift paddles, or a conventional lever on the floor.

Now that car was fast receding towards the horizon, without him. And everything else seemed to be, too.

What was Ashley's problem? For months they had been so incredibly close, as close as he could ever imagine two human beings could be. They shared the same humour, the same taste in food, drink, the same interests; they fancied each other like crazy, making love whenever they could snatch a few precious moments – and on a couple of occasions coming perilously close to being caught by Michael. She was an amazing girl, smart, super-bright and yet so loving and caring. He had never met anyone remotely like her, and could not imagine life without her.

So why was she being so short with him now? OK, it had been stupid to get drunk at the wedding and to be rude to the smartarse cop. But all this talk about killing Michael really worried him. Murder had never been on the agenda. Ever. Now she was talking like it had been all the time. Her words of half an hour ago in the trattoria echoed in his head.

There's never been any question of him getting out alive, has there?

And yes, he'd gone along with her plan. Not actually to murder Michael – just to – to – to—

Not murder. Definitely not murder.

Murder was when you planned things, wasn't it? Premeditated? This had all just been circumstance. Burying Michael alive, then the accident. He had no love for Michael. Michael was always first in every fucking thing. At school, Michael won the 100 metres and just about every damn thing else. He was the one who got to score the goals in football; he was the first of their group to lose his virginity – women always gravitated to him, always, always. Mark would find himself standing next to Michael in a crowded bar, and a couple of beautiful girls would come up to Michael, and he would say, 'This is my friend, Mark!' And the girls would smile and say, 'Hi, Mark!' and then turn their backs on him for the entire evening. It didn't happen once, it happened time and time again.

It had been the same with Ashley, in the beginning. In that first interview six months back it had been Michael, as usual, who had done all the talking and Ashley had seemed captivated by him, barely even casting Mark a glance. (Later she'd told Mark that it was all an act, because she had so desperately wanted the job and had been tipped off that it was Michael who really controlled the company.)

During the first month or so, Mark had been able to see how interested Michael was in Ashley. He knew his friend well enough to read the signs – he was flirting with her through his jokes, questions, flattery, stories about himself, exactly the way he flirted with all the women he fancied, and Mark had watched Michael's continuing flirtation with her with huge amusement – and satisfaction. It was the first time ever he had pulled a girl that Michael had fancied – and it felt terrific, liberating, as if finally, after fifteen years of their friendship, he no longer felt under Michael's thumb.

The plan had been Ashley's idea. Mark had had no qualms about any of it, except the notion of Ashley and Michael on honeymoon. That he had found so hard to bear. That, he knew in his heart, had been the reason he'd driven out into the forest last Thursday night and removed the air tube.

But now to let this madman torture and mutilate his friend? To death? He wasn't sure he had the stomach to do that.

He unlocked his front door, and as he stepped inside, the landline phone rang. He slammed the door shut, ran across the room, glanced at the display, but there was no caller number showing.

'Hello?' he answered.

The same Australian voice he had heard before said, 'Hi, mate, Vic here. I'm a little curious about the copper who popped round to see you earlier. Thought I told you about not speaking to the cops.'

'I didn't,' Mark said. 'This is a Detective Superintendent investigating Michael's disappearance – I had no idea he was coming.'

'I don't know if I believe you or not, mate. Want to have another chat with Mike about it, or are we cool?'

Trying to follow what he meant, Mark said, 'I think we're cool.'

'So you are going to do what I tell you?'

'I'm listening.'

'Just go to your office right now, open the safe, take out the documents signed by you and Mike giving power of attorney to a lawyer in the Cayman Islands called Julius Grobbe and fax it to him. At the same time you phone Julius Grobbe and tell him to transfer one million, two hundred and fifty-three thousand, seven hundred and twelve pounds from your bank account there to the numbered account in Panama I have already faxed to him. I'll phone you back here in exactly one hour and you can tell me how you got on. If you don't pick up the receiver, your friend loses another bit of his body, and this bit will *really* hurt him. Copy?'

'Copy.'

One million, two hundred and fifty-three thousand, seven hundred and twelve pounds was the exact total Mark and Michael had in their joint account.

76

Roy Grace and Glenn Branson – who had arrived back at Sussex House just as Grace was leaving – sat down in Ashley's cool, minimalistic sitting room and studied the very badly texted message on her dinky Sony Ericsson phone.

*aliVe. *£ cAlll ponlice*

Ashley sat opposite them, wringing her hands, her face pale, eyes watery. She looked as if she had been out somewhere, Grace thought, staring at her ragged cream blouse, her hair, linen skirt, and smelling the powerful aroma of perfume she exuded. *Where? With whom?*

He ought to be feeling sorry for her, he knew. Her fiancé had vanished, their wedding had been called off and tonight, instead of being somewhere on honeymoon, she was sitting crying in her house in Brighton. But he didn't feel sorry, couldn't feel sorry. All he could feel was deep suspicion.

'Have you tried calling him back?'

'Yes, and I've texted him. The line just rings and goes to voicemail.'

'That's better than before,' Grace said. 'It didn't ring before, just went straight to voicemail.'

Branson was fiddling with the phone – as he was much better with gadgets than Grace. 'It was sent by Michael Harrison, phone number plus 44797 134621,' he announced, then pressed a button with his thumb whilst sucking in his lower lip in concentration. 'At 22.28, today.' Both Grace and Branson checked their watches. Just over an hour ago.

Twenty minutes before she rang, Grace thought. *Why did she wait twenty minutes?*

Glenn Branson dialled the number and held the phone to his ear. Grace and Ashley watched him, expectantly. After some moments, Branson said, 'Hello, Michael Harrison, this is Detective Sergeant Branson of Brighton CID responding to your text to Ashley Harper. Please call or text me on 0789 965018. The number again is 0789 965018.' Then he ended the call.

'Ashley, does Michael normally text you?'

She shrugged. 'Not a huge amount, but yes – you know – little love messages, that sort of thing.' She smiled suddenly, and in the warmth it brought to her face, and the beauty it seemed to animate, Grace could see her melting almost any heart she chose.

Branson grinned. 'Has he always been a crap texter?'

'Not usually, no.'

Grace stared again at the words. *aliVe. *£ cAlll ponlice*

It looked like an infant had texted them, not a grown man. Unless of course he had done them in a hurry, or while driving.

'What information can you get from this?' Ashley asked.

Grace was about to tell her, then decided not to. He surreptitiously touched Branson's leg with his own as a signal not to contradict him. 'Not a lot really, I'm afraid. It's good news in one respect, in that we know he's alive, but it is bad news, because he is clearly in trouble. Unless it is part of a hoax.'

Her eyes were all over the place, Grace noticed; he had

been watching every inch of her body language since she had appeared at the door; everything was considered, all done after a pause, nothing spontaneous.

'You can't still believe Michael is doing some kind of a hoax?' she said incredulously. Grace noticed something very forced and theatrical about the way this came out. He told her about the discovery of the coffin – all the details.

'So he's escaped – is that what you think?'

'Maybe,' Grace said. 'Or maybe he was never there.'

'Oh, right, so he like scratched the inside of the lid himself?'

'I think that's one possible scenario, yes. It is not necessarily the right one.'

'Oh, come on, get real! This text message is desperate and you are sitting here giving me a bullshit theory about a hoax?'

'Ashley, we are very real,' Grace said calmly. 'We have an entire team in the Major Incident Suite; we have over one hundred officers out searching for Michael Harrison; we are getting national media coverage – we are doing all we possibly can.'

She looked contrite suddenly, a little girl lost and scared. She stared meekly at the two police officers, eyes wide, and dabbed them with a handkerchief. 'I'm sorry,' she sniffed, 'I didn't mean to have a go at you; you have been so brilliant, both of you. I'm just so – so—' She began to shake, her face scrunched up against a flood of tears.

Grace stood up awkwardly, and Branson followed.

'It's OK,' Grace said. 'We'll see ourselves out.'

77

He made the call. But it took five attempts for the damned fax to go through. The first time, trying to do it too quickly, he hadn't loaded the letter in straight and it had jammed. He'd spent ten precious minutes trying to unjam it without tearing the letter.

He'd driven, which was stupid considering the amount he'd drunk, but it was too far to walk to the office and back in the time, and he hadn't wanted to risk not being able to get a taxi.

Now, bursting in through the door of his apartment with less than three minutes to the deadline, he made straight for the drinks cabinet, poured himself three fingers of Balvenie and gulped it straight down. He felt the burn in his gullet, then winced as it burnt his stomach even harder, closing his eyes for a moment.

His mobile beeped. A text message signal.

He pulled it out of his pocket and stared at the display.

Well done, mate! Just made it.

The phone was jigging in his hand from nerves. Where the hell was this man, Vic? He punched the *options* button, trying to see the source of the text. It was a number he did not recognize. Clumsily, he typed back, *Are we OK now?* Then pressed the *send* button. Instantly there was a soft beep, indicating the text had been sent.

The whisky wasn't working, at least not on his nerves. He walked unsteadily over towards the drinks cabinet. But before he reached it, the phone beeped again. Another incoming text.

Walk out onto your balcony, mate.
Look down at the street below!

Mark made straight for the patio doors, unlocked them and stepped out onto the teak decking, then crossed the narrow balcony, past two sun-loungers, placed his hands on the rail and looked down. Music pounded from a gay nightclub a few yards down the street, and he could see the bald domes of the two bouncers. A couple walked along arm in arm. Three drunk girls were staggering along, bumping into each other, giggling. A steady stream of cars drove past.

He looked at the far side of the street, wondering if that was where Vic meant, but all he could see was a couple snogging. Holding his phone in the palm of his hand, he tapped out, *I cannot see you.* And sent it. Again he scanned the street.

Moments later, there was another beep. The reply on his screen read: *I'm right behind you!*

But before he had a chance to turn, one strong hand grabbed the rear of his belt, and another his shirt collar. A fraction of a second later, both his feet were in the air. He dropped his phone, desperately trying to grab the balcony rail, but he was too high up, and his fingers clawed at nothing but air.

Before he even had time to shout, he was launched like a javelin over the rail and plunged down towards the pavement.

He landed flat on his back, with an impact that broke his spine in seven places and shattered his skull with the impact of a coconut hit by a sledgehammer.

One of the drunk girls screamed.

78

Grace and Branson heard the call on the police radio in Grace's car minutes before they arrived back at Sussex House. An apparent suicide jumper at the Van Alen building on the Kemp Town seafront.

They looked at each other. Grace pulled his blue light from the glove compartment, clipped it to the roof, and hit the accelerator. They raced through a speed camera which flashed at them, but he didn't care; he could sort that one out.

Seven minutes later he was forced to slow to a crawl as he drove onto Marine Parade. Ahead he could see a whole circus of flashing blue lights, a crowd of people and two ambulances.

After double parking, both of them leaped out of the car, pushed their way through the crowd and reached two uniformed constables who were busily putting up a tape barrier bearing the wording 'POLICE LINE, DO NOT CROSS'.

Flashing their warrant cards, they ducked under the tape and saw two paramedics standing uselessly by the crumpled heap of a man on the ground, with a dark pool of blood stained with yellow seeping from his head and another, larger, darker stain from his torso.

Under the amber glare of the street lighting Grace could see the man's face. It was Mark Warren, no question. Fighting the rising bile in his throat, he turned to one of the constables and showed him his warrant card.

'What happened?'

'I – don't know, sir. I just spoke to a witness – she was walking along with her friends when he landed, almost at their feet. She's in the far ambulance – bad shock.'

Grace glanced at Branson, who was looking unsteady, then down at the clearly lifeless body. Mark Warren's eyes were wide open, as if in shock.

Christ. Only a few hours ago he had been talking to the man. He had reeked of alcohol and seemed a nervous wreck. Suddenly Grace thought about Cleo. How she would be busy in about an hour's time at the mortuary, making him look presentable for some relative to come and identify him. He didn't envy her that one bit.

'Does anyone know who this man is?' said a voice.

'Yeah, I know him,' said another voice. 'On my floor. He's my neighbour!'

Grace heard a siren, coming closer. 'I know him too,' he said. Then corrected himself. 'Knew him.'

Robert Allison, a tough Detective Inspector – and former Sussex Police snooker champion – who Grace knew well, emerged from the front door of the building and Grace, followed by Branson, walked over to him.

'Roy! Glenn!' Robert Allison greeted them. 'What are you two stop-outs doing here?'

'Thought we'd swing by to catch some sea air,' Grace said.

'Dangerous thing to do around here,' the Detective Inspector said, nodding at the corpse. 'He thought he'd step out on his balcony and catch some sea air, too.' A police surgeon had arrived, and a police photographer. Allison spoke to them both briefly then returned to Grace and Branson.

'Any information about what happened?' asked Grace.

'Not yet.'

'I know him,' Grace said. 'I interviewed him earlier this evening. About eight o'clock. He's the business partner of the young man who's missing – the wedding prank – the four lads killed last week.'

Allison nodded. 'Right.'

'Can we get into his apartment?'

'I've just been up there – the porter has a key. Want me to come with you?'

'Yes, sure, why not?'

A few minutes later Grace, Branson and Detective Inspector Allison entered the apartment. The porter, a muscular-looking man in his fifties, wearing shorts and a singlet, waited outside.

Grace strode into the sitting area, with which he was already a little familiar, and walked over towards the balcony, which he had stepped out onto a few hours back. He went out again and looked down at the scene below. He could see the small crowd, the two ambulances, the police cars, the flashes of the police photographer's camera, the tape cordoning off the crumpled figure of Mark Warren, the dark stains like shadows leaking from his body and head.

He thought back to the wedding, when Mark had come up to him so aggressively. Then tonight when he was a drunken wreck. Grace knew from his experience that survivors of accidents in which others had died often got chewed up with guilt that they had survived; it could destroy some people. But had Mark Warren jumped over the balcony for that reason?

That night he had come back late to this apartment with mud on his car – had that been a guilt trip to the scene of the accident he should have died in with his friends? Possibly. But what was the damned aggression about at the wedding? That bit did not fit. He hadn't had a good feeling about Mark Warren. The best man who didn't know what the stag night plans were.

How likely was that?

He went back inside pensively. 'Let's just take a good look around for a few minutes,' he said, and began by walking over to the cupboard door Mark had kept staring at earlier. But all it contained were two dusty flower vases and an empty box of Cohiba Robusto cigars.

Steadily he worked his way through each cupboard, opening every door and drawer. Glenn Branson began doing the same, while Allison watched. Then Grace reached the fridge in the open-plan kitchen and opened the door. Casting his eye across the cartons of skimmed milk, yoghurt pots, clumps of fashionable salad leaves and several bottles of white burgundy and champagne, he almost missed the Jiffy bag on the third shelf.

He pulled it out and peered inside, frowning. Then he tipped the small plastic bag it contained out on the black marble kitchen work surface.

'Jesus,' Branson said, staring at the fingertip.

'OK,' Robert Allison said. 'Now this starts to make sense. I found it on the victim when I was looking for ID.' He pulled a folded sheet of A4 paper from his pocket and handed it to Grace.

Grace and Branson both read it.

'Check the fingerprints out and you'll find it is your friend and business partner. Every 24 hours I will cut an increasingly bigger bit off him. Until you do exactly what I tell you.'

Grace read it again, and then a third time. 'I think this tells us two things,' he said.

Both detectives looked at him, but they had to wait some while before he spoke, finally.

'The first is that I don't think we're looking at a suicide here. And secondly, if I'm right in that assumption, we'll be lucky to find Michael Harrison still alive.'

79

The phone was ringing again! The third time! Each time before he had hit the buttons, trying to stop it in case Vic heard. Then he had fumbled with the keyboard, dialling 901. And each time got the same damned woman's voice. 'You have no messages.'

But now her voice said something different. 'You have one new message.' Then he heard, 'Hello, Michael Harrison, this is Detective Sergeant Branson of Brighton CID responding to your text to Ashley Harper. Please call or text me on 0789 965018. The number again is 0789 965018.'

It was the sweetest sound Michael had ever heard in his life.

Again he fumbled with the keys, trying to text a reply in the dank darkness: *A'88m breing h$ld—*

Then dazzling, blinding white light.

Vic.

'Got a mobile you didn't tell me about, have you, Mikey? Naughty boy, aren't you? Think I'd better take that off you before you get yourself into trouble.'

'Urrrr,' Michael said through the duct tape.

The next moment he felt the phone being ripped from his hand. Followed by Vic's reproachful voice.

'That's not playing the game fair, Mike. I'm very disappointed in you. You should have told me about the phone. You really should have done.'

'Urrrr,' Michael mumbled again, shimmying in terror.

He could see eyes glinting through the hood above him, inches from his face, bright green eyes like a feral cat.

'You want me to hurt you again? Is that what you'd like, Mikey? Let's see who you were calling, shall we?'

Moments later Michael heard the police officer's faint voice through the phone's speaker again.

'Well, fancy that,' the Australian said. 'How sweet. Calling your fiancée. Sweet, but naughty. I think it's time for a punishment. Would you like me to cut off another finger – or clip the callipers back on your bollocks?'

'Noorrrrrr.'

'Sorry, mate, you'll need to articulate better. Talk me through what you'd like best. It's all the same to me – and by the way, your mate Mark is a rude bastard. Thought you'd like to know he never said goodbye.'

Michael blinked against the light. He didn't know what the man was talking about. Mark? Dimly he wondered where it was that Mark had gone.

'Here's something for you to think about, Mikey. That one million, two hundred thousand pounds you have salted away in the Cayman Islands. That's one hell of a nest egg, wouldn't you say?'

How much did this man know about him and his life, Michael wondered. Was that what he was after? He could have it, every damned penny, if he would just let him go. He tried to tell him. 'Urrrrrr. Ymmmgghvvvvvit.'

'That's sweet of you, Mikey, whatever it is you're trying to tell me. I really appreciate all the efforts you are making. But here's the thing, you see. Your problem is, I already have it. And that means I don't need you any more.'

80

Shortly before midnight, Grace drove back into the car park of Sussex House, giving a weary nod to the security guard. They had said little on the drive back from the Van Alen building; Grace and Branson were both wrapped in their thoughts.

As Grace pulled the car up, Branson yawned noisily. 'Think we can go home, go to bed, get some sleep?'

'No stamina, youth?' Grace chided.

'And you're wide awake, full of beans? Firing on all cylinders, yeah? I've heard when you get past a certain age you start needing less sleep; which apparently is just as well, since you spend half the night getting up to piss.'

Grace smiled.

'I don't look forward to old age much,' Branson said. 'Do you?'

'To be honest, I don't think about it. I see a guy like Mark Warren, lying all broken, leaking his brains out on the pavement, and I remember he and I were talking just a few hours before; things like that make me believe in just living one day at a time.'

Branson yawned again.

'I'm going back to work,' Grace said. 'You can fuck off home if you want.'

'You know, you can be such a bitch at times,' Branson said, reluctantly following him to the main entrance, through the doors and up the staircase past the displays of truncheons.

Emma-Jane Boutwood, wearing a white cardigan tied around her neck and a pink blouse, was the only person still in the Incident Room. Grace walked over to her, then gestured at the empty work stations. 'Where's everyone, E-J?'

She leaned forward as if to read some small print on her computer screen and said distractedly, 'I think they've all gone home.'

Grace stared at her tired face, and gave her a light pat on her shoulder, his hand touching the soft wool of the cardigan. 'I think you should go home too; it's been a long day.'

'Can you just give me one minute, Roy? I have something I think is going to interest you – both of you.'

'Anyone like a coffee?' Grace asked. 'Water? Coke?'

'You buying?' Branson said.

'No, the ratepayers of Sussex are buying this time. They want us working at midnight, they can buy us coffee. This one's going on expenses.'

'I'll have a Diet Coke,' Branson said. 'Actually, no, change that. Make it a full-strength Coke; I need the sugar hit.'

'I'd love a coffee,' Emma-Jane said.

Grace walked out, along the empty corridor to the rest area with its kitchenette and vending machines. Fumbling in his pocket he pulled out some change, bought a double espresso for himself, a cappuccino for Emma-Jane and a Coke for Branson, then carried them back to the Incident Room on a plastic tray.

As he walked in, the young detective constable was pointing at something on her computer screen, and Branson, leaning over her shoulder, seemed engrossed. Without turning his head, he said, 'Roy, come and take a look at this!'

Emma-Jane turned to Grace. 'You asked me to check up on Ashley Harper's background—'

'Uh huh. What have you found?'

Almost swelling with pride she said, 'Actually, quite a lot.'

'Tell me.'

She flipped a couple of pages on a notepad covered in her neat handwriting, checking her notes as she spoke. 'The information you gave me was that Ashley Harper was born in England, and her parents were killed in a car crash in Scotland when she was three; that she was subsequently brought up by foster parents, in London first, then they moved to Australia. When she was sixteen she went to Canada and stayed with her uncle and aunt – and that her aunt died recently. Her uncle's name was Bradley Cunningham – I don't have her aunt's first name.'

Still reading from her pad she went on: 'Ashley Harper returned to England – to her roots – about nine months ago. You said that previously she had worked in real estate in Toronto, Canada and that her employers were a subsidiary of the Bay group.' Then she looked up to Grace and Branson as if for confirmation.

Grace replied. 'Yes, that's right.'

'OK,' she said. 'Earlier today I spoke to the head of Human Resources for the Bay group in Toronto – as you may know they are one of the largest department store chains in Canada. They do not have a real estate subsidiary, nor have they ever had an Ashley Harper work for them. I did some further checking and found there are no real estate firms anywhere in Canada with the name "The Bay" in them.'

'Interesting,' Branson said, flipping the ring-pull of his Coke. There was a sharp hiss.

'It gets even more interesting,' she said. 'There is no Bradley Cunningham listed in any phone directory for Toronto, nor for anywhere else in the whole of Ontario. I haven't had time to check out the rest of Canada yet. But . . .' she paused to sip some chocolate-covered froth off the top of her cappuccino, 'I have a journalist friend on the *Glasgow Herald* in Scotland. She's checked back in the archives of all the principal Scottish papers. If a three-year-old girl was orphaned in a car crash, it would have made the news, right?'

'Usually,' Grace said.

'Ashley claims to be twenty-eight. I've had her go back twenty-five years, and then five years either side of that. The name Harper has not come up.'

'She could have taken the name of her foster parents,' Branson said.

'She could,' agreed Emma-Jane Boutwood. 'But what I'm about to show you reduces that possibility.'

Grace looked admiringly at the young DC. She seemed to be growing in confidence in front of his eyes. She was exactly the kind of new blood the police force so badly needed. Smart, hard-working youngsters with determination.

'I had the name Ashley Harper run through the Holmes network, as you requested,' she said, addressing Grace.

Holmes-2 was the second phase in a computerized database of crimes, linking all police forces throughout the UK and Interpol and, more recently, other police networks overseas.

'Nothing showed up under the name Ashley Harper,' she said. 'But this is where it gets interesting. Taking the initials "AH", and linking them to a broad category heading of "property", Holmes came up with the following. Eighteen months ago a young lady called Abigail Harrington married a wealthy property developer in Lymm, Cheshire, called Richard Wonnash. He was big into free-fall parachuting. Three months after their wedding, he died when his parachute failed to open during a jump. Four years ago, in Toronto, Canada, a woman called Alexandra Huron married a real estate developer called Joe Kerwin. Five months after their wedding he drowned in a sailing accident on Lake Ontario. Seven years ago, a woman called Ann Hampson married a property developer in London called Julian Warner. He was a high-profile society bachelor, with big holdings in London docklands around the time of the early 1990s property crash. Six months and two days after their wedding, he gassed himself in an underground car park in Wapping.'

She took another sip of her froth.

'Same initials,' Branson said. 'But what does that prove?'

'A lot of con artists keep the same initials when they change their names,' she said. 'I read about this at police training college. In itself it proves nothing. But here's where it gets better.' She tapped her keyboard and a black and white newspaper photograph of a young woman with close-cropped dark hair appeared. The face belonged to Ashley Harper – or her double.

'This is from the *Evening Standard* article on the death of Julian Warner,' she said.

There was a long silence while Grace and Branson studied the photograph. 'Shit,' Branson said. 'Certainly looks like her.'

Saying nothing, she tapped the keyboard again.

Another photograph, also in black and white, appeared. This showed a woman with shoulder-length fair hair. Her face looked even more like Ashley Harper. 'This is from the *Toronto Star*, four years ago, reporting on the death of Joe Kerwin.'

Grace and Branson said nothing. Both were stunned.

'This next one is from the *Cheshire Evening Post*, eighteen months ago, in an article about the death of Richard Wonnash. Abigail Harrington was the beautiful grieving widow.' She tapped her screen and a new photograph appeared, in colour. The hair was red, styled in an elegantly short razor cut. The face yet again was, almost beyond doubt, Ashley Harper's.

'Bloody hell!' Branson exclaimed.

Grace stared at the face, pensively, for a long time. Then he said, 'Emma-Jane, well done.'

'Thank you – Roy.'

Grace turned to Glenn Branson. 'So,' he said. 'It's twenty minutes to one. Which magistrate do you feel brave enough to wake up?'

'For a search warrant?'

'You worked that all out by yourself did you?' Ignoring Branson's grimace, Grace stood up. 'Emma-Jane, go home; get some sleep.'

Branson yawned. 'How about me? Do I get some sleep?'

Grace clapped a hand on his shoulder. 'I'm afraid, my friend, your day's only just begun.'

81

A few minutes later, Grace was on the phone to a very sleepy-sounding magistrates' clerk, who asked if this couldn't wait until the morning.

'We're investigating a possible abduction, and it's a potential life-or-death situation,' Grace informed her. 'I need an evidential warrant and I'm afraid it absolutely cannot wait.'

'OK,' she said reluctantly. 'The duty magistrate is Mrs Quentin.'

Grace smiled to himself. Hermione Quentin was one magistrate he particularly disliked, having had a run-in with her some months back in court over a suspect he had wanted to hold in custody; she had refused. She was the worst kind of magistrate in his view, married to a wealthy stockbroker, living in a vulgar ostentatious house, a middle-aged glamour queen with no experience of the real world and some kind of zealous personal agenda to change the way the police in general viewed criminals. It would give him the sweetest pleasure to get her out of bed to sign the warrant in the small hours of the morning.

Grace and Branson then spent a further ten minutes on the phone, organizing a team to assemble at Sussex House at 5 a.m. Then, taking pity on Branson, Grace sent him home to get a couple of hours' kip.

Next he rang DC Nicholl, and apologized for disturbing him, then instructed him to head for Ashley Harper's house and keep watch on it for any movement.

At 2 a.m., with the signed warrant in his hand, Grace arrived back at his home, set his alarm for 4.15, and crashed out.

*

When he hit the alarm button and jumped automatically out of bed in the dark room, he could hear the first twitterings of the dawn chorus, reminding him as he stepped into the shower that, although summer had not yet begun, they were less than a month shy of the longest day, 21 June.

At 5 a.m. he was back at Sussex House, feeling remarkably perky on his two and a bit hours' sleep. Bella and Emma-Jane were already there, as was Ben Farr, a round-faced, bearded Sergeant in his late forties who was to be the Exhibits Officer, and Joe Tindall. Glenn Branson arrived a few minutes later.

Over cups of coffee, Grace briefed them. Then, shortly after half past five, all wearing protective waistcoats, they set off in a police Transit van and a marked car, which Branson drove, Grace in the passenger seat.

Reaching Ashley's street, Grace told Branson to pull up alongside Nick's unmarked Astra, and wound his window down.

'All quiet,' Nicholl reported.

'Good boy,' Grace said, noting that Ashley Harper's Audi TT was in its usual place outside her house. He told Nicholl to cover the street behind, then they drove on.

There were no free spaces in the street, so they double parked beside the Audi. Grace gave Nick Nicholl a couple of minutes to get in place, then, leading the posse, marched up to the front door, in full daylight now, and rang the bell.

There was no response.

He rang again, then, after a minute, rang yet again. Then he nodded to Ben Farr, who went over to the Transit and removed a heavy-duty ram, the size of a large fire extinguisher. He hefted it up to the front door, swung it hard and the door flew open.

Grace went in first. 'Police!' he shouted. 'Hello? Police!'

The silent, winking lights of the hi-fi system greeted him. Followed by the rest of his team, he walked up the stairs and paused on the first-floor landing. 'Hello!' he called out again. 'Miss Harper?'

Silence.

He opened one door, onto a small bathroom. The next door was to a small, bland spare bedroom that didn't look as if it had ever been used. He hesitated, then pushed the remaining door, which opened onto a master bedroom, with a double bed that had clearly not been slept in. The curtains were drawn shut. He found the light switch and turned it on, and several ceiling spots lit up the room.

The place had a deserted feel, like a hotel room waiting for its next occupant. He saw an immaculate duvet over a queen-size bed, a flat-screen television, a clock radio plus a couple of Hockney swimming pool prints on the wall.

No Ashley Harper.

So where the hell was she?

Feeling a stab of panic, Grace exchanged glances with Glenn Branson. They both knew that somewhere along the line they had been outsmarted, but where and how? For a moment all he could think of was the bollocking he would get from Alison Vosper if it turned out he had woken a JP in the middle of the night to get a search warrant for no good reason.

And there could be all kinds of good reasons why Ashley Harper wasn't here tonight. For a moment he felt angry at his friend. This was all Glenn's fault. He'd suckered him into this damned case. It wasn't anything to do with him, not his problem. Now he owned the fucking problem and it was getting deeper.

He tried to recap, to think how he would cover his arse if No. 27 hauled him in. There was Mark Warren's death. The note. The finger in the fridge. Emma-Jane's findings. There was a whole ton of things that were not right. Mark Warren, so belligerent at the wedding reception. Bradley Cunningham, so smooth, so upmarket at the wedding.

'Actually the pants are killing me . . . rented this lot from your wonderful Moss Bros, but I think I got given the wrong pants!'

From the time he had spent in the United States and in Canada, and the conversations Grace had had about the differences in their language, he knew that classy Americans and Canadians might call ordinary trousers 'pants', but they would called dressier trousers 'trousers'. It had been an instant giveaway that Bradley Cunningham might not be who he made himself out to be.

Not that that slender hypothesis would satisfy Alison Vosper.

'Take this place apart,' he told his team wearily. 'Look under every bloody stone. Find out who owns this place. Who owns the televisions, the hi-fi, the Audi outside, the carpets, the wall sockets. I want to know every damned detail about Ashley Harper. I want to know more about her than she knows herself. Everybody understand?'

*

After two hours of searching, so far no one had found anything. It was as if Ashley Harper had been through the place with some kind of super-Hoover. There was nothing other than the furniture, a bio yoghurt pot in the fridge together with some soya milk, a bunch of radishes and a half-drunk bottle of Sainsbury's own-label Scottish mineral water.

Glenn Branson came up to Grace, who was busy lifting the mattress off the spare bed. 'Man, this is so weird – it's as if she knew we were coming, know what I mean?'

'So why didn't we know she was leaving?' Grace asked.

'There you go again. Another question.'

'Yes,' said Grace, tiredness making him snappy now. 'Maybe that's because you're always giving me questions instead of fucking answers.'

Branson raised a hand in the air. 'No offence, man.'

'None taken.'

'So where the fuck is she?'

'Not here.'

'I figured that one.'

'Roy! Take a look at this – I don't know if it's of any use?' DC Nicholl came into the room holding a small piece of paper, which he showed to Grace.

It was a receipt from a company called Century Radio on Tottenham Court Road. On the receipt was printed: 'AR5000 Cyber Scan, £2,437.25'.

'Where was this?' Grace asked.

'In the dustbin in the back yard,' Nick replied, with pride.

'Two thousand, four hundred and thirty-seven pounds for a scanner?' Grace asked. 'What kind of scanner costs that much? Some kind of computer scanner?' After a few moments thought, he added, 'Why would anyone throw away the receipt? Even if you couldn't charge the scanner to your business, sure as hell you would keep the receipt in case it went wrong. Wouldn't you?'

'I sure as hell would,' Branson agreed.

Grace looked at the date on the receipt. Last Wednesday. Time of purchase showed as 14.25. On Tuesday night, her fiancé disappears. On Wednesday afternoon she goes out and buys a two-and-a-half-thousand-quid scanner. This didn't make sense – yet. His watch showed that two hours had elapsed so far, it was now just past 8 a.m. 'I don't know what time Century Radio opens – but we need to find out about that scanner,' he said.

'You have some thoughts about it?' Branson asked.

'Plenty,' Grace replied. 'Too many. Far too many.' Then he added. 'I have to be at Lewes Crown Court by quarter to ten.'

'For your good friend Suresh Hossain?'

'I'd hate to think he was missing me. How about some breakfast? A big fry-up – the works?'

'Cholesterol, man, bad for your heart.'

'You know what? Right now everything's bad for my heart.'

82

As Grace entered the large, bustling waiting area for the three courtrooms housed in the handsome Georgian Lewes Crown Court building with plenty of time to spare, he switched his phone to silent. At least Claudine seemed to have got the message and had stopped texting him.

He yawned, his body feeling leaden, the massive fry-up he'd just eaten sapping his energy rather than fuelling it. He just wanted to lie down somewhere and have a kip. It was strange, he thought. A week ago this trial had dominated his life, his every waking thought. Now it was secondary; finding Michael Harrison was all that mattered.

But this trial did matter a lot, too. It mattered to the widow and children of Raymond Cohen, the man beaten to a pulp with a spiked stick, either by Hossain or by his thugs. It mattered to every ordinary decent person in the City of Brighton and Hove, because they had a right to be protected from monsters like him, and it mattered a very great deal to Grace's credibility. He had to shed his tiredness and concentrate.

Finding a quiet corner in the room, he sat down and returned a call to Eleanor, who was dealing with his post and email for him. Then he closed his eyes, grateful for the rest it gave them, and cradled his head in his hands, trying to catnap, trying to block from his ears the swinging of doors opening and closing, the cheery banter of greetings, the clicks of briefcase locks, the murmured voices between lawyers and clients.

After a couple of minutes he took two deep breaths, and the oxygen hit gave him an instant small boost. He stood up and looked around. In a moment he might find out whether he would be needed or not today. Hopefully not, and he could get back to Sussex House, he thought, looking around for the person he needed to speak to, Liz Reilly from the Crown Prosecution Service.

There were a good hundred people in the room, including several gowned barristers and assistants, and he spotted Liz at the other end of the room, a smartly dressed, conservative-looking woman in her early thirties, holding a clipboard and deep in conversation with a barrister he did not recognize.

He walked across and stood near them, catching her signal that she would be with him in a moment. When she finally broke away from the barrister, she looked excited. 'We have a possible new witness!'

'Really? Who?'

'A call-girl from Brighton. She rang the CPS last night saying she's been following the trial in the papers, and alleging that Suresh Hossain beat her up during a session with her. The sex session was on the night of February 10th last year, in Brighton.'

February 10th was the night of the murder for which Suresh Hossain was on trial.

'Hossain has a cast-iron alibi that he was at dinner in London with two friends that night. Both have testified,' Grace said.

'Yes he has, but they are both employees of Hossain. This girl isn't. She's terrified of him – the reason she hasn't come forward before is she's been threatened with her life if she does. And there's a problem, which is she doesn't trust the police. That's why she rang us, rather than the police.'

'How credible do you think she is?'

'Very,' she said. 'We'd need some high-level witness protection for her.'

'Whatever she wants. Anything!' Grace wrung his hands in excitement. He wanted to hug Liz Reilly. This was wonderful news. *Wonderful!*

'But someone's going to have to go and convince her that the police won't bust her for – you know – her trade.'

'Where's she now?'

'At her home.'

Grace looked at his watch. 'I could go and see her right away. Is that possible?'

'Go in an unmarked car.'

'Yes, and I'll take a WPC with me who can stay with her. We don't want to give Hossain any chance of getting at her. I want to go and see her and persuade her to come in right away.'

'If you play her carefully, you'll be pushing on an open door.'

Suddenly, Grace wasn't tired any more.

83

It was shortly after midday when he arrived back in the Incident Room. The witness, Shelley Sandler, was good, he thought. Mid-twenties, intelligent, articulate, vulnerable, she'd be highly credible in court. Just so long as she didn't panic and change her mind at the last minute, as so often happened. But she seemed determined to get back at Hossain. Very, very determined.

This was such good news. After a shaky few days last week, it now looked to Grace as if getting the verdict he so badly wanted was going to be achievable.

The full team were at the work station, plus two new assistants, a young male constable and a middle-aged female assistant, so he called a briefing meeting, telling them all to stay seated.

Keeping his voice low, as the other work stations were occupied also with teams hard at work, Nick Nicholl spoke first. 'Roy, the receipt we took earlier this morning from Miss Harper's house, two thousand, four hundred and thirty-seven pounds for a scanner?'

'Uh huh.'

'I got all the information on it from Century Radio.' He handed a few printed sheets off a web page to Grace. 'The rest of us have seen this.'

Grace looked at it.

AR5000 Receiver 'Cyber Scan'. Incredible 10Khz–2600Mhz Frequency Range! The AR5000 advances the frontiers of performance, providing excellent strong signal handling, high sensitivity and wide frequency coverage with microprocessor facilities to match including 5 independent VFOs, 1,000 memory channels, 20 search banks, Cyber Scan fast scan and search – including all mobile frequencies. Scanning and search speed is 45 channels or increments per second . . .

He turned to Branson. 'You're the best techie I know. I think I have already guessed what this thing is – can you confirm?'

'It's a state-of-the-art radio frequency scanner. It's the kind of thing used by Citizens' Band radio nuts to find new friends, to eavesdrop on police radio networks or on mobile calls.'

Grace nodded. Then to Emma-Jane Boutwood he said, 'Do we have any evidence that Ashley Harper was ever into Citizens' Band radio either in her current incarnation or any previous one?'

'We don't,' she said. 'No.'

He looked at the colour picture of the scanner. A large silver box on its own legs, with a dial on the front, and the same perplexing array of knobs and buttons you'd find on any complex piece of radio kit. 'So, on Tuesday night her fiancé disappears. Wednesday afternoon at two-thirty she legs it to London and buys a radio scanner for two and a half thousand quid. Any good theories why? And how the hell did she knew how to use it?'

'Desperation?' volunteered Nick Nicholl.

'I don't buy that,' Grace said.

'She obviously genuinely did not know where he was,' Bella Moy suggested.

Grace nodded distractedly. That made sense, but to him it did not fit.

'She might have known that Michael Harrison had a walkie-talkie. Perhaps it was to try to communicate with him?' Emma-Jane Boutwood said. 'Or – how about – to listen in to who else he might be communicating with?'

Grace was impressed. 'Yes, good thinking.' He looked around. 'Any more theories? OK, let's park this for a moment. Any other progress?'

'Yes,' Nick Nicholl said. 'After you left Ashley Harper's house, Joe Tindall started pulling up floorboards. We discovered an envelope full of receipts behind a chest of drawers we moved – it might have fallen there accidentally or it might have been hidden. Most of the receipts don't seem that interesting to us, but there is one here you should see.'

It was for £1,500 from a company with a Maddox Street, London W1 address, called Conquest Escorts. Underneath the name was the legend 'Discreet, charming male and female escorts for every occasion'. Two dates were shown – the previous Saturday, the intended day of Ashley Harper's wedding, and the previous Monday.

'Turn it over, Roy,' Nick Nicholl said. 'Take a look at the other side.'

Grace turned it over and saw written in ballpoint pen the name Bradley Cunningham.

His mind shot back to the conversation he had had with Ashley, in her house, on Friday night. He could remember her sitting there so dejectedly, talking about her Canadian uncle, saying, 'We adore each other . . . he took the whole week off just so he could be at the rehearsal on Monday.'

'She's faked an uncle?' he said, puzzling.

'She's faked a whole lot more than just an uncle – E-J

will tell you in a minute,' Glenn Branson said. 'Take a look at this first.'

He handed Grace a photocopied sheet of A4 paper. It was a faxed instruction to Bank Hexta, registered on Grand Cayman Island, to transfer the sum of £1,253,712 to a numbered account at Banco Aliado in Panama. The instruction was signed by both Michael Harrison and Mark Warren, and the date and time at the top showed 11.25 p.m., the previous day.

Grace read it through twice then frowned at Branson. 'This is about twenty minutes before he went off his balcony.'

'Yes, correct.'

Grace thought about the note found in Mark Warren's pocket. 'So he went and transferred the money in order to save his friend's life. Then he goes and tops himself?'

'Maybe they had some big debt to pay. Panama could be tied up with Colombia – the Colombian mafia – maybe they got themselves into shit on a loan? They pay it off, and Mark Warren then tops himself?'

'It's a reasonable theory,' Grace said. 'But these two guys have been doing pretty well. They have this huge development at Ashdown – twenty houses – that could make them several million. Why top himself for – what would his share be – a few hundred thousand pounds?'

'So he makes the transfer and then is killed.'

'That's a more elegant theory,' Grace said. 'I spoke to Cleo Morey at the mortuary just now. There's a Home Office pathologist on his way down. We might have a bit more information later today.'

DS Bella Moy then told Grace she had some information from the phone company. Vodafone had logged activity from Michael Harrison's mobile between 10.22 p.m. and

11 p.m. the previous night, and there had been several 999 emergency calls made from Michael Harrison's phone, but on each occasion the operator could not hear anyone at the other end and got no response to her questions.

'What about the cell mast?'

'I was just coming to that, Roy. Vodafone have been very helpful this morning, and we already have from them the location of the closest cell radio mast to Michael Harrison's phone,' she said.

'Where is it?'

Her face fell a little. 'This is not such good news – it's in the town centre of Newhaven, and the one mast covers the entire town.'

'Well, it's some help,' Grace said. 'Any coincidence that Newhaven is a Channel seaport?'

'I've already put out an all-ports alert,' she said.

'For what?'

'For Ashley Harper and for Alexandra Huron – that's the name she was using in Canada four years ago.'

She clearly had more to say, so Grace let her go on.

'I checked on her Audi TT car. It was leased by her, in her own name, from a dealer in Hammersmith a year ago. All payments are up to date and kosher. Same with her house, leased, but the lease expires at the end of this month.'

'To coincide with her wedding?' Branson suggested.

'Quite possible,' Emma-Jane said. 'Then on a hunch I had our new recruits do a trawl of all the car and van rental firms in the area, and gave them all of Ashley Harper's previous names in addition to her own. Nothing showed up under the name Ashley Harper,' she said. 'But at ten past midnight – this morning – a woman called Alexandra Huron rented a Mercedes saloon from a local Avis at

Gatwick Airport, using a Toronto Dominion Bank of Canada credit card. The assistant who dealt with the customer has now positively identified her from photographs as Ashley Harper.'

'CCTV cameras,' Grace said. 'What I—'

Glenn Branson raised a hand. 'We're already on the case. We're already having every camera checked between Gatwick and Newhaven from the time she picked up the car.'

'She left her house about an hour before you went there, Nick,' Grace said to DC Nicholl.

'Yes.'

'Do we know how she got to the airport?'

'No.'

Grace fell silent. For a few moments no one had anything to say. He was busy thinking through all the timings last night – when he had been to see Mark Warren, when he and Glenn Branson had visited Ashley. Mark Warren being taken out to the forest to help locate the grave. The money being transferred. Mark Warren's death. Ashley renting the car under a different name.

Now he knew what her game was; that was clear enough. And he knew that they needed to find her. Absolutely nothing else mattered at this moment than to do that.

And quickly.

If it wasn't already too late.

84

'Strewth, woman, four fucking suitcases – what's the matter with you, Alex?'

'What do you mean?'

'I'm not helping you lug four fucking suitcases, that's what I mean.'

'So we'll get a porter.'

'And what about the excess baggage charge?'

'We're travelling Club, Vic; they have a big baggage allowance. Relax.'

'Fucking relax? Why can't you just leave all this shit behind, buy new stuff in Sydney – they have shops there, you know!'

Ashley, in a Prada denim trouser suit and high heels, standing between her suitcases in the living room of the small detached house in Newhaven, placed her hands defiantly on her hips and stared out of the window. The view from the rented house's remote hill-top position took in almost the whole of the town, and much of the port that was part of it.

She watched the Seacat cross-Channel ferry slipping past the harbour mole, heading out to sea. It was a flat, grey day, and humid; she was perspiring, which added to her bad mood, and her period was about to start, which made it even worse.

She turned on him, her voice rising in acidity. 'Really? They have shops in Sydney? You mean shops you can walk into and buy things from?'

'Oh, fuck off, you stupid cow – don't speak to me like I'm some fucking servant.'

'You fuck off! Why should I leave all this stuff behind? This is my life.'

'What do you mean *this* is your life?'

At five foot, seven inches, Vic stood barely half an inch taller than Ashley, but he had always seemed to her to be much taller. He had the wiry, muscular build and the persona of a fighting man, with tattooed arms, crew-cut hair and a rough-hewn, handsome face. His clothes added to his military persona; at this moment he was dressed in a combat jacket over a black T-shirt, baggy khaki chinos and what could have been black marching boots.

'Do you mean Michael is your life? Mark? These two gits have been your life, is that what you mean? Have I got something wrong here – I thought I was your life, you stupid bitch.'

'I thought you were too,' she said tightly, holding back tears.

'So what the fuck does that mean?'

'Nothing,' she said.

He grabbed her by the shoulders and turned her round to face him. 'Alex, relax, OK. We're nearly there, home free; let's just calm right down.'

'I'm perfectly calm,' she said. 'You're the one who's all wired.'

He pulled her towards him. Stared into her green eyes. Then tenderly pushed some stray strands of her hair back up her forehead. 'I love you,' he said. 'I love you so much, Alex.'

She put her arms around his neck, pulled his lips up against hers and kissed him passionately for some moments. 'I love you too, Vic. I always have.'

'And yet you happily went off and screwed Mark, then Michael. And a whole bunch of guys before them.'

She stepped back angrily and almost fell over a suitcase. 'Jesus Christ, what's got into you?'

'What's got into me? We've fucked up this time, that's what. OK?'

'We haven't fucked up, Vic; we have a result.'

'A lousy one-point-two million quid? Half a year of our lives for that?'

'Neither of us could have foreseen what was going to happen – the crash.'

'We should have played it differently. You could have got Michael out, gone through with the wedding, and then we'd have had half his money, and his partner's.'

'And that would have taken months, Vic – maybe years. They still have some planning issues on their big development. As it is, we got a quick result. And if you hadn't gambled away half our goddamn money, we wouldn't have even needed to be here at all in the first place, OK?'

Sheepishly, he looked at his watch. 'We have to get going if we're going to make the flight.'

'I'm ready.'

'You don't have any idea how fucking painful this stuff is for me, Alex, do you? What we do? My sitting on the sidelines, knowing this year you're screwing Michael and Mark, before that you were screwing that jerk Richard in Cheshire, not to mention Joe Kerwin and Julian Warner.'

'I can't believe I'm hearing this, Vic. I did what I did because that was my part of our bargain, OK?'

'No, not OK.'

'You've always had your sweet revenge on them in the

end – so what's your problem? And this way, I get to spare you and me from a honeymoon with Michael.'

He looked at his watch again, anxiously. 'We'll talk in the car – I have one more thing to do before we leave.' He lugged her suitcases out into the hall, then went back into the sitting room and moved the sofa right across the room. Then he knelt down and peeled back a corner of the carpet.

'Vic,' she said.

He looked up. 'What?'

'Can't we just leave him?'

'Leave him?'

'He's not going anywhere, is he? He's not going to get out – he can't even speak, you said.'

'I'm going to finish him off, put him out of his misery.'

'Why not just leave him? No one's ever going to find him.'

'Take me ten seconds to crush his neck.'

'But why?'

He glared at her. 'You are sweet on him, bitch, aren't you?'

Blushing she said, 'I am absolutely not sweet on him.'

'You were never worried about me getting rid of any of the others. What's so special about Mikey boy?'

'Nothing's special about him.'

He let the carpet fall back in place, stood up, and rolled the sofa back to where it had been. Then he repositioned the coffee table. 'You've got a point, Alex, about him not getting out. Why show any mercy on the little bastard by putting him out of his misery? We'll just let him starve to death all on his own in the darkness. Happy with that?'

She nodded. 'Have you checked today's papers?'

'No, I've been cleaning the place out. Got all yesterday's – nothing to worry about. We'll check today's at the airport.' He grinned. 'Then after that, no worries, right?'

Five minutes later the Mercedes was packed with Ashley's four suitcases and Vic's large holdall. He locked the front door and pocketed the keys.

'Do you think we should drop them back in to the agency?'

'We have five more months to run on the lease, woman! You want people going in there and sniffing around? Because I tell you one thing, it ain't going to smell too good in there in a week or two.'

She said nothing as she clipped on her seatbelt, watching the house out of the window for the last time. It was a strange house, perfect for their purposes because of its isolation – the nearest neighbour was a quarter of a mile away – and in fact doubly perfect in the light of events last Tuesday night. You could never in a million years call it a pretty or stylish house. Built on scrubby wasteland – which hadn't changed – in the 1930s, it looked like one truncated half of a pair of semi-detached houses, as if the other side of it had never been built. Originally there had been an integral garage, but some years back that had been converted into what was now the sitting room.

He started the car. In an hour they would be at Gatwick Airport. Tomorrow, or later today – she always had a problem with the time zones – they would be back in Australia. Home. Specks of drizzle pattered onto the windscreen. Regardless, she slipped on her new Gucci sunglasses. Vic had cropped her hair – no time to go to a salon – then she had put on this morning a short, dark wig. If there was any search at all at the airport, they would be watching for Ashley Harper. There was just the smallest possibility they might be looking for Alexandra Huron. But as she looked at the passport in her handbag, which still had two years to run, she smiled. Certainly no one would be looking for Anne Hampson.

Vic put the gear lever into *drive*, then fumbled around. 'Where's the fucking brake?'

'It's a handle; you pull it.'

'Why the fuck do they have a handle? Why didn't you rent a normal car?'

'How much more normal than a Mercedes can you get?'

'One with a proper parking brake!'

'For Christ's sake!'

He slid down his window and shouted out, 'Bye, fuckwit. Have a nice rest of your life!'

'Vic?'

'Yeah?' He accelerated away fiercely down the potholed road, which the council seemed to have forgotten. 'What's the matter, missing your lover boy's dick already?'

'You know something? It's bigger than yours!'

He lunged out at her, slapping her face, the car swerving onto the overgrown grass verge, then back onto the road, lurching through a pothole.

'Does that make you feel good, hitting me?'

'You are just a fucking slapper.'

They reached a T-junction and turned right by a modern housing development, the trees still saplings.

'And you're just a bully, Vic. You're a sadist, you know that? Does that make you feel good? Is that how you really get your rocks off, tormenting someone like Michael?'

'And you get your rocks off by screwing him and knowing that one day you are *really* going to screw him?' He turned to glare at her, then pulled out onto the main road.

It happened so fast, all she saw was what felt, for an instant, like a sudden change in the light. There was a tremendous bang; she felt a fierce jerk; her ears went numb; and the interior of the car filled with what looked like feathers, and reeked of cordite. At the same time the horn began to blare.

'Oh shit, oh shit, shit, shit!' Vic hammered on the steering wheel with his fists; the driver's air bag hanging like a spent condom from the wheel boss, and another air bag limp beside his head.

'Are you all right?' he asked Ashley.

She nodded, staring at the bonnet of the car, which was raised jaggedly up in front of her, the Mercedes star that had been on the end now invisible. There was another car, white, stopped at a crazy angle in the middle of the road a few yards away.

Vic tried to open his door, and seemed to be having difficulty. Then he threw his weight against it and, with a scream from the hinges, it opened.

Ashley's door opened without a problem. She unclipped her belt and stepped out shakily, then pinched her nose and blew hard to clear her ears. She could see a bewildered-looking grey-haired woman behind the wheel of the other car, a Saab, with much of its nose crumpled.

Vic inspected the damage to the Mercedes. The offside front wheel was crushed and buckled and pushed right into the engine compartment. There was no chance of the car being driveable.

'You stupid fucking bitch!' Vic yelled, above the blare of the Mercedes horn, at the Saab.

Ashley could see another car coming up the road, and a van coming from the opposite direction. And she could see a young man running towards them. 'Vic,' she shouted urgently, 'we need to do something, for Christ's sake!'

'Yeah, right, we need to do something. What do you fucking suggest?'

85

Back at the Incident Room, Nick Nicholl suddenly yelled at Grace. 'Roy! Line seven, pick it up, pick it up!'

Grace stabbed the button and lifted the receiver to his ear. 'Roy Grace,' he said.

It was a Detective Sergeant from Brighton police station called Mark Tuckwell. 'Roy,' he said, 'the Mercedes you have an alert out on, blue saloon, Lima-Juliet-Zero-Four-Papa-X-Ray-Lima?'

'Yes.'

'It's just been involved in a RTA in Newhaven. The occupants, one male, one female, have hijacked a vehicle.'

Grace sat bolt upright, the phone clenched to his ear, adrenaline exploding. 'Have they taken hostages?'

'No.'

'Do we have descriptions of the two people?'

'Not great ones so far. Man stocky, Caucasian, cropped hair, mid-forties; the woman has short dark hair, late twenties, early thirties.'

Grabbing a pen, he asked, 'What are the details of the vehicle they've taken?'

'A Land Rover Freelander, green, Whisky-Seven-Nine-Six-Lima-Delta-Yankee.'

Scribbling this down, Grace asked, 'Any contact with this car so far?'

'Not yet.'

'Exactly how long ago was it taken?'

'Ten minutes.'

Grace thought for a moment. Ten minutes. You could get a long damned way in ten minutes. He thanked the Detective Sergeant and told him he would call him back in a couple of minutes and to keep his line clear.

Then Grace quickly briefed his team. Handing the vehicle details to Nick Nicholl he said, 'Nick, circulate the vehicle details to all the surrounding counties – Surrey, Kent, Hampshire – and also the Met. Now!'

He thought for a moment. The roads to the east of Newhaven went to Eastbourne and Hastings. To the north were the fast roads to Gatwick Airport and to London. To the west was Brighton. Most likely, if they stayed with the Land Rover, they would head north. Turning to DS Moy he said, 'Bella, get the helicopter up. On the assumption they are heading away from the area, get it positioned to cover the roads ten to fifteen miles north of Newhaven.'

'Right.'

'When you've done that, get a watch put on all CCTV at the railway stations in the area, in case they try to ditch the vehicle and get a train.'

He drank a swig of water. 'Emma-Jane, call the Road Policing Department and get some vehicles up on the A23 on look-out for this car immediately. When you've done that, alert the police at Newhaven Harbour and Gatwick and Shoreham Airports.'

He ran through a mental checklist: *stations, seaports, airports, roads*. Often, he knew, when people hijacked cars they would only drive them a short distance, ditch them and take a different car. 'Glenn,' he said, 'get the whole surrounding area of Newhaven flooded – we want to make sure they haven't abandoned the car yet. Also get a couple of our patrol cars here on standby.'

'I'll do it now.'

Grace rang through to the Ops Room and informed them he was taking command of the incident. The clerk there told him there was one update that had just come in. A car matching the description had sideswiped several cars at a traffic light as it had cut past them on the pavement to get over the Newhaven swing bridge seconds before it opened. This information was just two minutes old.

86

Vic Delaney stabbed the brake pedal hard as they came into a right-hander on the winding country road that was much sharper than he had realized. The front wheels locked and for a sickening moment they carried straight on, towards a poplar tree, while he wrestled with the chunky steering wheel. Ashley screamed, 'Viiiic!'

The car lurched violently to the right, the front slewing round, the rear wheels breaking way, then he over-corrected and they were heading at another poplar. Then back, the top-heavy car swinging like a weighted sack, their luggage crashing around in the rear. Then they were back under control.

'Slow down, Vic, for God's sake!'

There was a massive truck ahead, crawling along, and in a moment they were on its tail, with no room to pass. 'Oh, fucking Jesus!' he said, braking, hammering the steering wheel in frustration.

It had all gone wrong. *The story of my life,* he thought. His dad had died of drink when he'd been in his teens. Shortly before his eighteenth birthday he'd beaten up his mother's lover because the guy was a punk and treated her like shite. And his mother had responded by throwing him, Vic, out.

He'd drifted into the services in search of adventure, and instantly felt at home in the Marines, except he'd also acquired a taste for money. Lots of money. In particular he liked fancy clothes, cars, gambling and tarts. But above all else he liked the feeling he got – all that respect – when he walked into a casino in a sharp suit. And what better massage for a man's pride could there be than to get comped at a casino for a steak dinner, maybe a room, too.

A lucky streak in the casinos during his second year in the Marines netted him some big loot, then an unlucky streak wiped him out.

He'd then teamed up with a bent Quartermaster called Bruce Jackman, in charge of the ordnance supplies, and found an easy way to make fast money by selling off guns, ammunition and other military supplies via a website. When that was in the process of being rumbled, he'd garrotted Bruce Jackman, and left him hanging in his bedroom with a suicide note. And had never lost a night's sleep over it since.

Life was a game, *survival of the sharpest*. In his view humans made the mistake of trying to pretend they were any different to the animal world. All life was the law of the jungle.

That didn't mean you couldn't love someone. He'd been deeply, crazily, besottedly in love with Alex from the moment he had first seen her. She had it all: real class, style, stunning beauty, a great body, and she was a dirty cow in bed. She was everything he had ever wanted in a woman and way more. And she was the only woman he had met who was more ambitious than himself – and who had a game plan to achieve her simple goals: make a fortune when you are young, then spend the rest of your life enjoying it. Dead simple.

Now all they had to do was get to Gatwick Airport and catch a plane.

The interior of the Freelander stank of diesel fumes from the exhaust of the massive lorry in front of him, crawling at less than 30 mph. He pulled out to see if he could pass, then pulled back in sharply as a truck thundered past in the opposite direction. Increasingly impatient, they followed the truck through a sweeping, dipping, S-bend, past a quarry sign, then up a hill, the truck slowing even more. He slipped his left hand over into Ashley's lap, found her hand, squeezed it. 'We'll be all right, angel.'

She squeezed his hand back, by way of a reply.

Then a blue sparkle in the mirror caught his eye. And a cold sliver of fear whiplashed through his belly.

He watched the mirror carefully. Tarmac, grass and trees unspooled behind them. Then the sparkle of blue again and this time there was no mistaking it. *Shit.* Any second it would come into sight around the corner.

Pulling out again, he suddenly saw to his right a wooden public-footpath signpost, and a wide track, and in one swift jerk of the wheel, swung the Freelander right across the path of an oncoming van and onto the bumpy, overgrown track, the car crashing into a deep, water-filled pothole, then out the other side. In his mirror he saw a police car flash past in the opposite direction, much too fast, he hoped, to have seen them.

'Why have you turned off?'

'Police.' He accelerated, felt the wheels spinning, gripping, the car lurching forward, sliding up the ruts, then down again. They passed a farmyard, with an empty horsebox outside and a silent tractor, and a corrugated iron structure filled with empty sheep pens.

'Where does this go?' Ashley asked.

'I don't fucking know.'

At the end of the track he turned left onto a metalled lane; they drove past several cottages, then reached a very busy main road. Vic, winding down his window and dripping with perspiration, said, 'This is the A27 – it takes us to the A23 – straight up to Gatwick, right?'

'I know. But we can't go on the main road.'

'I'm thinking – the best way—'

Both of them heard the clatter of the helicopter. Vic stuck his head out of the window and looked up. He saw a dark blue helicopter bearing down out of the sky straight towards them. As it arced round, the sound even louder, it was low enough for him to read the stencilled white 'POLICE' beneath the cockpit.

'Bastards.' There was no break in the traffic, so he judged it too risky to go straight over. Instead he made a left turn, accelerating hard out in front of a Jaguar, which proceeded to flash him with its lights and hoot, both of which he ignored, staring fixedly ahead, his brain in panic mode. The traffic was slowing down ahead. Shit, it was coming to a standstill! Pulling out to the right a fraction and peering past the traffic, he could see the reason for the jam, despite part of his view being obscured by a tall caravan.

A police car had blocked off the road, and there was a large blue 'POLICE STOP' barrier either side of it.

87

'They just rammed through a police barrier at the Beddingham roundabout,' the Ops Clerk, Jim Robinson, informed Grace, 'and are now proceeding west on the A27. Their next turn-off options are the roundabout in one mile, where they have a choice of a right turn towards Lewes or left towards Kingston village.'

'Have we got anyone at the roundabout?'

'A bike on its way – might just get there in time.'

'A bike's no use. We need to get them boxed in. At least they're not in a fast car, so we can catch them. We need four cars – where are the nearest four located?'

'We have two heading for the A23 junction, one on its way from Lewes, ETA four minutes, one on its way over from Shoreham, ETA three minutes to the A23/A27 junction, two here at Sussex House ready to go, and one coming in from Haywards Heath, ETA two minutes.'

'The helicopter still has them in sight?'

'Right above them.'

Grace closed his eyes a moment, visualizing the road. Right now the villains, whoever they were – and he had the strongest suspicions about who one of them was – had made the error of picking the road on which he drove to and from work every day, and knew better, probably, than any other road on the planet. He knew every turn-off, every opportunity, adding in the fact they were in a vehicle with off-road capabilities, and although the ground was fairly soggy from all the recent rainfall, there would be plenty of opportunities to get off the road and across farmland if they wanted.

'Can we get a couple of police off-roaders into the mix as well?' Grace said. 'Position them as close to the A27/A23 junction as you can.'

He looked at his watch. A quarter to two. Tuesday. There would be a fair amount of traffic on the move and one consideration was other road users. The police had had a lot of bad press in recent years over reckless car pursuits and some tragic deaths of innocent people in the process. He needed to keep this pursuit as safe as was possible in the circumstances.

Boxing them in would be best: a car in front, a car behind, one either side and slowly bring their speed down. That would be the textbook happy ending.

Except he hadn't known too many happy endings since he'd grown too old to enjoy fairy tales.

88

Barrelling down a long, curving hill in the fast lane, with the speedometer needle flickering past 125 mph, Vic knew the A23 junction would be coming up in a minute or so, and he was going to have to make a decision. For the past couple of minutes, aware of the constant shadow of the helicopter, his mind had been occupied with one thought: *If I was a cop what bases would I be covering right now?*

Airports were not going to be an option. Nor ferry-ports. But there was one thing that the cops probably had not considered – probably because they didn't even know about it. But to get to it they needed to lose the damned chopper. And there was a place, just a few miles ahead, where he could do that.

The dual carriageway rose dramatically uphill, with undulating open Downland countryside to his right, and the vast urban sprawl of Brighton and Hove to his left. And ahead, some miles yet, the tall chimney landmark of his intended destination, Shoreham Harbour. But that wasn't going to be his first stop.

'Why've you carried on, Vic?' Ashley asked nervously. 'I thought we were going to Gatwick.'

Vic did not reply. A little old man was pottering along in the inside lane in a bronze four-door Toyota that looked a good ten years old. Perfect!

The tunnel was coming up any moment now. From memory it was about a quarter of a mile long, cutting through the Downs. They passed the 'No Overtaking' warning sign and entered the dimly lit gloom of the tunnel doing a good 110 mph. Instantly, Vic swerved into the inside lane and stamped on the brakes, slowing the car down to a crawl and putting on his hazard flashers.

'Vic – what the hell—'

But he was ignoring her, staring in the mirror, watching a line of cars flash past. And now the Toyota was approaching. Vic tensed, knowing he had to get his timing absolutely right. The Toyota indicated that it was going to pull out to overtake, and began moving out, but instantly there was a flash of lights and the blare of a horn as a Porsche hurtled past, and the Toyota, braking hard, swerved back into the inside lane.

Beaut!

Vic jerked on the Land Rover's handbrake as hard as he could, knowing it would stop the car without the brake lights showing. 'Brace yourself!' he shouted, releasing the brake and accelerating.

There was a scream of tyres behind, but by the time the Toyota struck them, they already had some forward momentum again. There was a small impact, just a tiny jolt that he barely felt, and the sound of breaking glass.

'Out!' yelled Vic, hurling open his door, jumping down, running back and surveying the damage. All he was concerned with was the front of the Toyota. It looked fine – the grille was stove in and a headlamp gone, but no oil or water was spewing out.

'Get the fucking bags!' he yelled at Ashley, who was walking, startled, towards him. 'The fucking bags, woman!'

He wrenched open the driver's door of the Toyota. The driver was even more frail than he had looked when he had driven past, well north of eighty, with a liver-spotted face, wispy hair and spectacles with bottle-glass lenses.

'Hey, what – what do you think – what—?' the old man said.

Vic unclipped his seatbelt, aware that a car was pulling up behind them, then removed his glasses to disorient him. 'I'll get you into the ambulance, mate.'

'I don't need a bloody—'

Vic hauled the man out, hefted him over his shoulder and placed him on the rear seat of the Land Rover, then shut the door. A pot-bellied, middle-aged man who had just climbed out of a Ford people-carrier that had pulled up behind the Toyota came running up to Vic. 'I say, do you need any help?'

'Yes, poor bloke, I think he's had a stroke – was swerving all over the place.'

A lorry thundered past, then two motorbikes. Ashley shouted out, 'For God's sake help me, Vic, I can't manage these bloody cases on my own!'

'Leave the fucking things!'

'One has all my papers in it—'

Vic saw the pot-bellied man looking at Ashley oddly and decided the fastest solution was to deck him. He knocked him out cold with one punch, and propped him up against the front of his Ford.

Then they hastily loaded Vic's holdall and two of Ashley's cases into the Toyota and jumped in. Vic found *reverse*, then, with a grinding noise coming from what he presumed was the fan belt, he eased the car back several feet, then he found *drive*, and the car juddered. He checked his mirror, then accelerated, pulling out past the Land Rover, and accelerated as fast as the distinctly clapped-out old Toyota would go towards the rapidly widening light at the far end of the tunnel.

Ashley was staring at him in shock. 'That was clever,' she said.

'Can you see the fucking chopper?' he asked, squinting as they came back out into bright light.

She squirmed around in her seat, craning her neck upwards through first the front windscreen, then the rear. 'It's not following!' she exclaimed. 'It's hovering over the front of the tunnel – wait – great – now it's going back to the rear!'

'Fucking A!'

Vic took the first exit off the dual carriageway, which came up a mile on. It took them down into the mixed urban and industrial sprawl of Southwick, the suburb separating the city of Brighton and Hove from Shoreham. They had a few minutes' head start before the police got an ident on this car, and maybe with a bit of luck the old git who owned it couldn't remember the licence number, Vic hoped.

'OK, so where the hell are we going, Vic?'

'To the one place the police aren't looking at.'

'Which is?'

'Michael and Mark have a boat, right, a proper yacht. You've been on it?'

'Yes, I've told you – I've been out on it a few times.'

'It's big enough to cross the Channel, right?'

'The guy they bought it from sailed it across the Atlantic.'

'That's fine. You and I know how to sail.'

'Yes.' Ashley remembered several sailing holidays they'd had in Australia and in Canada, chartering a yacht, going off on their own. Some of the few happy and peaceful moments of her life.

'So now you know where we're going. Unless you have a better idea?'

'Take their boat?'

'We'll sail after dark.'

They were now on a busy main road, with semi-detached houses on each side, set well back. He slowed down as they approached a red light and could see a shopping parade ahead on both sides of the road. Then, as he halted, his face fell. Brilliant white light filled the rear-view mirror. He heard the sharp blast of a two-tone siren. Saw a blue flashing light, heard the blip of a loud throttle; then a police motorcyclist pulled alongside his window, signalling for him to get out.

Instead, he floored the accelerator and shot straight over the lights, right across the path of a heavy truck.

'Oh shit,' Ashley said.

Moments later, siren on, the motorcycle was alongside again, the cop signalling sternly for him to pull over. Instead, Vic turned the wheel sharply to the right, deliberately striking the bike, sending it hurtling over on its side; in his mirror he caught a fleeting glimpse of the cop, unseated, rolling across the road.

Panicking, Vic saw a pillar box ahead, and a quiet-looking side-street. He turned sharply into it, hearing the sound of the bags sliding across the back seat, then accelerated down the tree-lined avenue. It was starting to rain again, and he fumbled around with the switches until he found the wipers and got them working. They reached a T-junction, with a church ahead.

'Do you know where we are?'

'The harbour can't be far,' he said. He drove on, through a maze of quiet residential streets, then suddenly they came out into a narrow, bustling high street, with traffic crawling down it. 'There!' Vic pointed ahead. 'That's the harbour!'

At the bottom of the high street, they came to the junction with the main coast road that ran all the way along Brighton and Hove seafront, past Shoreham Harbour and then along the banks of the River Adur.

'Which way's the boat?'

'It's at the Sussex Motor Yacht Club,' she said. 'You have to go left.'

There was a bus coming, quickly. He was going to wait to let it pass when a glint of white light in his mirror caught his eye; almost in disbelief, he saw a police motorbike weaving through the jammed traffic behind him. The same damned cop he had just knocked off his machine?

He pulled out in front of the bus, tyres screeching. Then, moments later, out of nowhere, a black BMW with a flashing blue light on the dash and more flashing blue lights inside its rear windscreen, hurtled past the bus and his Toyota, cutting in front of him, forcing him to brake sharply. Above its rear bumper the words, in flashing red lights, appeared: 'STOP POLICE'.

In complete blind panic he swung the car round in a U-turn, accelerating back the other way, weaving through the traffic, which was slowing down ahead at a roundabout. The motorbike was right behind him, siren howling. Putting two wheels on the pavement, jamming his hand on the horn, making pedestrians leap out of the way, Vic squeezed past the line of cars and a van and reached the roundabout. There were three choices: right seemed to go back into the maze of houses; straight on the traffic was clogged up. Left went over a metal-girdered bridge spanning the river.

He turned left, the motorbike glued to his tail as he accelerated as hard at the Toyota would go, the fan grinding, shrieking, the noise getting worse every second. Below, the tide was right out, the river just a slack brown trickle between the mud banks, with moored boats lying on their sides, many of them barely looking as if they were capable of floating when the tide came back in.

On the far side of the bridge the road was clear. But within moments the BMW was coming up fast behind him. The motorbike suddenly whipped in front of him and then decelerated, trying to force him to slow. 'Thought I fucking gave you a lesson already,' Vic muttered, accelerating, trying to ram it, but the rider was too quick for him, darting forward as if anticipating this.

Vic, trying desperately to think straight, looked at the landscape to either side. On the left was a garage, a parade of shops and what looked like a large residential area. Over to his right he could see the flat expanse of Shoreham Airport, used mostly by private aircraft and a few small Channel Islands airlines. The entrance was coming up.

Without signalling he swung right, onto the narrow road. There was a concrete wall on his left, and the open expanse of the airfield to his right, dotted with hangars, with small planes and helicopters parked in front, and the white Art Deco control tower building, in need of a lick of paint. The thought now going through his head was that if he could just shake off the cops for a few minutes, they could hijack a light aircraft, like the twin-engined Beechcraft he could see coming in now – just drive straight over to it, grab the pilot.

As if anticipating exactly that, the BMW pulled alongside, then swung into him, forcing him into the concrete wall. Ashley screamed as the car slammed against it, grating along it with sparks showering past them. 'Vic, for Christ's sake do something!'

He sat, gripping the wheel for dear life, clenched up in

concentration, knowing they were hopelessly underpowered against the BMW and the bike. There was a tunnel coming up ahead. He could guess exactly what the BMW had in mind – to go in it ahead of him and then stop. So he stamped on the brakes. Caught by surprise, the BMW shot past, and instantly he swerved behind it, off the road and onto the airfield itself.

The bike stayed with him, and moments later, the BMW was behind him as well. He drove across the bumpy grass straight towards the first row of parked aircraft, weaving wildly in between them, trying to shake off the cops behind him, trying to spot someone walking to a plane or getting out of one. Then, as he headed for a gap between a Grumman executive jet and a Piper Aztec, the BMW suddenly rammed him hard, jolting them both forward, Ashley, despite her seatbelt, cracking her head on the windscreen and crying out in pain.

He heard the BMW revving. The runway was right in front of him, and he could see the twin-engined plane bearing down, yards away from touching down. He floored the accelerator, lurched across the runway, right through the shadow of the plane. And then, for a brief moment, no bike and no BMW in his mirror! He kept going, flat out, the car lurching, the grating from the engine getting worse and accompanied by an acrid smell of burning now, straight toward the perimeter fence and the narrow road beyond that.

'We need to get out and hide, Vic. We're not going to outrun them in this thing.'

'I know,' he said grimly, panic gripping him again as he couldn't see a gap anywhere in the fence. 'Where's the fucking exit?'

'Just go through the fence.'

Taking her advice, he continued driving flat out at the fence, slowing just before they struck it, the wire mesh making a dull clanging sound, and ripping like cloth. Then he was on the perimeter road, with the mudflats of the river to his right and the airfield to his left, and the bike and the car were right behind him. A Mercedes sports was coming the other way. Vic kept going. 'Out the fucking way!' At the last moment the Mercedes pulled over onto the verge.

They were coming up to a T-junction with a narrow road that was little more than a lane. To the left there was a removals lorry parked outside a cottage, unloading, blocking the road completely.

He turned right, flooring the pedal, watching in his mirror. At least this lane was too narrow for the BMW to get past. The bike was getting in position. Any moment it would whip past. Vic swerved out to warn it off. They were doing seventy, seventy-five, eighty, approaching a wooden bridge over the river.

Then, just as he reached the bridge, two small boys on bicycles appeared at the far end, right in the middle of the road. 'Shiiiiiiiit, oh shiiit, oh shiiit,' Vic said, stamping on the brakes, thumbing the horn, but there was no time; they were not going to stop, and there was no room to get past them. Ashley was screaming.

The car slewed right, left, right. It struck the right-hand barrier of the bridge, veered over and struck the left, pinballed off it, doing a half pirouette, then rolled over onto its roof, bounced in the air, clearing the safety barrier, bursting through the wooden side of the bridge's superstructure, splintering it like matchsticks, and plunging, upside down, the rear doors flying open, and the suitcases hurtling alongside the car towards the mudflats below, which were as soft and treacherous as quicksand.

The motorcyclist dismounted and, limping from his leg injury from when he had been knocked off his machine only a few minutes earlier, hobbled over to the hole in the side of the bridge and peered down.

All he could see protruding from the mud was the grimy black underbelly of the Toyota. The rest of the car had sunk into it. He stared at the metal floor pan, the exhaust and silencer, the four wheels still spinning. Then, in front of his eyes, the mud bubbled all around the car, like a cauldron brewing, and moments later the underbelly and the wheels slipped beneath the surface and the mud closed over it. There were some deep bubbles which broke the surface, as if the underwater lair of some monster had been disturbed. Then nothing.

89

The incoming tide was hampering their efforts. A wide cordon had been thrown around the whole area where the car had gone in, canvas sheeting only partially obscuring the view from a swelling crowd of curious onlookers on the far bank. A fire engine, two ambulances, half a dozen police vehicles, including a crash recovery tender, were all parked down the lane.

A crane had been driven onto the elderly bridge despite concerns about how much weight it could stand. Grace stood on the bridge himself, watching the recovery proceedings. Police frogmen were working hard to get the hooks of the lifting gear dangling from the crane onto secure fixings on the Toyota. The sky, which had been delivering spots of rain on and off all day, had lightened in the last hour and the sun was trying to break through.

The tightly packed mud had made it impossible for the frogmen to get down any further, and the only hope that the occupants were alive rested on the windows having stayed intact and that there was air trapped inside the car. The amount of shards of glass strewn over the bridge made this seem more than a long shot.

Two suitcases had been recovered from the abandoned Land Rover Freelander, but all they contained were women's clothes; not one scrap of paper that could give a clue to Michael Harrison's whereabouts. Grace had a grim feeling this car would yield something.

Glenn Branson, standing next to Grace, said, 'You know

what this reminds me of? The original *Psycho* – 1960. When they winch the car with Janet Leigh's body in out of the lake. Remember?'

'I remember.'

'That was a cool movie. The remake was shit. I dunno why people bother with remakes.'

'Money,' Grace said. 'That's one of the reasons why you and I have a job. Because people do an awful lot for money.'

After a few more minutes the hooks were in place. Then the lifting began. Against the deafening roar of the crane's engine, Grace and Branson barely heard the sucking and gurgling sounds of the mud, beneath the waters of the rising tide, yielding its prize.

Slowly, in front of their eyes, and washed clean by the water, the bronze Toyota rose up in the air, its boot-lid open and hanging. Mud oozed slowly out of all of the window frames. The car looked badly smashed and the roof pillars were buckled. It didn't look as if one single window had remained in place.

And as the mud fell out, some in slabs, some in squitty streaks, at first just the silhouettes of the two occupants became visible, and then, finally, their inert faces.

The crane swung the car over onto the bank, lowering it on its roof a few yards from a rotting houseboat. Several fireman, police officers and workmen who had come with the crane, unhooked the lifting gear then slowly righted the car. As it rolled back onto its wheels, the two figures inside jerked like crash-test dummies.

Grace, with trepidation, followed by Branson, walked down to it, squatted and peered in. Even though there was some mud still stuck to her face, and her hair was much shorter than the last time he had seen her, there was no question it was Ashley Harper, her eyes wide open, unblinking. Then he shuddered in revulsion as a scrawny, long-legged crab crawled across her lap.

'Jesus,' Branson said.

Who the hell was the man next to her, in the driving seat? Grace wondered. His eyes were open also, a powerful, thuggish-looking man with a shocked death mask.

'See what you can find on her,' Grace said, wrenching open the driver's door, and checking the man's sodden, muddy clothing for ID. He pulled out a heavy leather wallet from inside his jacket and opened it. Inside was an Australian passport.

The photograph was the man in the car, no question. His name was Victor Bruce Delaney and he was forty-two years old. Under *emergency contact* was written the name *Mrs Alexandra Delaney*, and an address in Sydney.

Glenn Branson wiped mud from a yellow handbag, unzipped it and after a few moments also pulled out a passport, this one British, which he showed to Grace. It contained a photograph that was, without doubt, Ashley Harper, but with close-cropped black hair, and it bore the name Anne Hampson. Under *emergency contact* nothing had been written.

There were credit cards both in the man's wallet and in a purse inside the handbag, but nothing else. Not a clue about where they had come from or where they might be headed.

'Houston, we have a problem,' Glenn Branson said quietly to Grace, but there was no humour in his tone.

'We do.' Grace stood up and turned away. 'It's suddenly a whole lot bigger than it was two hours ago.'

'So how the hell are we going to find Michael Harrison now?'

After a moment's silence Grace said, 'I have an idea, but you're not going to like it.'

Glancing uncomfortably at the occupants of the car, Glenn Branson said, 'I don't like anything much at the moment.'

90

An hour and a half later, Grace helped buckle the diminutive, wiry figure of Harry Frame into the front seat of the pool Ford Mondeo he and Branson had used this afternoon.

The pony-tailed, goatee-bearded medium, reeking of patchouli oil and wearing his trademark kaftan and dungarees, had a street map of Newhaven laid out in his lap, and held a metal ring on a length of string in his right hand.

Grace had decided to leave Glenn Branson out of this. He didn't want any negative vibes, and he knew that Harry Frame's energy was sensitive at best.

'So did you bring me something, as I requested?' Harry Frame asked Grace as he climbed behind the wheel of the car.

Grace dug a box out of his pocket and handed it to the medium. Frame opened it and removed a pair of gold cufflinks.

'These are definitely Michael Harrison's,' Grace said. 'I took them from his flat on my way here.'

'Perfect.'

It was only a short distance along the coast from Harry Frame's Peacehaven home to Newhaven. As they drove past the seemingly endless sprawl of shops and takeaway restaurants, Harry Frame was holding the cufflinks in his closed palm. 'Newhaven, you said?'

'There was a car we were interested in that was involved in an accident in Newhaven earlier today. And

Newhaven is where Michael Harrison's mobile signal came from. I thought we'd drive to that spot and you could see if you pick anything up. Is that a good idea?'

In his effusive, high-pitched voice, the medium said, 'I'm already picking up something. We're near, you know. Definitely.'

Grace, following the directions he had been given, began to slow down. Some tyre marks, a spill of oil on the road and a few sparkling shards of safety glass showed him where the Mercedes had been in the accident, and he turned right into a modern housing development of small, detached houses with immature gardens, then immediately pulled over and stopped.

'OK,' he said. 'This is where the accident happened this morning.'

Harry Frame, holding the cufflinks in his left hand, began to swing the pendulum over the map, taking increasingly deep breaths. He closed his eyes tightly and after a few moments said, 'Drive on, Roy, just drive straight on. Slowly.'

Grace did as he was instructed.

'We're getting closer!' Frame said. 'Definitely. I see a turn-off to the left coming up shortly – might not even be a road, just a track.'

After about a hundred metres, there was indeed a track going up to the left. It had been metalled, very many years ago, but had fallen into a state of total disrepair. It went uphill, through wind-blown, scrubby wasteland, and it did not seem from here, at least, that it was going to lead to anything.

'Make a left turn, Roy!'

Grace looked at him, wondering if he was cheating by peeping through his eyelids. But if Harry was looking anywhere, it was down into his lap. Grace turned onto the track and drove up it for a quarter of a mile, then a squat, ugly detached house came into view just on the crest of the hill. It had fine views over Newhaven and the harbour beyond, but little else to recommend it.

'I see a house, all on its own. Michael Harrison is in this house,' Frame said, excitement raising his voice even higher.

Grace pulled up outside. The pendulum was swinging fast in a tight circle, and Harry Frame, eyes still tight shut, was juddering as if he had been plugged into an electrical socket.

'Here?'

Without opening his eyes, Harry Frame confirmed, 'Here.'

Grace left him in the car, then stopped at the front gate, staring at the neglected front lawn and the flower beds, which were a tangle of bindweed. There was something odd about the house, which he couldn't immediately figure out. It looked as if it had been built in the 1930s, or maybe early 1950s, and the design was strange, lopsided.

He walked up a path of concrete slabs with weeds sprouting between the cracks, and pressed the cracked plastic front-door bell. There was a shrill ring, but no one came to the door. He tried again. Still no answer.

Then he did a circuit around the house, peering into each window as he went. It had a forlorn, neglected air about it, both inside and out. All the furnishings looked twenty or thirty years old, as did the design of and appliances in the kitchen. Then he noted, to his surprise, that there was a stack of newspapers on the kitchen table.

He looked at his watch. It was just gone 6 p.m. He ought to get a search warrant, he knew. But that would take another couple of hours – and with every minute that passed the chances of finding Michael Harrison alive were shrinking.

How much did he trust Harry Frame? The medium had been right on several occasions in the past – but he had been wrong on just as many.

Shite.

The thought of what Alison Vosper would say to him if he was caught breaking into a house without a warrant bothered him.

He didn't have enough to back his judgement up, but it would have to do. Time was running out for Michael Harrison.

With a loose brick from the garden, he smashed a kitchen window pane, then wrapping his hand in his handkerchief, he removed the pieces of glass that remained lodged in the putty, found the window catch, opened it and crawled in.

'Hello!' he shouted. 'Hello! Anyone home?'

The place felt and smelled dingy. The kitchen was clean, and other than some newspapers, all bearing yesterday's date, there was no sign of anyone having lived here recently. He checked out each of the downstairs rooms. The large sitting room was drab as hell, with a couple of framed prints of seascapes on the walls. He noticed there were lines on the carpet, as if someone had recently moved the sofa. He moved on into a dark dining room, with an oak table and four chairs, and flock wallpaper, then on to a small lavatory, with a 'God Bless This House' cross-stitch hanging on the wall.

Upstairs felt equally unloved and unlived in. There were three bedrooms, all the beds stripped to bare mattresses with old, yellowing pillows, without slips, lying on them, and a small bathroom, with a geyser boiler and stained washbasin and bath.

Above the bed in the smallest room was a loft hatch. By placing a chair, precariously, on the mattress, then standing on it, he was able to push open the hatch and peer in. To his surprise there was a light switch just inside the hatch, which worked, and he could see in an instant there was nothing up here. Just a small water tank, an old carpet sweeper and a rolled-up rug.

He opened every cupboard and cabinet door. Upstairs, all the bed linen and bath towels were folded away in the cupboards. Downstairs, the kitchen cupboards contained basics – coffee, tea, a few tins, but nothing else. It could easily have been a year or two since anyone had been here. No sign of Michael Harrison. Nothing.

Nowhere.

He checked the hall cupboard, in case there was a cellar entrance in there, although he knew that few houses after the Victorian era had cellars. He needed to find out who owned this place and when it was last lived in. Maybe the owners had died and it was in the hands of executors? Maybe a cleaning lady came up here occasionally?

A cleaning lady who read every national newspaper?

Grace let himself out of the back door and walked around to the side of the house, where there were two dustbins. He lifted the lid of the first one, and instantly he had a different story. There were egg-shells, used tea bags, an empty skimmed milk carton bearing a sell-by date of today and a Marks and Spencer lasagne carton bearing a sell-by date that had not yet been reached.

Thinking hard, he walked round to the front of the house, trying again to work out what it was that was wrong with the design. Then he realized. Where there was now an ugly plastic-framed window to the right of the front door, there should have been an integral garage. He could see it now, clearly; the tone of the bricks didn't match the rest of the house. At some point someone had converted this into a living room.

And suddenly it reminded him of something from his childhood: his dad, tinkering with things. He liked to do his own servicing on his car, changing the oil, doing the brake linings, *staying out of the hands of the rip-off merchants,* as his dad called garages.

He remembered the inspection pit in their garage, where he had spent many happy hours of his childhood helping his dad service the succession of Fords he always bought, getting covered in oil and grease – not to mention the occasional spider.

And he thought about the lines on the carpet in the sitting room that he had just seen, where the sofa had been moved.

On just a hunch, no more than that, he went back into the house and straight to the sitting room. He lifted the coffee table aside, then pushed back the sofa along the tracks in the green floral carpet that had been made previously.

Then he noticed that one corner of the carpet was slightly curled up. He knelt and gave it a tug, and it lifted easily. Far too easily. And instead of dust and fluff beneath there was a thick underlay that was not like any conventional carpet underlay. He knew exactly what it was. Soundproofing material.

His excitement mounting, he glanced over his shoulder, then peeled the heavy grey material back, and saw beneath it a large sheet of plywood. He worked his fingers under the edges, with some difficulty, as it fitted flush into a groove in the floor, then prised it up, and pulled it aside.

Instantly he gagged from the stench that hit his nostrils.

A horrendous reek of body odour, urine and excrement.

Holding his breath and scared of what he was going to find, he peered into the six-foot-deep garage inspection pit and saw a shadowy figure at the bottom, bound hand and foot and across the mouth with duct tape.

At first he thought the figure was dead. Then the eyes blinked. Frightened eyes.

Oh sweet Jesus, he was alive! Grace felt an almost uncontainable feeling of joy erupt through him. 'Michael Harrison?'

A muffled 'Mnhhhh' greeted him.

'Detective Superintendent Grace of Sussex CID,' Grace said, lowering himself into the pit, oblivious to the smell now, just desperately anxious to see what condition the young man was in.

Kneeling beside him, Grace gently peeled the duct tape away from his lips. 'Are you Michael Harrison?'

'Yes,' he croaked. 'Water. Please.'

Grace squeezed his arm gently. 'I'll get you some right away. And I'll get you out of here. You're going to be fine.'

Grace scrambled up out of the pit, hurried into the kitchen and ran the tap, radioing for an ambulance at the same time. Then he climbed back down into the pit clutching a pint tumbler of water.

He tilted it into Michael Harrison's mouth, who drank it down in one long, greedy draught, with only a few drops spilling down his chin. Then, as he removed the glass, Michael looked at him and asked, 'How's Ashley?'

Grace stared back at him, thinking hard, then gave him a gentle, reassuring smile. 'She's safe,' he said.

'Thank God.'

Grace squeezed his arm again. 'Want more water?'

Michael nodded.

'I'll get you some, then I'll cut this tape off you.'

'Thank God she's safe,' Michael said, his voice weak and trembling. 'She's all I've thought of, all I – I . . .'

Grace climbed back out of the pit. At some point he was going to have to tell Michael everything, but this didn't feel like the time or the place.

And he didn't know how to begin.

LOOKING GOOD DEAD

Read on for an extract from the next

Detective Superintendent Roy Grace mystery

in the series

1

The front door of the once-proud terraced house opened, and a long-legged young woman, in a short silk dress that seemed both to cling and float at the same time, stepped out into the fine June sunshine on the last morning of her life.

A century back, these tall white villas just a pebble's throw from Brighton's seafront promenade would have served as weekend residences for London toffs. Now, behind their grimy, salt-burned facades, they were all chopped up into bedsits and low-rent flats; the brass front-door knockers had long been replaced with plastic entry phones, and litter spewed from garbage bags on the pavements beneath a gaudy riot of letting-agency boards. Several of the cars that lined the street, shoehorned into too few parking spaces, were dented and rusting, and all of them were bombed out with seagull shit.

In contrast everything about the young woman oozed class. From the careless toss of her long fair hair, the Ray-Ban sunglasses she adjusted on her face, the bling Cartier bracelet, the Anya Hindmarsh bag slung from her shoulder, the toned contours of her body, the Mediterranean tan, the wake of Issey Miyake tanging the rush-hour carbon monoxide with a frisson of sexuality, she was the kind of girl who would have looked at home in the aisles of Bergdorf Goodman, at the bar of a Schrager hotel, or on the stern of a fuck-off yacht in St Tropez.

Not bad for a law student scraping by on a meagre grant.

But Janie Ross had been too spoiled by her guilty father, after her mother's death, to ever contemplate the idea of merely *scraping by*. Making money came easily to her. Making it from her intended career might be a different matter altogether. The law was tough. Three years of law school were now behind her, two still to go. But for the next six months she was articled to a firm of solicitors in Brighton, working for a divorce lawyer, and she was enjoying that, although some of the cases were, even to her – *weird.*

Like the mild little seventy-year-old man yesterday, Bernie Milsin, in his neat grey suit and carefully knotted tie. Janie had sat unobtrusively in a corner chair in the office as the thirty-five-year-old partner she was articled to, Martin Broom, nervously took down notes. Mr Milsin was complaining that Mrs Milsin, three years older than himself, would not give him food until he had performed oral sex on her. *Three times a day,* he told Martin Broom. *Can't keep doing it, not at my age, the arthritis in me knees hurts too much.*

It almost hurt her too much not to laugh out loud, and she could see Broom struggling, too. So, it wasn't just men who had kinky needs. Seemed that both sexes had them. Something new learned every day, and sometimes she didn't know where she gained the most knowledge from – Sussex University Law School, or the University of Life.

The beep of an incoming text broke her chain of thoughts just as she reached her red and white Mini Cooper. She checked the screen.

2night. 9.15?

Janie smiled and replied with a brief *xx.* Then she waited for a bus followed by a line of traffic to pass, opened the door of her car, and sat for a moment, collecting her thoughts, thinking about stuff she needed to do.

Bins, her moggie, had a lump on his back that was steadily getting bigger. She did not like the look of it and wanted to take him to the vet to get it checked. She had found Bins two years ago, a nameless stray, scrawny to the point of starving, trying to lift the lid off one of her dust-bins. She had taken him in and he had never shown any inclination to leave. So much for cats being independent, she realized, or maybe it was because she spoiled him. But, hell, Bins was an affectionate creature and she didn't have much else in her life to spoil. She would try to get a late appointment today. If she got to the vet by six-thirty that should still leave plenty of time, she calculated.

In her lunch break she needed to buy a birthday card and present for her father – he would be fifty-five on Saturday. She hadn't seen him for a month, he'd been away in the USA on business. He seemed to be away a lot these days, travelling more and more. Searching for that one woman who might be out there who could replace the wife he had lost and the mother she had lost? He never spoke about it, but she knew he was lonely. And living a hundred miles away from him did not help.

Pulling on her seat belt and clicking it, she was totally unaware of the long lens that was trained on her and the whirring motor of the digital Pentax, over two hundred yards away, not even audible from here against the background hubbub of traffic.

Watching her through the steady cross-hairs, he said, 'She's coming now."

'Are you sure that's her?' His voice precise, and sharp as serrated steel.

She was real eye candy, he thought. Even after days and nights of watching her, twenty-four-seven, inside her flat and outside, it was still a treat. The question barely merited an answer.

'I am,' he said. 'Yes.'

2

'I'm on the train,' the big, overweight dickhead next to him shouted into his mobile phone. 'The train. T-R-A-I-N!' he repeated. 'Yeah, yeah, bad line.'

Then they went into a tunnel.

'Oh fuck,' the dickhead said.

Tom Bryce, hunched on his seat between this dickhead on his right, and a girl wearing a sickly sweet perfume, who was texting furiously on his left, suppressed a grin. An amiable, good-looking man of thirty-six, in a smart suit, with a serious, boyish face lined with stress and a mop of dark brown hair that flopped incessantly over his forehead, he was steadily wilting in the stifling heat, like the small bunch of flowers, rolling around on the luggage rack above him, which he had bought for his wife. The temperature inside the carriage was about ninety degrees and felt even hotter. Last year he had travelled first class and those carriages were marginally better ventilated – or at least less jam-packed – but this year he was having to economize. Although he still liked to surprise Kellie with flowers once a week or so.

Half a minute later, emerging from the tunnel, the dickhead stabbed a button, and the nightmare continued. 'JUST WENT THROUGH A TUNNEL!' he bellowed, as if they were still in it. 'Yeah, fucking INCREDIBLE! How come they don't have a wire or *thing*, you know to keep the connection? Inside the tunnel, yeah? They got them on some motorway tunnels now, right . . . ?'

Tom tried to tune him out and concentrate on the emails on his wobbling Mac laptop. Just another shitty end to another shitty day at the office. Over one hundred emails yet to respond to and more downloading every minute. He cleared them every night before he went to bed – that was his rule, the only way to keep on top of his workload. Some were jokes, which he would look at later, and some were raunchy attachments sent by mates, which he had learned not to risk looking at in a crowded train carriage, ever since the time he had been sitting next to a prim-looking woman and had double clicked on a PowerPoint file to reveal a donkey being fellated by a naked blonde.

The train clicked and clacked, rocking, shaking, then vibrating in short bursts as they entered another tunnel, nearing home now. Wind roared around the edges of the open window above his head, and the echo of the black walls howled with it. Suddenly, the carriage smelled of old socks and soot. A briefcase skittered around on the rack above his head and he glanced up nervously, checking it wasn't about to fall on him or crush the flowers. On a blank advertising panel on the wall opposite him, above the head of a plump, surly looking girl in a tight skirt who was reading *19* magazine, someone had spray painted the words *SEAGULLS WANNKERS* in clumsy black letters.

So much for football supporters, Tom thought. They couldn't even spell *wankers*.

Beads of sweat trickled down the nape of his neck and down his ribs; more trickled down all the spaces where his tailored white shirt wasn't already actually glued by perspiration to his skin. He'd removed his suit jacket and loosened his tie and he felt like kicking off his black Prada loafers, which were pinching his feet. He lifted his clammy face from the screen as they came out of the tunnel and instantly the air changed, sweeter, grass-scented Downland air; in a few minutes more it would be carrying a faint tinge of salt from the English Channel. After seventeen years of commuting, Tom could have told when he was nearing home with his eyes shut.

He looked out of the window, at fields, farmhouses, pylons, a reservoir, the soft, distant hills, then back at his emails. He read and deleted one from his sales manager, then replied to a customer complaint – yet another key customer angry that an order hadn't arrived in time for their big summer function. Personalized pens this time, printed golfing umbrellas previously. His whole ordering and shipping department was in a mess – partly from a new computer system and partly because of an idiot running it. In an already tough market it was hurting his business badly. Two big customers – Avis car rentals and Apple Computers – lost to competitors in one week.

Terrific.

The business was creaking under the weight of debts at the moment. He'd expanded too fast, was too highly geared. Just as he was over-mortgaged at home. He should never have let Kellie convince him to trade up houses, not when the market was moving down and business was in recession. Now he was struggling to stay solvent. The business was no longer covering its overheads. And despite all he told her, there was still no let-up in Kellie's obsession with spending money. Almost every day she bought something new, mostly on *ebay* and, because it was a bargain, in her logic that didn't count. And besides, she told him, he was always buying expensive designer clothes for himself, how could he argue? It didn't seem to matter to her that he only bought his clothes during the sales and that he needed to look sharp in his line of work.

He was so worried that he'd discussed her spending problem recently with a friend of his, who had been through counselling for depression after his divorce. Over a few vodka martinis, a drink in which Tom was increasingly taking solace in recent months, Bruce Watts told him there were people who were compulsive spenders and they could be treated. Tom wondered if Kellie was bad enough to warrant treatment – and if so, how to broach it?

The dickhead started again. 'Hello, BILL, it's RON, yeah. Ron from *PARTS,* YEAH, THAT'S RIGHT! JUST THOUGHT I'D GIVE YOU A QUICK HEADS UP ON – oh fuck – BILL? HELLO – ?'

Tom raised his eyes without moving his head. No signal! Divine providence! Sometimes you really could believe there was a God. Then he heard the wail of a Nokia ringtone.

His own, he suddenly realized, feeling the vibration in his shirt pocket. Glancing surreptitiously around, he pulled it out then, checking the caller's name, answered it in as loud a voice as he could muster. 'HELLO, DARLING', he said. 'I'M ON THE TRAIN! T-R-A-I-N! IT'S RUNNING LATE! He smiled at the dickhead, relishing a few moments of deliciously sweet revenge.

While he continued talking to Kellie, lowering his voice to a more civilized level, the train pulled into Preston Park Station, the last stop before Brighton, his destination. The dickhead and a couple of others in the carriage got off, then the train moved on. It wasn't until some moments after he had ended the call that Tom noticed the CD lying on the seat beside him which the dickhead had just vacated.

He picked it up and examined it for any clues about where to reach its owner. The outer casing was opaque plastic, with no label or writing on it. He popped it open and removed the silver-coloured CD, turning it over and inspecting it carefully, but it yielded nothing either. He would load it into his computer and open it up and see if that provided anything, and failing that, he planned to hand it in to lost property. Not that the dickhead really deserved it . . .

A tall chalk escarpment rose steeply on either side of the train. Then to his left it gave way to houses and a park. In moments they would be approaching Brighton station. There wasn't enough time to check the CD out now, he would have a look at his leisure at home, later tonight, he decided.

If he could have known the devastating impact it was going to have on his life, he would have left the damned thing on the seat.